Praise for The Summer of the Bear

'Author of the bestselling *Hunting Unicorns*, Bella Pollen dexterously layers the perspectives of Letitia's two teenage daughters (the dutiful eldest and the rebellious middle child) with those of the widow, her son and the bear himself to create a gently absorbing tale which smoothly splices poignant family drama with suspenseful Cold War thriller'
Daily Mail

'Bella Pollen's novel . . . has such an improbable mix of ingredients that you keep reading avidly just to see how the jigsaw fits together. There is a shell-shocked widow, a tame grizzly bear, some spooks getting up to no good in Cold War Bonn and three beautifully drawn children . . . the plotting is lucid, the dialogue crisp and the character-ization first-class. It is a pleasure to spend time in the company of such a relaxed, polished storyteller'
Mail on Sunday

'Pollen's fifth novel is the compelling story of a family rocked by loss and bereavement during the Cold War . . . Pollen is brilliant at portraying the bewilderment of the Fleming children . . . Part spy-thriller and part ghost story, the novel shifts back and forth between East and West Germany and the Outer Hebrides, where Pollen spent much of her own childhood. Narrated by each character in turn, including the bear itself, this is a gentle, haunting tale that stayed with me long after I finished reading'
Daily Express

Praise for Hunting Unicorns

'Hilariously accurate . . . brooding and elegiac . . . a gifted writer with a pithy poetic style'   *Daily Mail*

'A superb novel: sharp, poignant, redemptive and very funny'   *Daily Express*

'A stylish romantic comedy with very funny asides'   *Sunday Telegraph*

'A romantic comedy served with a rich sauce of moribund Englishness'   *Big Issue*

'A cracking romantic comedy with a Wodehouse feel'   *Irish Independent*

'Witty, urbane romantic comedy . . . engaging'   *Publishers Weekly*

'A word-of-mouth triumph'   *Independent on Sunday*

The Summer of
the Bear

Also by Bella Pollen

All About Men

Daydream Girl

Hunting Unicorns

Midnight Cactus

BELLA POLLEN

The Summer of the Bear

PAN BOOKS

First published 2010 by Mantle

This edition published 2011 by Pan Books
an imprint of Pan Macmillan, a division of Macmillan Publishers Limited
Pan Macmillan, 20 New Wharf Road, London N1 9RR
Basingstoke and Oxford
Associated companies throughout the world
www.panmacmillan.com

ISBN 978-0-330-51906-9

5 7 9 8 6

A CIP catalogue record for this book is available from
the British Library.

Illustrations by John Spencer
Printed and bound by CPI Group (UK) Ltd, Croydon, CR0 4YY

Visit www.panmacmillan.com to read more about all our books
and to buy them. You will also find features, author interviews and
news of any author events, and you can sign up for e-newsletters
so that you're always first to hear about our new releases.

For my mother

The Outer Hebrides, Summer 1979

It was the smell that drove him wild. As though the ocean itself was a tantalizing soup made from the freshest ingredients and he couldn't get enough of it. Oh, for a crust of bread big enough to sop up that wonderful bouillabaisse – the head of a mackerel, tails of lithe and saithe. As he swam on, each new flavour presented itself: an underlying broth soaked from the shells of mussels and winkles; a dash of seasoning from the juice of the sea anemone; a sprinkling of plankton for texture. When he jerked his head it was an involuntary movement, a simple greedy lunge for more. Still, it was enough. The cord snapped and instantly the pressure around his neck was relieved. He paused, trod water, understanding coming to him slowly.

Freedom.

In front of him lay the horizon, behind him the island bobbed up and down. He spotted a blur of a man, pushing to his feet out of the foaming lines of surf on the beach. The wrestler stood up and raised both his arms in salute and yet still he hesitated, torn. He might be a contented prisoner but a rope was a rope, whoever was tugging on the end of it. So he turned his back on the big man, dove under the salty waters of the Minch and, oblivious to the storm brewing on the horizon, swam on.

Part One

1

London

Traffic or no traffic, weather good or bad, the journey from London to the island always took three days. For the children to be confined with one another for such a lengthy period of time seemed nothing short of collective punishment and Georgie decided she'd rather be strapped to the roof rack along with the rest of the suitcases and take her chances with the rain and low-level bridges than feel the evil eye of her younger sister bore into her shoulder blades for one minute longer.

It felt like they were one of those eighteenth-century families being transported to Australia for the theft of a single plum, but at least Australia would be an improvement on what they had been condemned to: an unknown future with only the menagerie of gulls and a few lonely sheep for company. Last night, when her mother had turned on the television to check the weather forecast, Michael Fish had staked his usual ground in front of a map of the United Kingdom.

'A cool summer's evening, followed by a moderately warm day,' he pronounced, moving a couple of plastic suns onto southern England. 'And this band of high pressure will mean sun as well for the Midlands and the north.' He tossed a few more stickers towards Liverpool. By the time he had finished, the entire map of the British Isles had been covered by cheerful yellow suns – the entire map, that is, except for one spot. A solitary grey sticker marred the United Kingdom's perfect day, a cloud symbol hovering like a storm warning over their future, and beneath it was the exact place to which they were heading.

Her mother had been right about leaving early, though. There were hardly any cars on the road. A sudden flash caught her eye and Georgie turned to see the old Peugeot's reflection in the corrugated metal wall of an industrial building.

As long as she could remember, they'd had a variation on this kind of car. 'Always drive a Peugeot,' she could hear her father saying. 'Africa's favourite car! They're built in developing countries and have brought affordable transport to millions.' Quite why her father still felt obliged to sanction Africa's favourite car after they had moved to Bonn, she didn't know. Compared to the sleeker Opel and brand-new sedans driven by some of his embassy colleagues, the 1967 Standard 404 Saloon was something of an embarrassment, with its fin-tailed rear lights and jerry-built roof rack. Her father adored it, though, referring to it as a faithful old thing and complaining fondly about its arthritic gearstick and stubborn clutch as though it were a decrepit great-uncle who had been graciously allowed to live with the family and was now expected to piggyback them around the city limits in return for board and keep.

Anyway, it wasn't Germany that the reflection of the Peugeot reminded her of. Something about the dirty white paint with all those blocks of suitcases piled on the roof made her think of Liberia, her father's first posting. Exchange the car for a cart, add in the lines of people and the bundles of clothing and they could be any refugee family, fleeing from country to country, exchanging one life for another. Packing, sailing, driving, unpacking. She had never minded the idea that life was something you could gather up and take with you. That was the way it was in the diplomatic service and she had become used to the edge of impermanence it gave. Georgie closed her eyes. When she had been nine, her father had been posted back to London. They had sailed out of the Gulf of Guinea, all their belongings lashed and secured in the hold beneath them. When the packing cases had been unloaded into their new quarters, there had not been an inch of floor space left. Now all their worldly goods fitted onto a single roof rack. If you started with a boat and shrank to a car, then by the law of diminishing returns, what came next?

'Are you all right, darling?' Her mother was looking over at her.

'Fine.' She faked a smile before turning back to the window.

They were crossing the canal now, zigzagging up through the tree-lined streets of Little Venice into north London. Georgie took in a dozen moving images. A documentary of a city, blinking open its eyes at first light. A rubbish truck churned by the side of the road. A taxi driver queued for tea at a greasy cafe. Under the overhang of a garage, a security guard smoked a cigarette. People shadowed the streets here and there. What were they doing? Where were they going? Who was lost and who had a purpose? A city was such a mysterious place. All those closed doors, all those lives grinding away behind them. And who could say what might happen to turn them upside down? Somewhere right now, two people might be falling in love; the first spark might catch in a factory fire; a man could fly into a rage, pick up a paperweight and kill his wife. There was no telling who was happy and who was sad. And, like her, there was no knowing what secrets people were being forced to hide.

2

It annoyed Alba that people accused her of hating things indiscriminately. It wasn't true. She had her reasons for feeling the way she did and they were good ones. For example, she despised over-polished furniture, easy-listening music and shiny food, as represented by, say, the glaze on doughnuts or the sweaty sheen of a tomato ring. She resented fish, loathed any form of sentimentality and strongly believed that doors should be kept either open or shut, but never in-between. This short list, selected entirely at random, did not constitute the sum total of Alba's wrath at life. Far from it. Alba incubated a fresh grievance for each day of the week. In fact, if someone cared to ask her – and God knows, she often wished they would – she could dredge up a bona fide irritation for every letter of the alphabet.

Where these prejudices came from she had little idea, yet she recognized them as immutable – steadfast, too, was the scorn she felt for her fellow human beings. Vegetarians, religious fanatics, English teachers, weathermen – at one point or other all these pervs had been in her line of fire. Nevertheless, the person she despised the most, the

9

person who drove her absolutely *cjubulunga*, the person who was to blame for everything that had happened to their family, if she could only work out precisely how, was, without a shadow of a doubt, her brother, Jamie.

There he was now, sitting across from her on the passenger seat. Holy God, what a revolting sight. His breath smelt sour and the chalky residue of night dribble around his mouth turned her insides.

'Retard,' she whispered.

Jamie was rubbing his legs. Long smooth strokes, up and down, up and down, up and—

'Stop doing that!'

'Doing what?'

'Fondling your legs.'

'But I'm not touching you.'

'You're annoying me, which is worse.'

'Leave him be, Alba.' Her mother's hand snaked through the divide and connected with Jamie's knee. 'He's just tired.'

Alba scowled. This was it. Exactly it. Excuses were always being made for her brother. In her opinion, if he wasn't babied so much, he'd be obliged to grow up. Jamie was nearly nine years old but still unable to read or write and the only reason he could count to ten was because he'd been born with the visual aid of fingers and thumbs.

'Retard,' she mouthed at him as soon as their mother's attention was reclaimed by the road.

Alba enjoyed using the word 'retard'. In fact, Jamie aside, she enjoyed the company of actual retards. As a punishment for incinerating her games kit the previous term, the school had sentenced her to weekend community service and given her the choice of visiting old people or playing games with the mentally ill. Alba couldn't stand old people, with their tottering gait and rotting gums. She was repulsed by the milky colostomic smell hovering about their skin, let alone the sparse, duck-down hair, which gave the impression of trying to distance itself as far as possible from their scalps. Old people had been born a long time ago and understood nothing of the world she inhabited. Retards, on the other hand, turned out to be a lot of fun: jolly and uncomplicated, impervious to insult and physically game for as many rounds of 'What's the time, Mr Wolf?' as Alba cared to make them play. It was like having a group of friendly, pliable trolls to order about and Retard Round-Up, as she dubbed it, became a fixture for the rest of the school term. Jamie, however, was not a pliable, friendly troll. He was stupid, spoilt and whiny beyond endurance.

'Jamie,' she bellowed. 'You're doing it again.'

'I'm not,' he gasped.

'You are.'

'My legs hurt.'

'So what?'

'Rubbing them makes them feel better.'

'I don't care.' She fashioned her thumb and forefinger into a pincer.

'Ow,' he cringed in anticipation. 'Stop it.'

But Alba had no intention of stopping. Every slap and pinch was a reflex born of her irritation and for every one successfully delivered, she felt that much better.

'Retard,' she mouthed for the third time.

'Alba, for goodness' sake!' Now it was Georgie who turned round. 'Just be nice.'

'What's so good about being nice?' she retorted, then, when no one responded, added, 'Dada was nice to everyone and look where it got him.'

'Where?' Jamie asked, immediately alert.

'Alba!' her mother hissed.

'Alba, shhh.' Georgie threw a meaningful glance towards her brother.

'Oh, for God's sake!' Though gratified by the reaction, Alba was aggravated nonetheless. How predictable. It was always Jamie everyone worried about – as if he had somehow acquired sole rights to the family's grieving. What about her? Why did no one seem to care how she felt? Anger rose up through her stomach like milk on the boil. She was sick of being shushed before she had finished. She was sick of half-truths and unspoken truths and all the lame excuses in between. She didn't believe in God, she didn't believe in Father Christmas or the Tooth Fairy and she was damned if she'd believe any of the other lies that parents told their children.

3

It wasn't that he didn't have the vocabulary to fight back – Jamie Fleming's vocabulary was far more sophisticated than that of most boys his age – but Alba unbalanced him. She turned him into a juggler with too many balls, a pobble with a mass of toes.

'Store your words, then. Keep them in your head,' Nicky Fleming advised his son. 'Think of them as your secret army and one day you will be able to do battle with your sister.' Jamie liked the analogy, but oh, what an unruly Dad's Army of words they were. Stationed safely in his head, they kept themselves in an orderly line, ready for duty. But as soon as he gave the command to go, it was as if an internal siren had been triggered. However much he implored them not to panic, the words stumbled and butted up against each other in their haste to leave and by the time they left his mouth were in too chaotic a state to be of any use.

Alba aside, verbal communication didn't give him significant difficulties. Books and newspapers were a different matter. Jamie Fleming appeared to suffer a form of blindness, an inability to see patterns in words. As he stared at them on the page, instead of joining together to form sentences, they separated into a haphazard collection of jottings which, for all the sense they made to him, might have been Braille or Morse code or birdsong.

Then there were the bodily manifestations of his 'condition'. It was as though Jamie's internal wiring had been connected to a faulty electrical socket. Physically his timing was sporadic, his reflexes sluggish. Bats and balls fell regularly through his fingers – but if the sports field was a minor skirmish, the dinner table was a war zone. In Jamie's uncoordinated little digits, knives and forks managed to point themselves any which way except towards his plate. As with most eight-year-olds, he found that food was loath to make the precarious journey from spoon to mouth without first detouring to his lap, or parking itself in rebellious gobs on his chin.

'You are repellent,' Alba would shout at him. 'You are useless. You are *nugatory*!'

'What does "nugatory" mean?' Jamie had taught himself to collect words the way other boys jotted down train numbers and he was always up for a new one, however personally insulting.

'Who cares? Just say it.'

'I am nugatory,' he repeated obediently.

If Jamie sometimes felt his home life was hell, it was still a big improvement on school. There, each hour promised its own level of purgatory. He was the worst on the playing field, remedially the worst in class. The teachers attributed his learning difficulties to middle-class stupidity. Jamie Fleming, everyone privately agreed, was just plain dumb. Even Georgie, his chief protector, accepted his lack of intellect as a sad fact and told him it didn't matter. Only his parents stood fast, taking him to doctor after doctor in the hope that one might hold the key to unlock their child's ability to read and write.

'Of course there's nothing wrong with you,' his father reiterated after every specialist's appointment. 'It's just that your brain hasn't been properly switched on yet.'

'Oh no, you're quite wrong, Dada,' Jamie said, 'my brain is switched on *all* the time.' He grabbed his father's hand and placed it on the top of his head. 'Can't you feel it? It's humming.'

Jamie knew he wasn't stupid, whatever anyone said. Even as he committed the word 'nugatory' to memory, he could feel his brain growing like one of those miracle carwash cloths that boasted a capacity of ten times its size when immersed in water. How he longed for his family to understand the scale of his thoughts. They were big and grown-up but, without the ability to articulate them, he was destined to converse only with himself. His war of words frustrated him almost as much as it worried his parents. What if he could never read a book or write a story. Much as he enjoyed it in there, he couldn't live in his head forever.

'Don't worry. There's a word for what you are,' his father told him, and whispered it into his ear.

'Is that good?'

'Well, I think so,' his father said, 'but then I happen to be one too.'

But if Nicky Fleming's polymath abilities were put to use in the everyday world, Jamie's breadth of knowledge became the building blocks of a convoluted fantasy life, one peopled by an astonishing number of characters all of whom were interested in everything he had to say. Alba might call him what she liked but inside his head he was a brilliant raconteur, a storyteller capable of threading together titbits of conversation, snippets from the paper – anything that fired his imagination – into a sweeping plot of which, coincidentally, he was almost always the hero.

In Jamie's world anything was possible. Wolves spoke as men and goblins ruled governments. Waterfalls flowed upwards and inanimate objects made conversation with him whenever they pleased. And if his parents encouraged him, they were not alone. Children's heads are a terrible mess of truth and lies, receptacles for conflicting information, fragments of facts and half-formed opinions. Misinformation is every parent's tool for shielding their offspring from the adult domain. Real life, with its grubby ethics and rank injustice, is not considered a suitable place for a child to inhabit. From birth, Jamie's baby cage had been padded with fairy tale and strung above a safety net of make-believe, no clues handed out as to what should be accepted as absolute or dismissed as whimsy. Even time had been warped and truncated – 'just a minute', 'the other day', the concept of 'soon' – a whole lexicon of vagueness invented to further smudge the lines of an already blurred world.

There were so many clues that the crossed wires in Jamie Fleming's head would not spontaneously unravel.

The Summer of the Bear

Somebody should have noticed but nobody was paying attention. If only they had been. If only his family had understood the strange workings of that clever little mind, they would have watched him so much more carefully.

4

Letty Fleming was not a confident driver. She sat stiff in her seat, gripping the steering wheel as though scared that it might, in a moment of whimsical rebellion, decide to hurl itself out the window and roll merrily along the motorway. In the divvying up of marital chores, Nicky had bagsed driving while Letty had been allotted map-reading, a job she negotiated with more calmness and tact than most, considering the mild abuse that came with the position. Even when Nicky wasn't around, he was still dictatorial, forbidding her to drive in bad weather or after dark, and it had always suited her to accept this as a sign of love rather than a slur on her capabilities. Now, at the thought of the seven hundred-odd miles in front of her, a trench-size furrow of concentration cut into her forehead.

An atmosphere of quiet discontent pervaded the Peugeot. Surely car journeys had not always been like this? A grim determination to get from A to B. She missed the ragging and the giggles and the half-hearted threats that accompanied them. It no longer felt as if they were a family. More like a collection of damaged souls bound by a set of rites and rhythms over which they had little control – but then maybe that was the definition of a family. She'd never had to think about it before. Unless there was enough pain to keep them awake, people tended to sleepwalk through their lives, disregarding the present to wait for the future, capable only of happiness retrospectively – until something happened that was monumental and only then did life divide into the before and after. People were destined to become haunted by those moments when everything was perfect – if only they had known it. Before the bomb, before the flood, before the . . .

Letty felt brittle with exhaustion. If only Nicky could be here, if only Nicky could take over everything for her. If only. These were the words that governed her every waking moment and now she was terrorized by the force of her wishful thinking. If only she had known. If only she had done things differently, but the further back she tried to roll time, the more paths opened up to her. Painstakingly, she had gone down every one of them looking for a different journey, another road, but in the end they all led to the same place. Fate was fate precisely because its outcome could not be manipulated or changed. Who knew why some people's lives worked out and others' did not?

5

Bonn, West Germany

 Information was Nicky Fleming's religion. He respected it, he traded in it, he made his career out of it. He was the missionary who wished to convert all others to his faith and so, as soon as the Fleming girls were old enough to read, he announced that each of them should find an interesting story in the day's paper and discuss it with him. This new rule was an extension of, but by no means a replacement for, his habit of lobbing general-knowledge questions at them when they least expected it.

'What is tax?' he might demand as the children sat unsuspectingly down to the dinner table. 'What does it pay for and is it fair?'

All three children were in agreement. News was a drag, but their father was adamant. They were to take an interest in the world around them. Besides, he argued, there was bound to be one story, one headline, however small and insignificant, that would appeal to them, and thus a daily ritual was born. Every morning, along with the *General-Anzeiger Bonn* and the embassy's digest of all the main national newspapers, a copy of the London *Times* was delivered. Nicky worked his way through both broadsheets over a breakfast of boiled eggs mashed onto fresh baked *Brötchen*. After he was done, he would shuffle *The Times* back into pristine order with the skill of a croupier at a gaming table and the paper would be passed to the children in reverse order of age.

Jamie liked animal stories: the sighting of a grey wolf in the Bavarian forest; the discovery of fossilized dinosaur eggs; the story of a Hungarian dancing bear rescued from its persecutors. He was fascinated by pictures of natural disasters and spent long hours planning to save his family from them. He was particularly intrigued by earthquakes and the idea that the world could, and sometimes did, open up and swallow whole, people, buildings, cities.

In the evening, after Nicky returned from the embassy, he would sit in his favourite chair, a chaise longue with matching footstool that had travelled from country to country with them – a chair that had absorbed so many chapters of *Our Island Story* it was almost a historical expert in its own right – and he would invite his three children to sit with him and justify their pick of the day.

'So this earthquake,' Jamie would say after the article had been read to him. 'How did it feel to fall? How long did it take to reach the centre of the earth? Would everyone's houses and cars still be okay when they got there?' And Nicky, hardly wanting to think how it might feel to be crushed between the vengeful arms of nature, having no intention of describing the agony of a man whose lungs were being filled with pebbles while his bones were ground to dust, abandoned his passion for facts and turned instead to his imagination. No, people didn't die!

Of course they didn't fall forever! Yes, there was salvation down there, a terra firma, and not only was there terra firma but also entire cities where buildings had landed intact and precisely into their allotted space. There was a train station too, just like the one in Bonn, complete with uniformed station-guard who announced in loud staccato German the arrival times of new citizens. '*Herr Henkel, vierzehn Uhr!*' His lovely wife, twenty minutes later! Every parent does what they can to protect their children from the concept of death until such time as they can cope with it, and down in the centre of the earth, Nicky told his son, was a whole new world where people lived and worked and mined the earth's core for untold riches.

'But what happens if the people want to come home and see their children?' Jamie asked.

'They have to be patient,' Nicky declared. 'They must wait for another earthquake to split the earth and then up they climb, quick as they possibly can.'

Whilst he never tired of hearing about natural hazards or the poor maltreated *Tanzbär*, Jamie's real love, as he grew older, was the Cold War. *The* Cold War, the Cold *War*, the *Cold* War. He would roll the words around his mouth, giving them different emphases and inflections, sometimes adding a dramatic little chatter of his teeth for effect. Jamie's inability to read meant stories had to be picked for him, but he recognized the phrase 'Cold War' when it appeared in a headline and was entirely au fait with all its associated acronyms: CIA, KGB, NATO, MI6, SIS. For Jamie, as for most spy-mad boys, the Cold War conjured up a James Bond world of dissidents and traitors – of intrigue and deceit. Of the 'umbrella murder' and

Markov's fatally unaware stroll across a foggy London bridge. He had little idea that the Cold War was the actual world in which he lived. That a hop, skip and one very high jump away from the capitalist excesses of the Bonn embassy stood the physical and ideological divide of the Berlin Wall. And in this matter, as in the matter of those long-suffering souls diligently working the earth's core, his father was unwilling to bring anything even close to stark reality into his small son's life.

With Alba, such qualms were a waste of time.

Alba's taste ran to sensationalism. Nothing made her happier than the gory nihilism of a family murder or the brutality of an armed robbery. Her chief aim when choosing her story *du jour* was to find something so subversive, so blatantly unsuitable for Jamie's ears that her father would be required to fudge the more sordid details, whereupon Alba, with the self-righteousness of the child who catches her exhausted parent skipping pages of a bedtime story, would take a sadistic delight in correcting him. Fortunately for Nicky, Alba's preferred genre of news was not often to be found in *The Times*. Nevertheless, she used the newspaper sessions as an opportunity to milk her father for criminal know-how with the fervour of a lifer who'd suddenly discovered her new cellmate was a habitual escapee.

Finally, though, it would be Georgie's turn. There would be a redistribution of limbs on the side of the chaise longue, Nicky would slide his arm around his eldest daughter's waist and say, 'What about you, my George? What has caught your attention today?'

But Georgie was shy. The whole business of preference-stating had always made her self-conscious and besides, she could never dredge up a particular interest in any of the headlines, so she would fidget and tug at the piping of the loose cover and say, 'Um, I'm not sure,' all the while turning the pages of the newspaper as slowly as she dared, growing increasingly miserable, praying that something would jump out at her before it was too late. She knew her father to be a patient man, yet, as the minutes ticked by, the room seemed to go very still with the weight of his expectation. How she envied Jamie with his headlines, pre-edited and presented as multiple choice. Why couldn't she be of Alba's gothic persuasion? She desperately wanted her father to think of her as an intelligent child, but all she felt during these sessions was uninteresting and stupid.

'There must be something,' Nicky would urge as she stared in mounting desperation at the newsprint while Jamie fidgeted and Alba sighed until finally, when she could stand it no longer, she stabbed her finger arbitrarily at the nearest headline.

'President Defiant in Bucharest,' her father read. 'Why this one, Georgie?' he probed gently. 'What is it about this one you find so intriguing?'

And she would turn her head and blink back the tears while Alba groaned cruelly.

On 21 January 1979, no papers were delivered to the Flemings' house in Bad Godesberg. If they had been, the children would have found only one page of *The Times* to be of collective interest.

6

Outer Hebrides

 It was futile, his continued battle with the elements. For as long as he could remember he'd been pitted against a single adversary but the sea was an opponent that did not play by the rules and he was no match for it. Water was coming at him from all sides – enormous swells tossed and turned him, salt burned his throat. The undertow grabbed at his legs and cold squeezed his chest, leaving him no oxygen for the next round. Survival was an instinct lodged into every one of his bones so he conceded defeat, blinked his sore eyes and allowed the current to float him towards the island as though he were as weightless as a piece of driftwood.

It was not the friendliest of landing spots: a stone plateau, guarded by sentinels of rock that buffeted him between each other like the levers of a pinball machine. A wet tumble of seals barked at his approach. The swell withdrew, then in one almighty forwards rush propelled him up and out of the water, dumping him on land below.

There was a frenzy of splashing as the seals streaked by. A lifetime spent lolling on the rocks had not prepared them for such an oddity dropping unannounced into their world. But he was not the first creature to have under-estimated the power of the northern elements. At one time or another various migratory birds – a snowy owl, an African stork, even a flamingo – had found themselves in a gale so powerful that it skewed the delicate compass in their heads, resulting in a dizzying free fall and crash landing. Over the years this barren Hebridean isle had been a refuge for all manner of lost souls. Now it was his turn to be blown off course, and it was a late summer slot he was destined to share with an equally adrift family of four.

7

Bonn

The day after Nicky died, the machinery of the Embassy Wives' Club began to turn. The kindness of the women was as overwhelming as it was stifling but the order had come from the top. Letty Fleming was not to be left alone, not even for a minute. A rota was formed, food was purchased and cooked, the kettle boiled in shifts. A grieving widow, it was agreed, simply could not be made to drink too much tea.

Every afternoon at precisely the same time, the Ambassadress came to the house in person. Letty stared at the woman's ramrod back, at the way her knees were pressed together in perfect symmetry, and wondered whether she herself had overlooked the chapter entitled 'How to Sit Elegantly in a Pencil Skirt' in her guidance book of embassy etiquette. The Ambassadress poured the tea but, noting that Letty made no move to pick it up, gently took the younger woman's hand and placed the cup and saucer in it. 'Are you sleeping, Letitia?'

'A little, thank you,' Letty lied.

'And you're eating, I trust?'

Letty nodded. She had no desire to be either rude or

ungrateful. She knew she was supposed to find comfort, sanity even, in routine, but heaven knows there were only so many times a day she could answer the same questions without screaming.

'And the children?' the Ambassadress asked. 'How is little James?'

Letty turned her head to the wall.

'My dear, you must be strong. The children will take their cue from you. Too much emotion will only upset them unnecessarily.' The Ambassadress produced a handkerchief. 'Show them you can get through this, and they'll soon find that they can too.'

Letty blew her nose and promised to grieve quietly and considerately.

'There is one more thing,' the Ambassadress announced with the delicacy for which she was renowned. 'My dear Letitia. Naturally, I don't have to explain how these things work. You understand that a replacement for Nicky must be found.'

A film of ice began to form around Letty's heart. No, it had not occurred to her. There had been no time to think of England and the blip in its global diplomatic relations. Still, the Ambassadress was right. A gap had been opened. The business of Queen and Country could not shut up shop for weddings or birthdays or untimely deaths.

'Of course,' Letty murmured.

'There's a good man just arrived back in London,' the Ambassadress continued. 'He's spent the last three years as cultural attaché to the ambassador in Japan. Made quite a success of it from everything we're told. Excellent references. He was hoping to stay in England for a bit, but we believe he'll be willing to rise to the occasion.'

Letty projected herself into the future through sheer need. Nicky had left no will, made no provision for his family. The house, the children's schools, their entire way of life came courtesy of the government. Quite how courteous the government would feel towards them under current circumstances remained to be seen.

'How long, do you think?'

'Sir Ian believes we can bring him over by the end of next month.'

Panic rolled through her like a rogue wave. What was she to do? Where were they to go?

'So.' The Ambassadress placed her teacup carefully back in its saucer. 'You can manage that?'

It had not been a question. The Ambassadress patted her arm. 'Good for you, Letitia. Sometimes the thought of positive action is all it takes to make one feel a little better. I give you my word we will help you with any arrangements you might require.'

As always, the Ambassadress's word was her bond. Within a matter of weeks, the Fleming family were out of their residence and on a boat back to England.

8

Scotland

 Letty had come to resent borders. Those pencil-thin divides where culture, power and religion were destined to grate interminably against each other. She resented them for the intolerance they represented, for the secrets and lies they necessitated and above all for the amount of Nicky's time they had stolen. How much more pleasant would life be were borders treated as celebratory places – auspicious spots where flags were raised and flowers strewn. The Scottish border, however, was not such a place. Distinguished by a commonplace lay-by, it offered only a warped sign for Gretna Green and a van whose paintwork was jauntily stencilled with 'The Frying Scotsman'.

Letty bought bacon baps and sugary tea in stout paper cups. The bacon was spitting hot and salty, the inside of the rolls soft and warm. Even before the children had wiped their mouths of the dustings of flour, Letty ordered a second round.

A few miles short of Inverary they stopped at a petrol station for a lunch of sweets and crisps, and not long after that on the verge of the road for Jamie, whose stomach had suffered the consequences. Letty hovered a respectful distance behind, a clutch of tissues in her hand.

'It won't come,' he sighed apologetically. 'I want it to, but it won't.'

'Never mind.' She folded the tissue back into her pocket. 'Does your tummy still hurt?'

'A little,' he fibbed. He waited until his mother began picking her way back to the car before hastily taking the map from his pocket and concealing it under a large stone. It was the third such map he'd hidden since leaving London. Two had already been safely stowed, one in the petrol station, the other impaled on a fence post somewhere in Cumbria, but this was a long stretch of road without distinguishing landmarks and another clue would surely help his father to follow them. As Jamie straightened up and wiped his hands on his shorts, the shadow of a passing coach fell over him. To his utter amazement, he saw that its side was painted with an immense picture of a grizzly bear.

'Mum,' he squealed, 'look!'

'Mmm.' Letty had unfolded a scarf from her bag and was busy tying it around her hair.

'Did you see?' He danced an excited little jig.

'See what, darling?'

'The bear!'

'Darling, there are no bears in Scotland.'

'It was on a bus.'

'Was it, darling?' She smiled indulgently. 'I do hope it was off somewhere nice on holiday then.'

'Come on, Jamie.' Georgie wound down the window.

'Did you see it, Georgie?'

Whatever *it* referred to, Georgie shook her head. She loved her brother, but found him unfathomable.

'I was reading, sorry.'

'Do you think there's going to be a circus?'

'Jamie, why would there be a circus? We're in the middle of nowhere.'

'Get in the Godalmighty car, Jamie,' Alba said. 'Or there will be heavy corporal penalties.'

'Don't swear, Alba,' Letty murmured.

Alba rolled her eyes and withdrew to her outpost in the corner back seat. How much patience did one human require? The whole journey she'd had to listen either to the inane bleatings of her brother or the muffled crackle of the radio. Surely her mother could have fixed it before they'd left? Surely a trip to the garage wouldn't exactly have strained her capabilities? Surely she could make Jamie shut up for *once*?

'Did you see it, Alba?' Jamie reached the car and yanked open the door. 'Did you look?'

'Of course. As you know, I'm fascinated by every tiny thing you choose to point out.'

'You are?' Jamie found himself momentarily diverted.

'No, Jamie, I'm not. That was an example of the use of sarcasm. Now, I know how keen you are on spelling things correctly, so allow me to help you out. S. a. r. c. a. s. m.'

'But did you see the bear?' Jamie hid his confusion with perseverance.

'Ah, well, if you mean that large brown animal who was running along the road wearing a kilt and playing the bagpipes, of course I saw it. Why do you ask?'

'Do you think it was my bear?'

'I'm sorry, I wasn't aware you had your own bear.'

'Yes! The one from the *Zirkusplatz*! The one I have the picture of. The one Dada was going to take me to see the day he—'

'Oh Jamie, of course,' Letty intervened quickly. 'I know exactly which one you mean. He did look like an awfully nice bear.'

'Then can you drive faster to catch him up?'

'Darling, I can't drive any faster than I'm supposed to.'

Jamie swallowed his disappointment. He stared at the road ahead.

The bear was long gone. Even if his mother went over fifty miles an hour, which she never did, they would still not catch him up. He closed his eyes and concentrated on retrieving the image on the side of the coach. The starkness of the brown fur against the glossy white paintwork. The big grizzly had been standing on his hind legs, one colossal paw extended in a wave. Hesitantly, Jamie raised his own hand.

'Hello, bear,' he whispered.

9

Bonn

 There had never been much to do in the city at weekends. Despite the government institutions, the ministerial residencies, the sub-ministerial agencies, despite the Bundestag and the Bundesrat, the diplomats and the policy-makers, despite the journalists, the writers and thinkers and all the newly minted restaurants and cafes briskly opened up to accommodate them, Bonn was a town destined never to rise above its provincial roots. Even the glare of the international spotlight comprehensively failed to brighten up those dreary streets. Weekends in Bonn were quiet, boring affairs, and particularly so for a small boy. There was the Haribo factory of course, amiable strolls through the Naturpark and those damp, dragging walks along the Rhine, but the outing Jamie enjoyed above all others was a visit to the Museum Koenig with his father. As natural history museums go, it was both well curated and surprisingly inspirational, but Jamie was interested in neither of these commendations. What he cared about was the outrageously large stuffed grizzly presiding over its foyer.

Technically, the bear was mounted. 'Stuffed' was a

layman's term and one which would have undoubtedly irked the taxidermist in question, who had spent weeks preparing the bear's skin by meticulously peeling the hide from its body then soaking it in a pickling solution of salt and chemicals. Still, stuffed or mounted, it was an impressive creature, standing over nine feet high on its hind legs. Jamie was terrified by the mere sight of it.

'The grizzly is one of the largest of all land carnivores,' his father translated off the plaque on the wall, and Jamie could well believe it. Each of the bear's claws was the length of his hand and sharp as a machete. Its teeth were so yellow they might have been made of solidified poison, but it was the bear's eyes which scared him the most. It was five-year-old Jamie's first visit to a museum, his first grizzly bear, and he shrank behind his father.

'There's nothing to be scared of, old chap. This one's a nice bear.'

Jamie shook his head.

'No, really. The fangs and claws are only for show. The truth is, he was once a child's teddy who grew too large to keep in the house and so he left home to seek his fortune. He's in this museum today only because he became very famous and made his mark on the world.'

Jamie crept out from behind his father's back. 'What did he do?'

'Ah well, let's see, shall we?' Nicky pretended to consult the museum's information leaflet. 'It says here that his achievements are too numerous to be listed but I quite often sneak down here to have a chat with him when you're at school.'

'He can talk?' Jamie's eyes stretched wide.

'Of course. Bears are highly intelligent and this partic-ular one has been well educated.'

'Does he talk in English or German?'

'He speaks fluent German, perfect English, passable French and a smattering of Russian, which he picked up on a state visit.'

'How do I make him talk?'

'Well, you have to be introduced first. Like most people in the service, he's a stickler for protocol.'

'Can you ask him to talk to me?'

'If you like.' Nicky stepped up to the grizzly, cupped a hand towards the bear's musty ear and began whispering.

'What are you telling him?' Jamie demanded.

'That you're a pretty decent fellow and you want to have a quick word. Only don't let Rosa Klebb catch you.' He raised an eyebrow towards the turnip-faced security guard hunched on her stool in the corner of the room.

Jamie took a tentative step towards the bear.

'Go on,' Nicky encouraged. 'Don't be shy.'

'Hello, bear,' Jamie croaked.

Nicky covered his mouth with his hand and pretended to rub his chin.

'Hello, Jamie,' he growled.

10

The Highlands, Scotland

'This looks like it!' Letty steered the Peugeot down a muddied track. 'We came here once before . . . I expect you were too small to remember,' she added quickly, as Alba groaned on cue. The anger sparking from her daughter's eyes threatened to set the car's upholstery on fire and Letty fought a surge of panic. The drive to the islands had always seemed like such an adventure but this time she had felt the drag of the children's apathy at every turn. The previous evening they'd arrived in Fort William only to discover that their favourite hotel, the Alexandria, had been refurbished and hiked up its prices accordingly. She'd had to scout in ever-widening circles until she'd found a B&B that had trumpeted a vacant family room and bilious supper for the extra price of two pounds a head. Still, today would be better, she promised herself. Nicky had always been snobbish about lowland scenery, claiming that Scotland didn't really begin until the grass turned to tussocks and the moors raised themselves into hills, but now only a few miles behind them lay the purple heather of Rannoch Moor and in the distance, rising into the clouds, was the misty shark fin of Ben Nevis. They had already negotiated the pot-luck timing of the little Ballachulish ferry and the drive through Glencoe, where she and Nicky had once blown out two tyres simultaneously and ended up walking for hours through those menacing black hills while Nicky tried to spook her with blood-curdling stories of the massacre. As if he could. She'd been driving through Glencoe since she was a girl. She'd been in love with the west of Scotland her whole life. From Glencoe there had been the smell of wet bracken and a salty wind to blow them north until finally they were in reach of the coast road, the sea and the promise of the islands to come.

'No, no, I remember.' As always, it fell to Georgie to bridge the gulf between her mother's pretence at normality and her sister's mutinous rebuttal. It was hardly the weather for a picnic but she understood her mother's need to live in the past. After all, she spent a considerable amount of time there herself. And besides, it *was* a beautiful spot. The track petered out into a circular clearing on the bank of a river. A fish jumped, dragonflies hovered neurotically over clumps of desiccated reeds. The scene had all the ingredients of an idyllic summer's day – save for any genuine warmth.

Georgie wandered down the bank, rolled up her trousers and induced Jamie to pitch some twigs into the swirling eddy, but the water was cold, and as soon as she felt everything possible had been done to bolster her mother's feelings, she steered Jamie up to where Letty was attempting to make merry by laying their jackets on the heather and spreading a picnic on top. An emergency dash into Fort William had produced buns, hard-boiled eggs, thick slices of ham with a crumbly yellow edge and a bag of still-warm sausage rolls. Georgie sat cross-legged on her anorak and squeezed the last of the Primula onto her tongue. Jamie had sequestered the packet of Jaffa Cakes and moved to a rock he had deemed a safe distance from his sister. Had Alba liked Jaffa Cakes, no distance would have been safe, and Georgie was mildly surprised she hadn't already snatched the biscuits off him, if only for the fun of it, but that was the thing with Alba, just when her level of malice had you thumbing through the *Yellow Pages* for the nearest child-catcher, she would perform a bewildering volte-face, and was now curled into Letty's body, holding her mother's arm protectively around her. Georgie relaxed and allowed herself to tune into the near-silence – the rustle and munch of Jamie's chocolate fest, the sneery whine of a midge cloud. She decided she liked sitting up on the hill, with its prickle of heather, watching the river twist and flow towards the low grumble of the waterfall. It reminded her of Bonn and the first glimmer of spring when they would haul their bikes up the cellar steps and cycle to the restaurant on top of the Drachenfels, where you could sit under an immense arch feathered by ivy, admire the smoky waters of the Rhine below and gobble down buttery pretzels and frankfurters dipped in luminous yellow mustard.

Her eyelids had almost drifted shut when a flash of movement brought her back to the present.

'Mum?' She frowned at the roof of the Peugeot below them.

Alba sat up and shielded her eyes with a hand.

'Mmm?' Letty rolled sleepily onto her back.

'The car,' Alba said.

'What car?'

'It's moving. It's rolling backwards.'

'Mum!' Georgie cried.

But it was Jamie who was already up and running.

'Jamie, no!' Too late, Letty launched herself down the hill after him, but age had her at a distinct disadvantage. Jamie's body was oiled by youth. His eight-year-old bones were as supple as willows, his every sinew elastic and forgiving. He was not yet a veteran of life's wear and tear, not even a rookie. Uncoordinated, unsporting he might be, but compared to his mother, his feet were winged – and now the car was gaining momentum, its front end slowly tilting upwards as its back wheels connected with the bank's incline. 'Don't worry,' Jamie had yelled, 'I'll stop it,' and as it dawned on Georgie exactly what her brother was thinking, her heart pulsed with fear. Next to her, Alba was yelling and something must have penetrated, because Jamie glanced up, as in – what on earth was all the fuss about? But he quickly dismissed his sisters, because, let's face it, weren't they always shouting at him? Weren't they forever criticizing him, so much so that sometimes it was all he could do to think for himself? And besides, it felt good to have identified a problem and be dealing with it.

'It's down to you now, Jamie.' The Ambassadress had patted his head with her hard, flat hand. 'You must be brave and look after your mother. After all, you're the man of the family now.' Until his father returned, it was the truth. His grandfathers were dead. Jamie had no uncles or brothers. 'One by one the boughs of the Fleming family tree have withered and died,' he had once heard his father lamenting, and Jamie, willing to believe that the mystery of procreation began with an acorn, had projected to a time when he would seed a new tree. He would plant an entire forest of Flemings! Meanwhile, there was the more immediate problem of the car. The Peugeot was rolling into the river and strapped to its roof was his suitcase and inside his suitcase were those things that mattered most to him – the flyer from the *Zirkus*, the box of IOU promises from his father, his roll of comics – all destined to be lost forever. No! He would not let that happen. He would stand brave! Hold the car back from the brink. After all, how often had he witnessed his father jump-start the old Peugeot? Push it along the street from a standstill, one hand on the steering wheel? One hand! So he closed his ears to the screaming and powered on.

The car was almost in the river by the time Jamie caught up with it, but now the closer he drew, the bigger the car looked. Nevertheless, duty was duty. He stretched out his arms, shut his eyes and in the same instant felt himself blindsided by the full weight of his mother's body. There was a breath of wind on his cheek, thinner than a razor blade, as the car rolled by. The wheels hit water, the exhaust snapped with a muffled pop. The momentum of the car's backward roll drove it ten feet along the riverbed before it jammed to a stop. The current rose quickly, surrounded the roof rack and tugged at the elastic octopi, until, with a further succession of splashes, the suitcases slid one by one into the river and embarked on a docile bob towards the waterfall.

On his stomach, his face mashed into the soil, Jamie searched for air while his mother's voice reverberated with anger and fear around him. 'What were you thinking? How could you *be* so stupid?' Finally, she pushed herself off his crushed chest and only then, as oxygen sawed up through his deflated lungs, was Jamie able to burst into tears of rage and humiliation.

'I want Dada!' he wailed. 'Where is my Dada?'

Part Two

11

Bonn

This much Jamie knew: his father had suffered an accident. He'd gone away for some time, then somehow – Jamie didn't fully comprehend how – his father had got lost.

In the months that had passed since his father's disappearance, he had turned these facts round and round in his head, examining them for the sharp edge of a clue, a slight fissure of information, always on the lookout for something, *anything* tangible to hold on to.

That there had been an accident was unfortunate, but not necessarily odd. Accidents were nobody's fault. They were bad luck and you had to grin and bear them. Next, there was the question of going away. Jamie didn't like it, but he was used to it. His father travelled all the time. When Jamie had been smaller and noticed the suitcase packed and stationed by the front door, he would burst into tears, wrap himself round his father and beg him not to leave. 'Now, come along, fish-face.' Nicky would gently prise him loose. 'I'll be back before you know it.'

'But where are you going?'

'Ah, well, since you ask, I'm going on a mission.'

'Really,' Jamie breathed. 'A secret mission?'

'Naturally.'

'Is it dangerous?'

'No . . .'

Jamie's face fell.

'Well,' Nicky relented. 'Perhaps just the teeniest bit dangerous.'

'Do the others know?'

'No, and you mustn't tell them, either.'

'Why not?'

'Because it's to remain between us.' He tapped his finger to his nose and winked.

'But you will come back soon, won't you?'

'Of course I will, and when I do, I'll come and find you and maybe . . .' He picked up his son and swung him around. 'If you've been exceptionally good, I'll bring you a present.'

His father never told fibs. He always came back. He always came looking for Jamie and he always gave him a present. A Russian babushka, a slim waxed package of stamps, a lead soldier on a charging horse. This last time, however, everything had been different – and it had made no sense. No sense at all.

The last time Jamie saw his father had been one Saturday morning in Bonn, the day before the circus opened, and Nicky had been picking at his *Brötchen* and scanning the papers when Jamie asked for help with his homework.

'What's the subject?'

Jamie pushed over his exercise book. Nicky looked at the hieroglyphics of his son's attempt at the English language and sighed. There was already a mound of paperwork on his desk in the embassy that needed deciphering.

'When is it due in?'

'Monday,' Jamie said dolefully.

'Well, that's not so bad, is it? Do what you can on your own and we'll tackle the rest before supper this evening. That way it will all be done before we go to the circus.'

As luck would have it, the Circus Krone was being erected on the barren area of an as-yet-undeveloped piece of land behind the embassy. 'If I sneak up to the roof, I'll be able to watch them setting up the big top,' Nicky had told his son. 'I'll check every day and give you a progress report.'

'Promise you'll be back in time?'

'Cross my heart, hope to die, stick a needle in my eye,' Nicky sang, then, at his son's puzzled frown, scribbled a few words onto the top of his newspaper and ripped away the corner. 'Here.' He handed it to Jamie. 'Happy now?'

Jamie nodded as he folded the scrap into his pocket. His father did not fib and he did not break promises. 'My work can be hopelessly unpredictable,' he'd explained to his children. 'Things crop up, meetings drag on, so you mustn't ask me to make promises I might have trouble keeping . . . Oh, cheer up.' He'd laughed at their dismal faces. 'It's not so bad. When I do make a promise, I'll honour it. In fact, you can write it down and keep it in a box like an IOU.' But he hadn't come back in time for homework, or even for bed.

In the morning Jamie was up early, dressed in clean trousers and his favourite green alligator shirt. He extracted the paper flyer from beneath his pillow and smoothed it out onto his bed. The letters ZIRKUS were blocked over a picture of a cheerful-looking brown bear wearing a minuscule top hat and riding a unicycle.

'Can a bear really do that?' Jamie had asked his father.

'Oh, bears are wonderful creatures,' Nicky had replied. 'They can do almost anything – and if I happen to see him practising, I'll give him a friendly wave and tell him you'll be along soon to meet him.'

Jamie wondered whether to take the flyer with him, then, remembering that he'd torn it off a lamppost in the Münsterplatz when no one was looking and that, technically, this constituted stealing, carefully hid it under his pillow again.

The door opened suddenly.

'You're not ready,' Jamie accused his mother.

Letty touched her hand to her chest. Her heart felt as raw as butcher's meat.

'Jamie.' She sat heavily down on the edge of his bed.

'Is Dada ready?' Jamie demanded suspiciously.

Letty took his hand and rubbed the pads of his fingers with her thumb. Jamie decided something was wrong. His mother's voice had sounded reedy, thin – as though she'd left the bulk of it in another room.

'Jamie,' she said for the second time. She gulped at some air and squeezed his hand even harder. 'I have something to tell you.'

Jamie waited for the axe to fall. The circus had been cancelled. Perhaps his father had been detained at the embassy. It had happened before and the apology often came from his mother. 'Something important, sweetheart. I'm so sorry.'

But this did not happen where there was a promise. Never when his father had promised.

Jamie tried to crack the code of his mother's expression. She didn't look particularly sorry. If anything she looked scary. Angry almost. An unpleasant thought occurred to him. Had some inadvertent crime of his been discovered for which the circus treat was to be forfeit?

'Daddy's had an accident,' she said.

'Oh!' Jamie pulled his hand away. This was not what he had been expecting. He pictured his father tripping and spraining an ankle. 'Poor Dada,' he said sympathetically. 'A bad one?'

Letty hesitated. 'Yes, I'm afraid so.'

'Oh,' he said more thoughtfully. He upgraded the level of accident to the time his mother had sliced through her finger with a paring knife. She had been at the sink, cutting a garnish made from carrot, when suddenly she'd turned very white and held her finger under the cold tap for a long time.

'Did he cut himself?' Jamie ventured.

'No, Jamie. No, darling.' Letty drew in a breath. Every step of explanation felt like walking across broken glass. 'He . . . well . . . he had a fall.'

'A fall?' Jamie's brow cleared. Falls were painful, no doubt about that, but to a boy who had made a lifelong habit of falling, they were rarely cause for serious concern.

'What did he hurt?'

Letty had little experience with the terminology of death. Her own father had died the year before but despite her profound sadness, telling the children had felt natural. Their grandfather had been eighty-one. He had died in his sleep.

'Well, he hurt everything, really.' Letty struggled to regain control of her voice.

'Does he have to get stitches? Does he have to go to hospital?' Jamie faltered. A hospital trip meant high odds that the trip to see his unicycling bear would be called off.

The strength went from Letty's arms. The girls had cried themselves into a sleep from which they had yet to wake, but she could not close her own eyes without seeing Nicky on the ground, the pool of blood lacquered around his head. And now here was Jamie, and this was his moment. She was his knock on the door, his war telegram. Jamie was still living in the before while Letty would forever exist in the after and the gap between them was immeasurable. She knew she had no choice but to shatter his world – but into how many pieces was something she did have control over. She must find a way to tiptoe through the landmines of his age, his innocence, his very *strangeness*.

'Find words that won't frighten them.' The Ambassadress had put her arm around Letty's shaking shoulders and gently, firmly pulled her away. They hadn't wanted Letty to go to the embassy. Nicky could not be moved for some time. It was a question of jurisdiction, they said, of government formalities, but Letty couldn't bear for him to lie there on the tarmac, cold, alone. She had taken his coat to lay over him then knelt beside him, barely noticing the cramps or the pins and needles until finally, with the permission of the Ambassador, he had been loaded into an ambulance by the German authorities.

'Heaven only knows it's going to be hard enough for James without having nightmares to contend with . . . oh, the poor little boy. Oh, Letitia . . . oh, my dear . . .' The Ambassadress had gripped her hands and offered to come with her, but Letty had to be alone, if only for a few minutes. And now she summoned every ounce of steel she had remaining.

'Jamie, Daddy's not in hospital . . . Daddy's gone.'

'Oh, I see.' Jamie slumped down on his bed. He didn't see at all, but he matched his mother's solemnity of tone. 'When is he coming back?'

'Darling, Daddy isn't coming back. Try to understand.'

'But when will I see him again?' His voice began to rise plaintively.

'Oh, Jamie.' The fragile shell holding Letty together splintered and broke. 'Not for a long, long time.' She began to cry. 'I'm sorry, Jamie, oh God, I'm so sorry, but Dada's gone now and you have to be brave.' She pulled him to her and held him tight. 'We all have to be so brave.'

Jamie went very quiet. When he was finally released, he looked at his mother's tear-stained face with more than a trace of annoyance.

'Who's going to take me to the circus, then?'

12

The Minch

In the perpetual dusk of a summer's night, the ferry at long last shunted its way into Lochbealach harbour. Like some freakish sea monster, it opened its mouth, laid down the metallic tongue of its gangplank and began spewing out the contents of its belly. One hundred or so mildly traumatized sheep were the first off, followed by a windswept line of foot passengers.

It had proved an unexpectedly stormy crossing and the crew had taken several attempts to bring the ferry in. At one point, Letty, watching from the deck with the children, wondered whether the pier might collapse, such was the speed of the first approach. On the second try, the crew missed the pier altogether and their third attempt was foiled by a mischievous gust of wind that blew the boat off course at the eleventh hour. Once again the engines were thrown into reverse and, with a clanking of pulleys and chains, the ferry was dragged back into the choppy waters of the bay. Letty was not overly concerned. The crew of Caledonian MacBrayne were widely admired for their skilful handling of this particular strait and it was their determined 'What won't sink must float' attitude which was responsible for them having once set sail on Christmas Eve in a force ten gale, on the basis that it was every islander's God-given right to be returned home in time for a fine roast lunch. Opening into the Sea of the Hebrides, the Minch was a notoriously angry stretch of water and one the locals talked about as though it were a husband-bashing wife for whom the community held a grudging respect.

'Aye, she's a rough one all right.'

'She'll toss and turn a man at will.'

On the fourth attempt the crew manoeuvred in the boat with the tact and gentleness of a marriage counsellor and this time their persistence was rewarded. The wind and current momentarily aligned and the ferry surged neatly forwards, eventually butting up against the heavy fenders lining the pier.

Letty stood with the children on the upper deck and listened to the noise of the motors grind beneath the boat. She tilted her face upwards to catch the rain, falling in a light mist against her cheek.

It was finally behind them; the grisly little Pimlico flat; the handouts from the Diplomatic Wives' Fund; the negotiating of Nicky's pension; sorting out his affairs and sifting through his life. Oh, the endless bureaucracy and loneliness of it, and all the time not knowing, not being given any answers, wondering if there was a point, a life ahead of them, wondering even if there was a God. Now they were home. Everyone has a place where they fit into their skins, a place where they are able to make sense of the world, and the island was hers. There were no rules, no protocol, no politics or intrigue. There was no Cold War, no Russia, no spectre of power waiting to corrupt even the most morally recalcitrant of souls. On the island there was only sand and rock and the rain to wash over them.

'Why are you crying?' Georgie asked, alarmed. 'What's wrong?'

'It's only spray, darling.' She kissed Georgie's hand and quickly wiped her cheek. 'Come on, we'd better go.'

Considering its near-drowning in the waterfall, the Peugeot had made a miraculous recovery, drying out in the care of Macleod Motors, a dour father-and-son team who had arrived at the river with a tow truck and much simultaneous chain-smoking and head-shaking. Nevertheless, it had been a couple of days before the children were able to ease themselves gingerly back onto the damp, eggy-smelling seats. 'Aye,' Macleod Snr commented drily, 'best let the sea air blow through her.'

'But it's safe to drive?' Letty had asked. She'd spent the night punishing herself with every conceivable scenario, Jamie trapped in the car, Jamie pinned under the wheels, and her eyes were puffy with tiredness.

'Safe enough,' Macleod said. 'It's the interior that's taken the damage. I've stapled the carpet back but that plywood of yours will go rotten soon enough.' He handed her the worn leather key ring. 'I can pull it out for you now if you like. Give you more luggage room.' There followed a silence broken only by the clang of metal, a dropped spanner or rolling hubcap, and only then did Letty realize that Macleod was still peering at her with a mildly expectant air. She focused, snatched the keys. 'I'm sure it's fine, thank you.' Later she would recall a thread of this exchange that had jarred, a whisper in her ear to pay attention, but at the time there had been the ferry to make and the clock was already against them.

Unloading the ferry was almost as laborious a process as docking it, involving the lowering and raising of a metal turntable that lifted vehicles in groups of three from the car deck to sea level. The timing of this system was arbitrary and depended on some secret equation of lorries versus cars, versus height of tide, time of day and, most appreciably, the whim of the crew. Sure enough, it was a further three-quarters of an hour before Letty was given the nod to start the engine. She drove onto the metal turntable, where, dwarfed by a Mother's Pride truck, the old Peugeot was hoisted up and finally released into the brackish air of the Outer Isles.

13

The Outer Hebrides

When his strength returned, he pushed himself to his feet and took a look around. Ahead, the sea stretched to the horizon, its treachery and turmoil hidden beneath a sudden lull. Behind him a natural archway dead-ended in a crater, flanked on all sides by black rock in whose crevices several dozen fulmars were nesting. The cliff was sheer and the only section benign enough to climb – a spine of screed cushioned on either side by moss – offered no foothold within easy reach. Still, the crater was filling up like a kettle under a tap and soon the only way out would be to swim. His efforts at scrambling resulted in much feather-ruffling amongst the birds. A pair of them swooped down, distrust in their sharp yellow eyes, their stubby beaks thrust towards him. Scared, he dropped back to the bottom. Next he tried a running jump but the screed was impossibly crumbly and the rock slick from spray. The birds swooped ever lower until suddenly one of them opened its beak and hawked a putrid-smelling substance onto his head. Even more unsettled, he hastened back under the archway.

He more or less chanced upon the cave. Some trick of light and perspective made it appear as a shadow on the tunnel wall and it was only as he was tumbling backwards through the opening that he realized it was there. Once again, effortlessly floored by the elements, he lay still for a count of ten while his eyes adjusted to the dark. The cave was large, perhaps twenty feet long, with a floor sloping sharply upwards. The incoming tide was boiling past the entrance, but a happy combination of gravity and speed served to keep the water within the narrow confines of the channel. He peered back out of the opening and that's when he spotted it.

A small boat, hugging the shoreline. Travelling slowly, east to west.

They were looking for him.

Of course they were.

14

 The island's single road was a meandering tarmac track, barely wide enough to accommodate the chassis of the average car let alone a tractor or plough. Every half-mile or so, crescent-shaped passing places had been gouged from the verge but these appeared to be an afterthought to the island's civil engineering, as though the possibility of two-way traffic in such a remote place had been so laughable it had not been worth planning for.

After the dramatic pageantry of Scotland's west coast, the brooding hills of Glencoe, the Wagnerian scenery of Skye, there seemed precious little to admire of the island's flat, barren topography. There was instead the squat architecture of the townships; the islanders' predisposition to build modern bungalows right on the doorstep of their more picturesque crofts; the dumps of broken rusted cars; the dishevelled highland cattle grazing around them and then those never-ending barbed-wire fences that criss-crossed acres of bog-leaden ground. Pity the few day-trippers, lured to the Outer Isles by some 'Visit Scotland' guide's tepid promise of breezy sands and unique culture.

Why wouldn't they book themselves back to the mainland on the next ferry? How could they know that the ugliness was purely cosmetic, that the magic was hidden – that the *whole* island was magic?

Georgie breathed in the familiar smell of peat smoke. They had turned at the church and were juddering past the ghostly whitewash of Euan's croft and round the corner with its skyscraper of nettles.

'Look, there's Alick now!' Letty exclaimed as a swaying pinprick of light came into view at the end of the road. She slowed the car and wound down the window.

'Ah, Let-ic-ia.' Alick's rubbery face broke into a grin.

For as long as she could remember, Alick had met them off the ferry like this, his black serge jacket buttoned over a navy boiler suit, the handle of the lantern swinging in his hands. 'Welcome to the country,' he would always say, which, to Letty, was not only an affirmation of the island's isolation, but a reminder that the islanders themselves believed they came from a completely different world.

'Oh, Alick.' She took his hand and squeezed it. 'You're so good to wait for us.' It didn't matter how firmly she told him it was unnecessary, Alick was as stubborn as an ink blot and she knew perfectly well he'd been standing there, cold rain slanting across his face, for the full two hours the ferry had been delayed.

'Shall I help you in with the luggage, Let-ic-ia?' He hooked the remaining inch of a roll-up from his pocket, pinching it between oily fingers while he hunted briskly for a match. Possibly somewhere in his early forties, he was a short, wiry man, incapable of remaining still for more than two seconds at any given time. Letty watched him drawing noisily on the stub, his eyes flicking right to left, left to right as though constantly on the watch for enemy planes, and she thought how familiar every angle of his face was to her; the piercing eyes under mildly surprised brows, the sprigs of tightly coiled hair that looked as if they'd been blown back by the wind for so many years that they'd given up trying to grow in any other direction. He looked like a gnome. Alick Macdonald was her neighbour, friend and protector but he was as unpredictable as the weather. The last time she'd come up he'd been waiting for her on the road as usual, but he'd been visibly agitated and as soon as the car had been unloaded, had pulled her through the kitchen and into the passage where, to her astonishment, she saw that a long line of mice had been laid out on the carpet.

'Now, will you look at these wee mice, Let-ic-ia,' he said, as if she hadn't been already staring at them, mouth agape. The mice had been positioned with incredible precision, almost mathematically set apart and each facing the same direction, as though in preparation for a mass embalming. 'Thirty-six in total,' Alick had declared with satisfaction.

'Yes, I can see there are quite a lot of them,' Letty agreed, 'but what are they doing here?'

'I kept them for you to have a look at.' Alick dropped to his haunches and rolled one over with his blackened finger. 'They have such queer long noses!' His eyes darted in wonderment along the line of little synchronized bodies.

'I think perhaps that's because they're not mice,' she hazarded. They looked more like voles to her, although she did not feel altogether confident in her ability to identify small vermin.

'Of course they're mice!' Alick said with feeling. 'They're fairy mice, that's what they are!'

Letty knew better than to argue with Alick's conviction that the fairies or spirits were responsible for all of life's unexplained phenomena so she'd left it at that, hoping that whatever they were, he would, in the very near future, be removing their little corpses from the carpet.

'We'll unpack the car in the morning, Alick. It's late and I want to get the children to bed.'

'Can we put out the flag for you?' Jamie piped up.

'Aye, first thing. Put her out.' Alick ran a hand through his whorls of hair. 'Put the flag in the stone and I'll be down.'

'Thank you, Alick.' Letty gripped his arm.

'Ah, *mo gràdh*.' His sharp eyes softened. 'Welcome to the country.'

15

 Ballanish was neither a pretty nor structurally interesting house but it was a tough one, designed to take no nonsense from the elements. It didn't matter how violently it stormed – however hard the wind blew, the house simply arched its back, closed its eyes and blithely waited out each assault with such strength and patience that every time Letty drove up to find the roof intact and the doors on their hinges, she silently thanked the architect for his lack of creative inspiration.

'Georgie, you take Jamie. Alba, help me with the food. Everything else can wait until morning.'

Alba lugged the cardboard box into the larder. She hated this room with its pinching cold and lingering smell of mutton. Bad things happened to good food in larders. Butter became sullied by traces of Marmite and jam; bricks of cheddar cracked like heel skin; even the faintest hint of jellifying soup was enough to make her gag, and she held her breath as the stale air hit her.

'No, no,' she heard her mother say, 'not in there, Alba, put them in the fridge.'

'Oh, six hearty cheers,' Alba muttered. After the hours of proximity to her brother she needed to decompress in the sanctuary of her own room. *In the fridge*, she mimicked, backing out of the claustrophobic space. *The fridge*. She stood stock still.

Her mother was standing by the kitchen door, arm raised to the wall. 'Ta-da!' She pressed a switch and the room flooded with light.

'I don't believe it.' Alba forgot the pounding in her head. She forgot the cabbage soup smell of the car's upholstery. In the corner of the kitchen a brand-new Electrolux was humming with power. 'The whole house?'

Pleased, Letty nodded, but Alba, already regretting her momentary lapse into enthusiasm, frowned. 'Why?'

When, a decade earlier, electricity had finally made it to the Outer Islands, Letty had been one of the few to hold out against it. For what reason, no one was ever quite sure. 'Nostalgia,' Nicky diagnosed. 'Your mother appears to think there's some kind of romance to life in the Dark Ages.'

And life in the Dark Ages had been nothing if not impractical. While the rest of the township practised screwing in lightbulbs and flicking the on/off switch of kettles as though electricity was a mysterious foreign game recently adopted as the island's national sport, the Flemings continued to rake dead flies off the floor with a push-me-pull-you carpet sweeper and strain their eyes reading with torches under their blankets.

'I got some builders in from Skye,' Letty said. 'They made an awful mess, but they got the job done. What do you think?'

'You've kept the gas lamps,' Alba hedged.

'I couldn't bear to get rid of them. They give off such a pretty light. Besides . . .' Letty hesitated. 'Well, they remind me of your grandpapa.'

Up until then, Victorian glass sconces had provided the only light in the evening. Alba could picture her grandfather moving from one to the next putting a match to their muslin cones. The burning gas had emitted a comforting buzzing noise as though the whole place was inhabited by a swarm of beautifully house-trained bees.

'Look in the outside room,' Letty ordered.

Connected to the main house by a lethally draughty corridor, the outside room was home to an assortment of hardening oilskins and leaking gumboots. For as long as Alba could remember it had been the dumping ground for all family detritus. Shelves overflowed with fishing reels, amusingly shaped lumps of driftwood, splintered oars, duck decoys and a miscellany of unclaimed clothing items that had been soaked, dried and re-encrusted with sea water so many times they'd achieved the consistency of salted cod. Still, fishy, cardboard-ish, damp though it was, it smelt to Alba of freedom and summer. The new spartan hint of soap in the air unnerved her and beneath the virgin glow of overhead lighting, she saw that the shelves had been torn down and in their place stood a brand new chest freezer and state-of-the-art washing machine.

'Well?'

At the touch on her shoulder, Alba recoiled.

Letty dropped her hand, suddenly sideswiped by the memory of her daughter as a little girl. Hadn't she once been the most demonstratively affectionate of her three children? Granted, she'd presented herself as a foil to Georgie who, with an eldest daughter's classic obedience, had accepted her role as model daughter with good grace, studiously playing with dolls, assembling intricate and cosy homes for her teddies and freezing water in shoe-boxes to make fairy ice rinks. But then along came Alba with her piercing cries and colicky screams. As a baby, Alba had little power of veto over the smocked dresses and embroidered nighties foisted upon her, but she'd taken care to vomit on them regularly enough to ensure they could never be part of any future child's suffering. Then, as soon as she was old enough to discover she had a gender – and that some accident of nature had decreed it should be female – she turned suffragette, demanding sexual equality, staking her claim for muddy knees and bruising play. She had no problem with dolls, providing she was allowed to butcher their hair into amusingly asymmetric styles or remove their heads altogether. Only her father had ever been privy to her more malleable side. In the mornings she would leap onto his bed and wrap herself around him, revelling in his minor imperfections – tugging at a hair sprouting from a chest wart or fondly rubbing the wasteland of his bald patch. As he moved from bedroom to bathroom, brushing his teeth, or searching for socks, she would cling to him, forbidding his departure before he had been kissed two or three times and hugged many more. 'Oh, goodbye, Dada, I love you, I love you,' she would trill, but as her sucker limbs were forcibly pruned from him one by one, the wail would begin to rise, 'Oh no, please, don't go, Dada, please don't go,' until finally she would collapse in defeat on the floor, weeping and despondent. 'Oh, when are you coming back, Dada? When will I ever see you again?'

'In about half an hour,' Nicky would remind her sternly, whereupon Alba would dissolve into shameless giggles.

'Dada is my love-beetle,' Alba had once explained matter-of-factly. 'I love you too, of course, but I love Dada a little bit more.' And Letty had smiled. 'All girls love their father a little bit more. It will probably be like that the rest of your life.'

Now she could only stare in bewilderment at Alba's hard little face. The day before leaving London she had locked herself in the bathroom with a pair of needlepoint scissors. As Letty's eyes shifted to the blunt line of her daughter's newly shorn hair, she felt something twist in her heart. When had Alba become so hard, so lacking in compassion, and how had she not noticed it before?

'It must have cost a fortune,' Alba said accusingly.

As Letty's hand fluttered unconsciously to her throat, Alba noticed for the first time that it was bare.

'You sold Dada's *necklace*? Your *anniversary* necklace?'

'It was worth it, don't you think?'

Alba didn't know what to think. The significance of electricity was not lost on her. Even in their family's uncharted future, one thing was certain: without light and heat, life became untenable on the island after October, when daylight downed tools at three in the afternoon and did not punch its work card until ten the following morning. She had always loved summers on the island, but electricity lent a permanence to their situation that she'd been studiously ignoring. Holy hell, the present was a world she hadn't yet made sense of, let alone the future. She eyeballed her mother, willing her to answer all the suspicions she didn't dare voice. Were they poor? Were they in exile? How long was this for? And was it really conceivable it could be forever?

16

Within the laws of nature there is a hierarchy of elements and on the island it was the wind that ruled. It blew, gusted, breezed and roared, a soundtrack to everyday life, like a man with a terrible grievance he couldn't help airing. In the far north of the world, where evidence of a rising and setting sun could not be relied upon to mark the beginning and end of each day, the wind was always there to perform this task with enthusiasm. It was the last thing Georgie listened to before falling asleep and the first thing she heard on waking and she found it comforting or menacing depending on its mood. Sometimes it sounded like a ghost moaning or a tractor grumbling or a soldier with an agonizing war wound. On occasion it became so loud she would dream a tidal wave was rolling towards her and then she would wake, expecting to find an immense wall of water bearing down on the house, but there was always the same view on the other side of her window: the mist collecting over Loch Aivegarry, the rolling flats of the machair and the silver line of the sea beyond. Ballanish was perched on the western tip of the island, already Scotland's westernmost archipelago, and the only thing between the house and America was the vast emptiness of the Atlantic.

It was past midnight but darkness never truly fell during the summer. Instead, it was as though a rubber had been taken to a charcoal drawing of the sky, smudging the lines between night and day. Georgie loved her room with its brass bed and candy-stripe curtains. Every inch of wall space was covered with watercolours of island birds painted by her father. 'This red, black and white gentleman over your head is an oystercatcher,' he had told her, 'my favourite wader, and next to him is a red-throated diver – another delightfully elegant water bird.' Above the chest of drawers he had hung two studies: the head of a golden plover complete with scale measurements of its beak and a painstakingly detailed wing of a mallard.

'Why would you draw only the wing?' Georgie had asked, faintly revolted.

'To study the mechanics of it,' Nicky had said. 'I like to know how things work.' And this Georgie knew to be true. Her father devoured specifics and data with the same relish he reserved for smoked oysters on toast. Her eyes moved to the dawn landscape over the door. Underneath the birds, Nicky had recorded the minutiae of the morning's flight. *Widgeon rising, approx. 50–100 with small groups of teal and a few shoveller . . . tense nervous feeders,* he had gone on to note, *the marsh area is obviously the place that local birds come during high tide.*

'You know something, my little George?' he would whisper as he kissed her goodnight. 'That noise you hear at sunup is the drumming of the snipe, and have you noticed that the call of the corncrake sounds exactly like someone running their fingernail along the teeth of a comb?'

Even as she thought about it, Georgie picked up a faint rasping outside the window, but it didn't sound much like a corncrake. After a while she realized that the noise was coming through the walls of the next-door room and she fetched Jamie into her bed and curled herself around his trembling body.

'What is it, Jamie, why are you crying?'

'I don't know where Dada is.'

'Oh, Jamie.' She tightened her grip on him. 'Dada's in heaven.'

'No, no.' He pulled away, agitated. 'Why do people keep saying that? Dada didn't get to heaven.'

'Jamie, don't be silly! Of course Dada got to heaven.' But she was shaken. What did Jamie know? Had he heard something? Who knew what careless spills that absorbent little brain of his had mopped up.

'No, you're wrong,' Jamie wept. 'I looked for him there.'

'You looked for him in heaven?'

'Yes, but I couldn't find him. He wasn't there. *He wasn't there.*'

'Okay, Jamie,' she soothed, relieved to know what she was dealing with. 'It's okay now, it was a bad dream, that's all.' She stroked his damp hair and launched into a complex rationalization of heaven's geography and how its size and the distribution of its population made the locating of one individual impossible without maps and directions, not to mention a stringent set of rules and by-laws, until Jamie was sufficiently baffled to drop the subject. But even as it poured out of her, she couldn't help but wonder. What were heaven's rules of entry? Just how bad a crime did you have to commit to be denied? She wiped her eyes with the back of her hand. She was always careful not to cry in front of Jamie. Besides, what good were tears anyway? As a liquid manifestation of pain, salt water was hardly adequate for what she was feeling. There should be something stronger coming out of a person's eyes. Blood or poison or the molten steel of knife blades. 'Go to sleep now.' She buried her face in his neck. 'Take a big breath.'

Jamie rasped wetly.

'And another.'

Obediently, he gulped down air and immediately started hiccupping.

'Oh, Jamie,' Georgie said helplessly.

'I can't help it.' He hiccupped again. 'You'll have to scare me.'

'Don't be silly.'

'Tell me a story then. Tell me the Flora Macdonald story.'

'Oh, no, any one but that.'

'Please, Georgie.' His voice caught pitifully.

'All right.' She sat up, rubbing at her head with the knuckles of her fist. 'Well . . . let's see . . . years and years and years before Grandpa bought this house, it was owned by a rich islander called Captain Macdonald, and Captain Macdonald' – she settled Jamie in the crook of her arm – 'was a pig of a man.'

Jamie sighed in appreciation as Georgie went on. He loved this story, it didn't matter how many times he heard it. Captain Macdonald had been a notorious baddie, employing many of the islanders for menial jobs, such as rowing him out to distant islands, sometimes in appalling weather, in order for him to shoot a few duck. He was already a snobbish man but when it fell to him to welcome the King to the island for an official visit, he began to harbour dreams of scaling the prestige ladder and sent his only daughter to the annual ball on Skye in the hope of her catching the eye of one of the posh boys attending.

Flora had indeed caught the eye of a boy – not a grandee, but a young fisherman on the quay, and the Captain had been horrified. Swiftly deciding to marry her off to his Factor – the man who collected rent on his properties – he lost no time in arranging the nuptials. Neilly McLellan, Flora's fisherman, was heartbroken and sent word of his intention to rescue her from this unhappy fate. The plan was to wait for fine weather then row across the Minch and signal his arrival by shining a light from the mouth of Loch Aivegarry. Weeks passed while Flora pined, then finally, one moonless night, there it was, the beam of a lantern.

'Without hesitation, she wrenched open the window and, as you know,' Georgie said, 'under Flora's window – my window – is the only tree on the whole island and so Flora threw out her sack of belongings and climbed down it.'

'Is it true, though?' Jamie asked. 'Did she really climb down your tree?'

'Of course it's true.'

'But Alba says nobody could climb down that tree because it's covered in thorns.'

'A few thorns would never stop someone who was in love.'

'Alba says that the tree is too far away from the window and that Flora wouldn't have been able to reach it.'

'Jamie, why do you care about *anything* Alba says?'

'She doesn't lie about things.'

'Nor do I!' Georgie said, stung.

'You pretend, like Mum.'

'Look,' Georgie sighed. 'How old is Alba?'

'Fourteen.'

'Right. That means she only knows about things that happened in the last fourteen years, okay? This story happened ages ago.' Jamie's slavish adoration of his sister had always riled Georgie.

'Did the story happen more than seventeen-and-three-quarters years ago?'

'Oh, Jamie.' Georgie kissed the top of his head. Her brother's literalness, the unyielding pedantry that so enraged Alba, she had always found charming. She remembered him as a little boy, bursting into tears on his birthday after guests had been ordered to drink his health. 'Oh, not all of it,' he had pleaded. 'Leave some for me.' Another time, on being told to tidy up his room and use a bit of elbow grease, he had spent fruitless hours searching for the relevant tin in the cleaning cupboard. As he'd grown older, though, it worried her. Occasionally she caught a glimpse of something obscurely brilliant about her brother, but how would he survive in the adult world, with no irony or sarcasm, when his condition invited these very tools to be consistently used against him? She settled him back under her arm. 'Just listen, would you? Flora escapes in the rowing boat with her fisherman and two of his cousins and off they sail to Skye, but unfortunately a gale picks up and they're blown instead onto the southern shore of Harris. So, there they are, drenched, lost and scared. But they can see a light shining in the distance and eventually they get to a croft, knock on the door and guess who opens it?'

'Flora's auntie!' Jamie supplied.

'Exactly! Of all the bad luck! Of all the houses on all the islands! Flora's auntie had not been best pleased to find such a bedraggled collection of runaways on her doorstep. Even less amusing was the moment she recognized her niece amongst them. "Why, whatever are you doing here, Flora, lass?" she demanded, then, incensed at their story, dismissed the boys with a disgusted wave and kept Flora under lock and key until she could be safely returned to her father. The lovers, however, did not give up. The second time around, the plan worked. Flora and her fisherman escaped to Skye and from there to the mainland, where they eventually boarded a ship bound for Australia.'

'And lived happily ever after,' Jamie finished.

'Naturally.'

'People in stories always live happily ever after, don't they?'

Georgie's eyes slid to her dressing-table mirror, where a small snapshot was wedged between glass and frame. Their parents on honeymoon, leaning against the rail of the ferry, wearing sunglasses and grins. What a happy-ever-after day that had been, with a flat sea and a bronze gong of a sun slowly sinking into it.

'Go to sleep, Jamie.'
'Yes,' he said, but his eyes remained open long into the night.

17

Bonn

Protected from hard facts about his father, Jamie began to hoard scraps of information. He stitched each precious snippet together into a patchwork quilt which he used to keep himself warm at night, but it hadn't been until two weeks after the accident that the first significant clue came his way. A party was being given at the Ambassador's residence. Jamie understood neither what the party was for nor why he'd been required to attend. All he knew was that it was boring. Everyone was old and wearing black. There had been no music and no other children invited except Georgie and Alba.

A man wearing a black tail-coat handed round plates of cucumber sandwiches with neatly trimmed crusts. Jamie crammed four into his mouth, trying to satisfy the hollow feeling inside him, which he incorrectly identified as hunger.

He'd felt a hand drop onto his head and looked up to find Tom Gordunson standing beside him. Jamie liked Tom. He reminded him of a wolf with his shaggy head and crumpled suits. Tom was his father's oldest friend, the best man at his parents' wedding, and he always gave Jamie presents at Christmas even though, technically, he was supposed to be Georgie's godfather.

'How are you doing, old boy?' Tom asked.

'God supports us in our troublous life,' Jamie intoned.

'Ah, I see you've been talking to the vicar.'

'He said Dada has gone to a better place.' Jamie followed Tom's gaze to where the vicar was now chatting with the Ambassador, holding a cup of tea poised in the air. 'Has he?'

'Yes, I think he probably has.'

'Better than Bonn?'

Tom smiled faintly. 'Yes, better than Bonn.'

'But then why didn't he take us with him?'

'He couldn't take you with him,' Tom said gently. 'It doesn't work like that.'

'But I miss him, and I want him to come home.'

'Of course you do, old chap, of course you do.'

'He was going to take me to the circus,' Jamie said forlornly. 'He promised I could see the bear. He promised to help me with my homework.'

Tom dropped to one knee. 'Listen to me, Jamie.' He laid his big hands on Jamie's shoulders. 'Your father will always be with you. Always. Every night when you go to bed and say your prayers you must believe that your father can hear them.'

'Even now he's gone away?' Jamie noticed that Tom had missed a button on his shirt. Tom was always buttoning his shirts wrong. 'Tidy mind, though,' his father liked to say. 'Frighteningly tidy mind.'

'Especially now that he's gone away.'

'How though? Does he have special powers?'

'Yes . . . I suppose in a way he does.'

'Like a spy? Like James Bond?'

'Yes.' Tom smiled again. 'A little like James Bond.'

Jamie sucked in a breath. He knew it. His father had gone on one of his secret missions.

Tom Gordunson worked for the Foreign Office. He had one of the most important jobs in the whole of England. If Tom didn't know what he was talking about then no one did. 'I'm going to tell Mummy.' He tried to wriggle free but Tom held him back.

'Why don't we keep it hush-hush – just between you and me, eh?' He touched a finger to his nose and winked.

And there it was. His father's secret sign.

Tom did indeed work for the Foreign Office. Known as an intense, honourable man, he was a passionate defender of his country's sovereignty. He boasted a First from Oxford, a natural aptitude for maths and the kind of agile, lateral-thinking mind that allowed him to finish *The Times* crossword puzzle without bothering to fill in the answers; still he couldn't have known that this one simple gesture, coupled with the boy's fierce desire to believe, would harden into an unshakeable conviction that his father would be coming back.

Jamie hurried off. If he couldn't tell his mother, he would find Georgie. He bumped into a woman with a thickly powdered face and tight grey bun. She was a long-term intimate of Bonn society whose husband was a political commentator on the radio. Had anyone asked her, she would have crisply informed them that she did not approve of the Ambassador's 'wake' for Nicholas Fleming. There were few secrets in Bonn's diplomatic circles and a suspected traitor was as good as an actual traitor. Now, caught unawares by the turncoat's living, breathing offshoot in front of her, she reacted instinctively with a step backwards, then rallied with a fatuous question about school. Jamie answered politely. The fur stole around her neck interested him far more than social chitchat. The fox's head nestled on her shoulder while its legs dangled slackly down her back. The fox's eyes were glassy but alive-looking. He wondered about the nose. You could tell if a dog was sick from touching its nose and the fox looked pretty sick to him, but just as he stretched out his hand to test, he felt the acute sharpness of Alba's fingers.

'Don't do that, Jamie.' She pinched him again. Jamie started crying and the woman's awkwardness was dispelled. The relief seemed universal as everyone turned to look at the children – the one wailing, the other shushing. For the first time in this whole sorry event there was a focus for their embarrassment and pity. Poor bereaved children. Poor little fatherless boy.

Jamie never got to tell Georgie and he didn't dare tell Alba. Instead, he carried his secret with him wherever he went. To school in the mornings, to bed at night. It accompanied him on his mother's trips to the Marktplatz or her dreamy meanderings along the Rhine. In every one of these places he looked for his father, secure in the knowledge that it was only a matter of time.

But then they had left Bonn.

'Does everyone know we're going to London?' he asked his mother the night before they sailed. The house looked bare and unfriendly, stripped of their possessions.

'Everyone, who?' She labelled a trunk. 'Friends from school, you mean?'

'Will Dada know where we are?'

Letty stopped packing and drew him into a hug. 'Of course, darling.' He could feel her breath warm on his neck. 'Daddy will always know where we are.' And his heart had soared. His father had not lied. Tom Gordunson had not lied. His father was indeed on some kind of mission, and what's more, his mother knew about it.

'Mum,' he whispered. 'It's all right. I know.'

'Know what, darling?'

'Daddy's a spy, isn't he?'

It was as if he'd burnt her with a poker iron. Letty stiffened and held him at arm's length. 'Why do you say that, Jamie? Who told you that?'

'No one,' Jamie said, frightened. 'I mean, Tom said . . .'

'Tom?' she repeated incredulously. 'Our Tom?' Two red petals of anger bloomed in her cheeks.

'Yes.'

'And he said that? That Daddy was a spy?'

'Sort of, I mean, yes.' He had never seen his mother like this. Her mouth twisted, her eyes stormy. 'I'm sorry, Mummy, I was just trying to . . .'

'Don't you ever believe that.' She shook him, her fingers digging into him hard. 'And don't you dare say it,

either. Not to me, or anybody. Not ever. Do you understand?'

He had understood and he had felt ashamed. You were
not supposed to talk about secret things.

18

Ballanish

It was five a.m. but Letty was glad to be up. She felt Nicky's loss in every part of her life but it was as if an icy draught now occupied the other side of the bed and she couldn't prevent the cold from seeping into her, no matter how many blankets she slept under. Nights no longer promised the temporary respite of sleep but instead presented her with a marathon ordeal to be conquered in sections. Every time she switched off the light, she prayed for a means of fast-forwarding to morning. Mornings gave her some mindless chore to do – coffee to make or a letter to write – but night shackled her with its physical inactivity and her restless soul allowed her only short nightmarish dozes punctuated by long periods of wakefulness in which to forensically analyse them. Her dreams were always uneasy or suggestive. She rode on empty trains which travelled in circles. She was visited by a mutual friend, long since dead, as though his world was suddenly relevant to her. Then there were the recurring nightmares, always a variation on a theme. At times Nicky was standing on the roof looking down. Others, he was already falling in his endless drop through the weightless air. In this morning's version she was waiting with the girls at the top of the embassy stairwell when she'd heard her name being shouted and she had turned to find Nicky running towards them. He'd been agitated, as though burning with some vital news to tell her, but he'd come at them so fast that as they'd stepped out of his way the weight of his body propelled him over the metal guardrail and she'd watched him falling in dreadful slow motion, his white shirt flapping around his stomach. She hadn't screamed. Within the context of her dream, she had somehow known that Nicky was already dead. But then, from several floors beneath her, Jamie had suddenly stepped forwards, his thin arms extended to catch his father, and the force of Nicky's plummeting body had taken Jamie over the edge with him and Letty had woken herself with an anguished wail.

It was a beautiful morning, soft and gauzy with mist. A bird was beating a few plaintive chords from its chest. At the gate she turned west onto a sandy path lined by cotton grass and embroidered with cowpat splatters. Past the ruined croft, past the rusting carcass of the plough, until the road tapered out into a wide stretch of machair, pockmarked by rabbit holes and blanketed in wildflowers of every colour. Corn marigolds, purple clover, thyme, ragwort, wild pansies, kidney vetch and silverweed, she trailed a hand through them until there it was – the faintest tang of salt on the wind.

The Ballanish township was close to a strikingly beautiful beach, a mile-long curve of bone-white sand, free from the usual banks of seaweed or highways of tiny broken shells. Even its jellyfish were discreet and minimalist, squatting in transparent domes in the shallows. Letty stood on the tide line and stared out to sea. Around her, a scattering of ringed plovers and dunlins stalked the break of the waves on pin legs, pecking at the sand for lugworms and other juicy breakfast treats.

She felt quite dazzled by loss. The island had always acted on her emotions in the most elemental way and here, alone, she gave way to a backlog of noisy weeping. When Nicky had died she'd felt almost nothing. Shock, the body's natural anaesthetic, had kicked in. But then, alongside the numbness, there was guilt and then anger. More recently she had found herself banging her head against a wall of regret. She had tried climbing over it or crawling under it, but she always came up against the same irreversible truth. Nicky was dead and there was nothing she could do about it.

A wind was rising off the sea and along with it, the noise of quarrelling gulls. She turned and stiffened. There was somebody standing on the far point of the bay. Ballanish wasn't her beach, of course, but it had always felt that way. As she drew closer, the stick figure enlarged and thickened into a male form with a robust gut and pigeon chest. Closer still and she recognized the ginger beard and unclipped sideburns of Dr John. He was bent over a dead whale, his legs apart, hands on his knees, as though bracing himself against the stench, which even at a hundred yards almost took away her ability to breathe. The whale was nearly thirty feet long and half-embedded in the sand. The flesh had already been stripped from the bones, leaving the exposed ribcage arced skywards like a skeleton bridge anchored by a carriageway of vertebrae. The knuckles of each flipper were still attached by shreds of skin but at some point, the entire skull had been cleaved from the body. It was lying a few feet away, already picked clean by the birds and now acting as a handy stool for Dr John's tweed coat. He stood up at her approach and wiped the blade of his knife against his trousers.

'Why, Letitia,' he said, 'what a surprise indeed, and how are you keeping?'

'Fine, Dr John. How nice to see you.' She shook his outstretched hand. 'And you? You're well, I hope?'

'Oh aye, not so bad, not so bad.' He squinted down at the whale, then sank to his haunches and raised the skin off the head with the tip of his knife.

'What are you doing?' Letty asked.

'I'm looking for his teeth.'

'Oh, I see.' There was a short silence. 'Do you collect whales' teeth then?'

'Well, I was thinking I might sell them. Whales' teeth can be quite valuable, you know.'

'Yes, I'm sure,' Letty agreed, wondering who on earth he might find to buy a whale's tooth on an island where bones and skulls could be picked out of the ground as easily as potatoes. Watching him work she was reminded of her honeymoon, when poor Nicky had woken up with tonsillitis, a condition that had plagued him since childhood. After two nights without a break in his temperature she had sent for Dr John, who arrived holding what looked like old-fashioned sweetie jars, one under each arm, filled with a colourful pic 'n' mix of medicines. He'd shone a torch down Nicky's throat more or less from the doorway, then put an enormous and very thick-fingered paw into the jar and brought out a handful of pills.

'What exactly are you giving him?' Letty had asked.

'Why, penicillin, to be sure.'

'No, you mustn't.' She sprang forward. 'He's allergic.'

'Ach, no matter,' Dr John said cheerily. He poured the pills back into the first jar and sank his hand into the second. 'These others will do just as well.'

The doctor was still on his knees beside the dead mammal. 'It's early for you to be up and about.'

'I like the mornings,' Letty said. 'Quiet.'

'Yes, they are that.'

'How do you think the skull got separated?' She held her scarf to her nose.

Dr John grunted. 'Well now, I can't be sure, right enough. I expect the poor beast became disorientated and got hit by a trawler. There now.' He opened his palm to show her two lumps of gristly bone.

'Oh, well done!'

'Aye, a fine pair,' he said with satisfaction, slipping them into his jacket pocket. 'I was sorry to hear about Mr Fleming,' he added. 'He was a good man indeed. Well liked on the island.'

'Yes. Thank you.' She tried to smile but it was as though some neuralgic affliction was preventing her from calibrating her expressions. Had it been a mistake to imagine she might find peace here? Everywhere she turned the island reflected memories back at her. Behind them was the sand dune where Nicky liked to read. Anchored in the bay was the little green-and-maroon fishing boat and on the beach in front of it she could see Nicky writing in the sand with a stalk of seaweed. 'Lobsters for Ballanish House. Two, please.'

An awkward silence had grown around them but Dr John was a nice man and she wouldn't dream of offending him. 'You know,' she said, 'I never realized that whales had teeth. I rather thought they swallowed plankton or krill.'

'That'll depend on the kind of whale,' he said sagely.

'Of course. Of course . . . and what kind of whale is this?'

'Oh, I haven't a clue about whales.' Dr John scratched at the wiry hair on his cheeks. 'Not a clue at all.'

19

Seventeen years old and she knew nothing. Her entire life Georgie had been bookish, above-average clever. She thought of the sheer variety of knowledge she had absorbed – the layers of sedimentary rocks studied, the vocabulary memorized and grammar mastered, all those ghastly verbs and their petty little conjugations. And for what? What use was any of it? Okay, so maybe the cure for cancer would be found in the backbone of a stickleback, but it was a long shot and everybody knew it. No, she'd been taught everything, except the one lesson she really needed – what to do when your father died. Now, to add to her confusion, her mother had turned turtle. Pulled in her arms and legs and drawn a hard shell over her head and Georgie didn't know how to reach her.

Letty was sitting at the table, a pile of blank white envelopes scattered in front of her. She had always been an inspired letter writer. She picked up a pen the way a violinist might take up a bow but whereas letter writing had once been a hobby, now it was an obsession; lawyers, the Home Office, banks, insurance firms. She had written to every person Nicky had ever worked with or studied alongside, looking for answers they might give or clues they might offer. She wrote looking for a resolution, praying for absolution, waiting for intervention and, yet again, Georgie was overcome with an urge to grab her and tell her about Berlin – because the knowledge was heavier than she thought possible and she was sick of hauling it around with her, day and night. Christ, her mother already had emotional blood leaking from so many wounds, what difference would one more quick stab make?

'Mum.' She laid an emphatic hand on her mother's shoulder. *Forgive me, Georgie*, her father had begged.

Startled, Letty turned. 'Darling, sorry, million miles away.'

Georgie searched her mother's face. The wide forehead, the freckle high on one cheek. She was as beautiful as she'd always been. Her features remained unchanged – except there was nothing behind them. It wasn't indifference, or disinterest. Just blankness.

'Who are you writing to?'

'Oh, you know . . .' She gave a dismissive little wave, but Georgie knew. She hadn't been writing to anyone. There was no one left to write to.

'Mum,' Georgie whispered. *You realize we're being watched, don't you?* her father had said. Strange how she'd once thought this a joke.

'Sleep all right, darling?' Letty asked vaguely.

'Fine,' Georgie lied. 'You?'

'Fine,' Letty lied back, then smiled brightly to prove it.

20

 He tended towards anxiety in new situations so for the first few days he stayed put. Time would come when he'd have to search out food and water but in the meanwhile there was plenty to keep him occupied, listening to the wind and watching the birds freewheeling in the sky. Fulmars were Olympian gliders, they were trapeze artists, acrobats of the air, swooping through the narrowest of cliff openings at impossible angles. On the ground, they led more prosaic lives, passing their time in domestic disputes, bickering and cawing and knocking their beaks together in irritation. They were a thuggish, foul-mouthed crew, yet he continued to watch them, mesmerized. These birds enjoyed the kind of freedom that he, trapped in his cumbersome body, could only dream of. From time to time his thoughts strayed back to that small boat chugging by and he couldn't help but wonder – what had led to that heartbeat of an impulse, to hide?

Meanwhile he arranged and rearranged his new quarters to his liking. The cave was a repository of sea booty, a lost and found of global treasure. From various corners

he piled up a wooden box from the Ukraine; remnants of Irish naval uniforms, bleached almost white by sun; a shoe made in Russia and a shampoo bottle from Denmark. There were also a variety of colourful plastic containers, three frayed lengths of rope and a terminally rusted mine to which he intuitively gave a wide berth. Every tide promised some new object, a maritime refugee that had been bobbing, corroding and disintegrating for years until suddenly it was brought to the end of its journey. One day, as he was sitting there, waiting for the tide to recede, there was a popping noise and a glass bottle bounced over the lip of the entrance. He examined it curiously. If the Atlantic rollers had the power to grind shells to the silky consistency of sand, it seemed impossible that such a delicate object could be granted safe passage. He rolled the bottle around and sniffed it, and in doing so, noticed a piece of paper origamied inside. It was, of course, that most romantic of things – a message in a bottle. An ocean-gram delivered by the great sea god himself. He smashed the bottle and played clumsily with the piece of paper. It was a map of Europe, drawn in black crayon. A single dot marked the north-west of Germany and from there, tiny red arrows marched across France, forded the channel and made their way to London, where they turned sharply right to Scotland. On and on they advanced, up the west coast, across the Minch – and had he been adept at the art of map-reading it might have occurred to him that the line of red arrows led almost directly to his cave. Except the map didn't depict a cave. X marked the spot over a house, its name childishly written and hopelessly misspelt.
BALERNICSH

July 1979, the map was dated. And underneath the date, a message.

To Dada, was written in a barely legible scrawl.

To my Dada. If yu ar lukin for uss . . . we ar heer . . .

21

It was quite an ordeal kissing Alick's mother. Firstly, it went on for an astonishing amount of time; then there was the odd bristle to contend with; thirdly, the kiss itself was of the wet, full-lipped variety and accompanied by some exploratory and often painful rubbing of the chin. Nevertheless, it was an unspoken requirement of the Ballanish township that visits to Alick's parents be made on the first day of the holiday and so the children held their breath and duly surrendered to Mrs Macdonald's embraces. She met them at the door of her croft, a warm-hearted woman with ample bosom, wearing sheepskin slippers and a pinafore tied over a tweed skirt. 'And how is the mammy today?' she cried, hugging Letitia and ushering them all into the croft to shake hands with Alick's father. Euan was a neat, self-contained man with ear muffs of white hair and long elegant fingers, which from time to time stole into the pocket of his serge jacket for a Jew's harp, a strange contraption, more resembling a dental brace than a musical instrument.

Once inside, the children were positioned on the

wooden bench for the ritual of present-receiving. Mrs Macdonald had worked for many years at the knitwear factory and every summer produced a triptych of unusual-coloured jumpers from the seconds pile, all of them boasting a surprise deformity that only revealed itself as the children, encouraged by their parents, attempted to try them on. This year it was a polo neck in egg yolk for Alba, a slime-green tank top for Jamie, and a dung-coloured V-neck for Georgie. Mrs Macdonald's own dimensions blunted her ability to judge the size of others. If she was large, all other adults were small and children were smaller still. Thus, as Alba's shoulders became danger-ously embedded in her sleeve and Jamie attempted to push his head through an opening more suitable for an elf, while Georgie found an asymmetric flare under her armpit, they were compelled to endure the enthusiastic endorsements of their mother. 'Why, they're lovely, Mrs Macdonald, how very generous of you.' And there was nothing else to be said, because it was astonishingly gen-erous of her, but what little money she had the children fervently wished she would not spend on them, as it only made her poorer still and them increasingly guilt-ridden. Afterwards, weak from the exertion, they sat roasting gently in front of the fire while Mrs Macdonald set about making the tea. 'I'm surprised the ferry came in at all,' she said. 'Quite a storm it was, Letitia, and it's been that way all winter, right enough. Many's the croft that lost a roof, and a fishing boat struck the rocks near St Kilda, why, no' more than a for'night ago.'

'Did it sink?' Jamie asked.

'Aye, three men gone and with their bodies not yet

recovered.' She transferred the kettle to the hotter of her two griddles.

'Will they wash up on the beach?' Jamie asked.

'You'll no' be wanting to find them if they do, young Jamie, they'll have been tossed around plenty so there's no telling what they'll look like.' She turned to encounter Letty's strained face and remembered herself. 'Though it's more likely God will have taken them before that.'

'Taken them where?' Jamie asked eagerly.

Mrs Macdonald collapsed onto a stool and squeezed her hands together in an effort to milk inspiration out of them. 'They say that sailors and fishermen who drown at sea come back as seagulls and the sky and the ocean become their kingdom. Ach, you can imagine them swooping down, with the sky always blue and the fish plentiful for the rest of time. There now.' She snatched a scone from the trolley and pressed it into Jamie's hand. Letty smiled gratefully, but she didn't know, how could she possibly know, what a child like Jamie could do with imagery like this?

The Macdonalds' tea trolley was a three-tiered affair that would not have looked out of place in the finest hotel in Edinburgh. The teapot and crockery were kept on the top, a bowl of carrageen and a plate of sand-wiches below and on the very bottom a basket of warm scones. Mrs Macdonald's scones were famous on an island already famous for scones, but her tea trolley was approached in strict hierarchical order from above. Tier one presented no problem as the children were not deemed old enough to drink tea; however, the question of how to endure their itchy knitwear receded in the face of carrageen, a quivering blancmange of a dish made by boiling milk and seaweed together for days. Even should this feat be accomplished, there were other foodie dragons to slay. Mrs Macdonald's sandwiches were grouted with a thick layer of margarine and an even thicker layer of tinned luncheon meat. How to avoid them was a subject often discussed in the Fleming household and inevitably Letty now found herself working her way solo through the white triangles, feeling the benevolent eyes of Mrs Macdonald and Euan upon her.

Alick's parents might have five sons, but Letty was their spiritual daughter and they treated her accordingly. In turn she loved Euan for his gentle manner and thoughtful mind. No matter how many times she heard his stories, she was always eager to hear them once more. How his eight siblings had all died of smallpox. How the London and Port Stanley Railway had conned him along with many of the islanders into emigrating to America to make his fortune. How he'd arrived instead in Canada in the bitter depths of winter to find he was not to be given papers to cross into the USA. How snow was as easy to drown in as a bog . . .

Euan held himself straight and spoke slowly and quietly, for which Mrs Macdonald more than compensated by delivering a ceaseless stream of news, and the news that she was currently preoccupied with was the closure of the seaweed factory.

'Plenty of people lost their jobs in that factory, Letitia,' she said. 'It's created a terrible unemployment on the island. There's only the lobster and the knitwear now.'

'And the knitwear is no job for a man,' Euan said darkly.

'But can't they do something about it?'

'The councillors called a meeting in the school and the whole township came. Back in May it was, Letitia, but it didn't make a bit of difference.' Euan sucked his teeth. 'No, indeed it didn't.'

'It's a terrible shame,' Mrs Macdonald said indignantly. 'And with all the products it went into.'

'A seaweed shortage,' Alba smirked. 'How tragic.'

'It'll no' affect the carrageen, don't you worry.' Mrs Macdonald emptied a shimmering second helping into Alba's bowl. 'I can fetch seaweed from the water myself, but that factory stuff went into all sorts. Soap, postage stamps, even the froth on the top of beer. Why, it was a very useful thing, that seaweed.'

'They started importing it from Tasmania. They said it was cheaper.' Euan shook his head sorrowfully. 'But how can it be cheaper? Bringing it in from such a far-off place, why, Letitia, it makes no sense.'

'No sense at all,' Mrs Macdonald echoed.

The first week on the island, Jamie found it hard to decipher what anybody was saying. A mainland Scots accent sounded sharp and clear, as though each word had been carved from a man's vocal cords with a knife, but the Hebridean accent was muffled and heavy enough to tip a word to the left or push it far to the right. Although Nicky claimed that the islanders' use of English was so spare and precise they might have been 1920s Cambridge undergraduates, when they actually spoke, it was as though a wind was blowing through their mouths.

Even for the Flemings, whose ears were attuned to it, Euan could make English sound as foreign as any language spoken in the corridors of the Bonn embassy and mistakes in translation were just as easily made. When Letty remarked that the ferry appeared to be new and asked Euan what had happened to the old one, he replied, 'Whell whell, Le-ti-see-ya, they say it's been sent off to Tourrkey, rroight enuff.'

'Turkey? Has it really?' Letty said, enjoying a wonderful vision of the shabby little ferry berthed in the glinting heat of the Sea of Marmara with the skyline of Istanbul behind it. Still, much as the image appealed, she couldn't quite reconcile it with the logic. Why on earth would a Scottish ferry be sent to Turkey – and indeed, on closer investigation, it turned out that the ferry was not in Turkey at all, but enjoying semi-retirement in the less salubrious port of Torquay.

Jamie sat quietly on the bench feeling his scalp prickle from the heat. The image of the fishermen turning into seagulls preoccupied him. It seemed so odd. Why couldn't they remain as fishermen in their heaven and still be rewarded with plentiful fish from the ocean? And what of the fish? Were they real fish or heaven fish? And if they were heaven fish, then how would it be fair for them to get eaten all the time? And what if a particular fisherman in real life had hated being a fisherman? What if the swell of the ocean had made him seasick and the sight of those bloody entrails on the deck iller still? What if you were a fisherman who had more ambitious dreams? Were heaven's rewards always career-appropriate? Would a fireman's heaven be smoke-free and flame retardant? But how would that work for a fireman who had loved his job? Wouldn't it be better for him to go to hell, where his expertise would really come in handy? But before Jamie could push these thoughts through to any conclusion he found his face being marinated in another of Mrs Macdonald's kisses and then suddenly the door to the croft was miraculously opened and Alba was shoving him towards the light and the blessed coolness of mist against his skin.

22

Bonn

It was thought better that Jamie did not attend the funeral.

'He's been through so much already,' the Ambassadress said. 'What purpose will it serve to upset him further?' And Letty, quietly sinking into darkness, was fast losing the ability to make judgements for herself. Despite the prickle of warning in some closed-down part of her brain, she had to concede that the Ambassadress was probably right. Jamie had come to the funeral of his maternal grandfather and suffered nightmares for weeks afterwards.

'Doesn't it hurt to be burned?' He had clutched her hand in the crematorium.

'Oh, my darling, of course not.' Letty had been stricken with remorse. Nicky bent down to his son. 'Nothing hurts after you're dead, fish-face.'

'How do you know?'

'Because when you die your body and mind switch off completely, and you don't feel pain.'

'How do you know?'

'I just do, and you have to believe me.' He put his arm round Jamie's shoulder. 'So don't you worry.'

Jamie remained unconvinced. How could anybody know? What if the idea that a dead person felt no pain was simply wishful thinking on the part of the living? Hadn't Alba once told him that a severed head knew it was a severed head for at least a minute after it got chopped off?

Every night he dreamed of those purple curtains. Of his grandfather waking to find himself locked in his wooden box. Of sparks catching in his thick white hair. Jamie watched, trapped in sleep's helplessness, as his grandfather tried to beat out the flames on the sleeves of his favourite red checked jacket, and Jamie had wept for him.

So Letty spared him the funeral – if that's what the small, awkward, under-attended service in Bonn could be called – and she spared him her tears. She tried to spare all three children the talk. Heaven knows there had been plenty of that.

Appropriately, it had been the press attaché who found the letter. It was the morning after the accident and a methodical search of the embassy had yielded a piece of paper in Nicky Fleming's office and the smoked end of a cigarette on the embassy's roof. The letter was a draft, clearly an unsatisfactory one, crumpled into a ball and left on the desk. It had been addressed to Letty, but neither its existence nor its contents were disclosed to her for a further six days, by which time it had been examined and re-examined, its implications discussed and every word analysed for nuance and meaning.

My darling love, it began.

How wrong it feels to be writing this, when all I want to do is take you in my arms and tell you everything. It's ironic, really, given how much of my job is spent talking to strangers, that I have not found a way to reach the one person I love above all others . . .

And there the letter ended. Below this single paragraph, however, were a number of disjointed phrases, some crossed through, others underlined or scrawled at odd angles – and it was these that Letty read over and over again, until they were running through her head on perpetual loop.

Something I've been keeping from you, something that's been preying terribly on my mind

protect you and the children . . . in doing so I fear

a moment of madness

taken the only way out I thought possible

for which I am finding it hard to forgive myself

Forgive me, my love

An internal investigation was immediately launched into 'the matter of Fleming'.

Letty could not understand why the questions that consumed her were not pertinent to anyone else. Situated on an industrial allotment between Bonn and Bad Godesberg, the British embassy was a low, rectangular building with a flat roof. Certainly if you fell unhappily you would be killed, but a person intent on killing themselves? Moreover, how could anybody be so impatient for death that they fail to finish a suicide note? Nicky was a methodical man. He could not tolerate unfinished business. He was a neat man who might have crumpled a letter merely because he hadn't liked the slant of his handwriting. The letter was a private matter, she argued. It proved nothing. But according to Nicky's colleagues, it said everything.

Over the previous few years, indeed for much of the time that the Flemings had been stationed there, Bonn had suffered a number of 'irregularities', which, once discovered, had become increasingly hard to ignore. The leaks were small, often unconfirmed – yet suspicion persisted. Was a file missing or misplaced? Had an apparently chance meeting really been contrived? Distrust settled over Bonn like a thin layer of dirt. The Ambassador and those directly under him were emissaries between the British and the local governments and as such were privy to enormous amounts of intelligence. Enough alarm had been generated to warrant surveillance on one or two individuals but nothing concrete had been turned up. Still, diplomats, particularly high-ranking ones, did not often jump from the roofs of their own embassies. Now, fingers were quick to point. Nicky's polymath abilities, that unusual, God-given skill for absorbing information, had been one of the reasons he'd risen so fast in his job. Oh yes, everyone agreed, Fleming had been extravagantly well informed. So what secrets had he access to? And why had no one picked up that he might be 'unsafe'? Suspicion lit its own fire and it was only a matter of time before it burned a trail towards the greatest sin of all. Betrayal of Queen and Country.

To Letty, a woman for whom trust and loyalty were as

much part of her everyday life as bread and butter, it came as a shock – the speed with which Nicky's colleagues lined up to condemn him. Who knew, they argued, what clever, considered Nicky Fleming had really been up to? Who knew what cards he'd been holding or even what game he'd been playing? People were regularly expelled from the service – for spying, for being unsuitable, for being unsafe. To his colleagues, he was just another fallen angel of Britannia. In a world where deceit was the norm, the fact that Nicky Fleming was popular, respected and trusted only made his betrayal worse.

A week after Nicky's death, Letty was collected by car and taken to the embassy where she was questioned by two men from MI6. The more senior of the two, Porter, did most of the talking. He was a stocky man in his early forties with a metallic sheen to his skin, a damson smudge of tiredness beneath each eye and an expression in them that seemed untroubled by even a flicker of uncertainty about the world. His subordinate, Norrell, was a good deal better looking if you discounted the hint of scurf salting his collar. He stood, back to the door, while Porter conducted his questioning.

After he had finished, Letty stared at Nicky's letter on the table in front of her.

'My husband's stepmother, Gisela, the woman who raised him, was born in East Germany,' she said eventually.

'Yes, we know,' Porter agreed.

'On her twenty-fifth birthday, she stepped outside her house and tripped over a phosphorus bomb. Her leg was so badly burned that three months later, when the Russians came, she still found it hard to run.'

The MI6 men bowed their heads in dutiful respect. Letty noticed Norrell surreptitiously moving the arm of his suit upwards to check his watch, but she didn't care.

It had been 1945 and everybody knew the war was over. News was being funnelled over the radio and no one left their living rooms, desperate for some clue to their fate. Rumours had spread like a virus and panic followed. The English, French and Americans were coming. The Russians were coming. It was pure speculation how the Allies would divide up the occupied country, but Gisela's family lived in the east and they understood only too well the brand of respect Russian visitors held for family and property. Stalin's army was near starving, hungry for vengeance, and now it was to unleash its barbaric fury at the gates of Berlin. Terrified for the women, Gisela's grandfather sent them on ahead with barely an hour's notice. He himself stayed behind to bury the silver and the jewellery, with the exception of a brooch, which he gave to a local farmer in return for his family's passage in the back of a cart. If the scabby regrowth of melted skin on Gisela's leg was inflamed by the straw, Gisela's younger sister, an asthmatic, nearly suffocated under it. The farmer took them as far as the Elbe and instructed them to swim to a train on the other side. Of the forty-two people who tried to swim the Elbe that day, twelve drowned, including Gisela's mother and sister.

'The Russians slaughtered Gisela's grandfather. They expropriated the house, stole the farming land and handed it over to a collective,' Letty finished.

'Yes, yes, it's all a matter of record,' the man from MI6 reassured her, almost tenderly.

'And yet on the basis of this – ' she touched the edge of the letter – 'you're suggesting my husband is a traitor.'

'Tomorrow we would like to speak to your eldest daughter.' Porter checked his notes. 'Georgiana.'

'No.' Letty's jaw felt tight from lack of sleep. 'Absolutely not.'

Neither Porter nor Norrell appeared to feel the need to contradict her.

'What can you possibly want to talk to my daughter about?'

'Berlin,' Porter said, and Letty blinked at him.

'Your husband has recently spent considerable time in East Berlin, has he not?'

'He's part of an allied delegation there,' Letty said, unconsciously slipping Nicky back into the present where he belonged. 'He's to and fro all the time.'

'Effectively giving himself a channel of both travel and communication within East Germany.'

'What do you mean?' she said quickly. 'No, it's not like that at all. He's involved with that industrial accident.'

'Schyndell,' Porter supplied.

'Schyndell, yes.' There had been an explosion at a nuclear power plant in East Germany. The initial response of the Soviets had been to play it down, deal with it on a national level, but it had grown too big, too complex. The plant was experimental and in the process of being shut down when the accident occurred, releasing into the air unknown quantities – *curies*, she seemed to remember Nicky telling her they were called – of radioactive isotopes with few resources in place for clean-up. 'Of course, it was very bad propaganda for the Soviets to come to us cap in hand and by the time they did, the damage had already been done,' Nicky had said grimly. 'Yet another consequence of Cold War isolationism.'

'This was your husband's second term in Bonn, correct?' Porter said.

'Yes.'

'Four years as First Secretary.' Porter consulted his file. 'A stint in London in the news department at the Foreign Office. Back to Bonn this time as Counsellor.'

'The Ambassador requested him specifically,' Letty said.

To return had been the last thing she'd wanted. She had prayed for a different posting, but the personnel department had put pressure on Nicky. *I hope you're not going to be difficult about this* was the exact phrase they'd used. You can say no to them once, Nicky had cautioned, but career-wise, I'm not sure it would be the most prudent thing. Perish the thought, we're banished to Luxembourg or somewhere worse next time. So they'd returned to Bonn and almost immediately Schyndell had happened. A delegation of scientists, safety experts, technicians and diplomats had been assembled by the allies, effectively doubling Nicky's time away from home.

'A little coincidental,' Porter said. 'A little convenient, don't you think?'

'I don't understand'

'Was your husband asked to be part of the delegation or did he perhaps apply?'

'Nicky speaks fluent Russian and German. He knew he could be of help.'

'Quite,' Porter said. 'And at Schyndell he would have

had access to a considerable amount of information. Sensitive information.'

'On what?' Letty asked.

'Nuclear technology.'

'As would everyone on the delegation, surely.' Fear made her voice deepen.

'Which is why the question of trust is so significant.' Porter said silkily.

Norrell stepped forwards to the table and pulled out a chair. 'And then, of course, this most recent trip with your daughter was just after your husband heard about Rome,' he said.

Schyndell, East Berlin, Rome. Why were they throwing place names at her like darts? 'Rome?' she repeated almost crossly. Porter cleared his throat.

'The position there.' Norrell clarified. 'Minister.' Close up, his features were extraordinarily nondescript.

She frowned. 'But that hasn't been . . . what's that got to do with anything?' She'd been aware that Nicky was in the running. It was a posting they'd both been anxiously waiting to hear about, but he'd never said anything about it being announced. Was it possible he hadn't *told* her?

'Mrs Fleming, your husband would not be the first official operating at top level found guilty of corruption of some kind.' Norrell looked at her intently. 'Men "turn" for all sorts of reasons, ideological, fiscal, sexual. Men are turned by inadequacy, by disillusion or jealousy. They betray their country out of greed, revenge, self-loathing, desire. But sometimes,' he said gently, 'all it takes is a little disappointment.'

23

Ballanish

When Letty forbade Alick to touch any of the new white goods she could see from his bemused expression that he was at a loss to understand why. He sat at the kitchen table, a mug of coffee between oil-stained fingers, while Georgie read and Jamie crayoned and Alba stared moodily out of the window.

'Well, Let-ic-ia.' Alick drew her name out to its full polysyllabic form. 'And what if they break down?'

'They're brand new, Alick, and they're under guarantee. If you take them apart, the guarantee won't be valid any more.' Letty was well aware of delivering a crushing blow to his pride but she remembered only too well coming home to find Alick lying on his back on the kitchen floor surrounded by every single component part, down to the last nut and bolt, of the Raeburn, ranked by size and cross-referenced according to function.

'Alick, why have you dismantled the oven?' She'd been aghast.

'Ach, just to see if I could,' had been the reply.

Alick was a genius of a mechanic. There was nothing

he couldn't fix or build. When *Modern Times* had come to
Bonn's old theatre a few years earlier, Letty had watched
Charlie Chaplin being transported around the wheels
and between the cogs of his factory-assembling machine
and all she could think of was Alick. Like Chaplin, Alick
would have whipped out a spanner and tightened bolts
and spools as he went, unable to resist improving the
efficiency and speed of anything mechanical. Unlike
Chaplin, whose proletarian hero was struggling against
the onslaught of the industrial age, Alick would have sold
his soul for such technical opportunity and advancement.
Had life been fair and designed to reward the brilliant, a
man of his capability might have made his career with
Ford in Detroit or been snapped up by NASA and found
himself party to the colonization of space. But life was not
fair and it was particularly inequitable towards a man
born in the Outer Hebrides. There was limited scope for
his energy and imagination on the islands so he was
obliged to content himself with whatever Letty needed
doing around the house – mowing the lawn, bringing in
the peats, tinkering with the Peugeot or the old Land
Rover, one of which managed to break down almost every
other day – but there were times when Letty caught him
looking wistfully up at an aeroplane, cutting its trail
through the sky, as though here was daily proof that his
ambitions were too lofty to be within reach.

'A guarrrrantee, eh?' Alick rolled his tongue suspiciously around the word as if examining it for contractual
flaws. He dropped some tobacco into a cigarette paper
and began working the thin tube between his thumb and

middle finger. 'Well,' he declared grandly, 'I'd like to see this so-called guarantee take a spanner to the pipes when she blows.'

'Don't be offended, Alick,' Letty teased him. 'It's so good to see you. Tell me how you've been.'

'Aye, not bad,' he grinned, mollified. 'Not bad at all.' He struck a match to his roll-up and leant forwards in his chair. 'What do you think of the beast then?'

'The beast?'

'Aye, the beast in the garden.'

'What beast in the garden?'

'What bloody garden?' Alba banged her head against the window, startling a wounded starling that crouched miserably on the outer sill. 'Bet that bird will be dead before lunch.'

'What bird?' Jamie looked up from his drawing pad.

Alba jerked her chin towards the bog where a feral cat was on the prowl.

Jamie dropped his pen. 'Can't we bring it in? I don't want it to get eaten.'

'Too bad,' Alba said briskly. 'Nature is cruel.' She flicked at the starling through the glass. The day had turned uniformly wet. Clouds the colour of graphite were suspended under the sky. Water ran in rivulets down the guttering and clumps of sheep's wool were caught on the barbs of the wire fence. The perimeter of her world had shrunk to this – this one sodden, depressing view. People loved to say that life was too short. Well, they were bloody well wrong. Life was far, far too long.

'Have you no' seen the beast then, Let-ic-ia?'

'A beast?' Jamie stopped drawing again. 'Does it have horns?'

'It's a young beast, Jamie, barely two years old.'

'Is it a lion?'

Alick stowed his ciggy end in his breast pocket. 'Why, I've never heard tell of a lion on the island.'

'Is it a dragon, then?'

'Maybe it's an ugly hobgoblin like you,' Alba grumbled.

'Aye, it's a dragon, right enough.' Alick jumped to his feet. 'A dragon with great big teeth. Come in the garden and I'll show you.'

The garden was a fancy name for an acre of thistle enclosed by a ruined stone wall. From time to time Letty tried to encourage Alick to grow lettuce and vegetables there but Alick's heart beat for metals, not soil, and it didn't matter how much time she took choosing seeds and bulbs, only the potatoes ever survived.

Jamie pushed past Alick as he opened the gate. A baby dragon would be wonderful. He could feed it and keep it warm until its little pink tongue grew and split to a fork, until its teeth pushed through its jaw and lumps of sharpened bone rose like miniature volcanoes to the surface of its tail. Jamie extended his arm and sent out a single command. A scorching length of fire shot from the beast's mouth. Behind him, Alba was consumed.

'There she is,' Alick said. 'Over in the far corner.'

Jamie squinted at the tumbledown section of wall. No dragon. Instead, a lone cow was breathing steam from its nostrils and stamping a foot like an impatient racehorse.

'Whatever is it doing in here?' Letty frowned. 'Is it trapped?'

'Ach, now you can get your milk here and not walk all the way up to my father's house.'

'Oh, but I don't mind the walk.'

'Indeed, but it's a lot of bother.'

'But it's good to get out and about.' The unpleasant possibility that the cow might be some form of present was only now occurring to Letty, and besides, fetching the metal churn from outside Euan's croft was a morning ritual she enjoyed. 'Oh Alick, you're not really expecting me to milk this thing, are you?'

'It's no' so hard. I can teach you in a jiffy.'

'I don't know anything about cows.'

'You'll get the hang of them soon enough.' He stuffed another cigarette in the corner of his mouth before approaching the cow with his bucket.

'Be careful, she looks awfully cross.'

As if to confirm this dim view of its mood, the cow punched out an irritated moo as Alick ducked between its legs.

'Does that creature belong to us?' Alba said.

'I don't think so.'

'Is Alick trying to sell it?'

'I should imagine it's on loan for a bit.'

'I bet he stole it.'

'Don't be silly. Alick hasn't got a dishonest bone in his body.'

'He stole those windscreen wipers.'

'That was completely different,' Letty said equably. The year they'd driven up to the island in a rented car, they'd barely switched off the ignition before Alick had exchanged the Fiat's brand new windscreen wipers for the knackered ones of their Land Rover. 'That's island economics for you.'

'What about the time he ran over that sheep and had it butchered and in the larder within two hours.'

'That's island common sense. What else are you going to do with a dead sheep?'

'See, it's easy, Letitia!' Alick was now wringing the cow's teats like church bells. 'She's a fine-tempered beast and this milk is as fresh as you'll ever taste, and all for a few moments' milking.'

'She doesn't look fine-tempered at all,' Letty said warily.

On cue, the cow twisted its head and aimed a hefty kick at the bucket.

'You bugger!' Alick roared. He staggered out, his boiler suit covered in milk. The cow bucked. Green saliva dripped from its mouth like watercress soup.

'Go, devil cow!' Alba roared delightedly.

'Alick, take her away,' Letty implored. 'I can't possibly deal with her.'

'I'll do it,' Alba said suddenly. 'It'll be something to relieve the tedium of my life.'

'Good girl.' Alick was still wiping froth from his trousers. 'But if she's to be your beast, then you'd best name her.'

Alba scrutinized the cow with something approaching respect. Its flanks were heaving like a pair of fire bellows. 'We'll call her Gillian,' she pronounced.

'Oh, I don't think that's a very suitable name,' Letty said faintly.

'Fine.' Alba turned her evil eye on her mother. 'In that case, we'll call her the Ambassadress.'

24

London

Early spring 1972 and the buds on the cherry trees were just beginning to unfurl. Nicky had been preparing to take up the post of First Secretary in Bonn when one of the more senior wives cornered Letty on the staircase of the FCO.

'Ah, Letitia! Precisely the person I've been looking for.' And with great flourish, she presented Letty with an official-looking hardback book.

'How very kind,' Letty said. 'What is it?'

'It's called *The Guidance*. It's a veritable bible of information. It details all modes of expected behaviour and I think you'll find it invaluable.'

'Behaviour?' Letty asked warily. Even at sixty, the woman's shoulders had a formidable erectness. 'What sort of behaviour?'

'Oh, everything one might conceivably need to know about being a good diplomatic wife. What one should and shouldn't do. What one can or cannot say. Why, it even gives advice on how to write a good thank-you letter!'

Letty closed the book with a snap. 'It's very thoughtful of you, really, but I'm sure I'll be all right.' She tried to hand the tome back but the old gargoyle pressed it upon her regardless.

'I think you'll find that embassy life in Germany is a little different from in Africa, my dear,' she said reprovingly. 'Believe me, you would do well to be prepared.'

'Of all the archaic, absurd . . .' Letty had leafed through the book later that night. 'It stipulates here I'm expected to wear hats and gloves on every occasion!'

'Even in bed?' Nicky quipped.

'I wouldn't be surprised,' she laughed. 'Surely they don't expect anyone to take this seriously?'

'Even if they do, I'm sure you *won't*.' He'd plucked the book from her and tossed it into an empty packing crate, but before long it became apparent that she'd been naive to dismiss the publication so cavalierly. Arriving in Bonn after a nightmarish journey with the girls, she and Nicky had been dismayed to discover that a diplomatic party was in full swing at the private residence of the Ambassador and that despite Alba's pneumatic cough and Georgie's tummy upset, despite their own utter weariness, they were expected to attend.

The Ambassador's residence was to be found on a hill overlooking the Rhine, discreetly set back from the road behind an old ivy-smothered stone wall. It was a charming, most unthreatening sight, but when the doors opened to a grand drawing room filled with over two hundred people, Letty had been thoroughly intimidated. 'Christ.' She gripped Nicky's arm with both hands. 'Don't leave me.'

'Hoy!' a deep voice boomed. A tall woman in a royal-blue shift was hastening towards them with a somewhat mannish gait. 'You're not allowed to stand next to your husband, you know,' she chided and before Letty could protest or even blink the stranger bore her off to the furthest corner of the room. 'I'm Gillian,' she announced, 'the Ambassador's wife.'

25

Ballanish

The first time she saw him, a stick insect in a boiler suit, Georgie had been standing in the wind and rain, waiting for Donald John to answer his door. The figure had been crossing the bog between Donald John's house and the graveyard and she could just make out the crucifix of oars strapped to his back and what looked like a pair of boots dangling by their laces from his hand. Sprinkled with patches of purple butterwort and myrtle, Donald John's bog was deceptively benign-looking, but one false step could land a person up to their waist in sucky black mud. Nevertheless, the figure hardly broke stride as he zigzagged from tussock to stepping stone. She screwed up her eyes and watched him until the bright blue door opened abruptly and Donald John appeared in front of her, stooping a little under the low frame.

'Donald John!' Jamie hurled himself at the islander.

'Why, Jamie!' Donald John caught him under the armpits and gave his head a vigorous patting. 'And Alba and Georgie too? Well, well. How today? How today?' He grinned and beamed and every version in between, ushering the children into the croft and shouting double commands over his shoulder. 'Come in, come in. Sit down! Sit down.'

'So, how are you, Donald John?' Alba enquired.

'Not so bad, not so bad at all.' He dusted off a bottle of Cherry Coke from his store cupboard and produced a plate of ginger nuts.

Donald John, their nearest neighbour and Alick's first cousin, was the youngest of a confusingly named line-up of brothers: John, John Donald, Donald and Donald John. He had lived alone in the croft his entire adult life but bachelorhood appeared to suit him. Despite his fifty-odd years, he hadn't a wrinkle on his waxy face and while most of the islanders treated their teeth like their farm machines, neglecting them until they rusted and fell into disuse, Donald John boasted an almost god-like smile of pearly whites. His voice was shrill and he tended to deliver everything in a gleeful shout accompanied by a selection of verbal paroxysms all of which were ruthlessly mimicked by the children as soon as they left the croft.

'So, Donald John, I could hardly believe my ears,' Georgie teased. 'Alick says you've actually been off the island this year.'

'Aye, I went to Inverness to visit my sister-in-law, but that was a good many weeks back now, a good many weeks indeed.'

'And did you like it?' Alba demanded.

'Well, the weather was just awful.' He shook his head vigorously. 'Oh, boo boo, it was just terrible.'

'Was it very wet?' Georgie said sympathetically.

'Not wet, Georgie, it was hot! Yes indeed, it was terrible hot.'

'Oh dear, was it really, Donald John?' Alba said. 'Was it, perhaps, say, a whopping sixty-nine degrees?'

'I canna' say it was as high as that,' Donald John tapped his head as though the edge of his brain had been so badly singed by his close encounter with the sun that it no longer functioned. 'But sixty-five degrees anyways. Oh, tse tse, what a day that was,' he reminisced, sucking air into his cheeks and noisily expelling it again. 'I hate the heat. It was awful.'

'Imagine if you had to go to a desert then. It's a hundred and twenty degrees in the Sahara,' Jamie said.

Donald John's eyes opened in horror. 'Ah, boo boo, I would be dead. Aye, dead, that's it!' Amongst his variety pack of exclamatory noises he pulled one out that sounded like a crow being throttled.

'But don't you want to see a desert, Donald John? Don't you want to go somewhere exciting, like abroad?'

'Abroad?' This warranted an extra strenuous slap of the knee. 'No, no, I've never been to that place,' he admitted gaily, 'and I'm sure I never will.'

The fact was that Donald John had been born on the island and would die on the island and he felt heartily sorry for anyone for whom this was not the case. The very concept of travel was abhorrent to his sensibilities. Should the children declare an interest in driving to a beach even a few miles to the north, he'd shake his head and try his best to dissuade them. If they mentioned a business trip their father had made, Donald John would adopt a terminally mournful expression. 'Paris? Well, well, poor soul, poor soul.'

Jamie loved Donald John's kitchen with its custard-coloured walls and shiny blue Raeburn. He sipped his cherry fizz and looked round at the never-changing objects on the mantelpiece – a school photo of his nieces, a postcard from Glasgow and the plastic clock whose twelve numerals were depicted by small songbirds. It was as though the clock illustrated the pattern of Donald John's life. When the big hand reached the wren, Donald John put on his cap and went out to tend the cattle. On the hour of the starling he prepared himself a dinner of bread, butter and herring. Visitors seemed to arrive between the thrush and the finch but when not entertaining Donald John spent his evenings in silence. No television, his radio switched off, just sitting in his chair, absorbing each tick of the clock and growing one second older with it. If the world slowed around grown-ups, Jamie thought, time crawled around islanders.

'So, Donald John,' Alba said, 'have you found a wife since we last saw you?'

'No, no.' He dutifully roared with laughter and reassured the girls he was saving himself for them.

'So come on, what other news?' Georgie asked. 'Any good gossip?'

'You'll have heard about the beast, I suppose?'

'Oh, yes, we love the beast!' Alba said.

'You've seen it, then?' Donald John sounded surprised.

'Alick took us.'

'Is that so, Georgie. Is that so?'

'Alba thinks it's deranged,' Jamie said.

'It *is* deranged,' Georgie agreed. 'It tried to kick Alick.'

'Ha ha, oh, I'm very sure it did.'

'Poor Alick was only trying to milk it,' Jamie said.

'Was he now!' Donald John began rocking backwards and forwards with amusement. 'Why, you'd have a hard job milking a wild thing like that, right enough!'

'Alba's going to try it next,' Jamie pressed on. 'Alick is going to teach her.'

'Oh, he'll make a fine teacher to be sure!' To the children's growing puzzlement, Donald John was now wiping tears, apparently of laughter, from his eyes. 'Well, you'd better not get too close, Alba, no indeed, it'll take your fingers off. Ach, it's to be expected. Why, it's not right to cage a beast up like that!'

'It's hardly caged up,' Georgie said. 'It's not like it would get much more exercise if it were loose on the machair. Besides, at least it has all the food it wants. It never stops eating, as far as I can see.'

'Aye, fifteen pounds of meat for its dinner every night!'

'Meat?' Georgie stole a look at Alba, an uncomfortable suspicion forming between them. Teasing was exclusively their department. It was not meant unkindly. It had never occurred to them that Donald John might find them anything but highly amusing but the truth was there wasn't a lot for them to talk about. Bonn, their schools, embassy life were of no more than polite interest to Donald John, who had little frame of reference for anything that happened off the island. Oh, perhaps if some seismic event occurred, say, an IRA bomb exploding or the discovery of life on Mars, there might be some minor 'oohing' and 'aahing', but even these paled in significance compared with news of MacCuish's lost cattle or the report of an islander having trouble with his wife. And this summer of all summers, Georgie found it a blessing. She dreaded anyone bringing up the subject of her father. What she didn't know was that Donald John felt uncharacteristically strongly about the matter and in so far as he was able to voice disapproval about anything, he had clearly been troubled by Letty's decision to bury Nicky in Bonn.

'It's where his mother and father are buried,' she'd told him.

'Aye, but who will visit him there?' Donald John asked, clearly troubled, and Letty had been unable to answer. She could not tell him the circumstances around Nicky's death. She would do everything possible to protect Nicky's reputation here on the island and the last thing she needed was more pity from friends who could no longer meet her eye. Georgie felt the same. Resorting to tried and tested jokes about wives and weather was safer for the girls – but this was the first time they had received any of their own treatment in return and it made them profoundly uncomfortable.

'What do you mean, "fifteen pounds of meat"?' Georgie asked tentatively.

'Why, he feeds it steak for dinner and bacon and eggs for breakfast. I've even heard it said the beast guzzles down coffee! You'd think it was a human the way it carries on.'

'Donald John, have you gone mad?' Alba said. 'Cows don't eat meat.'

'Or drink coffee,' Jamie added.

'And who's feeding it?'

'Why, Georgie, the wrestler is feeding him.' It was Donald John's turn to look confused. 'It's his beast an' all.'

'What on earth are you talking about?' The children stared at him in utter bewilderment.

'Why, the bear of course.'

'The bear?' Jamie stopped gargling his cherry coke.

The girls looked at each other in stupefied silence. 'We've been talking about a bear all this time?' Alba said. 'What kind of bear?'

'Well now, I'm not sure what *species* exactly,' Donald John said placidly, 'but a big one right enough.'

'Donald John,' Georgie said firmly, 'you're having us on.'

'Not at all. It is indeed a great big bear.'

'But we were talking about the cow Alick put in our garden.'

'A cow!' Donald John cracked out a laugh. 'Oh, boo boo, it's a lot bigger than a cow, that's for sure!'

'Are you saying there's an actual live bear on this island right now?'

'Aye, he belongs to that wrestler, Andy Robin, and he's quite famous. He even has his own bus.'

Suddenly, the loose wires in Jamie's head began to spark and fizz. He jumped to his feet. 'I've seen him.'

'You have not,' Alba said scornfully. 'Sit down.'

'I saw him on the way up here,' Jamie spluttered. 'He's my bear. He's a grizzly bear.'

'Jamie, you repellent troll, you're frothing at the mouth.'

'But I told you, remember?' Jamie wiped his mouth on his sleeve. 'It was on the road.'

'Why would anyone bring a bear up to the island?' Alba elbowed Jamie down into his seat.

'Oh, they say he's a hard-working beast, Alba. I've heard tell he's filming an advertisement – for Kleenex.'

'Does he do tricks?' Jamie asked. 'Can he ride a bicycle?'

'Oh, boo boo, I can't say, but I'm sure you'll be wanting to go and see him, young Jamie.'

But Jamie had already disappeared inside his head. How was it possible? The bear from the museum. The bear on his flyer. The bear waiting for him at the *Zirkusplatz* the day of his father's accident. And now here he was on the island. His island. His bear.

'Hello, bear,' Jamie whispered.

'Hello, Jamie,' the bear answered.

26

'Can we go now?' Jamie said feverishly. 'Can we?'

'In a minute, darling,' Letty whispered.

'How many minutes?'

'Oh, I don't know. A few, ten, fifteen . . .' Though increasingly aware of her son's need for precision, Letty was often unsure how best to supply it. 'As soon as possible,' she amended, turning back to the islander. 'So, how much do you want for it, Roddy?' Dolefully she eyed the wooden sideboard through the window. It didn't really matter how much he asked, they both knew she would end up buying it, just as she had ended up buying the unspeakably hideous wardrobe that was always going to be too big for the house; the iron bedstead that still languished in the outside room; not to mention the old peat-boiling cauldron whose handle had long since sheared off.

'Well now, I pulled it out of old Hugh's croft, down at Griminish. Oh, aye, terrible heavy it was.'

'I'm sure,' Letty murmured. Roddy bargained with a Gaelic adroitness and was not above a spot of emotional blackmail to hike up the price.

'Mum, pleeease?' Jamie said fretfully.

'Jamie, be patient. I'm having a cup of tea with Roddy.'

Jamie watched the old wall-builder as he spooned a fourth sugar into his mug. He was the oddest-looking man Jamie had ever seen. A unique genetic concoction, it was as if Roddy had pulled a face one day and deliberately ignored all warnings about an impending wind change. His head resembled something carved out of rock. His wiry eyebrows grew as untrimmed as a hedge of twigs. His lips were dark purple, his ears like handles of clay and the deep depression of lines etched into his cheek ran clear down to the prominent ridge of his jaw. The most startling aspect of Roddy's appearance, though, was not the epic cragginess of his face but the lump of bone on his back, which had bent his spine into an unyielding curve. No one knew for sure why Roddy was a hunchback. Most assumed he'd been born deformed, but the only time Letty had asked about it, Donald John had scoffed at the idea. 'Oh, boo boo. I was going to school with him when I was a boy. Ach, he was just the same as you or I. Straight as a plank. Then he started building walls and lifting heavy stones and the whatnot and that's when it must have started.'

To compensate for this dreadful physical burden, which would never allow him to get very far in the world, Roddy had been granted a more spiritual form of transportation. He was the seventh son of the seventh son and as such had been endowed with that most precious of island characteristics – second sight.

By rights, second sight should have opened up the universe to him, presented him with a visual history of mankind and the creation and destruction of forgotten empires. Second sight should have been his telescope to far-off lands, where mountains rose out of the sea and waves of sand burned under the desert heat. Instead of staring down at his dinner of boiled rabbit, Roddy might have peeked through the keyhole of history onto the great Viking feasts of Sigrblot, Vetrarblot and Jolablot but alas, none of this was so. Roddy's gift dealt only with the future and appeared to have been given to him for a more pedestrian use altogether – the prediction of births, deaths and who would be bringing home the prize for best cow at the Highland Games.

'I'll take twenty pounds for it,' Roddy said finally. Letty stole another glance at the sideboard. It really was an unconscionably ugly piece of carpentry. Twenty pounds! She didn't have twenty pounds. 'I'll take it for ten, Roddy,' she said firmly.

'Well, if my hard work is of no greater value to you,' Roddy removed his cap and scratched at the sparse hairs on his head, 'then, ten pounds it is.'

'Good.' Jamie pushed back his chair. 'Can we go now, Mum, please?'

'Where are you away to in such a hurry?'

'Jamie wants to see the bear,' Letty said apologetically.

'Oh, aye?' Roddy's voice was so deep it sounded as though it had travelled through all the peat bogs of the island before reaching his throat. 'Too late for that, lad.'

'What?'

'Aye,' Roddy said mildly. 'He's gone.'

'Oh no.' Jamie sank unhappily back into the chair. 'When?'

'No one knows for sure.'

'Are you positive he's gone?'

'Aye, it was last night I had news of it.'

'What kind of news?'

'Well.' Roddy noisily slurped at his cold tea. 'I'll tell you.' He leaned forward. 'I was asleep when I heard a terrible knocking on the door so I went to the door and there was this big horse waiting outside for me, and it could talk, this horse, you see, and it says, "Will ye come out with me, Roddy?" and I replied, "I can come with you right enough," and I jumped in the saddle. Soon enough, the horse was galloping along the field past Morag's house when he turns his black head and he says to me, "D'ye understand I'm the devil, Roddy?"

'"Is that so?" I replied and indeed when I take a look over my shoulder, there was room for another behind me on the saddle. So I says to the devil horse, "I see you have got another place here. Is it for poor Morag, then?"

'"Oh, no," the devil answers, cheerful as anything. "We're calling along the road to pick up old Fergus Mc-Kenzie."'

'Fergus with the white sheepdog?' Fergus McKenzie sang at *céilidhs* and always waved his stick in greeting from the door of his croft. Quite why he'd been consigned to the devil, Jamie couldn't imagine.

'Aye, it was Fergus he was after, all right,' Roddy said. 'They found him the next morning. Quite dead he was.'

'But how did he die?' Jamie was utterly transfixed.

'Well, that's the very same question I asked the devil horse,' Roddy declared grandly. '"Now, devil horse," I says, "Fergus McKenzie's in good health and no more

than eighty-nine so what business does he have in dying?"
And the devil horse turns to me, his eyes burning with red
fire and he says, "He's going to die of fright, that's what!"'

Roddy paused dramatically and raised his eyes to
Jamie's face. 'Of frrrrright,' he repeated awfully. 'Now,
can you imagine a death like that?'

'Yes, it would be horrid,' Jamie agreed politely, 'but
Roddy, what's it got to do with the bear?'

'Why, it was sight of the bear that killed Fergus, right
enough. Terrified him to death! No man's heart is strong
enough for a sight like that.'

'I don't understand.' Roddy's labyrinthine thought
process had finally led Jamie to a dead end. 'I thought you
said the bear had gone home.'

'I said the bear had gone all right, but I never said he'd
gone home. No, indeed.'

'Then where is he?' Jamie gripped the edge of the table.

'He's escaped.'

'He's what?' Letty stopped wiping down the table.

'Aye, the bear's run off and frightened poor Fergus
McKenzie to death. I'm surprised you've not heard!'
Roddy said with satisfaction. 'Why, the beast's escaped
and he's been loose and wild on the island these many few
days.'

27

 Over there, can you spot him? the islanders ask. Fishing in the loch; clambering up the rocky face of Taransay; running on all fours across the mouth of Aivegarry? Most are surprised he's still free. An eight-foot-four-inch anomaly loose on a sparsely inhabited, predominately flat island measuring twelve miles by fifteen.

The community divides into two groups. Those who see him but don't recognize him for what he is and those who have never seen him, yet identify him in every lump of seaweed or rusting oil drum. His is the dark shadow that falls across the window of their crofts at night. He is why their arthritis is flaring up or the reason they argue with their wives.

He is their demon chimera, their Frankenstein's monster.

And what a fleet-footed bear he is! Spotted coursing through the heather over at Loch Borrath, whilst at the same time taking a stroll ten miles east, across the ridged dunes of Stinky Bay. The wrestler's grizzly is a hostile bugger, an aggressive beastie. Every smashed lobster pot has been attributed to his foot, every carelessly mended gate to his unlawful entry. Then he is a skilled and ruthless predator, tearing the heads off salmon and strewing the island with the flesh of savaged red deer, and so now human and animal alike tremble at the mere thought of him.

In reality, though, he has yet to leave his cave. He has killed nothing. Eaten nothing.

And the hunger is beginning to hurt.

28

Bonn

Disappointment. That was the best the combined investigative powers of MI6 and the British government came up with. Nicky Fleming, disgruntled employee, passed over for promotion, had sought revenge on his country by filtering some as-yet-undiscovered information to an as-yet-undiscovered source. Then, unable to live with the guilt, he had confessed to his wife in a 'suicide note' and cast himself from the embassy roof. Simple. Tidy.

Six days after they had questioned Letty, Porter and Norrell returned to London. The autopsy report was clean. No abnormality detected. The verdict was recorded as suicide. File and case closed.

There was one flaw in the in-house trial of Nicky Fleming. That he was guilty was accepted as fact. But of what exactly, no one was sure. No recent documents had been discovered missing, there was no sign of files being copied. Evidence of an affair was not forthcoming. Nothing seemed out of place, except, of course, Nicky Fleming himself, dead and broken on the unforgiving ground, and then there was the letter. A confession, they'd argued. The investigation was as thorough as it was useless and by the end of it, there were no more answers than at the beginning.

'They can't leave it like this, Tom, they can't.' Letty paced the kitchen. 'You know him better than anyone. You know he wasn't capable.'

'Of course not.' Tom spread his hands in a gesture of helpless sympathy, but in the weeks following Nicky's death, Letty had become expert at picking up on the nuances of people's tones. Could she have imagined it? Tom was the last person from whom she would expect it – nevertheless, it had been there, the faintest hesitation in his answer. A certain inflection. She looked at him intently. She knew his face so well, the serious expression that masked a dry humour, the hawkish features, more suited to henchman in a film noir than a civil servant of the government. They had met by chance, on Piccadilly in a downpour, and ended up sharing the taxi they'd both been hailing. Had he courted her? She had never been convinced; certainly he was diligent in his friendship, taking her to the theatre, to the odd party, but then Nicky had come along . . .

'Make them dig deeper, Tom,' she said. 'Make them keep the file open until his name has been cleared.'

And there it was again. A flicker.

'Tom?'

'Let it rest, Letty, maybe it's for the best.'

'For the *best*! Dear God, how can it be for the best when everyone believes Nicky's a traitor?'

'The harder you push for answers, the deeper they'll dig. Every minute of Nicky's life, every aspect of your marriage will be under the microscope.'

'I don't give a damn. There's nothing there. Nothing.'

Tom was silent.

'You don't believe in him, do you?' Her voice began to rise.

'Letty, you must understand how ruthless the machinery of government can be . . . Nobody's life can stand up to this much scrutiny. I've seen it before. They will grind you down until there is nothing left.'

'It's not that,' she said hollowly. '*You* don't believe in him. I can see it in your eyes.'

'Letty.' He gripped her arm.

'No, don't touch me.' Once she started trembling she couldn't stop. She slumped in a chair and covered her face with her hands. 'How could you?' she whispered. 'You, of all people.'

A muscle ticked in Tom's cheek. 'Trust me in this, Letty, the last thing you want is for them to delve any deeper, for Nicky's sake,' he said. 'For everyone's sakes.'

Letty lifted her head. 'Protecting your position, Tom?'

'That's not fair.'

'Then what is it?'

He hesitated.

'Tell me, goddamnit!'

'All right, Letty, all right.' He sat down heavily. 'Look, about nine months ago Nicky and I had lunch at the Travellers Club. He told me he'd come into contact with someone. Someone he needed to help.'

'What do you mean? Who, where?'

'East Berlin.'

Letty felt a pain in her backbone as if her vertebrae were starting to crumble, one by one. 'Who?' she repeated.

'Letty, I don't know. He asked only whether he could count on my help.'

'For what?'

'He wouldn't say.'

'So what did you tell him?'

'That I couldn't possibly evaluate what he was asking out of context but that it was insanity to be involved in anything underhand, *particularly* in East Berlin.'

'But you agreed to help, of course.'

'I told him that whatever it was, he *must* talk to the Ambassador, go through the official channels.'

'You turned him down?' she said incredulously.

'Try to understand, Letty. A man in Nicky's position is particularly vulnerable. Nicky would have to assume that anybody with whom he came into contact would likely be an informant or a potential plant. You have no idea the internal soul-searching that goes on in assessing the risk factor of any chance meeting, let alone one in the GDR. For Nicky to become entangled with someone in East Berlin would mean going against all his instincts, all his training.'

'So why would you think him capable of such a thing? Why are you convinced it was underhand?'

'Because, had it been above board, there would have been no reason to ask for my help.'

'And yet he came to you.'

Tom stared unseeingly at the table. 'You think I haven't turned it over and over since?'

'Have you, Tom?'

'Letty.' He reached for her hand again and the briefest of memories came to her. A London dance, Tom's arm about her waist. One minute he'd been looking down at her, a smile in his eyes, the next he was looking over her shoulder and a shadow had passed over his face. It was as if he'd known, even then, before she and Nicky had ever met.

'You never wanted us to be happy,' she said. 'Right from the start.'

'That's not true.' Tom looked startled.

'You can never truly know someone, can you? You never know who your friends are until you really need them.' She watched Tom flinch. The thought had come from nowhere but as soon as she voiced it, it gained traction.

'Nicky was your recruit.' She was glaring at him now, her eyes brimming with misery, and as she cast around for an even larger stone to fling at him one came to hand. If Nicky was under suspicion then why not Tom, who had been so closely involved in Nicky's career. Tom, head of the Northern Department who came to Bonn all the time, travelled often to Berlin. *The leaks had been small . . . unconfirmed.* If Tom had crossed any lines then how expedient for blame to be laid at Nicky's door. 'Is there a reason it suits you to distance yourself from him now?' she said, and the accusation in her voice was impossible to ignore.

Tom pushed back from the table. 'Don't lecture me about loyalty or friendship,' he said bitterly. 'I have been a better friend to Nicky than you will ever understand.'

'No. You betrayed him, you betrayed us both.' She could see him trying to keep his temper in check, but she didn't care. She was in the grip of some kind of madness – and it felt so good to vent her own anger.

'You talk about knowing someone. Well, you're right,' Tom flung back at her. 'Nicky loved you with all his heart, but he has never been the man you thought he was.'

'How *dare* you.' She rose and slapped him in one swift movement. 'How dare you try to poison me against him, he was a better man than you'll ever be. I know one thing about my husband. You were his closest friend and he would have taken a bullet for you.'

Her hand was still raised when he caught her wrist. 'It doesn't matter about me, Letty.' And his voice was harsh. 'Hold on to what *you* believe. That's all that's important.'

29

Ballanish

'There's something wrong with my heart,' Jamie announced, skipping along the sandy path behind his sisters. He clutched his chest solemnly. 'Sometimes I feel the wind blowing right through it.'

'Then zip up your jacket, stupid,' Alba said, 'and don't fall behind.'

Jamie skipped faster. In spite of the ache in his chest, he felt cheerier than he had done in weeks. Fate could not have stuck its nose in his business in a more obliging way. Now he could search for the bear and keep a lookout for his father at the same time. He touched the bottle in his pocket. He'd already launched three maps from different points on the island, not including the one he'd dropped over the side of the ferry. If his luck held, maps in glass bottles would soon be bobbing on the ocean towards every corner of the globe.

'I say we do this methodically.' Georgie squinted towards the sea. 'A different beach each day. It's bound to be in hiding. So we'll have to track it.'

'Like check for footprints or poo?'

'Splendid idea, Jamie.' Alba grabbed her brother and

pushed his head towards the acidic splatter of a cowpat. 'Is this bear poo, Holmes? Is it? Is it? Take a sniff and tell us, why don't you?'

'I think this is cow poo,' Jamie offered nervously. He calculated the odds were low that his face might end up actually immersed in the steaming mass, but Alba's unpredictability was unnerving. At the penultimate moment, she released him with an amiable ear twist. 'Cows are utterly disgusting,' she declared.

'I thought you liked them.' Jamie moved discreetly to Georgie's side and took her hand. 'What about the Ambassadress?'

'The Ambassadress is different. We have an understanding. This lot are a bunch of Nazis. Look, why are they standing in a circle? Do you think they have a plan?'

'There's no plan,' Georgie sighed. 'They're cows.'

'I don't like the way they're rounding us up. Get away, you herd of hamburgers. Shoo!'

Jamie giggled. When Alba was in a good mood the sun shone into every dark corner of his world. And Alba was in a good mood. Now there was a purpose to the day; life had improved. 'By the way,' she mused, 'it's far more likely the bear will be tracking us rather than the other way round.'

'Why would it track us?'

'We're food, idiot.'

'The bear doesn't eat people. It eats steak.'

'A human can't get a steak on this island, let alone a bear.'

'It could eat fish.'

'It doesn't know how to catch fish. It's a tame bear. It

doesn't know how to do anything but wrestle. I'm telling you, when it gets hungry enough, it will track down the smelliest, most putrid thing on the island – you, Jamie – and then bingo, we'll be minding our own business and it will leap out from behind a rock.'

'But I want it to leap out from behind a rock.'

'And chew your face off?'

'The bear won't eat me.'

'It'll eat you if it gets hungry enough. I'd eat you if I was hungry enough. I'd eat you even if I wasn't hungry – just to get rid of you.'

'What if he tried to walk across the Bog of Stench?' Adroitly Jamie changed the subject.

'Then the Bog of Stench Men will drown him,' Georgie said, 'and no one will get the reward.'

'I don't care about the reward, I just don't want him to drown.' Jamie put his binoculars to his eyes and stared at the bog as though expecting to see the bear's paw being sucked down through the reeds.

The Bog of Stench was a stretch of wet marshlands between the house and the machair that had proved so dangerous to both people and livestock that the council had taken the unusually energetic measure of fencing it off. Bog of Stench Men, a creation of their father's, were ghosts of malevolent Viking invaders who rose up through the ground in order to prey on small children. According to Nicky, the Bog of Stench Men moved so quickly across the land that they left shreds of their skin on the sharp barbs of the fence. Whenever Jamie saw these black strips flapping in the wind, he would shudder with fear until

Alick told him they were bits of the plastic bags used by the islanders to transport silage.

Their father had been a master of scary stories but Jamie had never taken to the concept of being terrified. Alba, on the other hand, relished it. Once, when she'd been little, Nicky had driven her and Georgie to the farmlands of Liberia, and she'd asked him about the deep furrows in the sandy earth. 'Ah yes.' He knelt down and spread his hand over the undulating soil. 'These are made by a monster who lives under the land. Whenever he gets thirsty, which is often, he sucks all the moisture out of the soil until the ground collapses.' Alba had loved the idea of the soil-eating monster, but that night, when Nicky had come to kiss her goodnight, she had stared at him with burning eyes before turning her head to the wall.

'What is it?' he stroked her hair fondly. 'Why won't you kiss your old Dada?'

'Because you told me something scary,' she said furiously, 'and Mummy said it wasn't true.' Nicky had never understood that she wasn't cross because he had lied to her – she was cross because she had so badly wanted the monster to be real.

A bird was skimming low over the reeds. Distracted, Jamie followed it with the binoculars. 'Is that a curlew, Alba?'

'How the holy hell should I know?'

'What do you think though?'

'I don't think, and what's more I don't care. Birds are pointless.'

'No, they're not.'

'Jamie, you don't think you're pointless but that doesn't mean you aren't.'

'But I need to know for my bird book.'

'Why, so you can mark down that you've seen a curlew? How thrilling. But let's examine why it's so thrilling, shall we? Are you going to shoot the curlew and eat it? Are you going to adopt it or convert it to Christianity? The question you have to ask yourself is – will identifying this bird change your life in any way, and if the answer is no, then I think we can all agree that birdwatching is a pathetic hobby, and that birds along with cows are disgusting, soulless animals.'

'To you,' Jamie said with uncharacteristic spirit, 'but not to me. Can't you think about me for once?'

'Jamie, you think about you the whole time. If I were to think about you as well, it might create a dangerous imbalance in the universe.'

'It couldn't do that. Thinking doesn't weigh anything.'

'Fine, smarty-pants.' Alba snatched the binoculars from him and aimed them at the sky. 'Yup, it's a curlew.' She turned the glasses sideways and machine-gunned the bird. 'And now it's a dead curlew. Oh, dearie me.'

Jamie giggled. 'I love you, Alba.' He moved to hug her but she pushed him away. Jamie looked momentarily defeated then ran to catch up with Georgie. Alba was un-repentant. If she had her way, all physical manifestations of affection would be forbidden, but knowing that an out-right ban would bring some degree of censure from her mother, she had settled for imposing restrictions. Kissing was not allowed under any circumstances and hugging was rationed to one every third day. Still, sticking even to this Alba found irksome.

'Hey, there's someone on the beach,' Georgie shouted.

'What?' Alba ran to the top of the dune. Below them, a man and a woman were hovering over a small child who was troughing into a wet channel of sand with a plastic spade. 'Tourist pig dogs!' Alba narrowed her eyes. 'A pox on them and their plaguey brat!'

'Should we go and say hello?' Jamie said hopefully.

'No, they might think we're friendly.'

'Aren't we friendly?'

'No, we are not. In fact, I'm going to get rid of them.'

'Alba, wait!' Georgie called, but Alba was already zigzagging down the dunes waving her arms frantically at the small family. The couple looked up.

'I'm sorry . . .' Alba stopped, panting, in front of them, '. . . but I had to warn you.'

'Goodness, what?' They frowned.

'You mustn't let your child play on this beach.'

The couple stared at her. Alba stared back. They belonged to her least favourite anthropological category of hippy.

'Why on earth not?' asked the mother.

'Jellyfish.' Alba made a vague gesture designed to take in not only the entire length of beach, but most of the island too. 'They're poisonous this year.'

'Poisonous!' The couple exchanged a look. 'In Scotland?'

'Yes, I know, that's what we thought, but my brother, my beloved little brother Jamie . . .' she hung her head,

'. . . well, he was stung a few months ago. The jellyfish were only small, normal looking. No one knew . . . no one could have known.' She broke off and shamelessly began wailing. The couple, torn between scepticism, the grieving child before them and their own toddler pawing at the sand, perilously close, as it happened, to one of the beach's many harmless jellyfish, were taking no chances. Hurriedly, they scooped up the baby and thrust a tissue at Alba.

'Sweetheart,' the woman said, her own eyes brimming. She glanced desperately up and down the beach. 'Are you all right? Are your parents with you?'

'My mother's at home and my father . . . well, the thing about my father,' Alba continued in a tiny voice, 'is that he's dead too.'

The couple reeled back in comic unison.

A recently deceased parent had its uses, Alba had discovered. The merest reminder of her father's accident was enough to silence most people and the pity it invoked was a commodity that could be traded for all manner of benefits. A particularly stricken look she'd developed had saved her from school detention on numerous occasions and even the manner of her father's death could be embroidered or adapted to suit every eventuality. Over the past six months, she'd had him murdered, dying of a brain tumour, executed by the Red Army, falling out of a plane and rotting in a Siberian prison – although this last version had been a mistake, as the idea that he was still alive had made her feel the incomprehensibility of his loss far more than the fact of his death. She hadn't easily come to grips with the irony of these feelings, until she reminded herself that these fabricated stories were easier to believe than the truth. After all, look at the business her father was in. He knew so much about everything. It stood to reason that buried in all that knowledge was something dangerous, something he might have been killed for.

'How could he have fallen?' Alba had shouted hysterically that terrible night. 'People don't just fall. It doesn't make sense.'

Letty had hugged her close, crying herself. 'It was an accident, darling, no one's fault, just a terrible, terrible tragedy.'

And 'a terrible tragedy' had effectively been her mother's last word on the subject. But though Alba had spent the majority of her sentient years ignoring the feelings of others, she was not insensitive when it came to herself. As time went on she picked up on an undercurrent, a certain fear and reluctance on the part of her mother to explain. And not only her mother.

'What do you mean, they want to see you at the embassy?' she'd demanded of her sister.

'They just do.'

'There has to be a reason. They're sending a car for you.'

Georgie had shrugged. 'They want to know about Berlin.'

'Berlin?' Alba said indignantly. 'Did something *happen* in Berlin?' It was bad enough she hadn't been allowed to go herself, but the idea that something noteworthy had occurred there was too much to bear and when Alba caught the hesitation in her sister's answer, her already narrow synapses closed further, sending a sharp signal to her brain. Information was being kept from her – and it made her spit.

'Oh, my dear child.' The woman clutched her sandy angel to her breast and grasped her husband's arm for comfort. 'Oh, you poor girl. Look, we have a car. Can we take you somewhere? Why don't we drive you home?'

Alba had intended to round off the encounter with a theatrical blow of her nose, but suddenly her real feelings converged with her fake ones and she felt the welling up of actual tears behind her eyes. She shook her head and waved them away.

The thing was, some days it was all she thought about. The how and the why. Her father had died over six months ago. One day he had an office to go to, a suit to wear and a briefcase to carry. He had been a man with a job, a family to love and a set of ethics to live by. One moment blood had been pumping round his veins, his brain had been a mass of connecting thoughts, each one sparking ideas, evaluating problems, offering solutions. In the next moment, a moment that would only ever belong to him, he was gone. So what had he seen, her father, as he fell? The faces of his children? Had he flashed through his early years in Germany, then moved on to the cloisters of Eton, Canterbury Quad at Christ Church, the metal latrines of the army quarters? Had he tasted again his first kiss and subjected each of his life's successes and disappointments to the millisecond of re-examination allotted them? Alba thought not. Her father was a practical man. In the time left to him he would have tried to solve the problem of his impending death, considered how best to survive. Ingrained in his diplomatic nature was the desire to weigh all options evenly but perhaps this time, this one time, the necessity for a decision had come too fast.

'That was quick.' Georgie was always appalled by, yet at the same time secretly admiring of her younger sister's behaviour. 'Did you tell them there was a grizzly loose on the island?'

'A grizzly?' Alba quickly wiped her nose on her sleeve and swiped the tears from her eyes.

'Don't be ridiculous, Georgie, they'd never have believed that.'

30

East Berlin

The trip had been the month before her father died. It was the first time Nicky Fleming had ever taken any of his children away with him on business and Georgie experienced a degree of smugness at being the chosen one – a smugness which grew exponentially after Alba became inconsolable on discovering she was not to be invited. But then Alba did not boast her elder sister's credentials. On 13 August 1961, at the precise moment that armed military units of the GDR sealed East Berlin from the rest of the world and began construction of the wall, Georgiana Gisela Fleming was speeding through the underpass of her mother's womb towards a freshly changed hospital bed in St Thomas's, London. So it was Georgie's wall, too, and though conceived as a prototype, a semi-porous trial run of barbed wire and oppression, by the time the Flemings arrived in Germany it had grown into an impenetrable concrete barrier incarcerating East Germany's seventeen million inhabitants in an open prison of material and civil deprivation. Yet, even though the division of Germany was a national convulsion, it had not been the first thing Georgie studied when she'd graduated to the Bonn High School, nor, could it be said, was the war, with its fifty-five million dead, placed top of her educational agenda. This hadn't bothered Georgie. Despite the shared birthday, she had little genuine enthusiasm for the subject, and had begun studying it with the sole purpose of impressing her father. There were almost always references to East Berlin in the *General-Anzeiger*, snippets for her to latch on to during those agonizing newspaper trials on the chaise longue, and so she'd feigned an interest in Trotsky's perpetual revolution. She'd memorized quotes from Lenin, Churchill, Stalin, Truman and Hitler, those venerable fathers of Germany's bizarre game of modern-day politics, but in the end it was the Wall itself, with its metal plating, electric fences and creepy observation towers, that caught her imagination for real. She had found herself devouring stories of houses cut in two, of families leaping from the window of one country to the soil of another. Bonn was full of refugees who had fled East Germany at one time or another and her grandmother, Gisela, had been one of them. On surviving the river crossing, she had been rescued by widower Lieutenant Peter Fleming, who had bound her inflamed leg and married her within the year. By the time Georgie turned fourteen, the Wall wasn't just a physical divide between two opposing ideologies, it had become the very embodiment of danger and romance and she declared herself desperate to see it.

'Not now,' her father had said, 'but one day, yes.'

'One day, when?'

'Maybe when you're seventeen,' he'd joked, 'and beginning to get some lefty ideas, perhaps then I'll take you.'

'When I'm seventeen? Promise?' She watched him closely as he hesitated, weighing up the commitment.

'Yes, all right. I promise.'

It was the first and only time she thought he might break his word. Whether after three years, he'd forgotten. Whether it was the sheer inconvenience of having her tag along on one of his draining Schyndell trips, she didn't know – neither did it matter. She was holding a trump card in the form of a written IOU posted in her promise box and eventually she was forced to play it.

There had been much sucking of bureaucratic teeth when Nicky had applied for permission. 'A most unusual request,' the head of the delegation had apparently declared, but he'd turned out to be a fatherly old figure and eventually a concession had been made. Georgie had been ecstatic. East Berlin was West Berlin's evil twin and she was to go there for real. She was to lay flowers on her great-grandfather's grave, spend solo time with her father and Alba's tears be damned.

The first thing that struck Georgie about East Berlin was the fine yellow dust hanging in the air, which might have been mistaken for gold mist had it not been for the phosphorous smell that accompanied it.

'Lignite,' her father said as she wrinkled her nose. 'It's why car engines here are so noisy. That little Wartburg, for instance,' he said as a tin can of a taxi heaved alongside them emitting a succession of scatological explosions from its exhaust, 'is definitely running on lignite.'

'Why do they use it, if it smells so bad?'

'Because East Germany is rich in the stuff and they're not allowed to import oil. In fact they're not allowed to import coffee, fruit or anything. That's why we filled up the Peugeot on the other side.'

Her father almost always flew to Berlin, but at the last minute he'd changed his mind. 'A road trip will be more interesting. We'll make it fun, don't worry.'

Privately, Georgie recognized that her teenage brain had yet to make the necessary connections to appreciate the romance of a 'road trip'. Nevertheless, she had loved having her father to herself and on the journey there he'd done what he did best, chatted and joked, yet somehow managing in the process to impart a folder full of information – did she know, for example, that one in every six citizens was an informant? That hotels and taxis were uniformly bugged? That there existed a mortuary garage at one of the checkpoints where coffins were searched to confirm the occupants were truly dead?

As they approached the border, however, the atmosphere changed. Georgie had watched her passport travelling along a conveyor belt towards the processing building and experienced a strong urge to snatch it back and run. The border area was a no-man's-land, the police manning it looked like robots, prototypes for humans before God had breathed heart and compassion into their souls. The allied checkpoints, the East German Control point, the dismal corridor of the autobahn, the barbed wire, watchtowers and armed guards; it had felt like navigating her own nightmare with no hope of waking. The whole process had taken forever. When finally they'd been reunited with their papers and allowed to continue on their way, her father had turned to her and grinned. 'So, how was it?'

'What?'

'Your first experience of totalitarianism?'

Georgie had shrugged. Just before the trip, a rogue thought had crept into her head. Had the insane tyranny of the Cold War been exaggerated? Was it really so awful, this eternal battle where nothing appeared to happen and nobody took up arms? But that was before she'd seen the wall. It was the *Grenzmauer*, her father told her, the third wall, a new and improved version. Forty-five thousand sections of reinforced concrete bordering the raked gravel of the 'death strip'. Here was no romantic divide separating East Germany's Tristans from their West German Isoldes. Here was a sheer unscalable monument to fear.

At least that's what she told Norrell and Porter.

The questioning was routine, her mother had tried to reassure her. She was not to be scared. They were just ordinary people doing their job by an unbendable set of rules.

'But what do they want to know about Berlin?'

'In any government investigation there are bound to be questions. It would be the same process for the Ambassador or anyone else.'

'You do not tell my daughter about the letter,' she had said to Porter and Norrell. 'If you so much as put the idea of suicide in her head, I will come after you with everything I've got left – and please don't underestimate what that is.' It had been a bluff, of course. She had nothing left, but for the first time she had glimpsed a modicum of respect in their eyes.

It had not occurred to Letty that Georgie had anything to say to MI6 about her trip to East Germany. It had not occurred to Georgie either, but sitting at the table, facing the two men, it was easy to imagine herself back in Berlin. There she had felt under the same scrutiny – from the fish-eyed stare of the *VoPos*, from the guards staring down from their watchtowers. Even on the road home, she had been unable to shake the feeling that someone was watching them, listening to them, breathing over them.

Porter had directed the questioning.

Who had her father met? Had there been contact with anyone outside the convention? A cup of coffee? A chance encounter on the street? Georgie responded with the polite minimum. Her father's meetings in East Berlin had to be logged with the authorities in advance, that much she'd learned. 'The Russians and East Germans attached to the delegation are all spies,' he had told her, 'so they naturally assume everyone else is too.'

'Torsten,' she told Porter. 'Torsten was the only person my father met with.'

Up until that moment she'd answered them truthfully enough. How her father had checked them into the drab state-owned Interhotel. How the next morning, at the meeting of delegations, she'd been left to read her book in Room IV of some government headquarters. How the Peugeot had broken down and been towed to a garage . . .

Torsten was her father's friend on the delegation, a pleasant-looking man, with brown curly hair and an intermittent stutter that occasionally burst over his conversation like machine-gun fire. The conversation had been as interesting as watching sand trickle through an egg timer. Georgie read one chapter of *The Mayor of Casterbridge* while they reminisced about a convention in Birmingham where they had originally met, and a second chapter while they worked their way through the usual grown-up pedantries of their respective lives in Stockholm and Bonn. Nicky, however, was well aware that his daughter's expectation of the trip had been disappointed and, noticing she was restless, tapped the cover of her book with his pen. 'You realize we're being watched, don't you?' he whispered.

Georgie looked up.

'Ever since we sat down.'

'Really?' she said doubtfully. She knew her father well enough to suspect she was being set up.

'Trust no one,' he winked. 'They're all watching you.'

'Who?' she said, in spite of herself.

'Stasi.'

Instinctively, Georgie hunched behind her book. 'How do you know?'

'That's one there.' Her father tilted his head towards an ordinary-looking individual sitting at a nearby table. 'Another there.'

Georgie peered through to the reception area, where a man standing under an exit sign was attempting to straighten a map. 'They don't look like policemen,' she said uncertainly.

'Stasi are chameleons,' Torsten said. 'They understand how to blend in.'

'So how can you tell?'

'Oh, after a while, you get a nose for them,' he said airily.

'We've been under observation since the moment we arrived in Berlin,' her father said. 'Today, despite the fact that Torsten has attempted to dress inconspicuously, a precise record will have been made of what he is wearing, down to his rather dubious choice of footwear.' Torsten smiled the weary smile of a foreigner acknowledging himself to be the butt of an English joke. Georgie looked at the Swede's muddy-coloured nylon jumper, his khaki knit tie and orange shoes, which didn't look as if they were made of leather. If he had dressed to blend in, then fashion in East Germany was more woefully behind the times than she'd thought.

'The fact that we are here in this restaurant will have been logged, along with a record of exactly what we chose to eat. I, for instance, took milk in my coffee. You've been reading Thomas Hardy. All this information will be stored in a file, which, later on, some official will study and analyse.'

'Are you being serious?'

'Nobody is anything but serious in this city.' Torsten smiled grimly.

'But why do they care?'

'Guess.' Her father's eyes flickered almost imperceptibly towards Torsten and Georgie felt her pulse quicken.

'Really,' she breathed. She turned to him. 'You are?'

Torsten put a finger to his lips and glanced meaningfully at her school notebook, lying on the table. Georgie snatched up her pen. *Are you a spy?* she scribbled, then, fully expecting Torsten to laugh at her, blushed.

'Almost everyone else in East Berlin is one,' he said. 'I, however, am a nuclear physicist.'

31

Ballanish

Hunger made him leaner and fitter with every passing day. He swam for miles, island-hopping from one stretch of coast to another. The water was icy but the pain of it cleared his head and as he rolled through the chilled waters of the Atlantic he fantasized about bumping into his Kodiak brothers or comparing notes with those pale-faces, the polars. There were others he wanted to meet too. The walrus, for example, that wise old grandfather of the sea. All those rusted hulls of shipwrecks he'd explored, the whispered prayers of drowning seamen he'd heard. A walrus could follow the journey of a broken-off iceberg or play chicken in the fast lanes of the shipping highways.

So he swam on through shoals of bioluminescent shrimp and schools of minnows, their backs tattooed with silver. Twice he passed an orca, moving in graceful slow motion against the current. Another time he came across a basking shark, resting in deep water. He'd blown bubbles at it and splashed around with his paws, but the shark remained stationary, disinterested, like a submarine out of petrol.

The island was at its most beautiful just before dawn. A constant shifting of navy to grey. Once in a while the moon slid out from behind the clouds and shone a silver searchlight across the bay – a beacon signalling home. But when he returned to the cave it was not the thought of home or even the big wrestler that soothed him. It was the map. He would stare at the army of red arrows, at the misspelt words and badly drawn letters. These markings of language which looked so foreign, yet at the same time so achingly familiar.

32

How safe were memories? Letty tried to ward off paranoia but doubt was a tenacious emotion and she found it increasingly hard to judge what was real and what was not. After the row with Tom she found herself questioning even the most solid foundations of her life until the very ground beneath her feet began to shift and move.

There were good days, there were bad days and then there were the hopeless days, which outnumbered them both. On good days, she held on to what she believed. That there had been nothing underhand about this man she had loved, he was no liar, never a traitor. Instead, she focused her rage on Tom. *Men are turned by disillusion or jealousy*, Porter had said. If the British government were looking for a mole, then why not Tom? Why couldn't it be Tom? On good days she functioned on automatic, held her grief in check, but on bad days the weight of it simply rolled over her. Then she would smoke ten, sometimes fifteen cigarettes in a single sitting, grinding the butts into the sandy ground one after the other. At night, to help her sleep, she drank whisky from a bottle she kept under her bed. She had no appetite, barely spoke to the children. You could call it living, but only just. Her memories were prickly and uncomfortable. Suspicions about Nicky loomed, plausible, unanswerable. *He was never the man you thought he was*, Tom had said, and on bad days she believed him. Because if Tom was capable of turning his back on his oldest friend, then what had Nicky been capable of?

The rest of the time were hopeless days and a single question consumed her. Had it been a man or a woman for whom Nicky had risked everything?

'Marry me, and we'll travel the world,' Nicky had said, and she had imagined washing their clothes in the muddy water of the Ganges or nursing isolated Chinese villages through a cholera epidemic. She saw herself working tirelessly by Nicky's side, building dams, administering vaccines. At night, they would sink, exhausted, into a bed shrouded by mosquito netting and she had fallen for the idea of a love binding them together through passion and adversity. Had it been her and Nicky against the world, she could have borne anything diplomatic life threw at her. Liberia, their first posting – unofficially dubbed by the Foreign Office as the 'armpit' posting of the world – had embodied all the romance she'd attributed to the job. Liberia, for all its overpowering heat and unreliable plumbing, for all its dreadful poverty and the madness of its Third World bureaucracy, had been the place she'd been happiest.

There had been nothing romantic about Bonn's suburban spires and provincial formality. Her most immediate problem had been one of communication. Nicky absorbed languages like a plant taking in oxygen but Letty's ear tuned in to chords and scales. Had they been stationed in France, or Italy perhaps, she might have fared better but German was a noisy, industrial hardware of a language. Even with three lessons a week, the words that came out of her mouth still sounded like cutlery dropping onto a stone floor. And then there was the vernacular of diplomacy. It had come so easily to Nicky but Letty was constantly having to watch what she said, work on her formalities. Diplomatic life in Bonn was about entertaining at every level. There were endless dinners to attend, back-to-back functions to grace. The narrow requirements of dress code frustrated her. Always a brooch to be pinned onto a jacket. Always shoes to be matched to a dress. Even her hair required taming into diplomatic sobriety. She found the number of engagements exhausting and the adherence to rules a torture.

In the beginning she tried pleading childcare. 'I'm afraid it's just not done,' the Ambassadress informed her quietly.

'Heartless old ogress,' she said to Nicky. 'I think the children might actually be dying before she gives me the right to refuse.'

'Go on strike,' Nicky said. 'Everyone else does these days.'

But much as she was taken with the idea, she knew there was no place for a conscientious objector in embassy life. As the wife of the First Secretary, and then Counsellor, she had signed up for certain representational duties and some, of course, were worthwhile. If a train derailed or a plane crashed, it fell to the wives to comfort the survivors, but it seemed somewhat un-Christian of her to pray for constant national accidents for the sole purpose of keeping her from her chief duty – saving the Ambassadress from bores. At functions Letty soon learned she was required to draw the fire of the lesser guests, to laugh at their least amusing anecdotes, to free the Ambassadress for those who actually had something relevant to say. 'My role is to be the filter through which the uninteresting and the unimportant must not be allowed to pass,' she said to Nicky one evening.

'You're far too clever and beautiful to be allowed near anyone interesting. Gillian feels threatened by you – all the wives do, for that matter.'

'I don't know about that, but I swear to God, there isn't anyone less suited to the job,' she said ruefully. 'Conversationally, I have the knack of making a sow's ear out of a silk purse.'

'Rubbish, you charm everyone, and what's more, you know it.'

'No.' She kissed him. 'But as long as I charm you, who cares?'

'Anyway, you're an inspired listener, and that's all that most people want.'

She sighed. 'I miss Liberia.'

'I know you do.' He took her in his arms. 'The problem with Bonn is that its two principal industries are spying and *Gummibär*. There isn't much in between.'

The rest of the wives were a Stasi of well turned-out women who operated in a strict hierarchy according to the seniority of their husbands. They kept each other under constant surveillance and were never short of advice, whether solicited or not. Letty found their pettiness irritating. Her natural distaste for gossip prevented her indulging in the fruits of the intelligence grapevine, however juicy. From time to time there would be 'big' news. A divorce, someone who had cracked under the pressure. So-and-so's wife might be described as 'a bit unsafe'. 'She wasn't discreet,' the whispers went, 'she wasn't one of us. She wasn't . . . well . . . *diplomatic*.' These sorts of utterances, however, were too close to the bone for Letty and so she kept her own counsel.

The problem was, though, that if you weren't inside the circle you were outside, and so Letty had no way of knowing that the other women quickly began to whisper about her, and the softest whisper of all was that Nicky Fleming might never make Ambassador because of his wife.

33

The thought came to him violently. His time was finite and he was wasting it. The sea was a seductive distraction and what he was looking for was not to be found there.

So now he left the cave for land, and only at night, when visibility was grainy and uncertain. Barely a hop, kick and a splash away was a grand curve of a beach overlooked by high dunes that led to a machair, an immense sanded prairie blanketed in a mosaic of wildflowers, and from this starting point he explored the island, taking each arrow of the compass in turn. To the north were the shadowy hills of Lewis and Harris, the promise of a colder wind and harsher light. On the far side of treacherous bogs and salt flats covered in pink thrift were the stone causeways to the southern islands. Then there was the east with its hopscotch of fresh-water lochs and heather-covered hills pimpled with rocks, but the east he found faintly oppressive, as though it were somehow tainted by its proximity to the mainland. So it was the west he kept returning to, the west with its seductive loneliness, the iridescent turquoise and emeralds of its bays and those startling bleached-bone sands.

And wherever he went, he searched.

He saw Jackson, who worked at the lobster factory, hiding bottles of whisky in the sleeves of his Sunday suit. He witnessed Archie the gamekeeper, who sang at weddings in a soulful baritone voice, nearly cut off his thumb splitting driftwood. He was crouched in the byre when Hughie, the fisherman, who lived in unimaginable squalor in a croft with an upside-down pram on the roof, made love to his wife while she cried.

There were many times he could have been caught. Many times he would have welcomed it. Unlike other bears in captivity he hadn't had his teeth taken out. Unlike other bears, he was not trapped in a cycle of pain with his nose forcibly crushed and his sense of smell destroyed. He understood what it meant to be loved, to feel safe. Show a creature enough love and it will never harm you. This had been the wrestler's mantra and it was a brave one. Believe this and you have to believe that the instinct for love is stronger than the instinct to eat. You have to believe that the desire for love is stronger than the instinct to kill, stronger even than the instinct to survive.

34

 The Kettle was a nickname for a deep ravine in the Scolpaig cliffs, a couple of hundred feet inland from the sea. Some topographical quirk made this enormous gash in the earth invisible from a distance and a person not paying attention to where they were going, a birdwatcher, say, scanning the seas for a guillemot, might easily find himself dropping into the abyss before realizing that land and luck had unexpectedly run out. In recent years this had indeed been the fate of two people: the first, a stranger to the islands, caught in a rolling mist off the sea; the second, a vet from Skye, a man who really should have known better than to choose the Kettle as a suitable place to remove a thistle from his sock, a decision that cost him his left gumboot, his balance and shortly thereafter his life.

The sides of the Kettle were sheer but there was a way down. Bisecting the crater was a narrow slope, on wet days as lethal as the Cresta Run, but in dry weather . . . The children, of course, were forbidden to attempt it, but Nicky had once made the descent using clumps of tough grass as hand-holds. At the bottom, he had discovered both a cave and a tunnel, and it was through this tunnel, during a storm or spring tide, that the sea 'boiled', churning around the walls with such centrifugal force that it shot a frothy spray one hundred feet up through the Kettle's 'spout', covering those lying at the top in thick yellowing foam.

It was dead low tide by the time the children reached Scolpaig and the Kettle bottom was dry, save for the odd rock pool filled with green slime. Georgie and Jamie lay on their stomachs, the big Ordnance Survey map spread between them.

'You know what they should build here?' Alba rested her chin in her hands and gazed out to sea. 'A high-security prison. It's the perfect place. We're on an island in the middle of the Atlantic with no way off.'

'Except a ferry and a causeway and a plane once a week to Glasgow,' Georgie commented.

'The causeway leads to another island, so that's a dead end, and convicts aren't allowed to catch ferries or planes. Then the Minch is lethal to swimmers. It's like the Bermuda Triangle of the British Isles.'

'So?'

'So, there's no escape. We're stuck here for life with no parole and no visiting hours.'

'Perfect place for you, then,' Georgie said. 'Hey, look how clear St Kilda is.'

'Which is St Kilda?' Jamie asked.

'The one shaped like a witch's hat.' Georgie pointed at a shadow of land out to sea. 'Where the cliff game came from.'

Jamie squinted at the horizon. The cliff game was a

form of Russian roulette Alba had devised for playing when a gale blew at force eight or higher. They would all stand around the top of the Kettle, backs to the wind, then on a countdown from three, lean back and allow the wind to support their weight. If it did, they would step a few inches closer to the edge and try again until someone chickened out. The game filled Jamie with equal measures of excitement and dread. To be allowed to join in was an honour, a chance to earn Alba's respect, but he could never help wondering – what of those split seconds between gusts? What would it feel like to fall?

'If you wanted to get married on St Kilda,' Alba said, 'they made you stand on the edge of a cliff on one leg to prove you could support a wife.'

'That's silly.'

'They had no food out there, so they had to climb down cliffs to catch young fulmars and gannets.'

'But what happened if they fell?'

'Bad luck on them,' Alba said, chewing her hair.

'What happens if they didn't fall?'

'Then it was wedding bells and gannet pie for the rest of their life.'

'But why didn't they have any food?'

'Because they lived on a giant cliff shaped like a witch's hat,' Georgie said patiently.

'But why didn't they live somewhere else?'

'For God's sake,' Alba groaned. 'They lived where they lived.'

'But they can't only have eaten gannet pie.'

Alba lined up a row of sheep pellets and flicked them off the edge one by one. 'Of course not. For breakfast they had porridge with boiled puffin in it. For lunch they scrambled a few baby fulmars and they tore the feet off gannets and made jam out of them for tea.'

'That's horrid.' Jamie's brain flashed him an image of the head and shoulders of a puffin staring accusingly at him from the bowl. 'Why don't we send them some food?'

'Nobody lives there any more. They were evacuated.'

'I see,' Jamie said in his gravest voice.

'They asked the government to help them leave the island, although they didn't all want to go,' Georgie explained.

'It's pathetic,' Alba said. 'I would have refused.'

'But then you would have been there all by yourself,' Jamie said. 'You'd be lonely.'

'It's a question of principle, Jamie. I would have stayed, however lonely, just to show I couldn't be pushed around.'

'Well, you're the only one of us brave enough to,' Georgie said generously. 'Alba's been to St Kilda, Jamie; don't you remember?'

'And bloody awful it was, too,' Alba said.

It had been the summer of her eleventh birthday. There had been a surplus of crabs that year and Alisdair the fisherman took to bringing up tray containers of claws to the house. On hearing that Alba loved boats he offered to take her with him and Alba had been so excited that Letty had agreed without thinking through the implications. St Kilda was forty miles out to sea and boats had to leave at night in order to get a worthwhile fishing quota. As the day of departure drew closer, as the weather turned progressively nastier, she'd been plagued by doubts. Nicky had been delayed in Bonn and Alba, having shown off relentlessly about the trip, had been too stubborn to back down.

It was bitterly cold on the evening in question and Alba had felt sick just looking at the lines of white surf breaking out at sea. Perched on the boat's wooden bench, she watched her family growing smaller and smaller as they waved at her from the dock. Alisdair was typical of the island fishermen in that he was short of money and not entirely vigilant about the maintenance of his equipment, which meant his small boat wasn't quite as seaworthy as it might have been. By midnight a warm front had arrived bringing rain and three-foot-high waves. Nevertheless, the little boat toiled on against the prevailing wind and currents until eventually Alba found herself beneath the witchy brim of St Kilda's cliffs.

'So what was it like?' Jamie said.

Alba shrugged. 'The island is one massive rock. You beach the boat in the bay and walk up to these little stone huts where they dry the fulmars. Then you climb up and there's this patch of green that looks like a nice lawn, except it isn't a nice lawn at all, it's the other side of a really steep cliff and underneath the cliff there are about a billion gannets nesting. We only stayed a minute because we had to go fishing, although honestly, I wish we had stayed, as the fishing was awful.'

Alisdair had negotiated the treacherous narrows of St Kilda while Alba, lulled by the put-put of the outboard motor, watched the gannets above her head folding in their wings and plummeting one by one into the dense black sea. Finally Alisdair dropped anchor. The fishing rods were square biscuits of wood around which thirty feet of nylon line fixed with hooks was wrapped. Alba unravelled hers and waited.

By mid-morning the thrill of fishing had long gone. Alba's breakfast of bread and butter had been an early casualty of the choppy waters. Her hands were raw from pulling at the line. She was dotted in tiny metallic scales and her eyes stung from the salt water. A carpet of stiff and bloodied fish lay beneath her feet.

One of the mackerel had swallowed its bait so completely that Alisdair had been forced to cut through its mouth to retrieve the hook. Alba could barely watch. The fish hadn't been dead at the beginning of the operation and the noise the scissors made as they snipped through the cartilage was almost more than she could bear. And still they went on fishing. She'd been staring out to sea, her hand mechanically rising and falling, when she spotted them. Dark shadows rising up through the water like torpedoes. Two fins, a dorsal and a tail, twenty feet apart, circling the boat. Then, in frighteningly quick succession, four, five, six! Eight!

Alisdair froze. 'Basking sharks,' he hissed. 'They'll have us over.' Alba, too, had been in awe of their size, longer than the boat itself and so close she could have dropped her hand and touched their muscled backs. A tail splashed. The boat rocked. Alba lost her footing.

'Pull up the line!' Alisdair shouted, but it was too late. The sharks were already tangled. There was a tug so powerful on Alba's wooden handle that it wrenched her towards the boat edge. Alisdair, alarm written across his usually impassive face, snatched it from her and tossed it overboard.

'Quick!' He heaved a plastic container off the bottom of the boat. 'Pour this out! This will keep them away.' He grabbed a second container of paraffin and emptied it into the water. There was a frenzied thrashing. Alba caught a glimpse of a gargantuan mouth, then, as suddenly as they had appeared, the sharks submerged and were gone. 'The devil's messengers,' Alisdair breathed, white and trembling. 'Aye, sent by the devil hisself.'

'I've never had such a miserable day my whole life,' Alba later said. Even her mother's admission that she'd stayed awake all night, racked with fear and guilt, had not appeased her. Before that moment she'd had no idea that death was so close. Now she knew. Death shadowed everyone. Death was driving the bus when you stepped off the pavement. Death waited in the cold gloom of the sea when a monster rocked your boat. And when you tripped and fell off a roof, it was death who caught you.

'So you didn't drown, then?' Jamie said.

'No, village idiot, as you can see, I didn't drown.'

'Did you cry?'

'Yes.'

'Would you cry if it happened now?'

'No.'

'Why not?'

'Because I don't cry any more.' Alba shrugged. 'I can't imagine anything that would make me cry.' She looked away and Jamie, sensing the abrupt change of mood, leapt to his feet.

'Come on, let's play it now.'

'Play what?'

'The cliff game.'

'It's not windy enough,' Georgie said quickly.

'One go.'

'No.'

'Why?'

'Because we say so,' Alba said. 'Now shut up and sit down.'

But Jamie was already spreading his arms. 'Tell me when.' He took a step backwards. Alba seized his arm and yanked him down to the ground. 'Stoppit.' He struggled. She whacked him on the side of the head. 'You do as you're told, Jamie Fleming,' she said, gritting her teeth in sudden fury. 'Do you understand? You do as you're bloody well told!'

35

 There were three of them. Way above him. Silhouetted against the sky. They were worryingly
near to the edge and he risked a closer look.

Two were girls. One wearing a blue anorak, the other
red. Their long hair blew around their faces and caught
across their mouths. But it was the third child, the boy, that
made his heart skip a beat.

There's no point asking how he knew.

He just did.

'Hello, boy,' he said, and waited for a reply to come to
him on the breath of the east wind.

'Hello, bear,' the boy whispered.

36

Sometimes she hunted for memories of him. A postcard he'd received and used as a bookmark, a note he'd written and kept for no reason. She hoarded these fragments, stockpiling them for the future. It haunted her that she couldn't remember their last kiss or the last time he'd made love to her.

She'd found the canvas sorting through a builder's packing crate. It had been full of long-forgotten rubbish – boxes of old fishing flies, dried-up paint tubes, kites with knotted strings, a single rowlock for the little rowing boat they had kept on the church loch for a while. She took out each item in turn, intending to throw it away, but finding instead some spurious reason to keep it. The painting had been at the bottom, wrapped inside a plastic bag. It was one of Nicky's canvases, stretched over a wooden frame and neatly finished at the back with brown paper. The subject matter, the soaring white statue of Our Lady of the Isles set against the backdrop of radar domes, she had no trouble in recognizing as the missile firing-range at Gebraith. Given, though, that the strangely bright colours of the picture bore no relation to the weather on the day she and Nicky had climbed it, arguing all the way, it was obvious that Nicky must have returned at a later date.

The 'trip' to the statue had been years ago, on a washed-out monotone afternoon. Alba had been small enough to still be carried on her father's shoulders and that summer, for whatever reason, they'd decided to catch the ferry from Oban to Loch Baghasdail, driving up to the north island from the toe of the south.

When the white statue had unexpectedly come into view, Nicky had pulled the car into a passing place. 'That's it, isn't it?' he asked. 'Our Lady of the Isles. That's where the missile range is.'

'Yes,' she said shortly.

He switched off the engine. 'Let's walk up there. I've never seen it close up.'

Letty had been unwilling. The fact that it existed at all was bad enough. That Nicky should acknowledge its right to be there with a visit incensed her. In the late 1940s, the MoD announced its intention to build an army training base and rocket range at Gebraith. Initially the proposal was greeted with enthusiasm – jobs were scarce on the island – but everything changed once the islanders got wind of the sheer scale of the MoD plans, which extended from the middle of the southern island all the way to the north and required the 'relocating' of every islander in its way. The most impassioned critic of this scheme had been the local minister, who realized that not only would his parish be destroyed, but a way of life along with it. He had stirred up enough support to commission the building of a twenty-five-foot statue on a hill directly overlooking the intended military site. If the Free Church could admit to such things, then the statue was a godly act of defiance, a divine 'fuck you' to the MoD. The literature on Our Lady of the Isles described it as protector of the Gael. In times of trouble or threat they turned for help to Mary, Mother of God and 'miraculously', eight months after its completion, the Ministry of Defence announced a massive scale-down of their original plans. Even still, the range was an aberration. Giant twin golf balls perched on the hill, dwarfed by a radio mast. The very sight of it made Letty feel ill.

'First they appropriate St Kilda,' she fumed, struggling to pull Georgie up the hill behind Nicky and Alba, 'the biggest gannetry in the world, next they go ahead and build this . . . and do you know what they promised the locals? That during tupping and lambing season, the "use of the rocket firing-range will be kept to a minimum". Thank you very much. It's so bloody arrogant! I can't stand the way the MoD treats the Highlands and Islands like their own personal playground – look at this thing, it's a monstrosity and they only got away with it because they think the islanders are an easy touch.'

'A little simplistic, surely,' Nicky said mildly. 'Besides, you can't object to progress just because it doesn't suit your romanticized idea of how this island should be preserved. If it were up to you, no one up here would ever be allowed to join the twentieth century. People have to live and work and the range provides much-needed jobs for the locals.'

Letty bit her tongue. It was the very *insularity* of the island, its lack of ambition and blanket rejection of out-siders that had allowed it to remain a strange half-world, a closed world – but she knew that she too was an outsider, just as her father had been, and the unintended consequence that came with their class and money meant, by definition, they were themselves destroying the island by being part of it.

'If you think that a missile firing-range is suitable employment for the islanders then it shows you have no understanding of the kind of people who live here,' she said tightly.

'Or maybe you're as guilty of underestimating their intelligence as the MoD,' Nicky retorted.

'It's no use arguing with you,' she'd said resentfully. 'You won't hear anything negative about your precious government.'

'It's your precious government too, Letty,' he said gently. 'Don't forget that. You seem to have an innate distrust of your own country.'

'And you don't? With everything you know about their methods?'

'No,' he said quietly. 'I don't. I couldn't very well do my job if I did.'

And they had not spoken again until they'd arrived at Ballanish.

'Try to understand,' she'd told him later, 'this island is my sanctuary. It's where I belong, it's where I feel the possibility of hope and faith and every morning when I look out of the window I fall in love with it all over again.'

Now, Letty shook her head at the canvas, perplexed at the almost luridly bright blues and purples. Why had Nicky painted it and when? Had he gone down to Gebraith without her knowledge? CO-60, NI-60, MG-137. She squinted at his colour-codings, half-heartedly trying to match them to the tubes of old paint in the crate. Then, with a stubborn determination to find an answer to something, anything, she tried to match them to every other tube of paint she could find in the house, but none of the references came close. *I paint things to study them*, she could almost hear Nicky saying as she took the canvas to the kitchen table and set it down. *To understand how they work.*

And that had been her point, really. How Gebraith was going to work.

The range had been originally built to launch the Corporal missile, Britain's first nuclear weapon and a weapon, they'd argued, that was to be at the forefront of the Cold War defence. For the management and security of such a thing to be in the hands of islanders, whose inherent disposition allowed them to leave valuable machinery to rust outdoors and tolerate rubbish piling up all over their island, made her profoundly uneasy. What of human error? What if there was an accident? And suddenly, out of nowhere, the word appeared in her mind.

Schyndell.

The power-plant in East Germany. She sat down abruptly. There was no reason to make a connection, and yet . . .

Schyndell, Porter had said. *A little coincidental. A little convenient, don't you think?*

She tried to think back. Had Nicky applied to be part of the delegation, or had it been the other way round?

It was when she turned the canvas over again that she

heard it – an almost imperceptible shift of material, the noise of paper sliding against paper. The sound of suspicion. Nicky's paintings were crudely framed affairs with the raw edges of the canvas stapled straight to the wood. She stared at the double thickness of the brown backing paper, hoping for something, praying for nothing, hovering on the threshold of the before and after – it was so much easier to stay in the past where the knowledge of the present didn't exist, but it was too late now and she knew it. She punctured the corner of the canvas and ripped the paper away. A white envelope fell out. On the front was a single sentence written in Nicky's tidy script. *Everything and every event is pervaded by the Grace of God.*

She read the line twice, uncomprehendingly, then she turned the bulky envelope over and slit the flap.

37

An eight-hundred-pound grizzly with the run of a Hebridean island was a rare occurrence, and teatime most days found Donald John's small kitchen bulging with visitors all engaged in the island's most popular pastime: gossip. Weeks had passed since the flight of the bear and the excitement was beginning to die down. Nevertheless, when Jamie walked in, he found Peggy from the shop, Roddy and Mrs Matheson, who was married to the island stick-maker, all deep in speculation about the animal's fate.

'If it isn't wee Jamie,' the old lady broke off. 'Why, many's the long day since we've seen you!' She grasped Jamie's thin hands in her own complicated, knotted ones. Dolly Matheson was hopelessly crippled by arthritis and whenever the Flemings paid her a visit they had to steel themselves for an interminable wait at the door, accompanied by the sound of agonizing groans coming from within. After much dragging of feet the door would be opened with one final gut-wrenching cry by Mrs Matheson, who would then limp back to the front room where her husband, who enjoyed the rudest of health, was slouching in his favourite easy chair. 'Why, hello! Hello!' He would leap up to greet them in a sprightly manner before ordering his poor, creaking wife to fetch the tea as though she were a tin servant in need of oil. 'Aye, everyone's after that thousand pound reward,' she resumed as Jamie ran the gauntlet of head pats before squeezing himself next to Roddy on the bench. 'The army have got aerial photographs, helicopters and the whatnot, why, they've even got the coastguards in Skye looking for him on account of someone saying they saw him there.'

'Tse, so much fuss about that beast still.' Donald John produced a bottle of Cherry Coke for Jamie. 'He'll have gone over a cliff long before now.'

'No, he won't,' Jamie said. It made him furious when people said the bear was dead. The bear was a huge creature. *One of the largest of all land carnivores,* his father had told him. Nothing on the island could threaten it. If one hundred sheep armed with cudgels rushed it all at once, if all the cows and bulls ganged up and head-butted it together, the bear would still be stronger. As for the idea that he'd fallen off a cliff – bears weren't stupid! They didn't just trip over their claws. Bears lived in Russia, in Canada. They were used to cliffs. He didn't care if Georgie and Alba had given up. He had devised his own system for searching. The Kettle was his head-quarters. He wasn't sure why he was drawn back there again and again, but he was, and from the top of the cliffs he could see the flower-covered sweep of the machair, the headstones in the graveyard and the vast bog in front of it. He could see all the way to the road and up to the heathery tip of Clannach beyond. Way in the distance he could make out Donald John's croft and even the yellow gate of Ballanish. If the bear crossed in any direction, he would see it. If his father walked down the road to Ballanish, well, he would see him too . . .

In the last couple of weeks all Jamie's doubts had resurfaced. Despite his father's promise, despite Tom Gordunson's confirmation, despite all the prayers he'd uttered and the maps he'd folded into bottles and tossed off the rocks, his father had still not returned. While the family had remained in Bonn, Jamie had felt secure, but in England, in the unfathomable surroundings of a strange city, he had been assailed by new worries. In London, it had no longer been a question of his father finding him – the question was who, precisely, was looking for his father? In Bonn, the British Embassy had taken care of that. Everyone had been involved – the Ambassador, the two military policemen who checked passes, the BND, the third secretary – even the German *Militärpolizei* in their stiff leather coats. Jamie pictured them all, faces grave with concentration, listening for the tap of Morse code, waiting for the crackle of information, perhaps even interrogating suspects. In Bonn, he had held onto the idea that the entire city was secretly engaged in the effort to locate his missing father. He imagined the man behind the newspaper kiosk passing a stealthy note to the street cleaner standing outside Cafe Uhl, who in turn signalled the woman with the coiled bun sitting at her desk on the second floor of the office block, who immediately picked up a telephone to the embassy where every day, yes, *every single day*, new diplomatic channels were being opened to embassies in Paris, Istanbul, Madrid, Moscow. At night, when he had trouble sleeping, Jamie would spread out a map in his head and watch as red dots illuminated each capital until the whole world was blinking back at him in eager cooperation. Yes, in Bonn there had been a common cause, a single directive, 'Find Nicholas Fleming and bring him home,' but in London no one seemed interested. People stepped off pavements and ate in restaurants as though they hadn't a care in the world. Even his mother, who following his father's disappearance had yo-yoed between the embassy, the police station and the Ambassador's residence, seemed to become curiously inactive and, slowly, the dark truth came to him. No one was looking for his father any more.

And now people had given up looking for the bear. Angrily he took a slug of Cherry Coke and stared balefully round the room. Why was he the only person who believed in anything? Why was he always the only one not to succumb to the epidemic of hopelessness? Were faith and optimism things that disappeared when you grew up? His father was still lost, just as the bear was still lost and he, Jamie, would find them both.

'The beast isn't in Skye and he's no' dead either,' Roddy said. 'Why, only the other evening, I was listening to the wireless when I heard noises.' Roddy rubbed at the bags of loose skin under his eyes. 'It was a stormy night, right enough, but I went outside and there in front of me I saw the red eyes of the bear glowing in the dark. Ach, what a terrible sight! Why, if I'd only had a pitchfork to hand,' Roddy sighed mightily, 'indeed that reward would have been mine.'

'Alick said *he* should have got the reward,' Jamie

said, 'because he actually caught the bear a few weeks ago.'

'Did he now, the scoundrel!' Donald John bashed at his knees in amusement.

'Yes, but it got away,' Jamie said forlornly.

'Alick is always concocting stories,' Roddy scoffed. 'Why, once he comes into my croft with blood in his hair and he says to me, "I've got a sore head," and points to a dead sparrow lying there on the ground. "See that sparrow! It came flying straight at me just now and I got it right between the eyes." So I look at the dead sparrow on the ground and I says to him, "Why, that sparrow has been rotting on the ground for days, you liar."'

'Oh, tse tse, it's not just Alick,' Donald John said, 'there are many such yarns about the beast. Why, there's a fellow down south, they say slaughtered a sheep for his own use. It's illegal to home-kill a sheep now so he's been telling people that the bear killed the sheep hisself and ate its carcass. Well, that nice Sergeant Anderson took the wrestler along there and they found the sheep carcass hidden away in a back room and now the fellow's been brought to court and fined.'

'Serve him right, the scallywag,' Peggy said. 'That's what his lies did for him.'

'Maybe you should go out and look for it, Donald John,' Jamie said. 'You could get the reward.'

'Oh, boo boo, it would take a lot to tackle that bear.'

'The wrestler fights it all the time.'

'Aye, the wrestler can put that beast down all right, but he's a hardy man. Why, he's been out on the hills every day in the wind and the rain dressed in nothing more than his wrestling boots and trunks.'

'That's right,' Mrs Matheson said. 'Quite bare-chested. It's a wonder he hasn't taken a terrible chill.' She levered herself slowly to her feet. 'I must away, Donald John.'

'Right you are, then. Bye for now.' Donald John helped her to the door.

'Come on, Donald John,' Jamie said, following. 'Can you and me take the tractor and go now?'

'Ach, let it be. I'm not gallivanting round the island looking for a bear. If he's not dead, he'll be in hiding and I'm quite sure he's very hungry by now. There's no taming a wild nature like that.' He shook his head so vigorously it looked as if his neck was in danger of breaking. 'Why, if that beast turns renegade, it could be the end of us.'

38

Two small photographs had dropped out of the white envelope. Two passport-sized stamps of treason along with East German ID papers. Mechanically, Letty went on stirring the soup. Who was he, the blank face who stared out of them, and what did he represent? A trap? A double agent? Had Nicky owed him or needed him? She grated the spoon against the pan bottom. The split pea and ham soup was burning, but she couldn't raise the energy to do anything about it.

'Camel breath. Go and put out the flag for Alick,' she heard Alba ordering Jamie, and she identified the edge of claustrophobia in her daughter's voice.

It was nearly three weeks since the bear had run off and everyone was in agreement. The beast was dead. He had drowned in the viscous mud of the bogs or been carried out to sea and despite the repeated offer of a thousand pounds, most people had stopped caring either way. The children were defeated and listless and Letty couldn't blame them. They'd seen nothing in their searches. Not an ear, or stub of a tail, not one steaming mound of bear poo. And now there was nothing to fill their days except bickering and carping. Whatever suggestions Letty made were greeted with the enthusiasm of death row inmates being invited to sit in the electric chair. She steadied herself against the Raeburn. Summers had been so easy when the children had been small. They'd all potter round the house in the morning, then after lunch there would be an outing – dune jumping, digging for razor clams, a game of boules on the beach with washed-up lobster floats. If the weather was bad, they'd head to the tweed shop, or brave the cliffs of Scolpaig or go to Loch Portain to look for colonies of seals. Afterwards they'd drive home, the smell of damp wool settling around them, while Nicky wiped the rain off his face with one hand and negotiated the serpentine road with the other.

'Now darling,' she could hear him asking, 'was it an Arctic tern you thought you saw, or a cockyollbird?'

'You know perfectly well it was a skua.'

'Was it really? How unusual. Are you quite sure you weren't hallucinating? Oh do look, another car appears to want to share the road with us. Shall I stop to let him pass – what do you think?'

'I think it would be awfully decent of you.'

'I bet he doesn't say thank you, ill-mannered bugger.'

'Except he's giving you a wave, look.'

'Yes, yes, you're quite right. So he is.'

'A perfectly nice polite wave, too.'

'All right, don't rub it in,' Nicky said cheerfully. 'Although, I daresay he didn't mean it. Now, that's a new style of wave, isn't it? Two fingers raised slightly above the steering wheel. Shall I adopt it?'

'Oh darling, everybody was doing it last year. It replaced the single finger as the fashionable acknowledgement, surely you remember?'

'Nonsense, I've never seen it before in my entire life. I think you're hallucinating again.' He turned round to the back seat. 'Children! Your mother's gone mad! Oh look, darling, here we are at the Callernish Inn. Have I ever mentioned that you can get a very good haddock here?'

'It was perfectly disgusting the only time we had it.'

'Rubbish. I think you'll find they cooked it the proper way – in breadcrumbs and not batter.'

'It was still filthy.'

'Darling, I'm sorry to say you wouldn't know a good piece of haddock if it stopped you for speeding.'

'Have it your way. Now do concentrate, Nicky, and try not to hit that nice boy on a bicycle.'

'I actually think I might hit him. He's got a decidedly evil glint in his eye.'

'He's only about five.'

'Let's not forget *The Omen*.'

'Or you could drive a tiny bit slower, maybe?'

'Oh, darling, do stop grumbling.' And once again Nicky would turn round to include the children. 'On and on she goes, your mother. Never stops grumbling, it's quite extraordinary. You'd think there was actually something wrong with her life, the way she goes on.' Then he would smile secretly at Letty and take her hand in his.

Letty caught a rogue tear with her sleeve. She had to get through this, she had to, but how, when it was all spinning perpetually round her head? The painting, the missile range, the bleached-out face of the photographs. Why hadn't he confided in her? When had they stopped talking?

She was certain now that Nicky had done something wrong and the knowledge felt like a rock in her throat. She drank water, but no amount dislodged it. She stopped eating because it hurt to swallow. She found herself tired all the time, prone to napping at opportune moments during the day. Tom had called twice in the last month, each time getting one of the children, each time sending them to fetch her with a claim of urgency, but she had refused to come to the phone. What was she to say? Fear, suspicion, pride, loyalty, shame. She no longer knew what emotion was driving her. All she knew was that if she concentrated – if she concentrated really hard – she could sometimes pretend nothing had happened, but the feeling of unreality that accompanied her day and night had grown so strong that she thought it was amazing she still existed at all, amazing that she hadn't somehow cancelled herself out. Maybe this was why her children no longer responded to her. She had become invisible.

She stole a look at them. Georgie, pale as a piece of silk, her head in a book; Jamie, hunched in his woolly jumper as though it were actually knitted out of tedium. Alba was prowling the room like a caged tiger and the truth hit Letty like a body blow – this might be her home, but it was not *theirs*. Bonn was their home – Bonn, with its dinky houses and wet, leaf-stained cobbles. Bonn with its endless variety of oppressive weather – the mugginess, the mosquitoes and that infuriating level crossing. Bonn with its forensic politics, its armed police and cavalcades of black cars. Bonn was where their schools were, where their friends lived, and they needed those dreadful crêperies and Currywurst shacks in the same way that she needed the wind and the rain and the call of an oyster-catcher. The island offered them nothing more than a summer holiday. It was just the place where they were forced to live without their father.

She heard the rumble of the tractor. *Thank God for Alick.* Without Alick to take the children off her hands, she would have gone mad. Barely a day passed without one of them hanging their anoraks on the stick fixed into the old stone grinder in the garden. In the past the children had been forbidden to summon Alick for their own amuse-ment. *He is not a genie in a bottle, you know! Alick has other commitments besides us!* But this year, the anorak wrapped around the stick had been her literal SOS flag. As soon as Alick spotted it, down he raced and whisked the children off on whatever chore he happened to have that day. Cutting the peats, lifting potatoes or rescuing a calf stuck in the bog – God knows, she didn't care where he took them, as long as he took them away.

Covertly, she watched them through the window as they piled onto the trailer, Alba and Jamie perched in opposite corners, Georgie, steadfastly attached to her book, swinging her legs off the back. As soon as they were out of sight, she sighed with relief and stabbed a finger at the tape deck. Verdi. Puccini. Wagner. Anything would do. Opera insulated her heart from the chill of other emotions. *Men betray their country out of greed, revenge, self-loathing, desire* . . . Alick had taken the children and left her with another afternoon of empty hours in which she must try to work out which one of these had killed her husband.

39

Bonn

The afternoon the Ambassadress paid her a visit in Bad Godesberg, Letty had been preparing a dinner party. Eighteen people were coming and she had chewed her finger over possible menus before electing to serve tomato ring followed by a rack of lamb. At the bell, she'd opened the door to find the wretched woman outside, dazzling in a pastel tweed suit, and nervously Letty straightened her shirt. It always seemed as if the presence of the Ambassadress was carefully designed to downgrade her subordinates from ministers' wives to mice. Moreover, her timing was unfortunate. It wasn't so much the cooking of the dinner – the caterers would take care of that – as the infinite tedium of getting ready. The straightening of the hair, the choosing of the outfit, the musical chairs of the placement – that subtle art of fusing the intelligent with the self-regarding – Christ, the very thought of it made the pores under Letty's arm spontaneously open and begin leaking resentment. It was hers and Nicky's twelfth consecutive evening engagement and she would have given anything for a night of macaroni cheese with the children.

It could have been so different had she married a banker or a concert pianist. Sometimes, when they played Happy Families, she imagined herself and the children grotesquely caricatured alongside 'Fleming of the Foreign Office'. She tried to conjure up a different sort of family, but she had only ever loved one man in her life and could not see herself with Bones the Butcher or Grits the Grocer, so she pulled herself together, made Gillian coffee and offered her a chair. The Ambassadress proceeded to interrogate her with grace and ease about the children, their schools, their general health and happiness. Letty waited for the axe to fall, unaware that it had been dropping for some minutes in a controlled fashion towards her neck. 'And you, my dear, how are *you* getting on?' Gillian ventured. As always, her poise, the erectness of her back, even the symmetry of her knees, seemed a tribute to order and self-discipline.

'Oh, quite well, thank you,' Letty said, but Gillian was not to be fobbed off so easily.

'The welfare of the wives is one of my main obligations,' she reminded her, 'and of late I've been concerned. I know how isolating it can be for a woman to be shipped from pillar to post with a young family. Unhappiness is not unknown.'

'I'm sure,' Letty murmured.

'Perhaps you should try to involve yourself more in embassy life? Some of the other wives find it terribly rewarding, you know.'

'You're very kind,' Letty said, 'but I'd really rather devote my time to Nicky and the children.'

'Yes,' Gillian said gently, 'but you see, that's rather the reason I've come to see you.'

Letty felt her insides cramp with dislike. 'I'm not sure I quite understand.'

'Letitia, my dear, Nicky is being fast-tracked. He could go far, given the right circumstances – all the way, I suspect. As his wife you have a pivotal back-up role to play. A good diplomatic wife cannot afford to be too needy or distracting.' Gillian paused to remove a speck of fluff from her stockings. 'A good diplomatic wife must sacrifice her own desires and needs in order to allow her husband to get on and do his job.'

'And are you saying that I'm not?' Letty said, more archly than she knew she should.

'My dear, selflessness, self-discipline, are prerequisites of the position. Nicky really must be shielded from the trivia of domestic life.'

'Are you asking me to sacrifice the well-being of my family?' Letty said incredulously.

'Letitia, a post is coming up in Rome and Nicky's name has been put forward. Now, I know that you'll want to do anything in your power to support him,' Gillian said quietly, 'so, I want you to understand that you are equally under consideration. Think about what Nicky wants, think about how he would feel if he were passed over for, well . . . for the wrong reasons.' She stretched out a hand. 'The truth is, Letitia, a diplomatic wife can make or break her husband's career.'

Letty looked at the raised veins on the back of the older woman's hand.

She knew exactly why she and Nicky had stopped talking.

Rome. It was what Nicky wanted.

It was what she wanted for both of them.

40

Ballanish

Shoplifting was easy and great fun. The first thing Alba stole was a bar of Cadbury's Fruit & Nut. The second was a packet of Fruit Pastilles. As with the chocolate, the Fruit Pastilles had been a spur-of-the-moment thing. One minute she had been staring at them stacked on the shelf, the next they were in her hand and, without a thought to the consequences, she put her index finger to the tip of the green tube and propelled it up the sleeve of her Fair Isle in the manner of a magician preparing a trick.

The thing Alba liked about shoplifting was how very little justification it required. Stealing put her in a good mood and good moods, for Alba, were rare. And if that wasn't validation enough, items in this shop had no life or future. God only knew how long they had been consigned to the shelf like over-age orphans, hoping against hope to be taken into a loving home and eaten.

Then there were the hidden benefits to the crime. Now that the bear was missing, presumed dead, shoplifting was the only viable option for an afternoon's entertainment. Today, for example, her mother had gone on one of her hateful walks, but Alba had never understood the adult obsession with fresh air – as far as she was concerned, there was far too much of the stuff around. Georgie and Jamie had gone with Alick to the beach to chop up driftwood, but Alba was fed up with the beach and especially the persistence of sand, which liked to work its way into her hair, her nose, the crevices of her ears and even between her teeth. But even had she felt the need to do so, Alba was able to justify her shoplifting on the grounds that she was owed. She was owed for the death of her father and the zombie that passed for her mother. She was owed for the emptiness of her life and a future confined to this damp sponge of an island with nobody but her rhesus monkey of a brother for company. Then there was her sister. At the thought of Georgie, she could almost taste the bile in her mouth. It had been the week before, with everybody scattered to different parts of the island, when Alba, a prisoner of her ugly mood, had wandered round the house looking for something to destroy. She'd opened the door to the sitting room. It had been cold as a church and smelt of burnt ash. It was uneconomical, her mother claimed, to heat the house all day, and the sitting room was 'kept' for evenings. But how could peats be that expensive – it was only bloody earth for God's sake – and if they couldn't even afford fire, what would they have to forgo next? Food?

Alba snatched a picture of her parents off the mantelpiece. The photograph had been taken in Greece against a backdrop of ruins. She pressed her finger to the glass. The frame had been kept in direct sunlight and the image faded out in a way that suddenly seemed dreadfully symbolic. She put it back and opened the storage cupboard at the far end of the room where she found a few half-empty spirit bottles, greasy with neglect. Alba unscrewed the lid of the Vermouth and took a swig. It tasted sour – like medicine gone bad. She swallowed a second shot and grimaced as heat raced through her stomach.

The slam of the kitchen door sent the third shot circuiting her nose and sinuses. She moaned in pain and shoved the bottle quickly back in the cupboard.

In the kitchen, Angus Post Office had left a pile of letters stacked on the counter. Alba flicked idly through them before stopping at one addressed to Georgiana Fleming. *University College London.* For a moment, Alba stared numbly at the return address then she switched on the kettle and held the flap of the envelope to the spout.

Afterwards, she sat at the kitchen table for a long time, the university offer letter in her hands. Why hadn't Georgie said anything? Why hadn't she warned her? Two Bs and an A, that was all her sister needed. The whole world was about to open up to Georgie, while she would be left alone. She'd felt like grating her tongue or painting her body with black tar but after a while she had a better idea. She took the offer letter and envelope to the sitting-room fireplace and, shoving them deep into the pit of ashes, set them on fire. When and if the actual A level results came in, she resolved to do the same.

So now, standing in the aisle of the shop, she pondered her options. It didn't matter how many packets of sweets she pilfered, they simply couldn't add up to the debt that life was obligated to pay her.

The trouble was there was so little to steal. Alba ran her eyes over the cans of cock-a-leekie soup and Crosse & Blackwell stew. It was her turn to cook supper. The cooking rota had been her idea. A response to the disintegrating quality of family meals. Food in Bonn, whilst never inspired, had always been comforting, but ever since her mother had surrendered to this colourless version of herself, it was as though in some alchemical way all taste and flavour had also vanished from her cooking.

She wandered past the refrigerated section, whose hi-tech fringe of plastic hinted at sophistication, but there was only a pack of oily bacon and a single Scotch egg nestling cosily behind it. The purchase of meat necessitated a drive to the slaughterhouse where the stench of blood attracted a circling cloud of greater black-backed gulls and hoodies. The fruit and vegetable rack offered a choice between two furred and battered apples and a pitifully starved onion – charitable foster parent of abandoned food though Alba was, a line had to be drawn somewhere.

At the till, Peggy was gossiping with Morag. Alba moved along the aisle until the women's voices became no more irritating than the drone of flies. There were logistical problems to theft and she needed to think. Crisp packets were too crackly to store up her jumper. Tubs of ice cream gave her skin-freeze. She settled for two cans of tuna and a doorstop wedge of cheddar cheese. She would make tuna melts, a hot sandwich they served in the American Club in Bonn – one of her favourite places, where all the children of Ford cars and Procter & Gamble hung out and played baseball and ate exotic things like peanut butter and stacked sandwiches with tiny flags tooth-picked into the top. Alba pocketed the cans then headed for the front counter.

'Can you put this on Mum's account, please, Peggy?' She plonked down a loaf of Mother's Pride bread.

'Is Mammy not with you again today?'

'Evidently not,' Alba said rudely. Peggy was a committed gossip and theft required a fast getaway. The last time Alba had come in, the old bag had delayed her with a ten-minute soliloquy about the ill deeds of the beast and the irresponsibility of the man who owned it. So now Peggy owed her, as did the wrestler *and* his rotten dead bear . . .

'Strange that I've no' seen her these good few weeks.' Peggy noted down the Mother's Pride in her ledger.

'Well, she doesn't go out much . . .' Alba shrugged. 'You can imagine . . .'

'Ach, it's no surprise she's taken it hard, poor soul, what with your grandfather only last year and all. Aye, Sir Walter! People still tell of that submarine of his and as for your father, well, a man of the highest order, Mr Fleming was. Always a kind word for everyone, yes indeed.'

At the mention of her father Alba had intended to issue a warning growl but to her surprise she felt an unwelcome stinging behind her eyes. He'd become a forbidden subject at home. The submarine had been one of his favourite anecdotes and suddenly she felt his arm around her and the grate of his chin against her cheek.

'It was close to the end of the Second World War.' Nicky had first told her the story when she was seven or eight. 'Your grandfather was on leave, wounded in the head and knee. He set off for the islands with his friend, a Royal Marine Lieutenant who had a piece of shrapnel embedded in his shoulder. So this fine pair with their slings, bandages and walking sticks found themselves making the crossing on the Caledonian MacBrayne ferry known as the *Plover* and manned only by a skeleton crew.'

Alba imagined her grandfather in his uniform limping across the empty deck and scanning the churning waters for basking sharks or a school of dolphins. 'The ferry got no more than halfway across the Minch,' Nicky continued, 'when a German submarine surfaced and began barking commands at it. "*Achtung!*" they cried, or perhaps, "Heave to or we shoot!" or whatever it is that German submarine commanders say in these situations. Anyway, whatever they said, the very minute the Germans started threatening them, the Captain and his four crew buggered off in the *Plover*'s only lifeboat, leaving their passengers stranded on the ferry. So Grandpa, still with the bandage round his head, grabbed the small gun mounted in the bows and, steadied by the lieutenant, promptly fired at the submarine. The sub fired back but the shell glanced off the side. Grandpa fired again, this time scoring a hit because the sub submerged and disappeared and the two men managed to bring the ferry into Loch Baghasdail without further incident. The following morning, the Captain and crew also made it to Loch Baghasdail in their little rowing boat. By then, of course, the whole island had been told the story and every time the Captain tried to bring the boat ashore the islanders shoved it off again with their spades and sticks, shouting, "Away with you, bloody cowards!" And eventually the Captain and his crew were forced to row themselves all the way back to Oban.'

'Did Grandpa get a medal?' Alba asked.

'Heavens, no,' her father chuckled. 'Your grandfather and the lieutenant went straight to bed and, phlegmatic Englishmen that they were, simply woke up the next morning and went shooting. In fact, your grandfather never even bothered to note the incident in his diary. The only account for that day was a record of how many duck they'd shot.'

After the submarine incident, Sir Walter was forever a hero in the eyes of the islanders. When he'd died, despite his memorial service being held in London, the township had taken it upon themselves to honour him in one of their own Gaelic services.

It had all been so different with her father. Every time Alba thought about it, she felt sick. Her father worked for the government. He might not have sunk a submarine but he'd served his country. Christ, hadn't he died serving his country? 'A dreadful accident', 'just one of those things', what difference did it make? He'd been in the embassy, on the Queen's business. Her father exemplified patriotic conduct and honour in everything he had ever done. Yet, while her grandfather's service had been held at the Guards Chapel in Westminster, her father's had been in a small church in Bad Godesberg. She didn't know the diplomatic equivalent of a military funeral but surely there ought to have been some kind of official ceremony? Volleys fired, or soldiers carrying reversed arms? Instead the service had felt almost furtive. She had been expecting friends and colleagues to stand and speak about character and achievements, but there had been nothing except for that creepy, awkward gathering at the Ambassador's residence. How *dare* the government treat her father so badly and how *dare* her mother have allowed them?

Unseeingly, Alba printed her name in the shop's ledger. It made no sense. There was something else. Her mother was keeping information from her just as Georgie was. She stared broodily at her gumboots. A ladybird was sculling along the slippery wooden floorboards towards the counter. Alba followed its progress for a couple of seconds then stamped on it.

Oh yes, even the ladybird owed her.

41

 The second time Georgie saw him was through a window. Most days after lunch she retired to the upstairs bathroom and locked the door. The window faced north-east and through it she could usually run her eyes along a flat three-mile strip of the island without seeing another soul. One afternoon, however, she spotted a toothpick of a figure, sitting on the wall by the corner of Euan's croft. He looked as if he was waiting. He looked like she felt. As if he'd been waiting forever. She watched him with vague curiosity then went on scanning the roads until she spotted what she was looking for: the red dot of the Post Office van. She held her breath as it approached the turn, then experienced a pinch of disappointment as it carried straight on. Any day now Angus's Post Office van would bring her an envelope and that envelope promised her A level results, and those results were her yellow brick road to a life – one that did not necessarily play itself out on the island.

Soon she would be eighteen. Surely a watershed moment for pep talks about prospects and opportunities? Instead, growing up and moving on felt like just another dirty secret she was hiding and the kernel of resentment inside her grew bigger. What did her mother imagine? That she would stay forever on the island and work in the knitwear factory, listening to Donald John boo-booing away until she was as old and bowed as everyone else? Oh, God help her . . . She heard the noise of an engine. The mobile shop was idling outside the gate and she watched Jamie exchanging money for comics with a dark-skinned man in a boiler suit. How a Paki had ended up in the Outer Hebrides was one of the island's great mysteries. Alba's theory was that he had set sail from Karachi to London only to be blown off course by a storm. It was even possible, she claimed, that he'd mistaken Lochbealach for London – after all, who knew the size of village he'd come from? Either way, within a month of his arrival, the mobile shop, peddling everything from long-life milk to library books, was a regular sight outside islanders' crofts. Georgie slid to the floor. If Jamie and Alba had their *Dandy* and *Beano*, no one would bother about her. She pulled out *The Story of O* from behind the pipe in the cabinet. Its broken spine flopped open randomly and she began reading. If her A level results promised her a future, then surely that future must also include losing her virginity. She had a blurred and indistinct longing for the dark corners of dance halls and the smell of a boy's skin. She unzipped her jeans and wiggled them down to her ankles, then, licking her finger, brought it between her legs and mechanically circled it in small button-polishing movements. She found a watery thread of sensation and chased it for a while but it gained no traction. She dragged up her jeans and looked at her face in the mirror. More than half a year had passed since her father's death but she looked no older. It was as if she had frozen in time. She felt like a dropped watch that had stopped ticking and she needed someone to pick her up, align their beating heart with hers and kick-start her into living again. It was lonely keeping secrets. It was lonely being the oldest. On her sixteenth birthday, her father had released her from the daily bind of his news round. At the time she had considered it her best present ever. Now, though, through the prism of nostalgia, those awkward moments were the ones she yearned for most. She would have given anything to put her arm around her father's neck as he turned the pages of *The Times*.

Come on, my George, what is it that's caught your attention today?

Creeping into her mother's bedroom, she opened the chest of drawers and dragged out an old Viyella shirt. It smelt of mothballs. Quickly she stuffed it back and tried a jumper instead. The wool smelt of oil and linseed. She yanked open drawer after drawer, pulling out bits of clothing until at last, there it was, on a handkerchief – a lingering trace of her father's scent. His very own piece of Stasi muslin . . .

'You have to understand that East Germany is a country run on suspicion,' her father had told her on the drive to Berlin. 'The East Germans are incorrigible trainspotters when it comes to surveillance and there's nothing they're more talented at than fascist bureaucracy. East Germany deals in information. It's their currency. It's what makes their little hearts beat faster. Surveillance is this country's biggest industry. It keeps thousands in work.' He picked up the map from the divide and squinted at it. 'They say that in another decade, the Stasi will have generated more surveillance documents since 1949 than documents of any other kind printed in Germany since the Middle Ages. Think about that for a minute because it's a staggering statistic. Spare a thought for all those trees cut down, think of the crates of pens, the oceans of ink and miles of typewriter ribbon. Imagine all those people sitting at their desks poring over endless transcripts filled with the daily minutiae of other people's lives. Monday, 3.04 p.m. Georgiana Fleming walked into her bedroom (noted: untidy) picked up a black-handled hairbrush (noted: dirty) and brushed her hair using fourteen long even strokes. Monday, 3.07 p.m. Georgiana put down her hairbrush and picked her nose.'

'I do not pick my nose.'

'Try denying that under interrogation,' he teased.

'So, who was worse, the Gestapo or the Stasi?'

'Hard to say. East Germany slithered straight out of Nazism into Communism. Twelve years of Gestapo terror has been replaced by three decades of oppression and subversion. The Gestapo were more immediately sadistic, but it wouldn't be a whole lot of fun to be interrogated by the Stasi either.' He'd adjusted his rear-view mirror. 'They aren't just happy collecting documents on people, you know. They collect their smells too.'

'That's disgusting,' Georgie said doubtfully. 'And probably not true. You can't collect people's smells.'

'Indeed you can. If the Stasi suspect you of some infraction, let's say you've been seen associating with the wrong people or reading seditious literature – who knows what might send the buggers into a rage – they'll pull you in for questioning. They put you into a room where they make you sit on a seat with a muslin cloth underneath. Then they interrogate you, sometimes for hours on end until you've sweated out half your body weight in fear alone. After that, in the event they decide to let you go – and there is absolutely no guarantee that they will – your sweat-saturated muslin is whisked away and stored in a glass jar.'

'What do they do with it?' Georgie had been as revolted as she'd been fascinated.

'Well, every jar is labelled with the name of the poor brute they've scared half to death, and should that person ever abscond in the future, the Stasi simply whip the appropriate cloth from their storage facility and have them followed by the dogs.'

As always with her father's stories, Georgie had suspected an element of exaggeration for her amusement. Nonetheless, she added the Specimen Museum of Smells to the picture book of oddities he had already logged in her mind: the Dressed Fleas in Tring, the two-headed calf in the Museum of Lausanne. Life was supposed to make more sense as you grew up; instead the world became an odder and more unrecognizable place with every passing day.

'You deal in information,' she'd told him, 'so what's the difference?'

He had reached for her hand and squeezed it. 'The difference is that I'm one of the good guys.'

One of the good guys, he'd said.

It had all been so different on the journey home. Half an hour after they'd passed through the border, her father had stopped the Peugeot, stumbled from the driver's seat and thrown up violently by the side of the road. Georgie decided he couldn't have been feeling well for some time. He'd been ill at ease the whole day and she'd noticed his hand trembling as he twisted the key in the ignition.

'Are you all right, Dad?'

'I'm so sorry, George,' he'd said tersely. 'I'm so terribly sorry.'

'Don't be silly,' she protested timidly. 'You're the one who's sick. It must have been all that horrid food.'

He lowered his head to the steering wheel and banged it once, hard against the leather.

Georgie sat very still. Lord knows, the minute the lights of West Germany had appeared she too had felt like throwing herself to the ground and kissing the soil. She had expected the uneasy atmosphere to fade with every mile, but instead she could feel the raised hairs on the back of her neck. Try as she might, she couldn't shake the feeling that they were still being watched. She wanted to ask her father what was wrong. She wanted to ask him about the church. About whether the Stasi had followed them inside and recorded what they'd seen. She wanted to ask him why at the checkpoint the Grenzer, disregarding her father's diplomatic card, had waved the Peugeot into an inspection pit and initiated a search, only to abandon it abruptly after receiving a phone call – but more than these she wanted to ask her father about the look on his face as he'd been ordered out of the car and directed towards the small interrogation booth. He'd told her a couple of times that the harassment of visitors and searching of cars was standard procedure and this had made his expression all the more shocking to her. Because there had been fear twisting his face. Raw, unconstrained fear.

'Yes,' he agreed. 'The food.' He took her hand and held it to his cheek. 'Forgive me, my little George, forgive me,' and his voice had dropped unrecognizably low. 'I should never have brought you.'

She was not stupid. She was not a child. MI6 had reports to write and boxes to tick. What boxes could there possibly be? Accident. Suicide. Murder.

She buried her face in her father's handkerchief. There was another explanation. There had to be. For the trip to Berlin, for the meeting in the church and the whispered handover that accompanied it.

'My father is not a traitor,' she whispered. 'My father is not a traitor.' For a second her spirits lifted, then she remembered. Her father was dead. She would never know. She would live the rest of her life not knowing. She rushed back into the bathroom, swept the hair off her face and, just in time, knelt down over the loo.

42

'Good day to you, Letitia, and how are you keeping?'

Letty smiled blankly at the stranger on her doorstep. 'Well, thank you,' she replied, trawling her brain for a clue to the woman's identity. The ready use of her first name threw her, hinting, as it did, at more than a passing acquaintance.

'Why, it must be several years since we last had the pleasure.'

'Indeed.' Letty's diplomatic training snapped in. 'Come in, do, please.'

Her visitor was middle-aged and wearing face powder a fraction too bright for her complexion. The powder suggested non-islander. Letty herself had not worn make-up since the day she'd arrived and the idea of Peggy or Morag coyly applying blusher whilst totting up receipts at the shop seemed almost ludicrous. Then there was the expensive scarf she was draping over the back of the chair while her smart trousers, with their echo of easy-press, were decidedly more the patina of lowland style than island.

'Oh, but I'm glad to get out of that croft for a while,' the women confided. 'They're pretty enough from the outside, I'll give you that, but inside, well . . . to be honest, I don't know how they stand it. The ventilation is completely inadequate. It will be some time before I can wash the smell of peat out of my hair.'

Letty made some general noise of sympathy and plunged the switch on the kettle. 'So you're here visiting, I take it,' she fished. 'Holiday?'

The woman let out a mirthless tinkle. 'As if this would be anybody's choice for a holiday! Why, it's only when I visit that I remember the island is half a century behind civilization.' She sighed. 'It's queer to think that when my husband went to school there were precious few who even wore shoes!' She accepted the cup of tea with thanks. 'Though naturally it's hard for you or me to comprehend.'

'Yes, quite,' Letty murmured. 'So, where are you staying?' She slid a plate of chocolate digestives onto the table.

'With the Macdonalds, of course.' The stranger looked surprised. 'It would never do to offend them, though if ever a place was crying out for a good motel it would be this island.'

Letty gave up. What had she expected? Eighty per cent of the island sheltered under the umbrella of the Macdonald clan. Besides, whoever she was, she seemed determined to honour Letty with an extended visit. Outside the window, a sparrow was huddling anxiously on the sill. Patches of ochre-coloured lichen were mushrooming in the cracks of the render. It had stopped raining and a needle of light hung over the south island. She had always loved days like this, every colour soft and muted. In the far distance, Beinn Mhor rose out of the mist like a humpbacked whale. She risked a look at the clock. Two thirty. Her mind went to the beach and the virgin expanse of sand waiting for her. The tide would be on its way out – and still the woman was prattling on. 'All those heavy scones and sandwiches. It seems downright penny-pinching to be still using margarine when I've seen with my own two eyes that butter can be bought in the shop. Aye, Spam too! Why, none of the wives I know would touch the stuff! I don't know about you, Letitia, but I can barely keep it down.'

Letty began to shift irritably in her chair. She was no fan of the islands' Spam cult, but to say so outside the family was disloyal in the extreme. 'So you live down south, I take it?' The woman's polyglot accent was hard to place.

'In the Midlands. We moved there from Glasgow, why, let me see – a good year ago now.'

'That's nice.' As the woman embarked on a lengthy boast about the superiority of the south, its inhabitants, weather and bingo clubs, Letty drifted away again. She needed her time on the beach. It was where she went to think. Every day she looked at the small photograph and the painting. CO-60, NI-60, MG-137. Sometimes she drew the colour codes in the sand with a piece of seaweed and stared at them, waiting for meaning of some kind to come to her, but nothing ever did. *Cobalt, nickel, magenta.* Blues, silvers, purples. Sky, sea, heather. They were the colours of the island, that's all.

'Oh, it's hard to find an excuse to leave the croft, but with Murdo away to Eileandorcha today I said to myself: May, this is a good moment to pay your respects to Letitia.'

'Murdo?' Letty choked on her biscuit. 'Murdo Macdonald?' She stared at the woman with dawning recognition. Only a few days ago, she'd been sitting in the kitchen when she'd heard the noise of gunshots and instinctively she'd looked for Nicky. She saw him so often in her dreams that had he appeared at the gate, duck in hand, she would not have been remotely surprised, but all she could see was the blue square of Alick's tractor parked on the machair. The children were lifting potatoes, Nicky was dead and the shots were being fired by a flesh-and-blood poacher with a pocketful of cartridges, so she'd pulled herself together, thrown on a coat and hurried down the sandy path until she'd spotted him. A stocky man, crouched on a tiny islet in the middle of Aivegarry, waving his gun about his head, letting off shots at every bird in the sky. Letty shouted. She was answered by another shot, this time aimed low across the ground. An oystercatcher swerved and dipped in shock. Incensed, she splashed over the wet sand until she reached him.

He acknowledged her presence with a jerk of his chin, then lifted his gun again.

'Oi!' She positioned herself in front of it. 'What are you shooting at?'

'Anything that moves.' He was a bullish-looking individual, with wide nostrils that flared aggressively when he spoke. Generally Nicky turned a blind eye to poaching, reasoning that it was the islanders' right to shoot for the pot, but she was stung by the man's rudeness. 'Well, I move, my children move, so what on earth do you think you're doing shooting so close to them?'

'It's my God-given right to shoot anywhere I wish.'

'It's not your right. You don't have the shooting here. Who are you?' Then, adding as imperiously as she dared, 'And what's your name?'

'My name?' He laughed and she smelt the beer on his breath. 'Well, you might ask. Certainly not a Sassenach who owns the half-acre of land her house sits on and not a square inch more. Don't you be telling me where I can and can't shoot, Letitia Fleming. My family has lived on this island for hundreds of years.'

'How do you know my name?' Warily, she stepped back.

'Ach, you're all I hear about night and day. Letitia this, Letitia that.'

'Well.' Letty was completely wrong-footed '. . . You still can't shoot on this land, so please go.' To her relief she saw Alick hurrying towards her – there was nothing Alick liked better than a good fight – but instead of throwing himself into the fray, he'd pulled on her arm, agitated. 'Let's away home, Let-ic-ia.'

'Alick?'

'Aye, leave him to it.'

'Alick, what is it?' she said in a low voice. 'Why are you so fussed?'

'Don't you bother, Alick.' The poacher snapped the cartridges from the barrels of his gun. 'I'm away myself. Although you should be happy for a man about the place, Letitia Fleming, especially with that bear prowling around. Why, by now it must be hungry enough to take a cow, let alone a child.' He strutted off without another word.

'Alick, my Lord – who was that man?' Letty watched him go. 'Was he drunk?'

Alick shoved his hands deep into his pockets. 'Murdo.'

'Murdo who? Is he an islander?'

'Aye, he's an islander, all right.' Alick gazed miserably at the ground. 'He's my brother.'

'Indeed, Murdo Macdonald,' May confirmed with some surprise. 'Goodness, you'll not have been thinking I was married to one of the other brothers all this time. First come, first served, and I always say I got the best apple in *that* barrel.' Her eyes flickered. 'Aye, I know you give Alick a little work here and there. I can't imagine what the poor thing would do without you.'

'I imagine he would do very well,' Letty said pointedly. 'He's an exceptionally capable man.'

'The drink makes him unpredictable,' May countered, 'but I suppose it must be hard being the only son who's not found himself a wife or even a steady job. Alick should have had the sense to leave the island and better himself in some way.'

'I beg your pardon,' Letty said coldly. She could dimly remember meeting Euan and Mrs Macdonald's eldest son. Almost twenty years older than Alick, he'd left the island as a young man and barely returned since. Perhaps it was what Alick should have done but she resented the implication of superiority.

'Of course, he's left it too late now,' May continued blithely. 'Though I must say, Murdo has been a very good brother to Alick, allowing him to live in the croft all these years.'

'Alick doesn't live in the croft, he lives in his caravan, which he bought with his own earnings. He looks after everything for Euan, the croft, the cattle, all the farming. Your husband is extremely lucky to have him there.'

'Well, who can say if it will be for much longer?' May pursed her lips.

'What exactly do you mean by that?'

'Oh, I mean nothing by it,' May said airily, 'other than that Euan is hardly a young man.'

Letty stood up abruptly. She was no longer a diplomatic wife whose every utterance had to be checked, cross-referenced and milked of any nuance that might conceivably cause offence. If she didn't want this woman in her house, then she would throw her out or throttle her, whichever proved the most enjoyable – but May Macdonald was already knotting her scarf under her chin. 'Alick certainly has a good friend in you, Letitia,' she said, a hard edge to her voice, 'a good friend indeed.'

'Why, yes,' Donald John consoled her later. 'As soon as Murdo married her and took her to England she got terrible grand, Letitia.'

'She's completely lost her accent,' Letty said indignantly.

'Oh, boo boo,' he agreed delightedly. 'She talks just like someone on the wireless right enough. The simple life is no' for her.'

'Oh, poor Alick. He must hate having them here.'

'Oh, tse tse, yes indeed. He's no' been down for a visit since the day they arrived.'

'Is he on a bender?' Alick's drinking sprees were intense, short-lived episodes, invariably followed by bouts of remorse.

'Aye, I'm afraid that's it, Letitia.'

'I don't blame him. Do you know what business Murdo has up here?'

'Something to do with the army; building contracts, I think,' Donald John said vaguely. 'Still and all, he'll be away to the mainland soon and Alick will be rid of them.'

'I hope so.' Letty tried to shake off a lingering feeling of concern. Even if he was on a bender, Alick was rarely absent this long. But then once, when he'd disappeared for a few days and she'd suspected drink, it turned out that he was secretly holed up in her own garage repairing the Peugeot after Georgie had smashed into a telegraph pole. Another time, she remembered him ploughing the machair with Donald John following behind, throwing rye and barley seed for the cattle out of a sack slung over his shoulders, and they'd both been alarmed to see the tractor lurching erratically from right to left.

'Why, the bugger's drunk!' Donald John had exclaimed. But in fact, the lapwings were nesting on the machair that year and Alick had been deliberately weaving in between the nests in order not to disturb their young.

43

Jamie stared at the knife in Roddy's hand. He watched as the old man, with calm precision, inserted the tip of the blade into the lower belly of the rabbit then forced it swiftly upwards. Seconds later, the long ribbons of gut had been yanked out and were sitting, leaking blood in a bucket while Roddy, holding fast to the rabbit's hind legs, relieved the animal of its fur with one powerful rip.

'Skin-a-bunny,' Jamie whispered as the origin of his mother's jolly bathtime mantra sank in. Roddy laid the rabbit on the table and reached for the next. Roddy's income from wall building and antique dealing was supplemented by snaring rabbits. After they'd been cleaned and skinned, he would pack them up, five or six at a time in brown paper, and post them off to the mainland. 'D'ye want to take a turn, Jamie?' Roddy held out the knife towards him.

'Oh! Actually, no, thank you very much,' Jamie said. His relationship with rabbits was complicated enough without having to butcher them. He was not averse to them stewed in a casserole dish with carrots and onions but he preferred them alive and hopping about the sand dunes, unless of course they had the mixy, in which case their bulbous eyes and drunken staggerings came back to haunt him at night. He tried not to look too closely at the pile of corpses on the table. Stripped of their fur, they were unrecognizable, their bodies thin and extruded, their flesh strawberry-rippled with capillaries. Jamie shuddered. Sometimes it seemed that death was everywhere he looked – it was in the whale on the beach, in the matted carcass of the sheep at the bottom of the cliff, even in the bones that were occasionally spat out of the bog.

'Roddy!' Suddenly he had an idea. 'You can see the future, can't you?'

'Aye, when the second sight grants it me.'

'If the bear was still alive, could you see where it might be tomorrow, or the next day?'

'I might. Who's to say?'

'What about my father, Roddy? Could you try to see my father in the future?'

'The day will come soon enough.' Roddy glanced dramatically towards the heavens. 'And when it does, I'll be sure to shake him by the hand and tell him you're doing all right, lad.'

'But if you don't mind, could you do it now, please? I mean, you saw my grandpa in the future and then he came back, didn't he?'

'Aye, that's right, Jamie.' Roddy wiped the knife on his trousers and laid it carefully on the counter. 'But that was a premonition, something else entirely – you know that story well as any.'

Jamie did indeed. It had happened many years after

Flora Macdonald had set sail for Australia with Neilly, her fisherman, and a much younger Roddy had been building the walled garden at Ballanish. Roddy disliked Captain Macdonald as much as the next islander, but he pitied him. Left with no possibility of seeing his beloved daughter again, the Captain regretted his cruelty and decided to plant a garden in her remembrance. Every flower he could lay his hands on – wild orchids, irises, daffodils – went into that sandy, barren ground. He sent away for exotic bulbs and seeds from the mainland and purchased a load of rich Irish soil that had been used as ballast on a ship, but nothing took. Storms uprooted every hopeful shoot until finally the Captain's sense of loss overcame his inherent meanness and he decided to build a high stone wall around the entire garden to afford it some protection. Roddy was the only wall builder on the island, but he was a master of his craft. His walls were sculptures, constructed from thousands of haphazardly shaped stones, each one meticulously graded and sized before being intricately slotted together. Wall building was a painfully laborious process, particularly for a hunchback, and Roddy had barely completed the east side of the garden when he spotted a lone figure walking towards him. The way Roddy told the story had him recognizing Jamie's grandfather as a distinguished sort of a gentleman merely from the manner of his gait. The man had sauntered down that road as though he hadn't a care in the world and Roddy had been intrigued. There wasn't a soul on the island he didn't know. A stranger was news and news was currency and currency paid for whisky. 'So your grandfather walks right up to me,' Roddy said.

'He makes a remark about the fineness of the day and then, polite as can be, tells me to stop work.'

'And you asked him why, didn't you?' Jamie prompted.

'Well, of course I asked him, and that's when he tells me he has bought the house off Captain Macdonald and he wants the wall built in a different place.'

Young Roddy needed no further encouragement to down tools and while away the remainder of the afternoon rolling cigarettes and ruminating on the house's new owner until he was discovered by the Captain himself.

'Why, you lazy bugger!' the Captain bellowed. 'What the bloody hell are ye doin'?'

Roddy related his story, duly receiving a cuff round the head for being a liar and idle bastard. The years passed, the grieving Captain grew old and infirm and was eventually transferred to a home on the mainland. Thistles and weeds destroyed Flora's garden, the wall was invaded by moss and lichen and a section of its southern corner was destroyed in the great storm of 1949, but Roddy remained the island's only wall builder and finally he was brought in by the estate to make repairs. He'd barely had time to edge his trowel between two stones before he chanced to glance up and, sure enough, there was a gentleman walking towards him down the hill.

Roddy recognized him at once – the man's gait, the fine clothes. There wasn't a single detail of that original meeting he'd forgotten. 'Aye, it was your grandfather, Jamie, twenty years on to the very day, and insisting on buying the house that very minute.' Roddy shook his head. 'Now that was a grand premonition, indeed it was.'

A grand premonition and a top-class opportunity.

Roddy, shrewdly assuming the role of land agent, instantly upped the price of the house from the few hundred pounds it was worth to the two thousand pounds for which Jamie's grandfather eventually acquired it.

'Aye, your grandpa was well liked on the island. Your daddy too, and more's the pity your father's no' resting here as there's many a soul who'd like to pay their respects to him.'

'I don't think my father is resting anywhere, Roddy,' Jamie said reprovingly. 'He's lost.'

'Oh?' Roddy's eyebrows lifted in surprise. 'Jamie, your father's not lost. Why, he'll be up in heaven, keeping an eye on you.'

'Oh no, Roddy, he's not in heaven.'

'And what makes you so sure?'

'I went to look for him there.'

'Did'ye now?' The old islander tilted his cap and fixed his eyes on Jamie's peaked face. 'And how did'ye get there if you don't mind my asking?'

'I took a taxi,' Jamie said.

44

London

Heaven.

The first time it had cropped up had been a few weeks after the family arrived in London from Bonn. One of the boys in Jamie's class asked him about his father's job and Jamie – yet to make a single friend at the school – had been sorely tempted to confide in him. A long minute passed while he considered the multiple-choice answers to this question.

My father works for the government.

Sometimes my father gets to be a spy.

My father is currently a prisoner of the Cold War.

This last one had set him thinking. Lately he had taken to wondering what exactly the Cold War was. That it was so dubbed because it took place in snowy countries like Germany, Siberia and Russia was obvious. But so far as he could glean, it was not a war that involved trench foot or parachutes or Lancaster bombers. He had yet to wrap his brain around the concept of an amorphous conflict of counter-ideology and misinformation and so he had no pictorial backdrop against which to imagine his father. Jamie was not the kind of child to complain but it hurt him physically whenever he thought about his father. Sometimes it felt as though the bones in his legs were being ground to dust, sometimes he complained about his chest. Occasionally, the pain was so intense it erupted out of his body via the colony of gumboils that lined the inside of his cheeks. Still, none of this was the point – the point was Jamie would have endured any degree of suffering in exchange for news of his father but he decided that giving information to Felix Thompson for no reason was without real benefit.

When Jamie didn't answer, a teacher took Felix to one side.

'Jamie's father has gone to heaven,' he heard her whisper.

Jamie had long accepted that certain aspects of life were kept from him. He had learnt to recognize the signs. Adults who stopped talking when he came into the room. Family dinners during which looks were exchanged instead of words. His mother waving him away when she was on the phone. But quite why important information should be kept from him when it was made readily available to another boy at school – a boy he scarcely even knew – was beyond his comprehension and, most unusually, Jamie was overcome by a surge of anger so ferocious it propelled him after the teacher as she walked away. He yanked her sleeve. Miss Stevenson spun round.

'Did my mother tell you that?' Jamie demanded.

'Tell me what?' Her eyes softened as she recognized who it was.

'That my father was in heaven?'

'No, Jamie,' Miss Stevenson said gently, 'I haven't spoken to your mother.'

'Then why did you say that? Who told you?'

The teacher looked down at the trembling boy in front of her. Tears of anger glistened in his slanted, strangely avian eyes.

'Don't you know that heaven is for dead people?' he demanded.

'I'm sorry, Jamie,' she said. 'I just thought . . . well, I know you've lost your father and I . . .'

'I am not supposed to talk about my father and I don't like other people talking about him either.'

'Of course not,' Miss Stevenson said. 'That's quite understandable.' In the teachers' common room, earlier in the term, she remembered Jamie Fleming being flagged as an odd child. 'We won't talk about him again,' she said. 'I promise.'

Nevertheless, once the idea of heaven had been mooted, Jamie's analytical mind was forced to examine the implications. He started where he always started. At the beginning.

The day of his father's accident.

The day of the circus.

When his father had been hurt.

Before he had gone away for a long time.

On a mission.

And then got lost.

But now his father was in heaven?

The jump between these last two statements made no sense because heaven was where you went when you were dead. Jamie understood about being dead. His grandfather had died the year before. There had been a service for him and after that he had been burnt.

Jamie had sat in the church between his mother and father and stared at the balls of dust trapped between the cassocks. In spite of a warm spring wind outside, the church had felt oppressively cold, but then churches were already oppressive and perhaps death made them colder still. His mother had cried throughout the service. He watched, concerned, as the tears washed through the tributary of grooves around her eyes. Once upon a time he had himself been an Olympian wailer, but this habit had brought the wrath of Alba down on him. Jamie had loved his grandfather but he found it difficult to associate the idea of sadness with the man who had held him upside down and tickled him, the man who had tried, with more patience than most, to teach him how to catch and throw a ball with his five-thumbed hands. Also, and rather shamefully, Jamie found himself preoccupied by hunger the entire service. At breakfast that morning there had been the usual cereals, toast and jams on the table but he had been unsure whether or not to eat them. It hadn't been as if anybody had said he wasn't allowed. It was just that his mother's sadness was so immense and communicable that when she pushed away her plate, Jamie felt he ought to do the same.

So, in as far as his grandfather was gone, Jamie understood that death was final.

But there had been no church service for his father. There had been no purple curtains or ashes to scatter over the island. More significantly there had been no talk of dying. Beyond his mother explaining to him about the accident, there had been no talk at all. Then, surely, he reasoned, if there had been a river of tears for his grand-father, his mother would have cried two oceans for his father. So no, what had happened to his Dada did not in any way resemble death. It was something more mysterious and complicated and pupils and teachers alike should jolly well mind their own business.

Still, he was the first to admit that he misunderstood things. Perhaps he had misunderstood the concept of heaven. Maybe you didn't have to be dead to go there.

So he asked around.

Heaven was floaty and dreamy.

Heaven was paradise.

Heaven was full of puppies and things to cuddle.

'There is no heaven,' Alba said.

'Yes, there is,' Jamie said. 'It's God's kingdom.'

'I don't believe in God.'

'I know there's a heaven, because everybody says there is.'

'If you know, then why are you asking me?'

'Because I don't understand where it is exactly.'

'Look it up in the phone book then,' she said flippantly.

His eyes widened. 'Do you really think it will be in there?'

'Why not?' She turned her back on him. 'It's probably just down the road and you can go and ring on the door-bell.'

'Thank you, Alba.' Jamie was struck by the brilliance of this idea. 'I love you, Alba,' he called over his shoulder as he ran from the room.

After he'd gone, Alba pulled at her hair so viciously that

a small clump came away in her hand. Occasionally, she glimpsed in herself the possibility of protector as opposed to tormentor of her brother – someone able to absorb his love and adoration and release it back to him, if not in a touchy-feely way, then from a safe distance, and only when strictly necessary – but unconditional irritation with Jamie had been hard-wired into her personality and she had never understood how to defuse it. Besides, why should she? The world was not as he believed. If she didn't get let off the butcher's hook of life's misery, why should he?

Jamie got his neighbour, Saul, to look Heaven up in the *Yellow Pages*.

'It won't be there,' Saul said.

'How do you know?'

'Because I don't think it works like that,' Saul said doubtfully. 'Anyway, heaven is for dead people.'

'I don't think heaven is *just* for dead people,' Jamie said. 'I think you're allowed to visit on special occasions. A boy at school told me that when his grandmother had a stroke last summer she got all the way to the door of heaven. He said she saw bright lights and singing angels and then she woke up and found herself back in the hospital.'

'Okay, but I still don't think you can just go to heaven whenever you want.'

'Why not?'

'Because I think you need a plane or a spaceship to get there.'

'I don't think so,' Jamie said doubtfully. 'Alba would have said so.'

'I promise you do. My sister saw a movie about it. She said that heaven was on the other side of the Black Hole but you had to be an astronaut to get there . . . or a robot,' he amended.

'How old is your sister?'

'Twelve.'

'Well,' Jamie said, 'Alba is fourteen so she probably knows a bit more what she's talking about.'

Saul, youngest of four, rigorously and occasionally painfully versed in the hierarchy of age, backed down. Dutifully he grappled with the copy of the *Yellow Pages* until he reached H, then, squinting through his glasses, he traced his finger up and down the lines, until suddenly, there it was! Artfully placed between Heating Engineers and Hebrew Translation. 'I don't believe it!' Saul was dumbfounded. 'It *is* in London.'

'I told you,' Jamie said proudly. 'Alba is very clever, you know.'

Getting to Heaven had required the breaching of several rules. Rebellion was not in Jamie's nature, but his mission was important enough to justify both truancy and stealing. His mother's wallet had been an easy target, sitting on the kitchen table and weighty with coins. Jamie felt no guilt. He knew his mother would pay anything to get his father back.

145 Tithe Street had revealed itself as an unprepossess-

ing house in a narrow north London street. The boys waited until the taxi had disappeared around the corner before walking up the steps. A purple bulb in the ground-floor window bathed the lace curtains in a promisingly divine light. Jamie rapped on the lacquered door then pounded resolutely with his fist and in time was rewarded by the creak of a bolt being drawn. The door half opened and a woman peered out, a cigarette smouldering between her fingers.

What had he been expecting? A uniform? A doorman with peaked hat and gold epaulettes? Heaven was special, that much he knew, but there was nothing special about the woman standing in front of them. Her eyes were puffy and a back section of her hair was macramied into a cobweb of knots. A pink blouse hung limply over the waistband of a pair of achingly tight white trousers.

'What do you want?'

Until this moment Jamie's excitement had not once been tempered by doubt. He checked the paper in his hand. 'Is this heaven?'

The woman snickered and glanced down the street. 'Who's asking?'

'I am,' Jamie said, then, fearful that she was looking for someone more authoritative, drew himself up. 'After all, I'm the one who's standing here.'

'Cheeky,' the woman commented. She took a meditative suck on her cigarette. 'Right. What do you want?'

'So is it?'

'Is it what?'

'Heaven?'

'Maybe it is and maybe it isn't.' She scratched her nose with the back of her hand. 'Why?'

'I'm looking for my father.'

'Oh, are you now?' She eyed him with vague interest. 'And what makes you think he might be here?'

Jamie was about to say Miss Stevenson had said so when it occurred to him that permission might be required from a higher authority than a geography teacher.

'My mother told me.'

The woman's eyebrows shot up. 'Oh, she did, did she? And what did she have to say about that?'

'Well, my mother doesn't like to talk about my father much.'

'Sensible woman.' She pursed her lips.

'So can I see him?'

'Who?'

'My Dada.'

'Listen, sonny.' She started to close the door. 'Your dad's not here.'

'Wait,' Jamie stepped quickly forwards. 'How do you know?'

'Because I know.'

'Come on.' Saul plucked at his sleeve. 'Let's go.'

Jamie brushed him away. 'How can you be so sure?'

The woman flicked her stub into the street and considered the boys in front of her. The silent one had crooked teeth and jug ears. The other was an underfed-looking thing with string bean arms and huge, rather piercing eyes. Nevertheless there was something endearing about them. Here was a pair of life's soon-to-be failures. Before her stood her future clientele in all its youthful guise and for a moment, she felt the stirrings of something approximating maternal instinct.

'What does he look like, this dad of yours?'

'He's got a thin face and browny hair. He looks a bit like me, but grown-up.'

'Well, he's definitely not here right now.'

'How can you be sure?'

'Because no one's here right now, sonny, except me.'

Jamie's self-assurance was rocked by a wave of confusion.

'But I don't understand. Is this God's kingdom?'

The woman snorted. 'I don't know about that.'

'Well, is it paradise?'

'Now that, young man,' she said with grand coquettishness, 'it certainly is.'

'Good.' Jamie felt better. God worked in mysterious ways. Stood to reason heaven did too. 'So will he be here later?'

'Shouldn't you be in school?' the woman asked curiously.

'If he does come later, will you tell him I'm looking for him?'

'What's your name?'

'Jamie. Jamie Fleming. And I've been trying to find him for ages.'

'Well, Jamie Fleming, are you sure your father wants to be found?'

'Of course he wants to be found. Everyone who's lost wants to be found.'

The woman snorted.

'So do you think he'll come later?'

'I expect so,' she said, managing to exhale and sigh in the same breath. 'Believe me, sooner or later they all come.'

After she'd withdrawn, Jamie stood looking at the door for a long time. Finally, he turned to leave. If this was heaven, he was glad his father wasn't there.

But that had been London and now here he was on the island, months and months later, and his father had still not found his way home. How lost could a person be? His mother had said his father had hurt 'everything' in the fall. Could he have hit his head and 'lost' his memory? Jamie dared not provoke his mother by asking questions. Besides, his mother was so different these days. Oh, the familiar acts of love were still available to him – her arms still went round him, she still pulled him onto her lap or dropped an absent-minded hand onto his head – but it wasn't the same. Her love for him used to feel so huge and all-consuming it was as though he lived inside her very heart, but now there was an invisible barrier around her. He was too young to understand that she was not cross with him, but only sunk in her own sadness. All he knew for certain was that his world had changed.

So, first Georgie's and now Roddy's re-introduction of heaven came as a relief. It gave him something to think about, a trail of breadcrumbs to follow.

Heaven was where fishermen turned into seagulls.

It was where you went when you were dead, or a place

you visited when you were sick. Heaven was an address in Tithe Street, London. Jamie realized he'd been too quick in dismissing the notion his father might be there. Clearly there was more than one kind of heaven.

45

Ballanish

'How could you, Alba?' Letty stared down at her daughter. 'How *dare* you! Here, on the island. Of all places!'

Alba sat on the sitting-room sofa, every muscle tense with defiance. 'Alba, look at me!' Letty ordered.

Alba raised her head. Her mother was white, her cheeks hollow. Alba had never seen her like this. It was as though her anger had sucked all the oxygen out of the room and for a second Alba felt herself sag. Then she looked her mother straight in the eye and very deliberately drew her own eyebrows into a derisive arch.

'How dare I what?'

Letty kept an unsteady grip on herself. 'Don't you understand? Stealing is about the worst crime you could commit here. First, taking things from the mobile van and then, I heard from Peggy this morning that you've been in the shop almost every day.'

'Peggy's a sneak and a gossip,' Alba said dismissively.

Letty grabbed at her daughter's arm. 'Don't you dare speak like that about *anyone*. Peggy is an extremely nice woman. You're lucky she hasn't called the police.'

Peggy was an extremely nice woman, but, Letty conceded privately, she was a gossip and had doubtless spread word of Alba's transgression around the island. Nevertheless, she'd been a great deal more understanding than Alba had any right to expect. 'Oh aye,' she'd informed Letty breezily, 'there's been the odd thing in her pocket she's forgotten to pay for, but she's had a bit on her mind I'm sure, and besides, I put them on the account, so there's no harm done.'

'That was very good of you, Peggy.' Letty had chewed her lip.

'Ach, it's no bother, Letitia.' Peggy laid a hand on her arm. 'She's a good girl right enough, still and all, you might want to have a wee word with her.'

'What's got into you, Alba?' Letty could not stop herself saying.

'Got into me?' Alba repeated coldly. 'Got. Into. Me?' She cocked her head to one side in mock thought. 'Golly gooseberries. I wonder? I don't suppose it might have something to do with having to live in this godforsaken place, or, you know . . .' her voice rose dangerously, 'the fact that my father is dea—'

'Stop it.' Letty glanced at the door. 'Keep your voice down.'

'Why? Why should I keep my voice down?'

'You know perfectly well why.'

'Oh yes, because we don't want little Jamie upset now, do we?' Alba mimicked.

'No,' Letty said quietly. 'That's right. I don't.'

'Why not? Why are you so worried about Jamie being

upset? Why does he get to live in a bloody bubble? Can't you understand that he *should* be upset. That we should get him in here.' She glanced at the door. 'Make him really cry,' she yelled.

Letty sank into a chair, mute with despair. She had a sudden flash of an eight-year-old Alba. The burning eyes, the passionate avowals of love. Alba, leaping off the bed like a ballet dancer, forcing her father to catch her whether he was ready or not. 'Ah, Fonteyn in flight,' he would laugh, and cover her with kisses.

'I don't understand you, Alba,' she said. 'You have no reason to be this unkind to your brother. Nobody was ever unkind to you in the way you are to him.' She rubbed at her face tiredly. 'Where does it come from, this . . . this . . . desire to hurt people?'

Alba worked her finger into the frayed hole of the loose cover.

'Talk to me, Alba,' Letty said, 'please.'

The questions ran through Alba's head like ticker tape. *Tell me why. Tell me how. Tell me what I don't know. Tell me something, tell me anything, but please, please, tell me what it is you're keeping from me.* She tried to speak but she couldn't force the words over the block of pride jamming her throat. She closed her eyes and took herself back to her bedroom in Bonn – back to the safety of her bed and under the darkness of its covers. 'Almost everything that goes wrong in the world is due to people not knowing how to talk to each other,' she heard father saying. 'Humans are continually struggling to find ways of expressing themselves and sometimes, with the best will in the world, we forget how to do it, or our problems become so severe that we can't bear to talk about them any more. This is where diplomacy comes in. In fact, this is the sole reason why I studied so hard to became a diplomat – so that I could negotiate peace between you and your mother.'

Alba had been sent to her room in a tantrum. She'd felt the bed dip as her father leaned forwards to smooth her hair behind her ears. Anger, he had gone on to argue, was the default emotion for the lazy. Reason, logic and patience, conversely, all required harder work than most people were prepared to commit to.

'But what happens when you can't agree on things?' Alba sniffed.

'Well, humans fight and countries go to war. This is why diplomacy is important, because diplomacy is all about using words and not weapons.'

'But words are weapons,' Alba said, not because she particularly understood the meaning of the phrase but because she remembered her father saying it before and she knew he'd be impressed.

'Clever girl. Yes, they can be. But so is silence. So is anything you do to manipulate people. Bad moods, charm, sulking. So you see, you have to be careful how you use these things.'

'So your job is a weapon.'

'Very much so. But diplomacy is a good weapon. Countries talking to each other is a good thing. People talking to each other is a good thing – which is why, my little tree frog, you must apologize to your mother when she comes up to kiss you goodnight.'

*

'Alba . . .' Letty pleaded. Her bright flash of temper had already expended its battery life. All she wanted was to take Alba in her arms and hold her tight, keep her safe.

Alba's nose had blocked with mucus from the effort of not crying. She turned her head away and parted her mouth to breathe. Apologies had come so cheap when she was little, the price of a kiss or a hug – not any more. She no longer knew how to talk to her mother and her mother didn't know the person that she had become. She had no idea, for example, that Alba smoked cigarettes or that she had finished one of the half-empty bottles of gin in the sitting-room cupboard. Her mother had not noticed that she needed a bra and she had no idea that two weeks after the death of her father, as if further proof was needed to confirm the end of her childhood, Alba had pulled down her pants in the school lavatory to find spots of blood on the thin white cotton. Her mother had no idea that her daughter was currently in collision with her own puberty. She had no idea about anything. Alba's nose began dripping. She would not apologize to her mother, she would not. Her nose dripped harder and the silence between mother and daughter stretched long and shrill.

46

'Just get it over and done with.' Georgie rammed her hands deeper into her pockets and gazed up at the mottled sky.

'You're saying you want me to knock on the door.'

'That is the conventional method for entry.'

'Just walk up the path and knock on the door?'

'Why are you making such a fuss about it?'

Alba shrugged and stamped her gumboots on the wet tarmac.

'For God's sake. Bang on the door, say you're sorry, then run like hell.'

'Easy for you.'

'Well, he's not going to hear you shouting it from here . . . unless, of course, you go and shoplift yourself a megaphone or something.'

'You're hilarious.'

'Well, get on with it then. Besides, you got off lightly. He could have had you arrested.'

'Oh right, as if there's a single policeman on this island.'

'There's nice Sergeant Anderson.'

'Who's probably still searching for that bloody dead bear.'

'He could call for back-up.'

'From who – Dad's Army? Your friends at MI whatsit?' she said sarcastically. 'God, why is everyone making such a fuss about this?'

'Mum, you mean.'

Alba scowled.

'You don't think she has enough to worry about without you being a thief?'

'It's none of her business.'

'Don't be so stupid.'

'I could have paid the money back. She didn't have to make me *apologize*.' Alba spat out the word like a bullet.

'Of course she did.'

'If it's so easy, then you do it.'

'I would if it had been me stealing.'

'No, seriously, you ought to do it. Its embarrassing for me.'

'And it wouldn't be embarrassing for me?'

'No. You didn't do the crime. It would be more like an acting job for you. Besides, aren't you even slightly curious to know what it feels like to be in trouble?'

Georgie sighed. This was Alba's magic trick. Making her own guilt disappear like a rabbit back into a top hat.

'I'm not doing your penance for you.'

'Why not? The Paki doesn't know the difference between us.'

'Forget it, Alba.'

Alba yanked up her hood angrily. Rain was breaking

like cold metal needles against her face. 'What you don't seem to appreciate, Georgie, is that shoplifting is factored into the retail price of goods. Every Mars Bar the Paki sells has got a shoplifting percentage added onto it and since I'm apparently the only one that has ever stolen anything from him, he's defrauding the rest of the islanders. I mean, think about it, do you think he lowers his prices just because there's so little shoplifting here?'

'It's not going to work, Alba.'

'You think it's good for me to be forced to apologize. You think I need punishing. But I'm not sorry, so what's the point? A forced apology is just a lie dressed up in pretty clothes and lying definitely won't stop me stealing. So, as I already said – pointless. If you do it, though, I'll give you something in return and then we'll both benefit.'

'What could you possibly give me?'

'Why, will you do it?'

'Depends.' An idea was occurring to Georgie. There *was* something she wanted from her sister.

'What about if I do your cooking rota for the next few weeks?' Alba offered.

'For a start.'

'Shake on it.' Alba prised a hand from her pocket.

But Georgie had no intention of selling herself cheap. 'Yes, that,' she said coolly, 'plus you have to be nice to Jamie.'

Alba withdrew her hand. 'Define "nice".'

'It's not a word that normally needs defining.'

'Define "nice", and for how long exactly?'

'Alba . . .'

Bella Pollen

'How long?' Alba repeated harshly.

Georgie held her ground. 'You have to be really properly nice to Jamie and do my cooking until the end of the month.'

Alba scowled. She glanced at the Paki's house and tried to imagine forming the word 'sorry'. Most emotions were hateful, but humiliation had to be the most hateful of all. She was furious that Georgie had got the better of her, but then she remembered the neat pyramid of ash of her recently arrived A level results and felt better.

'The end of the month. But not one day, one hour, not one single minute longer.'

'Don't worry, Alba,' Georgie said resentfully. 'God forbid anyone should expect more of you than the bare minimum.' She began trudging up the stony path. Was empathy supposed to be optional? It was hard to say how anybody might turn out in the end, but not for the first time, she wondered whether her sister might be a sociopath. Once, she remembered asking Alba whether she would sacrifice her family for a cure for the common cold and without hesitation Alba had replied yes.

Georgie knocked on the door then pressed her nose to the window. She wanted to leave, but unless one of them wore Alba's hair shirt the whole unpleasant episode would have to be repeated. She sighed heavily and picked her way through wet thistles and nettles towards the mobile van parked to the side of the property. The back was rolled up and she peered inside.

It was the third time Georgie had seen him but he was now no longer a distant scarecrow figure, but a flesh-and-blood boy, slumped against a packing crate, reading a book, his long thin legs stretched across the worn floor like broom handles.

'Oh,' Georgie said. She took in the dark skin and the wild afro. Of course, it made sense. Son of Paki. Had to be.

Equally startled, he scrambled to his feet, tipping his book onto the floor.

'I'm so sorry,' Georgie said. 'I didn't mean . . .'

'I wasn't expecting to see anyone.' He brushed down his trousers. 'We're not open.' He was staring almost rudely at her.

Georgie pushed a strand of wet hair off her face. Standing, the boy was a gangly, thinner version of his father. The trousers of his boiler suit stopped well short of his ankles and his feet were bare. His hair was so bushy it could have been used to sweep cobwebs from the van's ceiling.

'Why are you in here if you're not open?'

'Reading.' He shrugged.

Only a year ago, Georgie's whole life had been about boys. How to meet them, when to meet them, in which cafe she and her girlfriends would congregate to get the best glimpse of them. Her mother had not approved of her wearing make-up, so she took to bringing a tiny palette of watercolours to school with her and as soon as she turned the corner from the house she would wet her finger and swipe her eyelids bright green. After her father's death, she had avoided boys – she had avoided everyone, but boys especially – and now it was as if she no longer remembered how to choreograph her body in their presence. She picked his book off the floor. '*Under Milk*

Wood,' she muttered, feeling hopelessly self-conscious. 'I had to read that for A levels. I even got to be Captain Cat in the school play.'

He continued to scrutinize her as though she was some exotic object the tide had washed up on his doorstep. 'Were you any good?' he offered finally.

'Awful, I've never been able to act. I think they only asked me because they felt sorry for me.'

'For being a bad actress?'

'No, no,' she bit her tongue. 'Mostly because I was new and . . . well, other stuff.'

The boy yawned and stretched one arm up to the roof of the van. There was something sleepy and fluid about him, Georgie thought, like a sloth that had woken up from a month-long nap only to discover it was bedtime again. 'The school here never puts on plays,' he said. 'They just made us read, day in, day out. I used to hate it.' He felt around in his pockets and produced a packet of cigarettes. 'Now, it's something to do when the weather's bad.' He glanced out at the clouded sky and grinned. 'I read a lot.'

'I like reading. You get to try out other people's worlds and see if they're any better than yours.'

'Are they?'

'Well . . .' she said carefully, 'not if you stick to the tragedies.'

The boy jammed a cigarette in his mouth and absently felt around with his foot for a boot. 'There's not much to learn about different worlds from *Under Milk Wood*. It might as well be set on the island.'

'I suppose so. I never really thought about it.' As it happened, she wasn't thinking about books at all, she was thinking about his subversive hair. She had seen hair like his before in newspapers. It was student-sit-in hair. Anti-war-protester hair, socialist-counter-demonstrator hair. If one day soon he drove the van through the township shouting communist slogans or preaching the evils of American-dominated global capitalism, no one on the island could claim that they hadn't been warned. She wished she had hair that stood for something interesting.

The boy found his boot and jumped off the van. 'So if you need anything, my father's doing the rounds tomorrow.' He rolled down the door and it occurred to Georgie that she'd missed her moment. The thing ought to have been done right at the beginning, a mumbled sorry and a lightning-fast exit. What a stupid idea apologizing for Alba had been. She suddenly felt tired by her adolescence. Why was navigating it so relentlessly hard and why was he making it harder?

'Are you saying that if I did want to buy something you wouldn't sell it to me because you're closed?'

'I've got no till.'

'What if I paid you the exact amount?'

'There's nowhere to put the money.'

'Couldn't you put it in your pocket?' Evidently she was only making matters worse but she couldn't stop herself.

'I suppose if you really need something that badly . . .'

'I don't, actually.' She couldn't work out why she was so cross. 'I was just making a point.'

'Look.' He glanced towards the house. 'It's not me. My father is fanatical about accounting. He would rather not make money than have it lying about in the wrong place or not know exactly what it was for. My father knows precisely how much money he's made every single day down to the last two-pence piece.'

'Oh.' Georgie's fingertips touched the edges of the coins in her pocket. 'I see.' No wonder Alba had been caught.

'It sounds crazy, but it's an obsession with him. When I was a boy, he would wait until he thought I was asleep, then he would whisper passages out of his accountancy manuals to me.'

'That *is* crazy,' she said unhappily.

'I don't care though.' He threw up the roller and jumped back in. 'You can get what you want. I won't tell him. Come on.'

Georgie looked hard at his hand before taking it. Unlike her light-fingered sister, she had never been inside the mobile van. The units to the right were tightly stacked with an assortment of sweets, tins and jams, while the other side housed a lending library with shelves of battered paperback books leaning flimsily against each other for support. There wasn't a lot of room for two people to manoeuvre in and Georgie could smell the peat and cigarette smoke on his clothes.

'Take anything you want.'

'I don't need anything.' She was flustered by his closeness.

'You've hardly looked.' Deftly he shuffled a few cans. 'We have beans, lentils, coconut milk, peppers, pygnolia nuts, you can't get any of these things in the shop, you know.'

'It's okay, thanks.' Then, worried she sounded snobbish, added, 'I mean you obviously have really good things.'

'You can pay me tomorrow if you didn't bring enough money.'

Georgie's head began to throb with resentment. Any minute now, he'd suggest turning his back while she swiped a can of sesame paste. 'Honestly, it's not why I came.'

'I don't understand.' He was towering over her, blocking her escape.

'I came to apologize,' she mumbled.

'For what?'

'For stealing from you.' Her pink cheeks mutated to crimson.

'Oh.' A spiral of hair bounced across his eye. 'Well, that's interesting.'

Georgie felt as vulnerable as a tortoise who'd been tricked into parting with its shell. Damn her sister. Damn her own pathetic lack of character for agreeing to take her place.

'I brought the money to pay you back.' She clanked her coins loudly and edged forwards in the hope that he might follow suit.

He didn't. And now they were even closer. 'It was only a comic,' he said.

'And a mint Aero.' Georgie could feel the damp under her armpits. 'Plus a book.'

'Well, the book she'll have to return. There are people waiting for it.'

And still he didn't move. Georgie prayed for deliverance. It was only because Alba had nicked the island's most popular read that she'd been caught in the first place. Quite why she'd snatched Alex Haley's *Roots* when there were already two copies at home it was hard to say. Her sister was probably a kleptomaniac as well as a sociopath. At school, there had been a girl in the year above her who could not stop stealing knives and forks from the school cafeteria. After she'd been rumbled, the teachers stormed her bedroom and discovered a cache of cutlery under her bed large enough for every Bonn resident to slice up their hams and cheeses.

'I'll get you the book.' Georgie raised her eyes to his with an effort.

He moved aside. The cool air felt like a poultice on her burning cheeks. 'Wait a minute.' Georgie found herself rewinding the conversation. 'You said "she". You said *she'll* have to return it.'

'My father said it was the younger sister. You're the older one, aren't you?'

'How do you know?'

'I saw you at the meeting in the school house.'

'The bear meeting? I didn't see you.'

'The whole island was there.' He shrugged as if a crowd of elderly islanders were the perfect camouflage for a six-foot-three smoky brown boy with bedspring hair. He was Mowgli, Georgie thought. No idea that he was being raised amongst wolf cubs.

She took a deep breath. 'I'm Georgie.'

'Aliz.'

'Aliz,' she repeated unconsciously. 'So, did you look for him? The bear?'

'Nah, I reckon it drowned at sea, otherwise someone would have spotted it.'

'That's what Alba thinks, but my little brother still goes

out searching every day.' For the first time she remembered Alba was waiting. 'Look, I have to get back.' She scrabbled in her pocket. 'Here. I'm really sorry by the way.'

Aliz took the change from her. 'How did your sister get you to do her dirty work for her?'

'I don't know, she's cunning that way. She's like Typhoid Mary, she infects everyone around her.' Georgie then concentrated so hard on finding a way to end the conversation that accidentally she began a new one. 'So why do you keep that old school bus in your garden?'

'It's not a bus, it's a greenhouse. Want to see?'

Out of the corner of her eye, Georgie noticed Alba grimly enlarging the circumference of a pothole in the road with the toe of her gumboot. 'I really ought to get back.'

'Take these for your little brother then.' Aliz produced a pack of Fruit Pastilles.

'No, no, please.' She waved them away. 'I don't have any more money.'

'Good.' Aliz took her hand and closed it round the sweets. 'That means you have to bring it tomorrow.'

47

Letty picked her way over the rubbery ferns and grasses of the dunes. The sea was as flat as polished glass. She slipped out of her clothes, folding them piece by piece and laying them on a dry patch of rock. The episode with Alba had shaken her badly. It wasn't the stealing. She understood that. It was the impossibility of communication that floored her. Alba had stopped talking to her, and now they moved around the house like two magnets repelling each other. Why was it so hard to reach out to the very people closest to you? If it were only possible to return to those moments when relationships went quiet and bang a noisy warning gong. It had been the same with Nicky. They had stopped talking and everything had changed.

Rome had been the posting Nicky had been after for some time. So after Gillian's little pep talk, and much as it went against her nature, Letty had made a conscious effort not to distract him with the mundane details of life.

At first, the difference in their relationship was so subtle, she barely noticed it. It was as though each sentence had one word less and each conversation was short of one sentence. Slowly but surely though, whole paragraphs began to disappear from their lives until information was being exchanged on a need-to-know basis only.

It was bewildering how lonely it made her feel. She was used to telling Nicky everything. From the day they'd met, they'd communicated like butterflies, flitting from one topic to the next, a whole garden of trivia to feed on. However dull Nicky's day, he always managed to find some funny detail or quirky observation, while Letty in turn amused him with the operatic power struggles of the wives, and the moods and whims of the children.

Communication operates according to the law of diminishing returns. The less there is, the less is generated. Lack of communication leads to misunderstanding, misunderstanding leads to resentment and the finger-pointing that inevitably follows leads to war. Nicky, busy negotiating with the rest of Europe, could not see that relations in his own tiny kingdom were in danger of imminent breakdown.

Letty waded into the sea. Happiness. Life. Family. Love. You only got one shot at it. Everything else was a re-try, a diminished version of. She gasped involuntarily as the water closed around her but it was too cold to remain still and she struck out purposefully, forcing her arms and legs into long powerful strokes. For a while she was hypnotized by the monotonous view of the horizon. A tiny part of her thought how simple it would be to keep swimming, but already she was aware of an ache in her chest. Her mind was filled with an image of Jamie's face and she quickly turned around.

She stood naked by the rocks and waited for the wind to blow her dry. Afterwards, when she was dressed, she crawled into the shelter of the sand dunes and curled up, trying to find warmth in her body. Why hadn't Nicky told her they weren't to be given Rome? She knew he would have hated disappointing her, but it wouldn't have mattered. Buenos Aires, Chile, back to Africa even. She could have been happy wherever they'd been posted. As long as it was away from Bonn; away from the Ambassadress. She should have reassured Nicky. She knew he felt the pressure of a new posting more keenly because of her, but after his and Georgie's trip to East Berlin, he'd been withdrawn. Overwhelmed with work, she'd diagnosed. And the more overwhelmed he'd seemed, the louder Gillian's warning came back to her. She must not be too needy or distracting. Nicky must be allowed to get on with his job. Besides, they were so nearly there. Seven years spent breaking rock in Bonn – they'd well and truly served their time in Germany. A new posting was imminent. Spring was on the way. Soon, the family would be together on the island, and everything always came right on the island.

Below her, a group of ringed plovers pecked at their reflection on the mirrored sand. The spring tide had deposited a tangled mass of kelp on the shore and suddenly the memories crowded in on her like an angry mob. Nicky whirling a ribbon of seaweed over his head. Nicky, doubled into a question mark, sifting through the lanes of broken shells for the prize of a single cowrie. Nicky pulling her down into a sand dune, kissing the brown mole on the mound of her stomach and then raking up her jumper and finding another, smaller mole on her ribcage. The first time they had made love had been in these sand dunes and she had been a virgin. She remembered the feel of his body close to hers, the taste of salt on his skin. She remembered how she unfurled under his hungry look. 'What if someone sees us?' she whispered, but nobody had been watching, only the nesting terns wheeling and screeching overhead.

The summer after they'd been married had been freakishly warm. They might have been holidaying in the West Indies for the cloudless skies and emerald waters swaying in and out of the bays. Nicky, walking a few steps ahead, bent down to pick something off the sand. The stone had been pure white, perfectly round, and he had turned it this way and that, examining it for flaws. When he was satisfied there were none, he hurried back and dropped it casually at her feet. 'Oh look!' he cried, pretending to spot it for the first time. 'A perfect stone! Fancy that.' He plucked it off the ground again and pressed it into her hand. 'We must keep it and treasure it forever.' He grinned at her and she'd looked quizzically at him.

'At least that's what penguins do, apparently.'

'You are silly. What do penguins do?'

'They drop pebbles at each other's feet. It's more or less what they say when they want to have a nice egg together.' He drew her to him and laid his hand gently on her stomach. 'You're pregnant, aren't you?'

She'd been shocked at his perception. She hadn't yet worked out why she hadn't told him.

He laughed. 'Don't you understand? Everything you do, everything you are, everything that makes you happy or sad, it's all there for anyone to read in your face.'

'For you to read,' she said, mortified by the idea. 'Only you, not everyone else.'

'But I'm right, aren't I?

'Oh Nicky, I wanted to be sure.'

'Well, you're lousy at secrets, you know that, don't you?'

Who knew, she thought bitterly, who knew that he would turn out to be so much better.

Something I've been keeping from you, the letter had said. *Something that's been preying terribly on my mind* . . . Once again she heard the sound of the envelope shifting in the canvas. 'Oh Nicky,' she said helplessly, 'what did you do? Tell me what you did, goddamnit! NICKY!' She shouted but the wind tore his name from her mouth and flung it with such force towards the sea she thought the line of the horizon might quiver back at her like sound waves from a radio. She closed her eyes, clenched her fists and roared until her throat burned. She didn't care what he'd done. Right then, she would have given everything she owned, she would have sold her soul to have his arms around her. To feel him move inside her. To know that he loved her.

A movement caught her eye. She scanned the top of the dunes. Had someone seen her? Heard her?

'Nicky?' she whispered.

She pushed shakily to her feet and stared out over the deserted sands. She pressed the pads of her fingers to her sore eyes then stared at the dunes again. 'Nicky,' she breathed, half in fear, half in hope. 'Oh God. Nicky, are you here?'

48

Why was he shadowing them? Sometimes the girls, sometimes the mother, but most often it was the boy he was drawn back to, the boy with his binoculars and little Bakelite lunchbox. Was he supposed to be keeping an eye on the family? He didn't know, but at least somebody should. Every day the tenuous threads that connected their lives frayed thinner. Did the children know, for instance, that their mother cried in the dunes most afternoons? Long, noisy bouts of crying, like a penance, like a prisoner breaking rock? Did she, in turn, have any idea that her eldest daughter was dreaming of a boy in a yellow school bus or that her son was riding on the trailer of an islander whose intake of alcohol doubled with every passing week, an islander who only the previous day swerved his tractor along the top of the cliffs with such abandon that two of its four wheels hung over the edge? And what about the time not so many days ago when he ferried all three children over the treacherous flats of Islay Sound but left the return journey so late that the channels of the incoming tide were almost too deep to pass? The children would not have been the first to drown in this way.

And so he continued to shadow them, guarding the house at night, watching the boy from his cave at the bottom of the Kettle, waiting for the girls to appear on the beach, and every day anxiety burned around the edges of his heart.

49

Jamie dangled his legs over the edge of the Kettle, and stared at the Penguin biscuit Alba had included in his lunchbox. He had noticed the change in her straightaway. It wasn't so much that the daily pummelling she liked to visit on him had abated. After all, he'd become so immune to her pinches, arm twistings and Chinese burns that his flesh scarcely bothered to bruise up for them any more. No, it was his pride that had taken fewer blows. Normally when Jamie opened his mouth in the presence of his sister, he did so in the full expectation of being sneered at one way or another. Sometimes her jibes were so crushing and numerous it felt as if she had taken his heart in her hand and squeezed it down to the size of an apple pip.

Jamie was used to being bullied. He had been mildly bullied at his Bonn school and more rigorously so at St Matthews, on the family's return to London. The trouble with Jamie was that he was eligible for bullying on so many levels; for being weedy, for being a dreamer, for his mal-coordination and laughable attempts to read out loud. In London, the chief perpetrator of his harassment was a boy called Fletcher who sat behind him in the class-room. Every time Jamie was called upon to stand up and open his book, Fletcher would issue a soft hissing noise through his teeth. The school's fondness for alphabetic order meant that Fletcher and Fleming were destined to be thrown together at every opportunity but nowhere was this more problematic than in the changing room. Jamie had no aptitude for sports whereas Fletcher was captain of both the cricket and rugby teams. If Fletcher handled a bat like Geoff Boycott, Jamie threw a ball as though he were a mechanical toy with a faulty repeat action. After each disastrous session on the field, Fletcher would corner Jamie and exact his revenge. Sometimes it was just your run-of-the-mill abuse, but other times he would lob the cricket ball at Jamie, taking him unawares in the chest, the stomach and once, painfully, on the edge of his kneecap. 'Oops,' he'd snicker, 'LBW. Fleming's out again!'

One day, fate intervened. Fletcher threw the ball at the precise moment Jamie opened his locker door. The ball ricocheted off the grated metal and back into Fletcher's face. There was a gasp, some fractured giggles from the other boys, then Fletcher sat down abruptly on the bench and plugged his fingers up his nostrils.

'I'm sorry,' Jamie stammered. 'I didn't mean . . .'

'Save it, Fleming,' Fletcher snarled. He waited till the bleeding had stopped, then he picked up his bat and trailed it softly across Jamie's shins. 'I'll be waiting for you outside.'

It was Jamie's turn to sit heavily on the bench. Fletcher was twice his size with purple-rimmed eyes and a thrusting overbite that was crying out for a pre-teen brace.

Jamie, conversely, was small for his age. 'We're a family of late developers,' his father had informed him as year after year he inscribed his son's lack of inches into the door-frame of his bedroom. 'You'll grow sooner or later, and it will happen quite suddenly, you'll see.' Jamie had believed him. Sometimes in his dreams, an abrupt tingling of his body heralded a wondrous lengthening of his arms until they burst through the ends of his clothes like spring shoots through winter soil. But it hadn't happened yet and he could not escape the fear that well into adulthood he would still find himself trapped in the same pygmy frame he was currently obliged to put up with. So after Fletcher left, after the other boys vacated, giving him the sort of looks familiar in the saloons of spaghetti Westerns after accusations of card-cheating, he rubbed the goosebumps on his legs and tried to work out what to do. Finally, taking a deep breath, he picked up his cricket bat, stepped out into the failing light of the afternoon and by some lucky chance found Fletcher, back to the door, momentarily distracted by a passing teacher. Without further ado, Jamie laid about his tormentor, breaking Fletcher's arm in two places. To Letty, summoned within the hour to discuss the incident, this had seemed like entirely justifiable behaviour, but Fletcher's parents, cold and hostile on the other side of the headmaster's study, took a dimmer view.

'Mrs Fleming,' the headmaster said crisply, 'bullying and violence cannot be tolerated under any circumstances. It is only in light of Jamie's recent loss that the Fletchers have generously agreed not to press charges.'

Letty knew she should have argued. Nicky, a champion against injustice and the tyranny of false blame, would never have accepted his son being sent home in disgrace, but as soon as she heard the word 'loss' she felt the habitual paralysis and she knew it was better to stand up and walk out of the room while she still had the use of her limbs.

However, for Jamie, the upside of the whole incident had been the unexpected approval it brought him from Alba. For the first time in a long while, she did not call him Spore of Satan, or remove his arms when he hugged her.

'Good for you,' she'd said. 'You mustn't let yourself be bullied. In fact, one of the main reasons I bully you myself is to toughen you up against this sort of thing.' Then, as if these accolades weren't startling enough, she had added, 'I'm actually quite proud of you.'

The glimmer of respect Jamie recognized in her eyes was a match flaring in the dark tunnel of his life and it illuminated a future in which he forged a magnificent relationship with his sister. Unfortunately, in his gratitude and joy, he pushed too hard. Nothing repelled Alba more than neediness and he'd woken the following morning to find the door to sibling love once again slammed in his face.

So as he carefully eased his finger under the metallic wrapper of the Penguin, his excitement was tempered by wariness.

Since the cricket bat incident he could not remember an act of kindness from Alba. As a general rule, 'nice' or 'helpful' were foreign concepts for her. Her cruelties were only occasionally curtailed by flu or extreme exhaustion. To trust his sister was to place his head inside the mouth of a sleeping lion, but the chocolate biscuit was no one-off. When he'd knocked on the door of her room a couple of days earlier, instead of randomly selecting a reply from her usual store of 'Choke on vomit, subhuman,' or 'I wish you'd died at birth,' she'd cried, 'Enter my domain!' in an almost genial manner. Added to that had been the two pats on the back, issued at separate times – the use of his name rather than 'spazz' or 'moron'. And, most thrilling of all, the introduction of special food allowances at meal-times. The previous night, wandering into the kitchen to find her mashing potatoes, he'd enquired what was for supper.

'Mum and Georgie are having winkles but I've made you a sandwich.' Then, adding a dob of butter and a sprinkling of salt, she'd scooped the potato from the bowl, spread it between two pieces of white bread and slid it onto a plate in front of him.

'I love you, Alba,' Jamie declared before he could stop himself, but instead of snubbing him or hitting him, she had merely responded with a triumphant little smile directed at Georgie. Jamie was the opposite of a futilitarian but even he tried not to put too much store by it. Still, the rekindling of hope was so seductive. The thing was, if Alba could love him, then the impossible became possible. The bear would be found. His lost father would come home, the hole in his heart would mend. Greedily, Jamie took a nibble of his biscuit and then a bite. He almost moaned with pleasure as the rich sweetness filled his mouth.

50

Alba was cooking mussels. She wrenched the lid off the big saucepan and sniffed. Beneath the steam, the water glowed a synthetic blue. She had never made mussel soup before and it didn't look precisely how she'd imagined, but Deuteronomy – it wasn't as if she was expecting any complaints.

Having exchanged her moral duties for Georgie's culinary ones, Alba had quickly realized that she'd as good as taken control of the kitchen in a bloodless coup. Her family would now eat what *she* wanted, *when* she wanted and while her flaws as chef might be legion, her skills as despot grew daily. Still, as with the administration of most dictatorships, there were logistical matters to consider and Alba's initial problem had been one of supply.

For obvious reasons she could no longer patronize the shop and because she was punishing her mother by not speaking to her, there was little question of demanding that the necessary provisions be bought for her. Given the dwindling cupboard supplies, it was only a matter of time before she hit on the idea of living off the land and, once she had, the beauty of it grew on her. She became evangelical about the procurement of food for little or no money and in this respect the island did not disappoint. Field mushrooms hovered like UFOs on cliff tops. Seafood, disgusting though she found it, could be had virtually gratis. Alick had long ago taught them how to whisk lobsters from underneath rocks with a broom handle and how to kill flounders by straddling the narrow channels on the incoming tide and stabbing them through with a pitchfork. Further away, under the causeway, buckets of winkles and mussels could be harvested and sometimes when the fishing had been especially good Alisdair would bring a sack of crab claws to the house. Added to these was the cow's yield with all its rewarding by-products. The bovine Ambassadress produced a bucket of warm rich milk a day, which, after a spell in a bowl on the top of the fridge, formed a thick layer of cream. Daily, Alba spooned off the drowned flies and attempted to make yoghurt from the curdling milk. Soon, with a little more practice, even crowdie would be within her repertoire. If all else failed, they could live on potatoes. With its whiff of famine, what could be more heroic than feeding her family straight from the soil? Island potatoes were the best in the world, so soft and floury they fell apart underneath the fork, and she had always suspected that the Irish had made a fuss about nothing. Anyway, the point was she would manage without the shop and she could manage without her mother.

'Indeed, we ate quite well before the shop came along,' Donald John confirmed when she quizzed him on the subject.

'Like what?'

'Well, this and that I suppose.'

'What specifically?'

'I was very keen on the salted herring,' he offered. 'They sold it on the mainland in barrels and it came over on the boat.'

'Did you fry it?'

'No, no, we boiled it.'

'How revolting!'

'No indeed, it was very good, Alba,' he said, faintly insulted.

'What about vegetables?'

'Ach, I've no use for vegetables.'

'Crab? Lobster?'

'I ate a crab once but I didn't think much of him.'

'Mackerel?'

'Mackerel are villains! Oh, boo boo, I'd rather eat my sheepdog than a mackerel.'

'Rabbits, then. Surely you eat rabbits?'

'Aye, you can snare a rabbit in no time. Ask Roddy. He'll teach you.'

'Is it worth shooting cormorants?'

'Well, they're very oily.' Donald John ironed his knees with his big flat hands. 'You have to take the skin off them because they're difficult to pluck. After that you can boil them in a pan with an onion. When I was a boy we used to poach plenty of duck and many's the goose your father brought for us too. He was a fine shot, your father, a fine shot indeed.'

It was true, Alba thought wistfully. For as long as she could remember her father had been engaged in a highly personal war of wits with the island geese. 'They're far more intelligent than people, of course,' he told her. 'See that formation of dots in the distance? Greylags. They're a cunning bunch and they probably suspect I'm waiting for them. However, the wind is coming off the loch today, so you and I have decided to face north.' He winked at her. 'That'll fool them, you'll see.'

He'd conscripted all three children into his plucking squadron. She could remember standing at the big table in the outside room pulling at the dead birds with brisk tugs while the radio crackled in the background and down floated through the air like dandelion spore. How fragile bird skin had been beneath its armour of feathers. You could rub skin off a snipe with the tip of one finger. Nicky used to keep the prettiest feathers in a cigar box under his bed. When he saw that Alba had developed an interest, he began taking her along on the morning flight and she would stumble behind him through the bogs while he tested the wind and planned the best place to hide to intercept the geese on their way to their feeding grounds.

She checked the mussels again. She'd picked them that morning, hitching a lift to the causeway only to find a big yellow digger idling on the bank and a man perched on the driving seat, alternately gnawing at a boiled egg and pulling on his cigarette.

'What are you doing?' Alba stared at the vast crater already gouged from the hill.

'Well now,' he said lightly, 'we're building a hotel, right enough.'

'You are not!'

'Aye, a casino in fact, and we're looking for nice young women like yourself to work in it.'

Alba giggled. 'No, come on, what are you doing really?'

'It's a quarry, lass. We're digging up the whole of this bank.'

'What for?'

'I haven't a clue. But the government is paying so we're doing it.'

'What are the government going to do with all this rubbish stone?' She kicked at the pile of rock.

'I don't suppose they'll do a thing with it, it's just that the money's there so they might as well spend it.' He winked. 'EEC grants and the like. There's nothing we won't dig up if we're paid to so you'll soon be seeing a fine lot of progress on the island.'

'But what about my mussels?' she asked suspiciously. On either side of the causeway where the tide was seeping back into the channels, the water appeared to be tinted with rainbow colours. 'Can we still eat them?'

'To be sure,' he'd replied cheerfully. 'A little oil in the water never hurt anyone.'

Alba lifted the saucepan lid and stared down at the clunky gumbo of black shells. The moules were more 'Liquide de Fairy' than marinières and when she drained them water frothed in the sink like the dregs of bubble bath. It was probably prudent to give them an extra rinse under the tap, but really, who could be bothered?

'Supper,' she yelled.

51

When Alick met them at Ballanish with the news that there was a ghost in Letty's bedroom, Jamie did not immediately appreciate the significance. The only ghost he could ever remember seeing was Casper the Friendly Ghost from the pages of his Harvey comic, a subscription for which Tom Gordunson had sent him as a Christmas present. Every Saturday in Bonn, it would appear on his pillow in a thin brown paper bag and although the words meant nothing to him, he could easily follow the pictures with his finger. In fact, he'd been so taken by cheery little Casper and his foxy friend playing happily by their graveyard home that one day after school, he'd been inspired to make a ghost outfit for himself. He pulled the sheet off his bed, found some scissors and snipped out holes for eyes. The result couldn't have looked more like a child's idea of a phantom, nevertheless Jamie was thrilled when both his sisters jumped after he burst into their room and he was even more chuffed when Alba suggested smuggling it that afternoon into the embassy where they were due to meet their father. Later, in Nicky's office, after the three of them had stuffed the sheet with newspaper, tied a string around its neck and then crept undetected to the flat roof, Alba clambered out and lowered the ghost down until it hung in front of their father's window.

Unfortunately for the children's comic timing, the mid-seventies was the high-water mark of the political activities of both the Baader-Meinhof and Black September groups. According to Nicky's somewhat stern lecture later that evening, Ulrike Meinhof, following her trial earlier in the year, had been found dead in her cell in Stammheim Prison. The Red Army Faction claimed she was killed by the German authorities and German embassies in most major cities, along with every international embassy in Bonn, were in the throes of dealing with threats against their staff.

The very minute Nicky drove through the security barrier of the embassy, he was met with news that an effigy had been delivered to his office by an unknown terrorist group and was swiftly led by a jittery attaché to see it. He'd taken one look at the stuffed sheet with its smiley face and inked-in nose and his shoulders began heaving.

'This is the work of my children,' he'd said, laughing, but no one else had found the incident funny. The children were promptly banned from the embassy and Jamie had not thought about ghosts again until he trailed into the kitchen behind his mother to find Alick pacing the floor and sucking at his roll-up in short impatient bursts like an expectant father in a hospital corridor.

'Ach, something terrible!' Alick exclaimed.

'What is it, Alick?' Letty said, not even mildly alarmed.

Terrible was one of Alick's favourite words and was applied with equal lack of discrimination to neighbours, slights, storms and joint pains.

'Upstairs!' Alick glanced up at the ceiling with apparent dread.

Letty saw at once that he was tipsy. His eyes were roving round the kitchen as if on the lookout for some mischief to cause and her heart sank. Under the influence of almost any quantity of alcohol, Alick quickly transformed from his gentle, sober Jekyll into the more impish Hyde and this persona in turn cast Letty into the unwelcome role of disapproving Victorian matron. Alick's four days' absence suggested a prolonged bender and his disappearing acts, whilst she understood that they meant nothing, still left her feeling oddly depressed, as though it was he who did the drinking while she was left to suffer the hangover.

'What's happening upstairs?' she asked calmly.

'There's a ghost up there.' Alick relit his cigarette end with trembling fingers.

'A ghost?' Jamie pictured Casper whizzing around his mother's bedroom like a balloon with its air abruptly released.

'Whatever do you mean, a ghost?' Letty took the lid off the stock pan and sniffed the steam.

'Come with me, Let-ic-ia.' Alick grabbed her hand and pulled her out of the kitchen. At the top of the stairs he paused, then, with the exaggerated gait of a vaudevillian clown, crept along the corridor until he reached her bedroom door. 'Ready, now?' he whispered.

'Yes, yes, we're ready.' Alick looked almost spectral

himself, Letty thought. The lower rims of his eyelids shone red against the pallor of his skin.

'Are you sure now?' His eyes darted over her shoulder to include Jamie.

'Quite sure,' she said firmly.

'Right you are.' He threw open the door as though surprise was the only way to catch whatever menace was lurking within.

Letty stepped briskly around him then stopped. 'Alick, what on earth . . . ?' Horrified, she surveyed the wreck of her bedroom.

The bed had been moved away from the wall and positioned in the centre of the room. Balanced on top of it, in one vast teetering pile, was every other piece of furniture along with whatever contents it had held: the small wicker chair and cushion, her bedside tables, books and alarm clock; the chest of drawers, with all the clothes spilling out. There were the medicines from the cupboard, including a sticky pink bottle of Pepto-Bismol, and poking out from under her pillows she could see the pair of wooden elephants that Nicky had bought for her from a roadside stand in Liberia.

'Alick, what happened?'

Running a shaky hand through his hair, Alick explained that he'd been fixing the hinge of the door when he'd heard a moaning noise coming from the walls – and it had been a noise so dreadful, so chilling, so unlike anything he'd ever heard in all his years, he had realized at once that it could not come from any mortal soul. Terrified, he'd run out of the house, across the garden and jumped over the yellow gate before even daring to look behind him, but when he had, he had spotted something he'd never noticed before.

'There was a window there, Let-ic-ia,' he said awfully. 'A secret window on the outside that canna' be seen on the inside.'

'Yes, it's a blind window, Alick,' Letty said with a trace of impatience, 'it's always been there.'

'Still and all, that's where the noise was coming from,' Alick said stoutly.

'Alick, it's just the wind. When it blows hard from the north-east, it sometimes makes a moaning noise.'

'It's no' the wind.' Alick knuckled the side of his head feverishly. 'I've been living with the wind since the day I was born. I'm telling you, Let-ic-ia, there's something very queer in this room, and I don't trust it at all. Not at all.'

'All right,' Letty asked reasonably. 'What do you think it is, then?'

'There's a secret place there.' Alick swayed backwards and forwards on his feet. 'Just like the one in that car.'

'What car? Alick, you're talking nonsense.'

'It's not nonsense, it's proof!'

'Proof of what?' Jamie said.

'A mer-derr.' Alick rolled the word off his tongue. 'It's the ghost of poor Flora Macdonald, strangled by the Captain and holed up behind that window.'

'Come on now, Alick,' Letty said. 'Everyone knows that Flora Macdonald ran away to Australia.'

'That's what they say.' Alick's eyes flashed. 'But who's to know what really happened? Why, I never believed that story anyways. Neilly McLellan was a rogue and a rascal, and he'd have had a job taking her all the way to Australia. In any case, ghosts canna' just appear and start their moaning for no reason. I'm telling you, she was mer-derred by the Captain and now she's trapped behind that window.'

'But why does she have to live behind a window?' Jamie asked. 'Why can't she go to heaven?'

'Because where there's sudden death . . . a *vi-olent* death – ' he leant his hand on Jamie's shoulder for support – 'there's unfinished business.'

'Alick,' Letty said uneasily, 'that's enough.'

Flora Macdonald's elopement with Neilly McLellan. She hadn't thought about the story for so long. It was an island myth, a love story, but it had become her love story too, and before she could stop herself she'd gone back to that evening again, the night she'd met Nicky. Tom had taken her to a dance in London. She could remember his arm about her waist, the smile in his eyes, then suddenly he was looking over her shoulder, his face briefly contorted by some emotion – what had it been? Resignation? Defeat? But she had no chance to process it before Nicky had cut in and waltzed her away. Letty had been startled at how strongly she'd reacted to the smell of his neck and the way his hair sat cleanly just above his collar. He was Tom's closest friend, she'd heard so much about him, but she had pictured another thoughtful, dishevelled wolf, a logical extension of Tom, not the slim, elegant man in whose arms she now found herself. She and Nicky were natural opposites. He loved Hoagy Carmichael and Thelonious Monk – or Melodious Thunk, as he liked to call him – while she had a passion for opera.

He was funny and gregarious; Letty was quiet, a little reticent. Nicky was being wooed by the Foreign Office, which was funding his studies in Russian while she, politically naive as a bar of soap, was working as a secretary for a legal firm in Piccadilly. For six weeks, they saw each other nearly every day. Then suddenly, Nicky was sent to Washington as a temporary replacement for a junior diplomat who had jaywalked a traffic light and suffered the consequences.

The week before he flew, Letty had introduced him to her father. They'd lunched at Scott's in Mayfair and she couldn't remember quite how it had cropped up, but her father had told him all about the story of Flora Macdonald and her midnight flight from the isle.

'It's a very good story,' Nicky had said later in the taxi. 'Who knows how much of it is true though . . .'

'Why do you say that?'

'I've heard it a thousand times and my father is constantly rewriting the facts.'

'Oh, do tell.'

'Well, sometimes it takes place in the nineteenth century, sometimes he bumps it up a generation or two, sometimes he has Roddy, the hunchback, building the walled garden, other times it's Roddy's grandfather. Occasionally it's a cautionary tale for overbearing parents, but usually it's just your everyday farce with drunken, lovesick sailors in completely unseaworthy boats endlessly criss-crossing the Minch. Once, I swear he even managed to bring Bonnie Prince Charlie into it, but he dropped that version pretty quickly.'

'So which one did I get?'

'You got the Shakespearean tragedy. Instead of living happily ever after, the illicit lovers are torn to shreds in the shark-infested seas of the Pacific.'

'A warning to his daughter's unscrupulous beau, perhaps?'

'No doubt, except you're about the least unscrupulous person I've ever met.'

'How dull. I must cultivate some hidden depths.'

'Well, in the meantime you can console yourself with the fact that the window in Flora's room, my room as a child, that is, and the one she is supposed to have jumped out of, makes the most hideous noise when you pull it up. Captain Macdonald would have had to be as deaf as a loaf of bread not to hear it, moreover the tree – the only tree on the island – is at most a gnarled stump of a thing and viciously thorny to boot. I wouldn't have climbed down it.'

'Not even for the man you loved?'

She'd smiled.

'You sound as if you don't want the story to be true.'

'Of course I do. I'm hopelessly sentimental, but we'll never know for sure.'

'I could find out,' he said eagerly. 'I could write to the Australian embassy, get the land registry checked. There would be records.'

'No, please don't.' She'd kissed him. 'I'd hate for my father to lose one of his favourite stories.'

But, now, as Alick continued to embroider his theory, she thought wistfully how much she would have liked to have known for sure . . .

'Don't you think you're being a bit melodramatic,

Alick?' she said. There had never been so much as a handbag snatch on the island, let alone a cold-blooded act of filicide. In fact the most heinous crime in recent years – discounting the illegal transfer of ten lobsters from Alisdair Mackinnon's pot to rival fisherman Callum's, an act that had been punished by Callum's ostracism from the community – had been her own daughter's extensive shoplifting spree.

But no amount of reasoning could deter Alick from his theory. 'Ach, poor Flora, poor soul,' he lamented, 'lost for all this time, not allowed to rest peacefully in heaven.'

It was this last statement that started Jamie's brain whirring. *Lost for all this time.* Disappeared, heaven, resting – here were the very same words struggling for order in his own confused lexicon. Wide-eyed, he turned to his mother, his mouth forming a question.

'Alick,' Letty said sharply, 'you're scaring Jamie with all this talk of ghosts.'

'No, no,' Jamie protested. 'It's just that . . . I want to . . .'

Alick grinned wickedly then lurched sideways. Letty put out her hand to steady him. 'All right, that's quite enough now.' She took stock of the precarious arrangement of furniture on the bed, of the mothballs rolling around on the floor like reproachful eyeballs, and resolved to sleep on the sofa downstairs. She could smell the sourness of whisky on Alick's breath and she suspected that to indulge him any further would inevitably lead to a second dram, which in turn would encourage a third. Jamie, however, had several searching questions for Alick on the nature and purpose of spirits but Alick seemed suddenly too dizzy to answer. Neither did he appear well enough to explain why he had thought that exorcism of Flora Macdonald's ghost might be achieved by pushing all the furniture away from the walls and, after a while, Letty quietly but firmly suggested that Jamie put it all out of his head.

52

It was a night of freefall insomnia. To Letty it felt as though the room itself was conspiring to keep her from rest. The sofa cushions were lumpy and unyielding, a vicious west wind yowled through the chimney, the blankets were scratchy and a taste of stale ash coated the back of her throat. For the first hour, she lay supine, trying to clear her mind, but gradually every unfamiliar creak amplified to a point where it jolted her body like an electric shock. She turned and sighed and sighed and turned, all the while trying to identify a nagging pinprick in her consciousness. She couldn't shake the feeling that there was something out of place, something important she'd overlooked. Twice she threw back the blankets, once to check that the small gas lever was turned to 'off', a few minutes later to make sure the pilot light on the Raeburn hadn't blown out. When eventually she broke the shell of sleep, this unease followed her into a viper's nest of dreams where she could only stand and watch, powerless to act as disaster after disaster befell her family. First it was the Peugeot rolling backwards with Jamie at the wheel. Then it was Gisela struggling to keep her head above the currents of the Elbe. Finally it was her turn. They were going to miss the ferry but damn it, Macleod wouldn't give her the car key. He stood in his garage, dangling it out of reach. *I can pull it out for you now if you like*, he was saying. *That plywood of yours* . . . Except it wasn't Macleod's voice any more, it was Alick talking, Alick's face leering at her.

The wall has a secret place, he said, *just like the one in that car*. And she woke with a start, her heart beating fast.

She hadn't needed the torch – the moon was out and almost bright enough to read by – but she was scared and the torch in her hand felt familiar and reassuring. She walked swiftly to the Peugeot, fighting a sense of unreality. *A secret place*, Alick had said. *A secret place*. The day Georgie had crashed the Peugeot was the first time she'd been allowed to drive the car on the main road. Letty had been away, down on the south island visiting her father's old cook. All summer she'd argued that Georgie hadn't been ready, but Nicky had taken her anyway. Barely a mile beyond the church loch, Georgie had whipped over a blind summit and swerved to avoid a duck. It was typical of Nicky's efficiency that he arranged for the car to be mended, the telephone company be appeased for the breakage of their pole and for parts to be ordered from the mainland before presenting her with the situation as a fait accompli on her return. There had been nothing for her to do but be thankful that neither of them had been hurt and allow Alick to get on with the repairs. *Damn her naivety*. She turned the key in the boot lock. The 404 boasted a spacious luggage section, or so Nicky always claimed when it came to the packing of the car. At the beginning of the summer this job had fallen to the girls and the fact that the boot had taken fewer cases than usual Letty had put down, in the fleeting second allotted to the thought, to the girls' rookie status. Nicky would have taken everything out and begun again, rigorously matching size and shape to space available, but she hadn't cared. The weight of inherited chores was just another measure of his loss. Grateful that the children had taken the initiative in the first place, she simply strapped the remaining suitcases on the roof rack and hoped for the best.

Her watch read quarter past four. It was cold and damp and the wind blew her nightdress round her legs. Shivering, Letty worked her way along the floor of the boot towards the back seat, feeling around the edges of the carpet. On the right-hand side the seam was more or less intact, but the car had gone into the river at a tilt and the left side must have taken in the bulk of water because here and there the carpet edge was disintegrating and between the new tacks of Macleod's repairs, shreds of glue came away under her fingers. She ran and fetched a screwdriver from the outside room then prised the staples out one by one until she was able to get some purchase on the corner of the carpet – enough to give it a good yank – and underneath, shining like the golden ticket in Charlie Bucket's chocolate bar, was the yellowy chip of plywood.

That plywood of yours . . .

That plywood of Nicky's . . .

It had been done so cleverly you would never know it

was there, cut to exacting standards and fitted at a slight inward slant, creating a false divide between the boot and the void underneath the passenger seat.

A void big enough for a person.

The wind was making a whistling noise through the hinges of the open boot.

Letty stared at the panel for a minute, then, putting the sole of her gumboots to it, kicked as hard as she could.

Afterwards she found she was shaking. First her hands, then her whole body. She hunched over, clasping her bare legs to her chest.

'Damn you, Nicky.' She blotted her eyes on the sleeve of her nightdress. She was cold through to the bone. A percussion of rain started up on the metal roof, yet still she couldn't move. God knows she understood the dangers of smuggling someone out of East Berlin, especially under the radar of the British Government. Nicky would have had no official cover. No safety net.

Whatever you're doing, involve no one, Tom had warned. Except that Nicky hadn't involved no one. He'd involved his own daughter.

53

 'It's so warm in here!' Georgie sketched a smiley face in the condensation on the bus window. 'I know. I'm sorry,' Aliz said.

'No, it's wonderful. Like being in some really exotic country.' Aliz's father was a genius, she'd decided. He'd converted a van into a shop/library and an old yellow school bus into a greenhouse. The bus had solar panels inserted into the roof and the rows of seats had been exchanged for trays of seed beds from which a tangle of greenery was rising like some John Wyndham-inspired jungle.

'Tomatoes, chillies, green beans . . .' The first time he'd shown her around, Aliz had pointed out every plant in turn. 'And these in here are herbs: coriander, parsley, fennel.'

'Why don't you sell all this stuff?'

'No one wants it.'

'I thought it was impossible to grow vegetables in island soil?'

'You can grow anything here but my father says the islanders are too feckless and, besides, they don't like vegetables.'

'My mother loves them.'

'So take her some.'

'No, no,' Georgie had said. She'd only just returned with the change for the Fruit Pastilles.

'Take something and come back with the money tomorrow.'

She cast a quick curious look at him. Was this a game they were both supposed to be playing?

'I don't think I can come back tomorrow.'

He'd slipped some tomatoes into her hand. 'You have to, or my father's books won't balance.'

Aliz's eyes were the colour of a peat bog. Georgie had looked down at the ripe tomato in her hand and had come back every day since.

She sat down on the slatted bench. The sun felt like honey on her back. She found it hard to believe that the island sun was the same as every other country's sun. It had always presented itself as a weaker, less dazzling member of the solar family. 'What's that?' She touched a finger to a purple bulbous-looking fruit.

'Aubergine. My father makes *kuku* with it but he complains it doesn't taste right. He says the aubergines don't get enough sun here, even in a greenhouse, so most of the time he strokes their skin and admires the colour. He likes to complain that the food on this island is all the same colour. White, grey or brown.'

'Last night my sister made spaghetti with Branston Pickle sauce.'

'And you ate it?'

'I had to! You have no idea what she's like.' Alba's

cooking was consistently inconsistent. She'd taken enthu-
siastically to food experimentation, rebuffing all questions
about what was on the menu with the ominous 'A little
something I've thrown together.' At mealtimes she stood
over the table, gimlet eyed, wielding her spatula like a
fly-swat, determined that every last mouthful should be
appreciated. Even so, Georgie found the tyranny of her
kitchen preferable to the tyranny of her moods. Her
mother, too, seemed prepared to sacrifice her digestive
system for the newfound truce between her children and
Jamie had never been happier. Sticking rigidly to the
smallprint of her contract, Alba had excused him from
her more ground-breaking recipes such as Razor Clam
Omelettes or Cottage Cheese Bake on the grounds that
he was too ignorant to appreciate the subtlety of their
flavours. Georgie knew she should consider her manipu-
lations a success but Jamie's rekindled hero worship of
Alba made her both jealous and uneasy. Time and time
again she had watched Alba open fire on Jamie's hopes
and the fallout was always the same – he would lapse into
misery, withdraw into a subdued state until he forgave or
forgot, at which point he would thrust his singed fingers
back into the very same fire. Each time, however, the
process took a little longer and each time she wondered
whether Alba would one day go too far. There was something about her sister's born-again sweetness that felt like
the lull before the storm. Sooner or later, Alba would
revoke Jamie's gift voucher of love once and for all and
Georgie was filled with a sense of foreboding. Then again,
if she hadn't made the deal, she would not have met Aliz.
Aliz who smelt of earth and minerals. Aliz who was sitting

so close to her now that she could feel his breath on her cheek.

'Food is what my father misses most about home,' he was saying. 'He talks about it all the time. Ice creams scented with rose petals or made with pistachio nuts. Lamb seasoned with cinnamon and coriander or fried with apricots and figs. At night I hear him tossing in his sleep, mumbling about salted cheeses and bitter lemons or the minted lentil dishes my mother used to cook for him.'

It was the first time Georgie had heard Aliz mention his mother. She had presumed Aliz's father was a widower. Alba claimed that he'd come to Scotland to find a new wife, although somehow the idea of Morag or Peggy being whisked on his arm through customs in their beige mackintoshes and emerging into the bustling streets of Karachi seemed a little far-fetched. She had less trouble imagining herself there, standing in front of some ancient mosque, waiting for a bull cart to trundle by. Accidentally, her knee touched his. 'What's it like in Pakistan?' she asked dreamily.

'No idea.' Aliz took out his tin of tobacco and began rolling a cigarette.

'You can't remember?'

'I've never been.'

'Aren't you curious? Have you asked your father?'

'My father has also never been to Pakistan.'

'What do you mean?' She looked sharply at him.

'We are not from Pakistan.'

Georgie's city of sandcastles crumbled to the desert floor.

'My father came here from Syria after my mother and brother were killed during the Six Day War.'

'But I thought . . .' she said, mortified. 'I'm sorry, I don't know why I . . .'

'Because everyone does. We're the Pakis who opened the Paki shop.'

Georgie hung her head.

'Don't worry, it doesn't bother me and my father likes the people here.' Aliz flicked a corkscrew of hair out of his eyes. 'He says many of the islanders haven't even been to the mainland, so how could they know the difference between Syria, Pakistan or the moon?'

'At the BHS, my school in Germany, we had American, English, African, Korean, Indian, even Finnish kids. The first thing we had to learn was which country everybody was homesick for.'

'I've been here since I was seven years old. I don't know where I should be homesick for.'

'Maybe that means you belong here now.'

'Well, everyone has to belong somewhere.' He severed the stem of the aubergine between his nails. 'Take this home with you, and some more tomatoes for your mother.'

'I should pay you.' Georgie didn't even bother to check her pockets.

'Yes. You must. Tomorrow my father will be completing his tax returns for the year.'

'I thought tax returns were completed in April – that's seven . . . no, eight months from now.'

'My father hates to be late,' Aliz said gravely.

Georgie rubbed the burnished skin of the aubergine with her sleeve. 'I'll come back tomorrow, then.'

'Good.' His chipped front tooth gave him an uneven smile.

Georgie smiled back. She felt young. She felt old. She had no idea what she felt.

54

He stood underneath the causeway, out of view from the road, and surveyed the dark expanse of mud in front of him. As a surface, it didn't look safe for a creature of his weight but he was hungry and there was food out there. He stepped forwards. Sludge oozed up between his toes. Clumps of seaweed covered the rocks like mermaids' hair. He threw one back, revealing a township of black mussels underneath. One yank and a dozen or so were in his paw. Hard to believe that such an odd-shaped shell constituted food, but he had watched the children throwing them into buckets and he had sorted through the empty shells dropped by the birds. They were food all right, but how to get into them? Closer inspection revealed a tiny hinged structure to one side and more dexterous fingers than his might have prised the halves apart, but he was too hungry for such niceties and instead stomped them underfoot. Inside was an orange fleshy thing that looked like an earlobe. He forced it down his throat as if he was a heron shucking an oyster. Ship-wrecked sailors, too squeamish to eat the eyes of fish or the raw flesh of turtles, were said to die of malnutrition despite the entire contents of the sea being available to them and it was possible that this would yet be his fate. He ate several more dozen, but they couldn't satisfy the cavernous void in his belly.

Grizzlies are omnivores, and not pernickety ones. Although fond of small animals, they will happily crunch down on anything from moths to root vegetables. Still, he was not an average grizzly and he did not like raw food.

Earlier in the week he came across a dead gannet washed up on the beach. He turned it over and over. It was, after all, meat – if the feathers could be discounted. Perhaps he should have eaten it, overcome his disgust and razored the flesh from the bones, but he couldn't bring himself to do it. How had it come to drown? Had it been too ambitious for its food? Smashed its skull against a submerged rock? He flipped the bird back over and waited for the sea to take it. The sea could absorb any manner of death and maybe, in the end, it would have to absorb his.

55

The betrayal lodged deep inside her.

And now all the tiny splinters of misgiving she'd been suppressing began rising painfully to the surface of her consciousness. Nicky's frustration with pen-pushers. All those minor acts of bureaucratic rebellion that had seemed so innocent at the time. *Diplomacy is a colourful profession which attracts maverick individuals*, he had once told her. *It's a world rife with deceit, infidelity and murder.* And now all the irreverent stories, the countless silly anecdotes came back to her as well. There was the Ambassador who'd spilled his country's secrets into the ear of a famous French actress. The disgrace of a young diplomat in Bucharest, expelled, it was maintained, because with his lisp he couldn't pronounce Ceauşescu; there was the story of the 'heroic' Air Force officer who had entered the diplomatic service just after the Second World War. When news came to light that he'd been a collaborator, he was swiftly dispatched to Africa where the official who'd been assigned to him suggested a swim to cope with the heat and lost no time in pointing him towards the nearest crocodile-infested waters of the Limpopo. For some reason

Letty had always imagined the poor brute in a pair of candy-striped bathers, standing in his canoe. Then came the arc of his dive, the pattern of circles in its wake, the stillness, broken by a discreet bubble or two, the almost imperceptible rise of a snout to the surface and the sinister swirl and roll of the feeding beast . . .

'A little unkind if all he did was tell a few secrets,' she had commented at the time.

'Well, that all depends on how you feel,' Nicky had replied. 'If you think that treason is the worst imaginable crime – as some do – then surely the punishment for treason has to be the worst imaginable as well . . .'

So, finally she had it. What she'd been fighting for – what she'd been demanding of the government. Proof.

Your husband would not be the first official found guilty of corruption of some kind, Porter had told her. Well, now she knew on what flimsy, self-deceiving grounds her principles had been built. She hadn't wanted the truth at all. Only a truth she could live with.

To Alick, she said nothing, other than to make him show her exactly what Nicky's 'modifications' had entailed. She'd stood next to him, watching a watery sun light up the grasses of the machair and feeling her world distort and spin further out of control as he enthused about the precision required for making a plywood template; how the switch he'd installed would cut the Peugeot's distributor and stop the car at any chosen moment. And if she marvelled at Alick's unquestioning nature, she could only deplore her own. Alick had little curiosity about what his adaptations had been needed for, his only interest was whether he was mechanic enough to achieve them. She had no such excuse. Had she chosen to look on the darker side of the facts, the signs had been there to see. Nicky's opting to take the car instead of flying, his resistance to taking Georgie with him. Then on their return hadn't there been some problem with the car? Hadn't the radio not been working or something? She forced herself to think back. Yes, it had definitely been the radio. Instead of making do with traditional speakers in the sides of the driver and passenger doors, Nicky had had the Peugeot upgraded some weeks before the trip, relocating the speaker cones on the wooden plinth of the back shelf and covering them with a strip of smart blue perforated leather. Now, at her insistence, Alick reluctantly cut through that leather and shone the torch downwards.

'Aye, they've been dislodged a wee bit.' He tapped the speakers with his screwdriver. 'See?'

'Yes,' she said shortly. 'I see.' Two of the four screws attaching the cones to the wooden plinth had been loosened and the speakers had been manually swung around and away from the perforated circles. No wonder the quality of sound had been poor. No wonder Alba had complained the whole journey up north. After all, Letty thought bitterly, a man had to breathe.

It was the single worst week of her life. She spent most of it in bed, away from the children, staring at the passport photo, passing her thumb over the stranger's face with increasing pressure as though some hidden clue to his identity might reveal itself like one of those novelty scratch cards Nicky had brought back from America. She couldn't bring herself to question Georgie; she dared not call Tom.

He was never the man you thought he was. The accusation came back to her again and again, but if Nicky wasn't who he said he was, then who on earth was she? Her whole life, everything she stood for, every memory she had held sacred unravelled until all she was left with were two hard knots of fury and grief.

One night, it was as if her brain could no longer purge the poison from her thoughts. Suddenly it was Tom's vice-like grip on her wrist that came to her. *Hold on to what you believe, Letty,* he'd said.

She switched on the light, reached for her cigarettes and smoked three in a row, hunched up in bed and trying to imagine a Nicky committed to treason, involved in subterfuge, a secretive, bitter man exacting revenge on his government, but she knew then with absolute certainty that she could never square this picture with the man she loved. She thought instead of Nicky standing beneath her bedroom window. Alick had brought the Flora Macdonald story back to life with his talk of ghosts, but Nicky had made it their story too, and now this memory on top of so many others had come back to haunt her.

'I'll make you a bet,' Nicky had said that day after lunch with her father. 'I bet you anything I can get you out of that window and down that tree without your father catching us.'

'This is assuming you'll be asked up to the island,' she teased.

'Whether I'm asked or not is irrelevant,' he said. 'The question is, will you take the bet?'

'What are the stakes?'

'Oh, I'll think of something,' he replied. 'Don't you worry.'

He'd been due to leave for Washington the following week and she was sure he meant to propose before he left, but he hadn't. And when the projected month in the US doubled and his letters continued to arrive less and less regularly, it had been to the island she'd fled to nurse her breaking heart. She'd not seen him for three months, she had almost forgotten the bet they'd made in the back of the cab, when she was woken by the noise of stones hitting glass. She'd looked out the window to find him grinning sheepishly up at her, his arms wrapped about his chest.

'Nicky,' she'd said faintly. 'Dear God, how did you . . . ? Nicky, whatever are you doing?'

'I'm here to rescue you!' he'd cried in a not entirely successful attempt at a Hebridean accent. 'Come along now, Flora lass,' he added when she seemed too shocked to move. 'Down you pop. It's bloody freezing out here.'

When it came to it, though, Letty had been right. The old tree, more bowed than ever from the unrelenting wind, seemed just that much out of reach.

'Jump,' Nicky said recklessly, 'and I'll catch you.'

'Nicky, no!'

'Climb over the ledge and then let go. I'll catch you, I promise.'

'It's too far.'

'Jump and we can elope.'

'Are you *proposing* to me from down there?'

'What does it look like, goddamnit?'

'Oh, Nicky.' She was half laughing, half crying. 'What if I say yes to the elopement thing, but come down the stairs?'

'No,' he said stubbornly. 'There are certain things that have to be done for love.' He stretched out his arms. 'Jump and I'll catch you. I promise.'

She'd looked down. The ground wasn't that far away, but it was the sort of uneven landing you could easily break a leg on.

'I'm scared.'

'No need to be scared, my love, trust me.'

'Nicky . . .' She faltered. She did trust him. God knows the thought of him made her bones feel stronger and her blood thicker. Nicky Fleming knew who he was and what he believed in. It was the quality she most loved about him.

'Letty, trust me,' he ordered, 'and let go.'

56

The problem was Jamie never put anything out of his head. All information received went straight to his 'brainbox' and from there was processed in a manner that made sense to him before any decision was taken on how to use it or where to store it.

Nominally earmarked for the file of his father, ghosts were new information, important information, if only he could work out why.

His father had had an accident. His father had gone away for a long time. His father was lost. Over the past months Jamie had tried to fit the clues together, but like a cheap cardboard puzzle whose pieces had been pressed in, the picture that had finally emerged made no sense to him. And all Jamie had ever wanted was a picture that made sense. Not good sense, not real sense or even common sense, but Jamie sense. For days after the Alick incident the connections between his father and ghosts perplexed him.

Ghosts were lost souls, and hadn't he heard his father described in the same way? Ghosts had not yet made it to heaven. Neither had Dada. Ghosts could not get to heaven if they had unfinished business down below.

Jamie thought back to the papers scattered across his father's desk in Bonn. He remembered the telegrams that arrived twice a day, the contents of the mysterious 'diplomatic bag', not to mention the help he, Jamie, had needed with his own homework. How could his father not have had unfinished business? And once again he found himself back on his unrelenting treadmill. His elliptical loop of sleuthing.

And then, the night of Georgie's birthday, the thing with the lobsters happened.

A long-standing tradition of the Fleming family called for the method of cooking lobsters to be decided by the winner of a race held before supper. First, each family member would choose a lobster and assign it an inappropriate name. Next, the rubber bands were snipped off their claws and the lobsters released onto the floor to begin their tentative scrabble across the cork tiling. The question of how most ethically to kill lobsters was argued passionately by both sides. Was the agonizing but virtually instant death of a dunking straight into scalding water more or less cruel than the prolonged torture of being placed in cold water and lulled into a coma over a low flame?

This year, however, there had been no race and no debate about comparative forms of death. Alisdair the fisherman delivered five lobsters in a sack and Alba dropped them without ceremony into the boiling water, cramming the lid on top of them with shouts of 'Die, you buggers, die!'

When the lobsters began to squeak, Jamie stuck his fingers in his ears.

'It's only air,' Georgie soothed, 'it's air escaping out of their shells.' But Jamie wasn't so sure. He stared at the giant saucepan. The lid was rolling and dipping on the bubbling water like a ship on stormy seas. To his horror, a single tentacle poked its way out. Oh dear Lord, one of them was trying to escape. He covered his eyes with his hands and watched between spread fingers. More and more tentacles crept over the edge of the saucepan like aliens emerging from a spacecraft. One appeared to be appealing directly to him for help while another was quite clearly attempting to locate the handle of the lid.

After it was all over, Jamie had gazed wonderingly at the steaming crustacean on his plate. Had it been scared? Had it watched Alba filling the huge saucepan and felt the dread of impending death? Did lobsters on the ocean floor threaten their children with tales of the giant saucepan to ensure good behaviour? Surely not, he reasoned, for no lobster lived to tell the tale. But then there was the ghost of poor murdered Flora Macdonald to consider. Where there was sudden death, violent death, Alick had claimed, there was unfinished business. Could lobsters become ghosts? If so, would the unfinished business of these lobster ghosts be to return to the deep in order to warn friends and family never to climb into lobster pots, no matter how deliciously putrefied the bait inside them? He touched the creature with his finger. Poor lobby. He wished it luck wherever it was going, it really hadn't had a nice time at all. Its shell was scalded a painful red and one of its tiny black eyes had fallen out and all of a sudden Jamie realized that there was one thing he knew for certain about ghosts. You had to die to become one.

So slowly, tentatively, he turned his attention to the question he least wanted answered.

What if his father was dead?

People died. It didn't matter how clever or strong you were. Death still happened. His grandfather had died. Even the bear, with all his strength, could have drowned. Jamie had put everything he had into believing in his father's return. He had believed in it with the sort of blind conviction people reserved for True Love or the existence of angels with proper wings. His father was a clever man, a brave man, but wherever it was that he had gone might have been a place too far. He might have been too weak from the accident. The mission could have been too dangerous. He knew his father would have tried his best to get back, but that didn't mean he hadn't failed. To Jamie's intense surprise, the idea that his father was dead did not much increase the unhappiness he already felt. The emptiness he carried around inside him remained the same. Over the past months the memory of his father had continued to fade even as his belief grew stronger that his father would return home, but until this moment his father's return could not be squared with the finality of death.

He had felt that there was something uniquely important about the Flora Macdonald story. The idea that she'd returned to deal with her unfinished business came to rest on the divide between his logic and imagination. And when Jamie couldn't find an answer to the preoccupations of one side of his brain, he always provided explanations from the other.

As he pushed away his plate, it dawned on him why ghosts were so important. This concept that you could die and return as something else.

Ghosts were a get-out clause in the contract with death.

57

Every day the air in the greenhouse bus felt steamier and more humid. Georgie liked the way her body melted in the heat. At home she sometimes felt so brittle she feared her bones might snap, but here with Aliz, surrounded by plants and earth and the smell of fermenting fruit, her arms and legs felt supple and her heart simmered and burned. He was reading to her from his book but the words swam past her like a shoal of the world's tiniest, most interesting fish. Her eyes were closed and she was dreaming of the sandstone facade of her future Syrian home, of the turquoises, reds and yellows of its courtyard mosaics and the explosion of colour from the garden. That's where they would sit all day, she and Aliz, under a jungle canopy of hibiscus listening to the clicking of the crickets, the shrill whistles of birds, the baby geckos scurrying across the floor. Just before she left Bonn, two of her friends had lost their virginity. A third had been put on the pill by her mother before she had ever been kissed. Georgie had been in awe of all three. They had passed to the other side, leap-frogged the continental divide between childhood and adult life.

Aliz stopped reading and leant his head against the wall. She looked at his chipped front tooth, at the sharp cheekbones and the wild springs of his hair, but she tried not to look at his mouth because whenever Aliz opened his mouth, Georgie thought about kissing and when she thought about kissing, her thoughts generally turned to sex. She found it safer to concentrate her mind on the upper half of the body. Anything south of the stomach made her nervous. At fifteen she had passed through a stage of obsessing about what grown-ups, more specifically grown-up men, looked like naked. The minute Georgie found herself in close proximity to any male, she began staring through the outer layers of his clothing with X-ray eyes. The more formal the diplomats, the more pompous their voices, the faster her eyes would drop from their faces and begin to burn through the cottons and wools of their trousers until the geography of their naked bodies was revealed. At night she tossed with feverish dreams in which she was running through a Maurice Sendak forest being pursued by grotesque monster-ministers. Hot on her heels was Fielding, from the Home Office, his chest pale and hairless as he coursed through the moonlight. Hiding behind a laurel tree was the *Chargé d'affaires*, scratching his crotch companionably . . .

It had been a miserable year on so many levels.

Assuming she was suffering from a teenage bout of extreme shyness, her father gave her several well-meaning lectures about looking people in the eye and being charming. 'You can do this,' he whispered, as he introduced her to the Spanish Ambassador. 'Find something of interest and ask them about that.' If only he knew! Georgie thought as she received the Spaniard's small damp hand obediently in her own. She tried to dredge up something pertinent to say about the Prado but, to her utter shame, found herself imagining him naked, running across the plains of the Sierra Nevada, the tips of his fingers trailing through the leaves of the olive trees while his pendulous balls swung between his legs like castanets. What an abysmal catch-22 she was caught in. The more she blushed, the more hands her father insisted she shake and the more her head was filled with the images of exposed diplomats, until England's entire foreign service had become a nudist camp to her.

Until one day, magically, it stopped. If this was what growing up meant, she thought, relieved, she wanted no part of it.

But now here was Aliz, with his dry skin and the musty smell it gave off and almost every physical part of him was fascinating to her. More than anything she wanted to touch the pads of her fingers to his, she wanted to put her ear to his heart and hear the rhythm of its beat. She couldn't decide whether his lips were blue or purple or the inside of his mouth hot or cold. All she knew was that she had a strong desire to put her tongue inside it and find out. It seemed quite unimportant that she barely knew him.

58

Letty disliked cleaning mussels. Tugging at their beards and scraping off the barnacles made her feel like a nurse cleaning up grizzled old men on a geriatric ward and she had always preferred to leave the chore to Nicky and the children. Now, as she dropped a gleaming shell into the saucepan of water, it struck her as a pleasantly mindless pastime. Outside the back door, protected from the wind, she could watch the sky change colour and keep an eye out for the black wing-tips of the male hen harrier that had already flown by twice that morning, probably on the lookout for a mouse or some other rodenty titbit for its lunch. The sun was warm on her face. Bluebottles were fretting around the moss in the render. The children had disappeared for the day with an assortment of picnic food stowed in their pockets. She had given up asking what they were doing. What did it matter, as long as it got them out of the house, as long as they weren't lolling around on the sofa, tearing her heart in two with their listlessness. She was aware of barely coping; she no longer knew how to.

She stole another look at Donald John, perched awkwardly on the far end of the bench. It was unusual for him to pay her a visit, and after a lengthy preamble about the weather, he'd slipped into an even more uncharacteristic silence.

'So, you're keeping well, Donald John?' she ventured.

'Aye, well enough.' He slurped at his coffee then stretched his neck towards the sky like a stork conducting a survey of possible routes south. Letty could dimly make out the sound of a plane. Donald John stared at the twin streaks of white cutting through the blue. 'These air-o-planes, where are they going? Forwards and backwards, backwards and forwards. Up in the sky . . . so high, so lonely.'

'They're transatlantic planes, Donald John. I expect they're on their way to America.'

'Aye.' He shook his oblong head in sympathy. 'Poor souls.'

'Yes,' she agreed. She too had no desire to be anywhere except on the beach, or trailing across the machair, blown by wind and rain. She understood why it was so hard for Donald John to leave. The island exerted a mesmeric pull. She had felt the magic of it all her life, but it was a magic that stayed on the island. You couldn't take it with you.

'Letitia,' Donald John began heavily, then broke off to gaze seemingly with great interest at an odd assortment of treasures stacked against the wall – glass lobster floats, whale vertebrae and sheep skulls, all bleached white by salt and sun. There was no particular reason why they'd been left there for so many years, but by the same token, there had never been occasion to move them.

'What is it, Donald John?' Letty pressed gently. 'What's bothering you?'

Donald John floated his big hands off his knees, then dropped them down again. 'It's about Alick.'

Letty laid down her knife. 'He's on the drink, isn't he?' she said quietly.

An islander's right to drink was inviolable, she accepted that. Within the community drinking was neither frowned upon nor encouraged. It was accepted as an everyday happening like breathing or the baking of scones. But since the ghost incident, Alick's behaviour had become increasingly erratic. He had taken to pitching up at ungodly hours, sometimes painfully early or just as Letty was deciding to go to bed. There was always a purpose for his visit. To show her a letter he'd received years earlier from a girl he'd admired, or to produce an obscure part he'd ordered for the Raeburn. Each time he'd take up position at the kitchen table, his sharp, inquisitive eyes flitting between each child in turn.

'Georgie!' he'd cry. 'Did I tell you about the time I was away in Aldershot?'

'Um, yes, actually, you did,' Georgie said uneasily. Alick's story of travelling to England to start his National Service, via tractor, hay baler, fishing boat, train, bus and finally hitchhiking was one of his favourites. He had eventually arrived two days late only to be bollocked by the signing-in officer, unimpressed by his explanation of having come from no small distance away. 'Where from, laddie,' he'd barked scornfully, 'Glasgy?'

'Och, no, Sir, ferther north.'

'Well, where then,' the officer rapped, 'Callander? Dundee?'

'No, no,' again Alick demurred. After a prolonged and increasingly heated game of Guess which Scottish Town, a map of the British Isles was produced and Alick pointed to the tiny speck off Scotland's north-west coast, which up until that point had been officially identified as a coffee stain. And how utterly in awe the signing-in officer had been! And hadn't Alick been declared the very hero of innovative travel!

Sober, Alick was a born storyteller. His head was a muddle of half-truths and whole truths and quarter-truths. Whether fabricating the reason why he'd missed the connecting bus or miming the Adjutant marching pompously up and down the room, Alick had the ability to spin the most riveting tale from the most commonplace happening. To begin with whisky enhanced his comic timing but as the bottle emptied, he slowly descended into the repeated telling of shaggy dog stories.

'Now, Alba.' He leant across the table. 'Did I ever tell you I was only a two-pound baby?'

'About a hundred zillion times,' Alba replied brutally.

'Although two pounds is a very small baby,' Jamie compensated politely.

'Aye, that's right, very small,' Alick mused, dropping his roll-up and fumbling for it under his chair. 'But I'm strong as an ox now. Aye, strong as that great bloody bear of yours!' He yanked up his wool jumper. 'Come now, Jamie lad, hit Captain Alick of the SAS in the belly. Hard as you can.'

'Alick, sit down,' Letty intervened. 'You're spilling your coffee.'

'I've no use for coffee, Let-ic-ia, we'll take a dram together!'

'No, we will not.' Letty pushed the mug closer to him. 'Now, drink up, Alick, for goodness' sake.'

'Let-ic-ia,' he sing-songed, 'did I tell you there's a terrible rascal on the island?' He looked around for matches, then, thrusting a hand into the lucky dip of his pocket, withdrew it clutching the prize of a dead mackerel. For a moment he gazed at it, truly confounded. The fish had been folded in half like a pound note and was stiff with rigor mortis. Then he stuffed it back in his pocket, winking at the children as though he were a co-conspirator in their efforts at schoolroom anarchy. Letty paid little attention. According to Alick, everybody was suddenly a thief or a tinker, out to get the better of him. But as the evening dragged on, as the children sloped off, one by one, to bed, it was always Letty left at the table, so tired it was as though her eyelids were lined with sand. She could not bring herself to send Alick away. As he talked and smoked and drank, she thought of all the years of selfless loyalty; she remembered every broken boiler or light he'd fixed, every errand he'd run. There was no question that Alick was the kindest, most capable man, but he was also a drunk. As she looked over at him, slumped at the kitchen table, the whites of his eyes veined with red, his oil-stained fingers hustling the wormy dregs of tobacco from his tin, she had a terrible premonition of an Alick to come: embittered and paranoid, his fierce spirit eroded, his independence drowned by alcohol. When the picture became too ugly to bear, she forced him to his feet and pushed him towards the sitting room with a pillow and a blanket.

'Now, I don't want to hear another word from you,' she said firmly. 'Just get some sleep and stop being so silly.' Because what else was there to say? Once, many years earlier, after Alick had disappeared on a bender, she'd accused him of being unreliable and never had she regretted cross words more. Alick had taken himself off and not returned for a week. It hadn't been his absence that had upset her, but the look of hurt bewilderment in his eyes. So, she would listen to all the long-winded stories. If necessary, she would even clean and gut the dead mackerel in his pocket, because she simply could not risk losing anyone else she loved.

'He's been taking the oil from you,' Donald John finally blurted out.

Letty stared at him. Had Donald John told her that Alick was wanted for war crimes she would have been less shocked.

'He's been stealing oil to pay for the drink.'

'I see.' Letty picked miserably at a mussel beard, untangling it strand by strand.

'Oil is terrible expensive,' Donald John commented.

'Yes. It is.' She hung her head and tried not to cry. Alick's drinking always meant trouble, but she had imagined a run-in with the church minister or a spat with his father, not this sucker punch of betrayal.

'Working at the croft all these years and nothing to show for it. Oh, boo boo, it's little wonder. And now with the cattle gone. Poor Alick never got a penny for all he did. Not a penny, no, indeed.'

'No, quite,' she said hollowly. Then, more sharply, 'What do you mean the cattle gone, Donald John?'

Donald John raised troubled eyes to hers. 'I was sure he would have told you.'

'Told me what?'

'Murdo has sold his father's cattle.'

'He's done what?'

'Aye, every last one of them, at the cattle sales.'

'But the cattle are Alick's livelihood. I don't understand. Did Euan ask him to?'

'Indeed, Euan had no idea, Letitia. No idea at all. Why, when poor Euan found out he took a terrible shock. Murdo had no right to them.' Donald John began to rock backwards and forwards in agitation. 'Murdo has the croft in his name but not the cattle.'

Letty's understanding of Scottish inheritance was hazy – crofting laws in particular were Gordian – but she dimly remembered talk of Euan turning the property over to his eldest son.

'Aye, Euan left the croft to Murdo,' Donald John's voice rose, 'but that didn't mean he got the moveables along with it. Euan never meant for him to have the cattle, no indeed, and Alick has taken it bad, right enough, working all these years, day and night, and getting nothing for his trouble.'

Letty bit her lip. 'He never said a word.'

'Well, it's put him on the drink and little wonder. Wee Alick was always the first to do a hands-turn for somebody. Oh my goodness, yes he was. He has been a very good worker these many years, both inside the croft and out.'

'Oh, Donald John, I wish you'd told me earlier.' She felt a surge of exasperation, though of course she had little right. Alick was Donald John's first cousin. God only knew what it had cost him to confide in her.

'You have your own worries, Letitia, but now there'll be bad blood in the family forever.'

'But why would Murdo do such a wicked thing?'

'They say he needs the money for his contracts, yes indeed Letitia, that's it. His company is involved in building that new army base.'

Letty frowned. The Eileandorcha army base was only a few years old. 'Why do they need a new one?'

'Well, I'm not sure if it's an army base exactly,' Donald John said thoughtfully. 'Angus Post Office says it might be some kind of nucular station.'

'Nuclear station! No, no. I don't think so. I mean, I think there must be a muddle of some sort,' she added tactfully.

'No one knows what it is supposed to be,' he conceded. 'Alisdair the fisherman had a letter from his cousin Duncan over in Lochbealach who said he'd heard it was a missile-testing range – like that one they built down on south island right enough – but old Jackson up in Clairinish thinks it's an early warning system for Russian bombs.'

Letty was staring at him. 'Donald John, are you quite sure?'

'Well, that's what I hear anyways, and they'll be starting with the building of it pretty soon.'

'But it will be the ruin of Eileandorcha,' she whispered.

'Oh, tse tse, Let-ti-cia, it's not going to be in Eileandorcha, no, indeed.' Donald John appeared fussed that he'd muddled her so comprehensively. 'It's going to be situated right here in the township.'

'In Ballanish?' Letty stammered.

He screened his eyes from the sun and pointed east. 'On the hill above the church loch. Yes, that's where they're going to build it, right enough, Letitia, just over there, at the very top of Clannach!'

59

 'Roddy, does everything get to be a ghost?'

'Well, I'm not sure I know what you mean.'

Roddy wiped the blood from his knife onto a piece of paper.

'This rabbit, for instance.' Jamie looked at the opaque, milky eyes of the dead animal. 'Will it get to be a ghost now it's dead?'

'No, no, I don't think so.'

'What about lobsters?'

'Lobsters . . .' Roddy appeared to give the matter of shellfish spirits some serious thought. 'Well, now, I can't say I've ever heard tell of a lobster ghost.'

'What about the bear, then? Would the bear get to be a ghost if it's dead?'

'Ghosts are for humans,' Roddy said firmly. 'Now, that's not to say that humans can't turn into rabbits or lobsters after they die, because they can and that's a fact.'

'Yes, I know,' Jamie said eagerly. 'Mrs Macdonald says that fishermen come back as seagulls after they die and that they have the whole sea to fish in.'

'Folks can come back as all kinds of animals, why, seagulls, rats, cockroaches even.'

'But how does anyone know if they're going to come back as a ghost or an animal?'

'Now that depends entirely on the circumstances. If someone's been very brave, they might come back as an eagle, or a horse. But if they've been very bad and disliked by enough people, then they might come back as a fly, or a mosquito.' Roddy tugged at a hair sprouting from his ear. 'Indeed, lad, there's many a wicked man I've ground under the heel of my boot.'

'But you've seen ghosts too, haven't you, Roddy?' Jamie tried not to be distracted by the creases in Roddy's earlobes. It was as though he had slept on a pillow of nails.

'Aye, plenty of them.'

'Alick thinks there's a ghost in mum's bedroom.'

'Well then,' Roddy said lugubriously, 'I'm very sure there is.'

'Roddy, where do people go when they don't go to heaven?'

'To hell,' he said serenely.

'And where is hell exactly?'

'Down in the depths of the earth.'

'Where the earthquake people live!'

Roddy lifted his cap and scratched his head. 'I don't rightly know about that, Jamie, but there's plenty of room down there for all sorts. Hell is where the wicked spend eternity. It's where the devil lives, right enough. Ach, the stories I could tell you about the devil.'

Jamie was well aware that Roddy boasted a special

kinship with the devil, that he seemed suspiciously privy to the devil's itinerary on any given day of the year, which he was happy to report to anyone who cared to ask, but Jamie had no intention of getting sidetracked. Roddy might choose to fraternize with the devil, but there was really no question of his father doing the same. In fact he imagined his father would take a very dim view of that sort of thing.

'What if you're not a wicked person, but you haven't made it to heaven yet?'

'Could be that a soul has unfinished business on earth. Folks can get trapped somewhere between the two until they see to whatever it is that's been bothering them.'

'Roddy,' Jamie took a deep breath, 'do you think it's possible my father's being a ghost or an animal somewhere?'

The hunchback eyed him thoughtfully. 'Well, that's hard to say, Jamie, indeed it is.'

'So who decides whether you get to come back as a person ghost or an eagle ghost?'

'It depends what you believe.'

'Yes, but what do *you* believe?'

'Well, now, I say if a man wants to come back as a ghost or an eagle, then that's his choice,' he pronounced philosophically. 'If it's a question of unfinished business, I would imagine it's whatever suits a man's purpose best, and if he's been a good enough fellow, why, who's to say he won't get what he wants?'

60

 His body ached. Hunger had dried out his eyes and stolen the marrow from his bones. It had morphed into a fiend inside him, one that grew bigger and more demanding every day and as it growled and whined, raking its claws up and down the inside of his stomach, he was overcome with the doubt that freedom and choice brings. Why not end it? Go home. Lumber into the township and wait for the net to close around him. Strength was something he'd always taken for granted, but as he began losing control over his body, something surprising happened. The shape and pattern of his thinking began to change. Idea overlapped idea. Was it possible to maintain life through will alone? He began to hallucinate. In a rush his head filled with memories he didn't recognize, images of places he had not seen and feelings he had never experienced. He didn't fully understand the journey he was on, but he sensed its magnitude and so he fought hunger and doubt as he'd never before fought any opponent.

From time to time, when energy returned to him in short concentrated bursts, he left the cave, slaked his thirst in the small burn that trickled into the loch, then made his way to the house, staying as long as he dared. He leant against the stone wall for support and reassured himself with the comings and goings of the family. But these forays tired him and were followed by extended periods of weakness spent in a trance-like state back in his cave.

Every night now he dreamt of the boy – that serious little face, his puppet and string form on top of the cliff, silhouetted against a thundery sky.

'Hello bear,' the boy said.

'Come to me, boy,' he begged and reached out, but in his dreams the boy could not hear him. In his dreams, the boy had yet to work out that he even existed.

61

Letty sat on her bed, chewing the inside of her cheek as wind rattled the glass in the window. She tried to imagine herself walking downstairs, picking up the receiver and dialling the Foreign Office. Yet it was eight months since they'd spoken, so how could she just say his name then stumble through small talk as if nothing had happened between them, as if nothing had been said? Still, what choice did she have? The long arm of the government had snaked north and tightened its acquisitive fingers around this tiny space, this one-third of a solitary acre that she'd carved out for her family, and she was damned if she was going to allow them to take it from her. The storm gave the window another shake in its frame and it was then she heard it, an eerie keening coming through the wall. She held her breath. It was as though the wind was tearing the grief out of her own chest and playing it back to her as a warning. Dear Lord, it wasn't Flora's ghost who would never be able to rest in peace, she thought wildly, it was her.

*

It had taken four telephone calls to secure the correct number for the MP for the Highlands and Islands and a further two to break through the protective guard of his staffers. Marriage to a diplomat had endowed her with an unusually high tolerance for bureaucracy and she was prepared for further filibuster from the man himself, but Edward Burgh had been depressingly forthcoming. Indeed, he confirmed, most people had little idea of the extent of MoD activities in Scotland. In the Highlands and Islands alone was St Kilda, the army base on Shillaig, the missile range at Gebraith. There was also the watch radar station in Theaval and a patrol boat stationed down in Loch Baghasdail. 'Over and above these,' he added, 'a number of other proposals are being considered. With those that do not offer significant job gains or threaten extensive upheaval, we are already arguing a perceived threat to the faith, language and culture of island people, but I have to advise you that the government is vigorously committed to the expansion of its military presence in Scotland.'

So Donald John had been right. After his visit that afternoon she'd gone straight to see Euan. 'Oh yes, Let-ic-ia, there's been talk of it,' the old man had said.

'On Clannach.' Her throat constricted.

'Aye, right up on the top.'

'But you'd be able to see it all over the island!'

'Aye, that's the truth.'

'But why Clannach?' She'd paced round the croft's smoky interior. 'Of all places, why here?'

'They say it's a very convenient place for tracking the enemy right enough.'

Euan looked ill, Letty thought. His eyes were watery and his whole physiology had changed, as though the iron spirit that had always supported him had been forcibly extracted leaving only a shell of flesh and blood. He'd taken his son's treachery hard, Donald John had warned her, and God knows, she understood. Why was it that the people you loved were capable of betraying you with such apparent ease?

'Have you talked to the town council? Surely if there was enough opposition, they could stop it.'

'Why, there's plenty of opposition, Let-ic-ia. There's many a crofter who's been complaining.'

'Yes, but to whom?' She knew perfectly well there would have been a great deal of sitting around in crofts, but precious little action. Was it fatalism or idleness, she thought bitterly, the islanders' utter inability to question authority, this placid acceptance of even the most outrageous impositions and restrictions to their lives?

'There was plenty of opposition to the military base on St Kilda and to that missile range above Our Lady of the Isles, but they went ahead and built those ones anyways.' He'd stared into the fire. 'Maybe it's no' so bad with the closure of the seaweed factory.' He raised his eyes pleadingly to hers. 'Murdo says the islanders would be involved in short-term building. He says the MoD might employ civilians there as drivers or security.'

'And you believe that?' But Letty knew he needed little convincing about the fickleness of his own government. At the beginning of the First World War, the MoD had made lavish promises to all Hebrideans prepared to fight for their country, first and foremost being the ownership of their crofts should any of them return alive. They had reneged on the deal and most of the survivors who managed to make their way back to the island, already profoundly demoralized by the horrors of war, had resignedly accepted the betrayal. But not Euan. He'd been swindled by the Canadian Pacific Railway, exploited by the Hudson Bay Company, and had no intention of being cheated by his own government as well. Incensed at how little control crofters had over their own land, he led a series of protests to establish their rights once and for all and found himself sentenced to prison for his trouble. It had only been on his release that the government caved in and he'd got his land but that had been the first and last time the islanders got the better of the MoD.

'Ach, the MoD has lied on more than one occasion,' Euan conceded unhappily.

Letty stopped pacing, struck by the miserable irony. What if there should be a job for Alick on Clannach and what if her meddling threatened it? She rubbed furiously at her eyes. She was damned if she did and damned if she didn't. What was it those MI6 pricks Porter and Norrell had said? *People betrayed their country out of greed, revenge.* She didn't believe the MoD promises, not for a second. She realized with a clarity that shocked her how much she loathed her own government for conspiring against her husband and everything else she held dear. If, right now, someone were to demand of her a quid pro quo for preventing this newest monstrosity from being built, there was nothing she wouldn't agree to. 'There must be someone on the island who can help.' She knelt by his chair. 'Someone with influence.'

The old man gripped her hand. 'There isn't a soul on the island with any influence with the Ministry, Letitia . . . except for you, *mo gràdh*.'

62

No one in the Fleming family was under any illusion they took baths to get clean, only to keep warm. Hot water was limited and the family took their turn in an unvarying but strict pecking order, youngest being last. Occasionally, Jamie talked his way up the list into his mother's slot, but there were disadvantages. The tub was not long enough for both of them, and although the water was hot, there was never enough of it to cover his body and the air that circulated around the inches of exposed flesh felt that much chillier by comparison. At least in the tepid soup of the family's collective dirt he could submerge himself completely and maintain the illusion of warmth, if only for a minute.

Under the water, Jamie's mind relaxed and his thoughts turned to the conversation with Roddy. Premonitions, ghosts, animals, insects. It seemed that people were able to return as just about anything. After some reflection, however, he decided he wasn't particularly keen on ghosts and didn't like the idea of his father returning as one. Apart from all the wailing and moaning, the practicalities of ghost life worried him.

Ghosts, for example, could not drive cars or buy ferry tickets and finally he understood the simple beauty of sailors returning as seagulls. What need would they have to maintain boats or untangle nets? To come back as a bird or animal made so much more sense and he could imagine his father appreciating the freedom of it, loving the sheer fun of it. Jamie stretched his foot towards the tap. Bath water, piped from the burn, was the colour of molasses. A thin trickle of hot ran over his toes. Yes, of all people, his father would have put considerable thought into the logistics of his return. There was no question of him coming back as a cockroach or a mosquito. His father was an important man, a good man. If he chose, he could be a unicorn or a golden eagle. Jamie closed his eyes and imagined his father swooping down and taking him on his back. He would hook his fingers through the soft vanes of the feathers, watch the wing tips twist in the wind, wait as they generated lift until together they would soar! His eyes snapped open underwater – but surely his father, of all people, would realize that there was more than one eagle on the island. If he fancied returning as a gannet, well, there were eighty thousand gannets on St Kilda alone, so it would be the same problem, only worse. His father was fond of great northern divers, describing them as magisterial with their swan-like necks and feathers so smooth and shiny it was as though they'd been combed through with hair oil, but they were strictly water birds and might lack the initiative to venture up to the house. He would never choose a snipe or goose for fear of getting shot and he would hate to be a black-backed gull or hooded crow because he had no respect for hoodies and referred to them as bloody vermin.

Remembering to breathe, Jamie came up for air. He tried to visualize other birds he had noted down in his book, wagtails, swallows, starlings, curlews, but all struck him as too insignificant. It was possible, he supposed, that he might choose a deer. Once, when they'd stopped the car to look at the Northern Lights, there had been a stag on the road in front of them. The stag had stared at them arrogantly, as if waiting for some explanation of their intrusion, before making off through the heather in languid bounds.

'Extraordinary,' his father had sighed and now Jamie's heart quickened as he scrambled out of the bath and grabbed a damp towel off the back of the chair. No longer constrained by mortal rules, his father might appear to him at any moment, in any form. And whatever he decided to return as, whatever sign he chose to give, Jamie now made his father a promise of his own.

He would be ready.

Part Three

63

Alba squinted out into the darkness. A blue-bottle was hurtling around the room. The buzzing was intolerable – like rounds of fire from an automatic rifle. She fumbled for the switch on her bedside light. The noise stopped. The fly was squatting on the inside wall of the lampshade. She examined it sourly. What disgusting vampiric creatures flies were. The swollen undercarriage of its belly glowed a fluorescent blue and it was rubbing its forearms together as though anticipating the joys of money to count or blood to suck. Slowly, deliberately, she reached for her paperback but the fly evacuated with a furious buzz and began a retaliatory dive-bombing of each wall from the safety of the ceiling. After several abortive attempts to kill it, Alba decided the more intelligent tactic would be to entice it from the room with a fresh electrical glow. She switched off her lamp and marched into the corridor. A cold draught was twisting up through the staircase. Christ, they might as well live in Siberia or the Ukraine. Through the window the sky had taken on a yellowish hue. She frowned, disorientated, almost giddy for a moment while she checked for the reassuring silhouette of Donald John's barn. Was it possible she was still asleep? Dreaming? What was she even doing out here? Her mind stalled then jolted. Yes, the bluebottle, the bathroom light. She crept on, then stopped abruptly outside her mother's room. A wedge of light was spilling onto the carpet. After a second's hesitation, Alba peered through the crack in the door.

Her mother was sitting up in bed, a letter in her hands. She appeared to be reading it fitfully, as though the contents were too painful to be absorbed more than a sentence at a time. As she put it down and picked it up again, her mouth and face contorted into expressions of sorrow and Alba found the effect disturbing, surreal. Suddenly, as though the letter had spontaneously caught fire and was burning her fingers, her mother threw it away, then, balling up her fists, she began to pummel her face. After that, the tears came in a seemingly unstoppable flow, bringing with them small dulled-down animal noises. Out in the corridor, Alba shivered in the cold air, intrigued, deeply suspicious, blinking like an owl into the failing darkness of the night.

64

The sheep trembled as he crossed the machair. 'Watch out,' he wanted to growl, *Ursus horribilis* coming through. The sheep's terror made him reckless, angry even. Maybe he should take a bite out of their necks, give the absurd creatures something real to bleat about but as he drew nearer, instead of huddling in groups or fleeing in their usual manner, they stayed still, transfixed, staring upwards, and suddenly he noticed the strange, almost luminescent colour of their wool. Above him the night sky was tinged an eerie swamp-green, but he found nothing surprising any more. He had grown used to the mind tricks that hunger played and his whole world had turned upside down. Even his flesh felt scratchy and painful as though fur was growing on the wrong side of his skin. How had it got this far? What had possessed him? But enough now. It was over. It had to be. He needed to eat, he needed to live. He began to run, but before long he realized that it wasn't only the sky and the sheep, it was the whole island. The fence post, the cow parsley, the machair – all were glowing a sickly green as though bathed in the landing lights of a UFO. Again he looked up, this time in fear. The sky was now a blaze of colour. Bands of electromagnetic light traversed the clouds. Stars dotted the atmosphere like particles of shattered quartz. Shapes and colours began merging with bewildering speed, one minute the smoky plumes of violet and red, the next, blues and greens were chasing each other in playful spirographic curves. Oh, it was beautiful, it was terrifying, it was awe-inspiring and he found himself trembling uncontrollably. He bounded on, up into the hills, up as high as he could climb, then he threw himself down behind a rock and lay there staring upwards as heaven slowly drifted closer to earth.

65

In Letty's dream the day was charged with electricity. A fierce toxic sun roiled across the island, polishing the slate roofs of the township and reflecting on the slick-wet sand of the bay. It burned clean through the surface of the lochs, warming even the blood of trout and salmon as they meandered through their watery cities of reeds and stones. Letty saw herself from the air, a dark speck silhouetted against the dull khaki fern of south Clannach. The wind toyed with the hood of her jacket while Alick pulled her by the hand up the hill's steep incline.

'Ach, there it is, Letitia!' he cried eagerly, as the twin funnels of a nuclear power station loomed into view. 'You'll not guess, but it was the fairies that built this!'

And now she was being transported to the school house where a meeting of the Ballanish township was in progress. The islanders were sitting in rows of chairs flanked by the military standing to unctuous attention for the Ambassadress. Gillian, impeccably dressed in her family's clan-appropriate tweed, stood on stage, one hand resting lightly on the burnished end of a warhead.

'It has come to our attention that a bear has been seen on this island,' she began. 'The bear is the symbol of Russia. Who knows how much information this enemy spy has already gleaned? Who knows how badly our existing defence plans have been compromised? The Outer Hebrides are now at the geopolitical axis of the Cold War and the facility we intend to build here will provide the integrated command and control system of Great Britain with early warning of approaching enemy aircraft. This will allow the government time to galvanize its defences in the event of nuclear attack.'

'How much time?' One of the islanders raised a tentative hand.

'Two minutes,' the Ambassadress shot back her reply. 'Now you must understand, the island is to be annexed for the greater good. There will be no back-door attacks by the Soviet Union. Ballanish might not be a natural capital of the British Isles but if the Germans can make it work in Bonn, we can make it work here, and for those of you who may harbour doubts as to the validity of this project, let me remind you that any community hosting a military facility will provide an essential service to the nation. This should be considered an honour for a people whose sole purpose up until now has been the cultivation of potatoes and the export of rotting sea matter.'

Letty's eyes snapped open. For a moment she lay still, dismayed to find that the horror of her nightmare had not been alleviated by waking. Then she glanced at the clock and threw back her covers. Tom's plane would be landing in just over two hours.

66

Georgie dipped her foot into the cold green water of the swimming hole. A zigzag of baby eels panicked and changed direction. Beneath her toe, a bright red sea anemone was stuck to the rock like a wine gum.

'I had no idea this place even existed.' Aliz took a drag on his cigarette and passed it to her. 'It's grand.'

'I've always come here,' she said. 'Ever since I could first swim.'

Along the coast a rising gale was inciting the waves to riot, whipping the sea into a foam, but within the protective curve of the cliff the rock pool was as calm as a millpond, the water clear, twenty feet down to its white sandy bottom. A bonxie, curving swiftly along the serrated shoreline, suddenly altered its direction.

'Look at the sky,' Georgie said. 'It's such a weird colour.'

'Looks polluted.'

'No, it's pretty. Like someone's placed a piece of tracing paper over the sun.'

'Ah, see the hand of God.' Aliz kicked at a limpet with the heel of his boot.

'What's that mean?'

'My father says it whenever he thinks something is beautiful, or when he cooks something tasty, when our egg yolks look particularly orange or his books balance perfectly, "Ah, Aliz, my son," he cries, "see the hand of God," and then he rubs his chin in wonder.'

'I love days like this,' Georgie said, 'when the weather is suspended and you know a storm is coming.'

'Wouldn't you prefer it sunny?'

Georgie shrugged. She found it strange that of all planets, the sun was most revered. The sun was a heater, the moon a torch and the stars merely a confetti of superfluous decoration. She connected with the earth. Soil. Mud. Rock. Sand. Somewhere, way below them, a magnificent geological pulse was sending electrical charges to every human being, keeping their hearts beating, keeping them alive. She pushed herself into the dip of the rock until she felt her chest constrict as the voltage passed though her. Maybe these were what growing pains felt like.

Aliz was leaning on his elbow, his bushy head propped up on one hand. She laid her arm alongside his. 'Look at your skin against mine.'

'Yours is so white.'

'Yours is dirty brown.'

'Mine is made of peat.'

'Mine is made of papier mâché. Or maybe it's been floating in the sea too long.'

'Mine looks like it's been stewing in the bog ever since the Vikings hacked it off and threw it there.'

Georgie laughed. 'Well, I still like yours better.'

'Take it, then.' He hooked it around hers.

She touched his skin. 'I don't like the hairs.'

'Pull them out.'

'It'll hurt.'

'I want it to hurt.'

'No.' Georgie sprinkled some sand onto his arm then ground it in under the pad of her finger. 'Besides, I have my own ways of making you talk.'

They lapsed into silence. 'Doesn't it feel strange?' she said after a while.

'What?'

'To be so different.'

'Because of my dirty peaty skin?' He looked at her and grinned.

'Don't laugh at me,' she said, offended.

'You don't know, do you?'

'Know what?' She reddened.

'It's not me. My family aren't the outsiders here. You're the ones the islanders talk about all the time. You, your sister, your father, grandfather.'

Georgie hugged her knees to her chest. 'What do they say?'

'I don't know,' he backtracked hastily. 'Lots of things.'

'What do they say about my father?'

Aliz hesitated.

'I want to know.'

Aliz gouged a hole in the sand and dropped his cigarette inside. 'Everyone has their own idea of what happened to him.'

'Like what?'

'My father heard Duncan saying he'd been assassinated. Chrissie thinks it was a plane crash. Peggy said he got the cancer.' He looked at her for a reaction, but Georgie's face was turned away. 'You know what everyone's like round here,' he went on uncertainly. 'Angus Post Office is convinced that Russians have hold of him and are keeping him prisoner.'

'I wish that were true.' There was a hard edge to her voice. 'At least it would mean he was alive.'

'I'm sorry. You must hate people asking about it.'

'No one *ever* asks about it.'

'Why?'

'I don't know, at the beginning my mother didn't want to upset my brother, but now it's as if . . . well, it's as if he's become a taboo subject.'

'I shouldn't have brought it up.'

'No, I want you to bring it up.' Talking about her father felt as if someone had clamped an oxygen mask to her face. She was giddy for more. 'Ask me anything,' she blurted out. 'Ask me how he died.'

Aliz looked at her, shocked.

'Go on. Ask me.'

Aliz dropped his eyes, touched the veins in the rock with his finger. 'All right then, how did he die?'

'He fell. From the roof of the embassy.'

'He *fell*. How?'

It occurred to Georgie, in that moment, that 'how' was the one word which encompassed all her torment. People didn't spontaneously fall from roofs. People fought and struggled and lost. People were pushed from behind or they leant against railings that gave way . . . she took a deep breath. 'I think he jumped.'

'Jumped?' Aliz stared at her. 'Why?'

'No one knows,' Georgie said. Secrets were lies you carried deep inside and they got heavier with each passing day. Aliz was still staring. Grains of sand glittered on the curve of his cheekbone.

'Except me,' she whispered. 'I know.'

67

 What had made her mother cry? A note from the bank? A letter from the embassy? All morning Alba brooded. Could Georgie have confessed her sneaky rendezvous with the Paki's son? Well, serve her mother right for opting so comprehensively out of her children's lives. Mechanically, she went about stacking the kitchen chairs on top of the table. She couldn't forget the way her mother had cried, the silent wailing, the desperate Gollum's hold she'd kept on that letter, reading, sobbing, reading, sobbing, a masochistic feeding of her pain. What the Deuteronomy was it all about? Wasn't there supposed to be a moratorium on emotion in their family? Weren't they supposed to have cornered the market in stiff upper lip? Either way she would make it her business to find out.

She fetched the broom from the outside room and slammed the door behind her, the violence making her feel better. Today all contractual obligations to her sister ended. No more family cooking, no more Jamie charity. From now on she would prepare her own meals and eat them in the peaceful solitude of her room. Hell, she would eat dust off the floor if it suited her.

She gave the cork tiles a cursory once-over. The section of flooring under the table was covered, most impractically, with a thick seagrass matting into which was embedded a mincemeat of squashed flies, the pin-like limbs of daddy long-legs along with a pick'n'mix of dropped food from the table, all of which were impossible to extract from within the mat's scratchy furrows. Alba amalgamated her dirt into a single pyramid then, lifting the corner of the mat, swept it underneath. She felt no guilt. Sweeping stuff under the carpet was a family hobby they were all becoming increasingly skilled at.

Her mother hurried through the kitchen, car keys and bag in hand. She hesitated when she saw her daughter and before Alba could turn away, stepped quickly forwards and cupped her cheek.

'My darling. You've been such a help to me these past few weeks. Thank you.'

Alba wavered. The touch of her mother's hand was unexpectedly calming; then she remembered. Anger was her refuge. It was all she had left.

68

'Alick, why don't you come any more when we put the flag out for you?'

'Well, I've a good many things to do just now,' Alick said.

Jamie looked doubtful. It was early afternoon, but Alick had only just got up. His wire-brush hair was sticking up and his eyes were red-rimmed.

'Is it because you're scared of Flora Macdonald's ghost?'

'Not at all.'

'Because Mum said that Flora Macdonald went to Australia with Neilly McLellan and it's just the wind that makes that howling noise.'

'If Flora and that rascal got to Australia,' Alick said bitterly, 'then they're a lucky pair of devils and that's a fact.' He scrabbled some loose tobacco off the table and looked around for his papers.

Jamie watched him unhappily. The electric blower was on full and he could hardly breathe for the cloying heat. Usually he liked the military tidiness of Alick's caravan. The caravan served as both house and workshop and Jamie thought that were a giant to pick it up and shake it, the fallout of handy household and mechanical items would shower the island with a hail of lethal metal. Today, though, the caravan wasn't orderly at all. The cushion Jamie was sitting on was haemorrhaging foam and a dirty plate sat on the linoleum-covered table with a fork insolently embedded into a mess of congealed eggs. Plus, the caravan smelt of something sour and mildewy. Attics and dead things, Jamie thought vaguely, attics and dead things. He wrinkled his nose and scratched impatiently at a midge bite while Alick struggled with the buttons of his boiler suit. It was already clouding over and a storm was brewing. There would be no use looking for stags in bad weather.

'Were you scared of ghosts when you were my age?'

'The will-o'-the-wisp,' Alick said grimly. 'That's what I was scared of. I only saw it once, but it was made up of a whole lot of lights right enough and so bright it seemed to move with the wind.'

'But what was it?'

'No one's exactly sure, but something phosphorous in the bog anyways. It must have been gases right enough, but still and all, we were terrified it would get us.'

Jamie looked out of the window. A small party of greylags had just landed in the flooded field. 'Alick, if you died and came back as an animal, what do you think you'd come back as?'

'Captain Alick is indestructible.' Alick flashed him a grin. 'So I'll not be dying anytime soon.'

'But do you think people can come back as animals?'

'Of course. Why there's a sheep out on the machair, I

swear is the very spitting image of Donald John's dead aunty.' Alick pushed open the door of the caravan and jumped down. 'Let's be off.'

'Can I drive?'

'Aye, if you don't put us in the ditch.' Alick climbed up into the tractor seat and pulled Jamie up after him. Jamie sat on his lap, put the tractor in gear and turned the stiff key. There were few pleasures in life as great as operating heavy machinery but, to his frustration, they'd gone barely a hundred yards before they were waved down by Peggy, a grim look on her face and a white plastic bag hanging from her wrist. Jamie's heart sank.

'If you're headin' to Hourghebost, Alick, will you give me a ride?'

'We're away to the Committee Road, Peggy.'

'To the Committee Road! At a time like this?'

Alick looked at her blankly.

'You've no' heard then?' Peggy was a determined competitor in the gossip race and nothing made her happier than being first over the line with the news.

'What is there to hear?'

'Why, word is all over the island,' she hedged. 'I'd be surprised if it's not on the wireless too.'

The real skill of the game was to delay the actual information for as long as possible while systematically building up interest. Peggy had plenty more teasers up her sleeve, but she hadn't allowed for the severity of Alick's hangover.

'Out with it, woman,' he commanded.

'Well, if you must know,' she said ungraciously, 'they've spotted the bear.'

'The bear?' Jamie spluttered. 'My bear?'

'Aye, the wrestler's bear,' Peggy said, only partially mollified by Jamie's reaction.

'Are you sure?' Jamie sprang out of his seat.

'Quite sure, and what an excitement, with everyone thinking he was drowned all this time.'

'I knew it.' Jamie punched the air with his fist. 'I knew he was still alive.'

'Alive and well indeed,' Peggy said placidly. Normal protocol at this juncture demanded a laborious Q and A, but Jamie, feverish with excitement, began bombarding her with questions. Where had they found him? Who had found him? Was he okay? Was he hurt?

Peggy relented. 'Old Archie down at Hourghebost was getting ready to go out with the sheep when he saw a wee furry ear sticking up behind the rock. Indeed, he reasoned at once it must be the bear and he had that nice Sergeant Anderson down in a jiffy bringing the wrestler with him. Why, the man was that keen to get here, they say he flew up in an army helicopter, all the way from Perthshire with half the press on his heels.'

'So they've caught him.'

'Why, no, that's it.' Peggy, still working her way towards the actual essence of the news, shook her head in feigned disbelief. 'It's the strangest thing. Archie says the wrestler put down a bucket of fish not fifty yards in front of him and the bear didn'a move an inch towards him!'

'Why not?' Jamie said.

'So he's still on the loose?' Alick squinted thoughtfully in the direction of Hourghebost.

'Aye, took himself off at a run,' Peggy said triumphantly, 'and with the reward still on his head.'

Alick stabbed at the tractor's starting button and stuck out a hand for Jamie.

'Come on,' he said grimly. 'We'll get after him.'

'Well, you'd best be careful,' Peggy said, unwilling to relinquish her audience without an encore, 'for it's the greatest likelihood he's gone mad.'

'Why do you say that?' Jamie couldn't stand to think of the bear in pain.

'Because if after six weeks that poor beast's not looking for his fish and he's not looking for his wrestler, then who on earth can he be looking for?'

Jamie almost heard the click in his head. He paused, his foot on the metal step of the tractor. 'What do you mean?' he asked slowly.

'Well, no doubt it was the commotion that scared him, but I heard Archie tell that the bear took off in such a hurry, why, anyone would think he had some kind of unfinished business to take care of.'

Now Jamie's brain was flashing like a circuit board. The bear . . . of course, the bear! Hadn't the bear been with him every step of the journey? From the *Zirkusplatz* in Bonn to the coach passing him on the Inverary road? If the Peugeot hadn't rolled into the river, wouldn't they have even crossed the Minch on the same ferry? Oh, he was stupid and stupider. It had been his father who'd made him love bears. The *Gummibär* sweets, the grizzly in the museum. The *Zirkusbär* balancing on his unicycle. His father who had told him that bears were princely animals. *Bears are highly intelligent*, he'd said, *and this one has been well educated. English, French, German and Russian*, and weren't these his father's languages? Hadn't the bear shared his father's hobbies of fishing and painting? Jamie felt his heart slam painfully against his ribs. If his father were to come back as an animal, then what else would he choose? Oh, Alba was right. He was a retard! He was *nugatory*. He felt like smacking himself in the face. Of course the bear wouldn't allow himself to be caught. Of course he would not be lured from his purpose by some smelly bucket of fish. His father had come back exactly as he'd promised. He had unfinished business, something to tell his family, and all this time, all these weeks he'd been waiting patiently for Jamie to find him, for Jamie to hear him. For Jamie to understand.

69

Bonn

After questioning Georgie for an hour, it had been Porter's turn to take notes. He moved quietly to the end of the table, his suit straining over his stocky shoulders, while Norrell repositioned himself casually next to Georgie, the very personification of friendly informality. I am no more threatening, his swinging leg seemed to imply, than an elder brother or school friend helping with your biology homework.

'So, why don't you tell us what he looked like?' Norrell asked her. 'This man your father saw. This Torsten fellow. Where exactly did you meet him and what was discussed?'

Georgie had fixed her gaze on the man's jacket. It was virtually without creases. A pen was hooked by the lid onto his lapel.

The door to the room opened. The Ambassadress entered carrying a mug of hot chocolate, which she set on the table. 'How are we doing?' she enquired. When there was no immediate reply, she stiffened her back. Protocol was not as clear as it might be on the interrogation of minors of deceased diplomats. She bore no particular fondness for either the secret ferrets of the government or Nicky Fleming's eldest daughter, with whom she'd had little contact over the years, but Fleming had died on her watch and she would see to it that there was fair play. 'Mr Porter?'

'Very well, very well,' Porter responded with weary heartiness.

'Georgiana?' Again Gillian waited for an answer but Georgie was staring over her shoulder. Framed in the shadow of the doorway stood the familiarly shambolic form of Tom Gordunson and she felt the tightness of fear loosen a notch. Tom would make it all right. Tom was family.

Or was he? As he stepped forward, she caught his brief nod to Porter and Norrell, before all three men turned once again to her. 'Are you all right, Georgie?' Tom asked. 'Would you like me to stay?'

Georgie's fraught brain whirled. *Trust no one*, her father had told her. *Can't you see? They're all watching you.*

'Perhaps a woman . . .' the Ambassadress was saying quietly. She took Georgie's limp hand in her own and patted it. She had two grown-up sons, both serving overseas. It was a long time since she'd held a child's hand out of love rather than duty, but empathy was an emotion she had practised assiduously.

Georgie withdrew her hand and pushed away the hot chocolate. She was no longer a child whose cooperation could be bought. The Ambassadress absorbed the hostile atmosphere and recalibrated her tactics accordingly. 'Georgiana, these men are here to help. They understand how difficult this is for you and they wholly appreciate your desire to be loyal to your father, but you must realize that anything you tell them now might help to put the record straight.'

'The record?' Georgie looked from the Ambassadress to the three men. It was a colossal gaffe and all of them recognized it. Georgie knew then she had been right to lie. That she would continue to lie.

'Just a turn of phrase, my dear.' The Ambassadress took barely a second to recover. 'I'm afraid that in the business we're in, even tragedy is subject to records and red tape. I'm so sorry.' She turned the handle of the mug towards Georgie and eased it gently in her direction. 'You'll tell them everything they want to know, won't you?'

Georgie nodded. The day she'd left East Berlin, she'd put it out of her mind, the echo of her feet on the stone flags in the church, the low whispers and the strained face of the man her father had met inside.

'Be careful, Georgie.'

She looked up. Tom was standing right over her. His suit was absurdly rumpled but then his eyes met hers. She felt weak with certainty. *He knows*, she thought. *He knows*.

'It's hot,' Tom warned. 'Take small sips.'

Georgie picked up the mug and gulped down as much liquid as she could. She winced as the scalding milk blistered her tongue and took the skin off the back of her throat. The pain was good. It made her less vulnerable.

'Don't keep her too much longer,' the Ambassadress

instructed Norrell, and for the smallest second it seemed to Georgie that the woman's composure had slipped. 'After all,' she added with infinite compassion, 'she's only a child.'

After Tom and the Ambassadress had left, Georgie told the men everything. How they'd walked into the hotel restaurant. How her father asked for a table and the waiter denied having one, and then, in response to her father gesturing towards all the empty tables, had said coolly, 'Your eyes deceive you,' and stared hard at the wallet in Nicky's hands. She told them that of the eight items listed on the menu, seven had been unavailable and that when her order of sausage and potatoes arrived, she noticed that the meat, too, gave off a lingering smell of lignite. The sausage had been as white and sickly as an albino's thumb. She told Porter and Norrell how none of the streetlamps worked and how dark and sinister and vast the Alexanderplatz had seemed. She told them that Torsten had been wearing a knitted tie and orange shoes that didn't look as though they were made of leather.

She took her time to answer every question. She overwhelmed Norrell and Porter with information, drowned them in detail, but as she watched them painstakingly transcribe every word, she could see the impatience in their eyes and she encouraged herself with the thought of them later, terse, chain-smoking, the insides of their mouths furred from too much coffee, scouring page after page of extraneous truths in the hopes of identifying the single one important lie.

'And what did they talk about, your father and this man?' Norrell, still deceptively relaxed, made a show of checking his own notes. 'Who did they talk about? Can you remember if they mentioned anyone in particular?'

'I was a bit bored, really.' Georgie matched her tone to his. 'I read my book most of the time. *The Mayor of Casterbridge*, we were studying it at the BHS last term and there was a test coming up.'

It was true, Georgie *had* read her book. Still, echoes of the conversation kept returning to her. Schyndell. Torsten and her father's frustration with regard to the factory clean-up. The apparently unanswered questions of who was at fault, who was to be blamed, whose head would roll? The determination of every tier of East German government from the Politburo down to blame management and for management to kick someone further down the ladder. She clearly remembered her father saying quietly and furiously, 'It's nothing more than a witch-hunt,' with Torsten's reply coming in an equally low voice: 'Yes. Apparently this is the last we'll be seeing of our friend Bertolt Brecht – I'm afraid he's going to be scrubbing institutional toilets for the rest of his life.'

'Why would Bertolt Brecht be scrubbing toilets?' she'd asked later. 'I thought Bertolt Brecht was a playwright.'

Her father had been distracted. The Peugeot wouldn't start and they'd been waiting over an hour outside the hotel for the garage to pick it up.

'He is a playwright,' he answered after a second or two, 'but all the players in our little industrial accident have pet names. It makes the meetings a little more lively for us.'

He had been play-acting at jolly, she'd thought retrospectively; even at the time, he'd looked tense and worried.

'Ah! Here they come at last.' He blew on his hands and stamped his feet against the cold as a breakdown truck swung round the corner.

'So, what happened in the church?' Porter asked.

Accident, Murder or Suicide. In the matter of her father, the government had boxes to tick and files to close.

You have to understand, Georgie remembered her father saying, *treason is the worst crime imaginable.*

Georgie's burnt tongue felt enormous in her mouth. She had sworn then and there. She would tell Norrell and Porter nothing. She would never tell her mother.

Towards the horizon, clouds were merging. Warm air from the high-pressure system meeting with cool air from the low-pressure system. A sudden confluence of weather-related phenomena. A rumble deep in the belly of the sea.

'My father was a traitor,' Georgie whispered.

Aliz was sitting cross-legged. The bone of his ankle jutted out from underneath his trousers, hard and round as a pebble.

'My father was a traitor.' She said it louder and his face closed down in acknowledgement.

Georgie lay back against the cold rock. She took Aliz's hand then lifted her jumper and slid it onto her stomach. Above them, the storm hovered in the sky like a temper about to burst.

70

Ballanish

Afterwards, when it was too late, Alba wondered at her capacity for cruelty. Where had it come from? When had it begun and how had it evolved into such a white-hot tool for her to wield against her family? She must have been born that way, otherwise why else would it feel so comfortable, so much like second nature to her? In some distant part of herself she knew Jamie had done little to deserve the brutality she consistently meted out to him, but if he couldn't help who he was then nor could she. They might not like each other, but they had learned to live together and Georgie should never have forced a change in the status quo. It wasn't that she had found the last few weeks of being civil to Jamie particularly arduous. It wasn't even that her contract had expired. It was that when he raced into the house – literally flew into the kitchen, with that ghostly white face of his so full of hope, Christ, so full of naked *want* – it had both enraged and panicked her. She'd been sitting at the table, her father's letter in her hand – or should she call it his suicide note, because wasn't that what it was? Dated the day of his death, confused scribbles of admission and regret

– for what, she had no idea, but hell, just add it to the list of everything else that had been kept from her.

Taken the only way out, her father had written, *forgive me, my love*. And then he had given up on them all. Alba choked on a sob. Had he really loved them so little that death was preferable?

She wanted to shred the letter into a thousand pieces, but she knew it would make no difference. You couldn't rid yourself of knowledge once you were in possession of it, but then hadn't she known already? Hadn't she *always* known there was something more? Grown men did not tumble off roofs. They did not fall to their deaths. But why? How could he have done such a thing? That her mother was somehow responsible, she had little doubt. Why else had she been hiding the truth from her children? Alba read and reread the terrible lines, stoking the fires of her rage, adding up all the minutes and the hours and the days her mother had *lied* to her, treated her like a child, treated her like an idiot, making her guess and search for answers. As if her father's death was a game of charades. As if it didn't make any difference *how* he'd died – as if she didn't have the right to know – and, on top of everything, daring to shush her when she'd had the audacity to question it, shushing her every time she mentioned his name. Of course she had concocted stories, of course she had invented fantasies, but of all the far-fetched scenarios, this had been the one that had never occurred to her. Her Dada had killed himself; Dada had jumped.

It had been at that moment, at the very apex of her anger, that Jamie careered through the door like a runaway truck. He'd opened his mouth and tipped a full load of his screwy thinking down on her like two tonnes of gravel until she could no longer breathe under the weight of it. She watched his mouth opening and shutting with the effort of coherent explanation. She heard intermittent snatches – bears, mosquitoes, caves, Roddy, ghosts, heaven – but his voice kept passing in and out of audio and there was no way it could compete with the roaring static in her head. Suddenly the noise stopped. She opened her eyes to find Jamie staring at her, a look of disbelief on his face.

'Alba, you're crying,' he stated flatly.

'Shut up.' She balled her hands into a fist.

'Alba, don't cry.' He took a hesitant step towards her. 'Don't be sad, it's okay.'

'Get away from me.'

Jamie saw that she was shaking and his heart ballooned with sympathy. He remembered every day he'd spent grappling with his father's disappearance. He felt the customary pains shoot up and down his leg. 'Alba, don't be sad, we'll go to the Kettle. You were right all along, that's where he'll be.'

The absurdity of what Jamie was suggesting meant nothing – but his face, shining, almost evangelical with conviction, was too much. How dare he have hope when she had none?

'I love you, Alba,' he announced simply. 'You were the first person I wanted to tell.' He plucked at her sleeve.

It had been a reflex. At his touch, her hand swung back and she struck him with the cumulated force of her atomic misery. Jamie spun backwards, his foot caught on the mat's curling edge and he landed hard on the floor. For a second he lay stunned then his hand floated slowly to his face. 'Alba?' The disbelief in his voice was pitiful.

'Get away from me,' she shouted. 'Just leave me alone.'

'Alba, I don't understand.' A scarlet weal shone on his pale cheek like a burn from an iron. 'I thought . . .'

'You thought what?' she spat contemptuously.

Jamie remained absolutely still. He felt watery, diluted. As if everything meaningful was slowly draining out of him.

'Oh, hell's teeth,' she said, shame driving her on. 'Don't start crying. What have you got to cry about?'

'It wasn't real.' He touched his raw cheek. 'You being nice to me. I thought it was real.'

Alba was almost frightened at how badly she wanted to hit him again.

'You're talking about people coming back as mosquitoes and bears and you're worried about whether me being nice to you was *real*?'

Her face was pinched, hard as granite, a thin blue vein pulsed on her forehead and despite the distance between them, he shivered at her coldness. It quenched the flame of his hero worship, it froze his unconditional love and in that instant it was over. He felt curiously lightheaded. Free.

'I'm going to the cliff.' He pushed to his feet. 'I'm going to find him.'

'Yes, well off you pop, Jamie. It's a marvellous idea. Go to the cliff in a storm, why not? In fact, you know what's an even better idea? Why don't you just jump off the bloody cliff and have done with it.'

Part Four

71

Even with his wretched shortsightedness he had known who it was. From the way he was standing, the way he was holding that bucket. And suddenly it was all over. The big wrestler had come for him. Home was no more than a few hours away and all he had to do to get there was put one foot in front of the other. The sight of the bucket worked like a crank on his hunger and he moved towards the wrestler, drugged by the promise of salvation, the smell of fish so intoxicating his eyes began to water.

What happened next, the fact of his stopping, no one would ever pretend to understand. All anyone could do was attribute it to the strangeness of the beast's half-human heart.

When the image first entered his brain, it was as faint as the muffled note of a piano or a Polaroid yet to develop. Then it sharpened and his mouth filled with the sour anticipation of tragedy. The fear was so strong it felt as though it had the power to cleave his skull in two, to prise loose the very soul from his body. For the image was not the one haunting him these many weeks – the children standing silhouetted at the top of the cliff, the girls with their bright anoraks and long hair blowing across their mouths, no, it was not that one, so familiar, so dear to him now. It was a new picture, a terrible vision, the boy lying at the bottom of the cliff, as still and lifeless as the washed-up gannet. He faltered. For a moment he didn't know where he was. Then, out of the blackening sky, the wind picked up and breathed life back into his numbed soul and finally he understood. Finally he recognized himself, and ignoring the shouts of the wrestler, he turned towards the cliffs and ran.

72

The waiting room was fogged up with cigarette smoke, the meaty fumes of frying bacon and industrial shots of steam from a catering urn that was dispensing tea to a shuffling line of people. Letty stopped in the doorway in surprise. She had never seen the airport so busy. Lonely-eyed army wives nursing babies were regulars, so too were the handful of islanders looking quietly terrified at the prospect of floating up in the sky with no visible support. But there were also huddles of men, bulky canvas bags slung over their shoulders, some queuing for the single payphone, several with cameras dangling around their necks and almost all woefully equipped for the stormy welcome the island afforded them. From the atmosphere of mild hysteria Letty guessed they were journalists. Every decade or so some minor dignitary paid a visit to the island, if only to check whether it was still there. Or possibly the Outer Hebrides were hosting a convention, Birdwatchers of Great Britain or some similar dubious collective, but suddenly there was a screech of brakes on the runway and the knot in her chest tightened as if a wrench had been taken to it. Over the last months, Tom had become synonymous in her mind with the government. Her hatred for both divided equally between the two, but from the moment she'd raised the courage to call him, she'd been surprised to find that although her fury hadn't diminished, the details of it had become blurred. Had their fight been weeks or days after the accident? Had Tom's refusal to help Nicky really been a betrayal rather than a desperate attempt to prevent his friend from risking his career? Then she remembered Tom's brutal denouncement of Nicky, Jamie's high conspiratorial whisper – *Daddy's a spy, isn't he? . . . Tom said* – and she was almost relieved to feel a spark, a rekindling of all her frustration and anger. What Tom had said had been unforgivable. Christ, why had she even called him?

She'd spent the drive figuring out what to say but now, faced with the sight of him, stooping a little as he levered his big frame out of the plane, she forgot her lines. Instead she found herself back in the London Ballroom, the music of the waltz all around her. She remembered the feel of his hand tightening on her shoulder even as Nicky cut in and danced her away and she felt a prickle of shame. It didn't matter what she told herself. She had known, she'd always known how he'd felt, but she'd never been brave enough to do anything but ignore it. She shook herself, tried to reorganize her thoughts, but Tom was already walking across the runway, his tweed overcoat blowing about his legs, and nothing felt natural. Should she wave? Not wave? Should she smile or frown? She darted into the loo and splashed cold water on her face. Her hair was damp and frizzy from the rain. Her skin freckled and brown. What would he think? Did she look older? Defeated? She swiped on fresh lipstick and, pulling herself together, went back out with the intention of waiting for him in a calm and collected fashion, but he was already standing right by the door, his hair blown over his face. When he said her name and took hold of her shoulders, to her utter mortification she burst into tears.

On the drive home, she tried to paper over the awkwardness with geographic reminders – look, there was the track down to Maleshare where Nicky had once taken him for a walk; on their right was the turning to the lobster factory, remember? But these dried up long before she reached the causeway and an unreasonably long silence formed around them.

'Letty . . .' Tom began judiciously, cleaning his glasses with his handkerchief. 'Letty, I'm glad you called.'

Letty gripped the wheel and frowned at the road.

'I tried to see you in London. I wrote to you.' He turned to look at her helplessly. 'I was never sure whether—'

'I got your letters, Tom.'

'But you never wrote back.'

'No.'

'Letty.' He pressed on in a low voice. 'Despite what you thought, despite what you may still think, I have always been Nicky's friend. I am still *your* friend.'

Letty stared straight ahead. The moment she had picked up the phone to the Foreign Office, she had decided. She would tell him nothing of what she had discovered. She would betray Nicky to no one. Tom was here for Clannach, and Clannach alone. Guilt was a powerful tool and she was not above using emotional blackmail to get what she wanted. 'There's no point dredging it up again, Tom. God knows, nothing can be changed now.'

'Letty,' he said vehemently. 'We *must* talk about this.'

Letty swerved the car into a passing place and switched off the engine.

'You want to talk about it.' She turned on him. 'Fine, we'll talk about it. You were not a friend to Nicky. You didn't help him or believe in him. You were as quick to condemn him as everybody else.'

'No.'

'You even tried to turn me against him and then you told Jamie. Dear God, of all people, you told Jamie.'

'Jamie?' Tom looked baffled. 'Told Jamie what?'

She gave a bitter laugh. 'That his father was a spy.'

'Good God, Letty, how can you say such a thing?'

'Jamie told me. He said he knew his father was a spy because you told him.'

'I swear on my life I did no such thing.'

'Jamie might be an odd little boy,' she said vehemently, 'but he's the most truthful child I know.'

'Letty, whatever Jamie thinks I said to him, or whatever I did say to him, he must have misunderstood. Surely you know me better than that.'

'You were his best friend,' she said, and the words caught in her throat. 'Whatever he's done, you should have *fought* for him.'

'Of course I fought for him. MI6, the Foreign Office, the Ambassador; I fought all of them, but you can't disprove suspicion. It's as futile as trying to prove you never received a letter.'

Letty bit her lip miserably. She had no appetite for this. No strength for it.

'Letty!' he implored.

'He would never have betrayed his country – and if you don't believe that, then you're no friend of his. *Nicky was never the man you thought he was.* Isn't that what you threw at me that day?'

Tom grimaced. 'It was a stupid thing to say, I've regretted it since.'

'But you meant it, didn't you?'

Tom sighed, pulled his overcoat around him. 'Letty, if Nicky had to choose between his family and his country, what would he have chosen?'

'I don't – ' She felt wrong-footed. 'What—'

'You want to know if I trusted him? Yes, I trusted him. As a husband, as a father . . . and yes, as a friend.' Tom's eyes refused to leave hers and Letty felt the colour rise in her cheeks. 'But a man signs up to work for his country, he thinks he understands what that means. He thinks it makes him a particular kind of person. He walks into the job with an unshakeable set of principles and the belief that he has the moral backbone to maintain them in some precise and unyielding order, but in the end it never works out that way. If you were to ask me whether I trusted Nicky to put his loyalty to his country over and above his wife and children? Then no. Most people are fortunate enough not to have to make that choice. Maybe Nicky wasn't.'

'Tom, what are you saying?'

'I think Nicky stuck to his own moral code, no matter what side of the line it put him on.'

Tears were rolling down her face. 'They never found anything. There was never anything to find.'

'Letty,' he said gently.

'No, I don't want to hear it.'

He handed her his handkerchief and waited while she dabbed it over her eyes. 'Did I ever tell you why I recruited him?' he asked softly. 'First-rate mind, an apparent ability to gobble up languages notwithstanding?'

She shook her head.

'At school he was assigned as my fag the first day. By lunchtime he'd talked me out of the practice. More than once I witnessed him persuading older boys not to bully younger ones. He was utterly protective of others, with a keen sense of right and wrong. He was idealistic, fair, passionate about Britain's democratic principles, loathed the Communist regime for obvious reasons. Nicky was a born diplomat – except in one respect.'

Letty suppressed a childish urge to put her hands over her ears.

'He was a romantic, an impulsive and occasionally reckless one, and there is nothing quite as dangerous as that.' Tom's expression was unreadable, and once again she was aware of the nuance. 'It's why he didn't get Rome, Letty. He wasn't ready. He may never have been ready.'

'Oh, Tom.' Tears welled up again.

He waited till she had finished. 'When you called me last week, I did some snooping. It's not my department, as you know, but, well . . . Letty, did Nicky ever mention this proposed site on Clannach to you?'

'No.' She blew her nose. 'Never. Why, do you think he knew?'

'It's possible. He was privy to so much information. It just seems like too much of a coincidence.' Tom was watching her closely.

A little coincidental, Porter had said. *A little convenient, don't you think?*

'I had no idea until I looked at the map,' Tom went on. 'Clannach . . . the range . . . it would be right on top of you.'

'Yes.' She held his look. 'It would be.'

'What about Gebraith, the missile firing-range? Did he ever mention that?'

'No.' She looked down at her hands. Of all people, she should know better than to underestimate Tom.

'Letty,' he said quietly. 'Don't make me do this on my own.'

A sudden wave of loneliness overwhelmed her. Her world looked so much less distorted through his eyes. Maybe it was better for everything to come out. The painting, the car. It was the not knowing, the half-knowing. Secrets were corrosive and they made the living of any kind of truth impossible. 'All right,' she said, defeated. 'All right.'

Tom reached into his briefcase and handed her a thin blue leaflet.

'Naval Protection Services.' She opened the report to a sub-heading on the first page. 'Outer Hebrides. Radio Mist Distance Indicators.' She flicked through pages of tables, technical data and graphs. 'What is this?'

'It's a safety report for Gebraith.'

'Our Lady of the Isles.'

'Quite. Where religion meets radar, as I believe it's been rather wittily dubbed.'

Nicky painted things he was interested in. He liked to find out how things worked. A study of a bird's beak, a missile firing-range. A nuclear power plant.

'When you called me,' Tom continued, 'I checked on the status of Clannach and I found the department's feathers were in a state of advanced ruffle about this report.'

Letty dug a nail into the palm of her hand. If Nicky had found out about the proposed plans for Clannach, he would have been in no doubt as to how she'd feel about them.

'The blueprint for Clannach is being lifted directly off the Gebraith model, but this report claims that Gebraith's surrounding areas, i.e. the hills, dunes and beaches, have all been contaminated by something called Cobalt-60.'

'Cobalt-60?' She frowned with recognition.

'Cobalt-60, or CO-60 as it's referred to in the report, is a radioisotope used to track missiles. The report claims that significant amounts of CO-60 have been leaked onto the launch pad during the course of the last ten years.'

'And this CO-60. It's dangerous?'

'Highly toxic. If this report is correct, it could have caused a great deal of harm to the island.'

Letty stared at him, appalled. 'What sort of harm?'

'Radiological.'

'Dear God.' She covered her mouth with her hand.

'The report claims to have been commissioned following an accidental spillage that was brought to the MoD's attention two years ago.' Tom shrugged. 'Apparently, the missiles on the range were not stored safely. The magnesium in the cone head connected with sea water and that's how the original leak occurred.'

She closed her eyes. So Nicky had known and said nothing. Magnesium. Cobalt. She saw the codings on his painting. CO-60, MG-137. They weren't colours. They were chemicals.

'Schyndell. Gebraith. One nuclear power, the other nuclear weaponry. Nevertheless much ties them together. Containment, waste treatment, risk of uncontrolled radiation—'

'We *talked* about this.' She shook her head in agitation. 'Nicky and I – we *argued* about it. This is exactly what I was worried about.' Operator error. She stared unseeingly at the report in her lap. 'What about the islanders, have they been warned?'

'Letty, you're missing the point.'

'But they'll need to be—'

'Letty, *listen*, will you? If this report is true, it will have implications for the Clannach project.'

'Why do you keep saying *if* the report is true?'

'When this came in, everybody was so busy reacting to the content, they didn't initially look into where it had come from.'

'Stop being so bloody cryptic, Tom,' she said calmly, though her heart was thudding. 'Where did it come from?'

'That's just it. No one knows. This report was not commissioned by the MoD, or any other government body for that matter. Look.' He took the document from her and flicked through to the last page. 'It's not even signed with a name, just initials. BB.' He looked at her keenly. 'Letty, I believe the report is fake.'

73

God rot the little bastard. Alba clenched and unclenched her fists as she checked the blackening sky. Rain was sluicing down the glass, wind howling through the pipes of the Raeburn. She went from window to window scanning for any moving smudge that might turn into a boy. The storm should have forced Jamie's return long before now. The little deviant was obviously staying out on purpose to land her in trouble. She could get away with a cuff round the head; she could get away with any number of pinches or dead arms, in fact, all forms of torture within the normal parameters of sibling warfare, but an unprovoked slap to the face was a major breach of the Fleming Geneva Convention. If Jamie was still out sulking in a storm when her mother returned, the crime would increase ten-fold in severity. It wasn't that she cared about being punished. She had already decided on solitary confinement for the rest of her life and her mother simply wasn't imaginative enough to top that but it would be better if Jamie came back. None of them was allowed to go to the cliffs on their own. Especially Jamie, especially in this weather. She scrutinized the landscape again. He knew to be careful, but it was raining hard and it would be slippery, misty as well. And then there had been that look in his eyes, a glittering brilliance she'd never seen before.

She had hit him hard, really socked him, and she felt the curdle of shame. She'd gone too far, but hadn't it been justified? Eight years she'd been forced to deal with her brother, more than half her life co-opted into mopping up his spittle, feeding him, watering him; Christ, mucking out a pigsty would have been less trouble. And all this time he'd been hopelessly indulged, allowed to grow up in a dream world. So, now if he was chasing about the island after some childish fantasy then why the hell should she get a soaking just to bring him down to earth? Let him take responsibility for once. Let him get cold and wet and frightened. His little milk teeth could chatter till they dropped out of his gums for all she cared. She remembered the time she and Georgie had got trapped at the mouth of Loch Aivegarry on the incoming tide and been forced to swim for their lives through the channels. When they'd arrived at the house, two frozen automatons, barely able to speak, had their parents been sympathetic? Not in the slightest. They'd terrorized them with tales of drownings and autoamputation of frostbitten toes, then forced them to squat in a cold bath into which they added hot water at a sadistic trickle. 'I told you to keep an eye on the tides,' Letty kept saying furiously. 'How many times have I told you?'

So no, she would not go after Jamie. She sat down at the table but the rain continued to fall from the sky and the clock ticked. With each passing minute, the ludicrousness of Jamie's outburst drifted back and she felt a sick uneasiness. What if he did something stupid, really stupid, as in attempt to climb down the Kettle to look for the bear? Suddenly a horrifying image of his foot sliding on the wet grass passed through her head and abruptly she knocked back her chair. 'All right,' she said grudgingly. 'Bloody hell.' Swearing calmed her. The sound of her own voice calmed her. Relief at having made the decision to go gave her the latitude to hate him even more. Giving in to his manipulation was a breach of her resolve and he would be punished for it, as Georgie and her mother would also be punished, because, as usual, she was getting the sticky end of the lollipop, and it wasn't fair. Meanwhile it was mid-afternoon, her mother would be back soon and she was supposed to have laid the table and heated up the slop that passed for lentil and ham soup. On the mantelpiece she caught sight of Jamie's collection of bird skulls. She identified a crow and a curlew, alongside something larger that he'd picked off Islay Sound – a cormorant, perhaps. On a whim, she placed the skulls on three separate plates, arranging them on the table flanked by a knife and fork. She tore a strip of paper from Letty's writing pad and bent it into a placement card. 'Enjoy', she wrote, then she propped up the card in front of her mother's plate setting and slammed out of the front door.

74

The weather was closing in fast. Jamie was thankful for his coat as he stumbled across the bog, hardly bothering to aim for stepping stones. More than once he sank to his knees but he was oblivious to both the wet and the cold. His body was on fire. His heart, too big for his chest at the best of times, drummed as if a moth were trapped against his ribcage and by the time he reached the cliffs, he was close to hyperventilating. He threw himself down on the ragged side of the Kettle and attempted to untangle the strap of his binoculars from his pocket. 'Bear!' he shouted. 'Dada!'

No reply, only the pattering of rain on his anorak hood and the wind playing Chinese whispers in his ears. He squirmed closer to the edge and peered over. The bottom of the Kettle was roiling with water. Out to sea, a long wave crested white, sending spray and specks of yellowing foam into the air.

'Dada!' he yelled again. The wind stole his voice and laughed in his face. A fulmar, hugging the ledge a few feet beneath him, looked up and squawked with distaste.

'Bugger off, fulmar,' Jamie said wildly, then giggled hysterically at his nerve. He tried wiping his jumper sleeve over the convex lens of the binoculars but the wind was gathering strength and it was no longer possible to hold them steady, and besides, the Kettle was too high and narrow for him to see into the tunnel. He stuffed the glasses back into his pocket and shuffled round the perimeter on his stomach. When he reached the ridged spine that funnelled down to the bottom, he stopped and appraised the descent with what he hoped was a professional eye. Alick had been down with a rope to rescue sheep and the day his father had climbed down had been the day he'd found the cave. Forbidden, dangerous, off-limits, yet . . . possible. And then Jamie couldn't rid himself of the notion that he was *meant* to do it.

It began easily enough. The heather at the top was bunched and thick enough to take his weight but as he progressed down the clumps grew sparser. After thirteen or fourteen feet, the spine narrowed and steepened and Jamie spread-eagled himself across its width, hugging the sides of the drop with both arms and digging his fingers into the soil. He was wet through and the sharpness of the rock pressed into his chest. He didn't feel quite as confident as before but scrambling back up seemed like an impossible feat and surely it was easier to cooperate with gravity than defy it? He took a deep breath, searched for courage and continued down, itsy bitsy spider, synchronizing his arms and legs, descending inch by precarious inch, but after another few minutes he discovered his left foot waving ineffectively in space and he was compelled to press his head into the mossy slope to stop himself falling.

'Dada!' he yelled, but when all he tasted was earth, the dread realization hit him. He was stuck.

The shriek of the fulmar came a fraction of a second before its wings brushed against the back of Jamie's head. Instinctively, he took a swipe at it and his body came away from the cliff like a winkle kicked off a rock. Down he plummeted, another fifteen feet. There was an intense pain in an indefinable part of his body, and at the same time his head jerked backwards and smashed against something solid.

And then everything went dark.

75

 Georgie stole a sideways look at Aliz. He was working the pedals with his boots undone and the laces dangled from the eyelets like spaghetti. When he turned and grinned at her, a loose electrical charge ran through her body. Love, sex, passion, longing, these things had always seemed inaccessible, adult emotions, and certainly the preserve of somebody less self-conscious, less graceless than her, but under Aliz's hesitant touch, every awkward curve and angle of her body made sense for the first time. She had placed his hand on her stomach and he had groaned. She could still feel the imprint of his fingers pressing against the arc of her ribs, his thumb hooking her white cotton pants over the small mound of her hip bone. There was heat between her legs and a graze where sand had rubbed between their lips. She touched it with her tongue as the mobile van clattered over the watery potholes of the road. She wondered about running away from home. Packing a bag, leaving a note. She thought of the huge backlog of things she had been storing up to tell someone and she thought of all the time she could take to say them. Suddenly every scrappy thing she knew, every tug of emotion she'd suppressed, every tiny bead of information in her abacus of knowledge felt relevant to her future and for the first time in a long time, the world glowed with possibility.

Out of the window, a flock of geese took wing. Georgie watched them assemble into a V formation, their long necks stretched out, their feathers glinting white under the thin seam of light in the dark sky.

Aliz stopped the mobile van at the yellow gate. When he blinked, his eyelashes closed down on his cheek like velvet claws. He took her hand and pressed the tips of her fingers one by one.

'Can you meet me tomorrow?'

Georgie nodded. She would meet him every tomorrow, she thought, and wondered whether she was already pregnant.

Happiness suffused her. She wafted into the house, floated through the kitchen door, his name whispering in her head, Aliz, Aliz, Aliz. Every time she said it, a tiny pair of bellows blew at her heart, making it glow red, making it spark and when she heard a voice telling her that she looked chilled to the marrow, that her clothes and hair were soaked from the rain, she assumed her mother must be talking to someone else. How could she be referring to a person whose heart and soul were on *fire*, but then she heard a strangely familiar voice and she plummeted down to earth with a jolt.

Tom Gordunson rose slowly from the kitchen table. 'So how's my favourite goddaughter?' He kissed her on the cheek and sized her up with a rueful laugh. 'Look at you, good God, you look radiant . . . and, well . . . a little damp.'

'When did you . . . ? Why are you . . . ?' Georgie looked from Tom to her mother. 'I don't understand.'

'It was all somewhat last-minute,' Tom apologized.

'I wanted to surprise you all, darling,' Letty said. 'It's been such a long time since we saw Tom and—'

'Has something happened?' Georgie interrupted.

'Come and sit with us.' Nervously, Letty pushed out a chair.

'Yes, and I want to hear all your news,' Tom added.

'No.' Georgie stayed standing, thoroughly spooked. She had finally shouted her secret to the sea and her words had summoned up Tom Gordunson like the ghost of miseries past. 'What's going on? Why are you here?' She glanced at the canvas lying between them. 'What is that? What are you doing with Dada's painting?'

Letty looked at the floor.

'Georgie, I want to talk to you about your father,' Tom said.

'No.'

'About Berlin.'

'I don't want to.'

'Georgie, believe me, it's all right.'

'No!' *Aliz, Aliz, Aliz*, she chanted in her head.

Letty looked upset. 'Tom, please,' she begged in a low voice. 'If she doesn't want—'

'Something happened there, didn't it?' Tom said urgently. 'Something happened in East Berlin?'

'No,' Georgie said again. She covered her face with her hands but she could remember the raw fear on her father's face as the Grenzer pulled them over. The jump and ring of the telephone in the interrogation room. She could smell the lignite in the air. She saw the albino sausages stagnating on her plate.

Georgie, my George, her father's voice had been teasing, but his face had been hard and set, even in the restaurant. *You really don't have to eat the damn things.* He'd signalled to the waiter. *Now, unless you want the pleasure of boiled tablecloth for pudding, let's go and fetch the car.*

There was always the before and after, Georgie thought; something monumental happens and life divides sharply. What little peace of mind her mother had left, she was about to blow apart.

'There is a time', Tom coaxed, 'when all secrets have to come out.'

'Mum?' she pleaded.

Letty touched the tips of her fingers to Georgie's hand. Her eyes were suddenly brilliant and clear.

'Whatever it is, Georgie, tell us.'

She began haltingly. Berlin was a long story hinging on a single moment. A short sentence and a swift handover. Tom asked a few questions, but listened attentively, drawing on a cigarette, his eyes never leaving her face. Once again Georgie was struck by the incongruity of his looks, the heavy eyebrows and shaggy head. His manner, his voice, were unfailingly gentle and measured, yet there was something almost animal-like about him, something sharp and dangerous beneath the undisciplined exterior, and now he leant forward as though sensing the moment had come.

The exchange had happened inside the church. After the car had been towed to the garage and their laborious paperwork had been signed, she and her father, Georgie told them, had walked through the empty streets, hand in hand.

She had stood at her great-grandfather's headstone and shivered with some vague sense of apprehension. She thought about Gisela, her leg scabbed and tender from the phosphorus, she thought about her battling the treacherous currents of the river as her mother and sister drowned in her wake.

Her father wanted to make an offering or light a candle, she couldn't remember which excuse he'd used. 'Stay here,' he ordered. 'I'll be back in less than a minute.' And she nodded, too cold to move and overcome with a powerful longing for home. Berlin was the saddest place she'd ever been. There was no spirit there, no hope or humanity. The city was in the thrall of a depression that had permeated even the hollow spaces inside her bones. How she envied Alba. Not singled out for a special trip with her father, going about her normal day, oblivious to a world more complicated than school and homework and fish-finger suppers. A minute passed and then five. The afternoon was closing in. She began picking her way through the dilapidated headstones towards the church. She wandered through the big doors and up towards the altar. When she reached the pulpit, she turned and headed down one of the side aisles but there was no sign of him and only the echo of her footsteps on the stone flags of the floor. Back at the heavy entrance doors, she exited, but he was not waiting for her outside. 'Dada?' she called a

little uncertainly. She came back in and started purposefully up the other side of the church, peering through
arches and around balusters. She'd spotted the shadow
of his overcoat before she'd actually seen him. He was
behind a pillar, speaking with someone in a low voice, but
she'd been so relieved to find him that she'd filed away the
conversation, just as she'd filed away every hateful detail
about Berlin. It hadn't been until Norrell and Porter had
posed the question of an illicit meeting that the scene
had returned to her with all its damning implications.

'Instructions, map,' she heard her father emphasize as
she crept closer. 'Take it,' he'd urged. Then again, stronger,
'My friend, time is running out.' Two more steps and she
could see him clearly. He was holding out an envelope,
thrusting it insistently towards someone still hidden from
Georgie's view. Suddenly, there was a fumble, the ring of
something metal dropping onto the stone and her father
had started. 'Dad!' she called in a whisper, and only now
as she moved closer did she catch sight of the second man
behind the pillar, stooped, then rising quickly from the
floor, the envelope already slipped into a pocket and whatever object her father had dropped enclosed by his hand.
'Dad!' she said again, but this time as the stranger reacted
to her voice and turned to look in her direction, there had
been no hiding the guilt on his face.

Neither Tom nor her mother spoke for a long moment,
then Tom reached for the papers on top of the canvas and
handed them to her. 'Is it possible that this is the man you
saw?'

Georgie frowned at the passport photograph. A
stranger, his features flattened by over-exposure, his eyes

Bella Pollen

dead-fish blank. 'Maybe,' she said, 'but I only saw him for a second . . . Eugen Friedrich Schmidt.' She read the name printed on the ID document. There were small tugs of memory attached to the name, but they dissipated before she could get hold of them. 'Who is he?' she looked up at Tom, but he shook his head.

'I don't know. I was hoping you might. His picture and papers were hidden in your father's painting.'

'Eugen Friedrich Schmidt,' she repeated. She picked up the canvas and ran her hand over the thick paint. 'Why in Dada's painting?'

Tom looked at Letty.

'Tell her,' Letty said.

76

It was quiet in Jamie's head. He was floating down the Rhine and the water felt as warm and protective as amniotic fluid. In the distance, the swells of the Siebengebirge were carpeted with the soft green of spring. He crossed his arms on his chest. He heard the cry of a seagull, the impatient horn of the barge, but after a while, nothing, just the persistent lapping of water around the edges of his consciousness. The silence spooked him. It was *too* quiet in his head. Something was missing and he decided it was the noise of the wind. *Aye, the wind has moderated*, a voice informed him. *The wind has dropped.*

'The wind has moderated,' Jamie whispered.

'Jamie!'

And now his name was being called.

'JAMIE!'

His eyes flew open. He was annoyed to find that the wind hadn't moderated at all. He could feel it, stinging and raw against his face.

'Jamie,' the voice ordered. 'Don't move.'

Alba.

He stiffened and his knee exploded with pain. Nausea rolled through him. He turned his head to one side and to his terror, saw that he was lying on a ledge barely wide enough for his body. A thin boy's body. Above him the sky was set hard as concrete. All around, black rocks were speckled with the white of nesting fulmars. He remembered the brush of wings against his head. He remembered letting go.

'JAMIE!' Alba's shout echoed around the walls of the Kettle. 'Can you hear me? Are you hurt?' Her voice sounded tinny and far away.

Threads of mist floated through the air like mystical spore. Overhead a fulmar cawed a warning. Time slowed while Jamie focused on this important question. Was he hurt? And if so, how badly? Certainly, his skull felt heavy. He pressed his hands into his chest. If before his heart had been thumping in overdrive, now it could hardly summon the energy to beat at all. Above his head, two fulmars circled in a holding pattern.

'Alba,' he wailed.

'Stay still! Don't move.'

Jamie felt confused. Profoundly disorientated. It was as if someone had turned reality inside out as an unkind joke. His heart had stopped beating and the rain felt hot against his face. None of this was right. He lifted his head to protest.

'Don't look down!'

He looked down. Sixty feet below him, the bottom yawned. Above him the clifftop swayed. Rain was free-falling from the sky. It slicked down the rocks, pooling in the crevices of his ledge, seeping between every stitch of his clothing. One of the fulmars swooped. The hostile yellow beak was coming straight for his eyes. Jamie whimpered and turned his face to the cliff wall. 'Dear Lord,' he intoned numbly, 'help me in these troublous times.' He groped at the ledge but it crumbled under his fingers and now he began to cry in earnest.

Forty feet above him, Alba stood, immobilized by panic. Jamie's sobbing sounded like the bleating of a lost sheep. Monotone, unstoppable, hopeless. She could barely see him through the mist. She needed to get help, but how could she leave him? Christ, if she could only trust him to stay still.

But Jamie could not stay still. He needed to move his leg away from the grinding ache of his pain. Another sliver of rock crumbled and fell. And now Jamie's body, his thin boy's body was wider than the ledge supporting it.

'Alba, help me!' he screamed.

There was a reciprocal yell but the desperation in it frightened him more than anything and this fear caused a seismic shift in his mind. His powers of logic began to shutter down and a feral, more animal thinking took hold. Instinct told him it was only a matter of time before the ledge gave way. Instinct told him he was going to die. Blood was roaring in his ears. He searched for breath as a black film slowly began to wash the colour from his vision. He was so tired of hoping, of not knowing. It was easier to accept – and accepting was easier than he had ever imagined. He looked down again, this time with something approaching resignation, and suddenly there he was. Oh dear God, there he was, waiting at the bottom. Jamie's vision cleared. A slow smile broke across his face.

'Hello, bear,' he whispered.

'Hello, Jamie,' the bear replied. And at the sound of his father's voice, Jamie felt all the fear and tension, all the misery, doubt, confusion and longing, bleed slowly from his body.

77

Georgie touched her hand to the scratched paintwork of the Peugeot's boot and felt a corresponding prickle on the back of her neck. She was scarcely aware of Tom waiting next to her, shoulders hunched, his hands thrust deep into his pockets. It was raining but she felt so disconnected from the present that she was oblivious both to the cold and the bitter wind augmenting it. Overhead the clouds were darkening, suddenly it was nightfall and they were driving away from East Germany, the atmosphere in the car thick with unease. In Berlin it had felt as though every eye in the city was turned to them and still she hadn't been able to shake the feeling they were being watched. Well, they *were* being watched. *I should never have brought you*, her father had said. And suddenly she gave a short laugh.

'Georgie?' Tom stepped forward and laid a hand on her shoulder.

She shook her head, unable to articulate her feelings, even to herself. Her skin was damp with sweat, as though she'd been in the grip of a prolonged fever which had only just broken, and strangely, she felt better.

It had been complicated and confusing to piece together but as Tom had worked through his theory, changing details, bending time lines, a story emerged that Georgie began to recognize as one that suited her father. It was the kind of story he would have liked. A fake report, an attempted defection, the very cloak-and-dagger, finger-to-lips drama of it all. And had it not been for the ending, it was precisely the kind of story he might himself have told his children. She laughed again, except this time she couldn't quite control her voice and hot tears rolled down her face.

'Come on.' Tom wrapped his coat around her shoulders and Georgie let herself be guided back into the house.

'I believe your father found out that the MoD had plans to build a missile firing-range on Clannach and I think he wanted to stop it,' Tom had said earlier, and Georgie thought she could almost see his brain slotting it together, a mental crossword puzzle with cryptic clues. 'As you know, he was already shuttling backwards and forwards to East Germany as part of the Schyndell clean-up, and I suspect he came into contact with someone at Schyndell who he thought could help him, someone who had a compelling reason to help him.'

Eugen Friedrich Schmidt. The name flitted through her head again and suddenly she found herself transported out of the kitchen and back to the big white chaise longue with her father's arm around her. *What about you, my George?* he'd said. *What has caught your attention today?*

Berlin, she said, without hesitation. *Berlin has caught*

my attention. And her brain unlocked. Her memory of the visit, the smallest needling details, the very smell of it opened up to her as chemically preserved and meticulously recorded as any Stasi cloth or file.

'Poor old Bertolt Brecht,' she said slowly.

Tom looked at her quizzically.

'Bertolt Brecht was going to be made to scrub toilets for the rest of his life. It was the nickname Dada and Torsten gave one of the environmental scientists at the plant. Torsten said the Schyndell investigation had turned into a witch-hunt and that this trip was probably the last time they'd see him.' Georgie reached for the passport photo and ID documents. 'Yes.' She stabbed her finger at the printed name. 'Don't you see? Eugen Friedrich Schmidt!'

'I'm afraid I'm not with you, Georgie,' Tom said.

'Bertolt Brecht's real name, the playwright's full name was Eugen Bertolt Friedrich Brecht.'

'Georgie!' Letty exclaimed.

'BB.' Tom nodded. For a while he sat smoking silently, then he cleared his throat and leant forward. 'Letty, if this Schmidt fellow was being blamed for the accident he'd have been desperate to get out. The trouble is, unless he was important or senior enough, well . . . we, i.e. the British government, wouldn't have helped him and his situation would have been impossible. Nicky must have been a godsend for him, his defection facilitated in return for providing credible scientific and environmental data of a toxic spill on Gebraith . . .'

'So Dada hid him in the car,' Georgie said. Her mind clattered over the potholes of the road. Her father, stopping the Peugeot, retching out his fear into the grass verge.

'Schyndell had already dragged on for so long. I imagine your father thought he had more time,' Tom said, his eyes trained on Letty. 'I'm sure he never intended the trip with Georgie to be anything but a dry run, but then Torsten tells him that Schmidt is about to disappear and, realizing it's now or never, he decides to take action.'

Letty said nothing.

Tom looked at her shrewdly. 'My guess is it started out as a business arrangement, but then Nicky got to know this man, liked him. The idea that he would be persecuted, turned into a scapegoat, would have been unconscionable to him.'

'I still don't understand how he could even contemplate doing something so risky,' Letty said tightly.

'It was less risky than it sounds,' Tom said slowly. 'As part of the delegation, Nicky would have had a degree of diplomatic immunity. Allied personnel are not supposed to be stopped in any zone, but that doesn't mean to say they aren't, from time to time. Nicky was working with no official cover. He understood the thinking of the East German government better than anyone. As far as they were concerned he was an interesting fish. He knew how closely they watched him on these trips, so he had to come up with some kind of insurance – an extra safety measure of sorts. He drives to Berlin in his conspicuous western model, which, with the aid of Alick's distributor switch, he breaks down in full view of his Stasi tails, knowing it would be towed to a garage, and knowing perfectly well that once it was, the Stasi would lose no time in bugging it. He hands over a key to Schmidt in the church – Georgie heard something metal drop – along with a map of the garage and instructs the scientist to get himself into the car that night. "It's your only chance," your father told him.' Tom turned to Georgie and she nodded. 'By the time the Peugeot is delivered back to the hotel the next morning, once again in full view of Stasi watchers, Schmidt is safely installed in the secret compartment.'

'But if the Stasi were bugging the car, then wouldn't they have heard him getting in?' It was surreal, Georgie thought, to be talking about her father as though he were the protagonist of a film they had all been to see but not quite understood.

'A Stasi listening device would most likely be fitted behind the dashboard or heater grill and powered by the battery. It would only be activated by the car being started. The point is, having bugged the car, the Stasi would never suspect that it would then become the means of exfiltration. As a rather ingenious example of hiding in plain sight, it was probably the *least* risky way to cross the border.'

'Except that we *were* stopped at the checkpoint.'

'And quickly released after a phone call. The last thing the Stasi would want would be some oafish Grenzer dislodging their handiwork, but it must have been a terrible moment for your father.'

Georgie bowed her head. *Forgive me, my little George, please forgive me*, he'd said.

'Letty.' Tom took her hand. She had not spoken for some time. 'It's entirely supposition. It might never have happened.'

'Except for the compartment in the car. Except for the report.'

'The report, yes.' He sighed. 'For poor old Bertolt Brecht it was the perfect quid pro quo, but for Nicky . . .'

'He hated bullies,' Georgie said suddenly. 'He always backed the underdogs.'

'Yes.' Tom smiled faintly. 'Commendably British in that respect but still, I cannot over-exaggerate the phobia our people have about dealing with anyone from the GDR. I still don't understand, why take *any* risk? There are plenty of silent protestors, some in our own government even, who are virulently against the building of further military sites. Nicky could have convinced one of them to write it.'

'No,' Letty said quietly. 'He would never have done that. That he would have considered a betrayal of his principles, a betrayal of his country. Nicky was no pacifist. He was motivated by personal not political gain.'

'But if the report is fake,' Georgie said, 'then why does it matter? Why does anyone care?'

'The MoD have a number of scientists contracted to them. When the report came in, they had these scientists look at the written characterization of the sand, soil and sediment samples. In other words, their particle size, pH, water-holding capacity, all technical details like that – and all of these were exactly as one might predict for the region.'

'Meaning what?'

'Meaning that the samples tested did indeed come from the Gebraith site. Moreover, and here is where it gets interesting – I think I mentioned this before, Letty – an earlier MoD document shows a reported incident of incorrect storage of the missiles, which apparently resulted in a leak of some sort. The vulnerability of the Gebraith site is clearly an issue the MoD have known about for some time and failed to act on.'

'Why?'

'Because it wouldn't have suited their agenda for expansion.'

'So the land, the beaches . . . are they contaminated?'

'That's the MoD's dilemma. They'd chosen not to investigate it before, but this report changes everything. They might not know by whose authority it was commissioned, but if so much of the *data* that it's based on is genuine, then there is a very real possibility that the results could also be genuine. In other words, yes, the Gebraith site *could very well be* contaminated. Faced with this possibility, the MoD would have no option but to commission their own safety report to check for certain. At least, my strong guess is that this is what Nicky was banking on. He knew the MoD had already suppressed information about the leak. He knew, therefore, that any kind of civil protest would be pointless. Forcing the MoD's hand was his best, if not only, option. If there were proven instances of toxic spillage in Gebraith, then, surely, not even the government would risk it happening again at Clannach.'

'So did it work?' Letty asked eagerly. 'Have they commissioned a report?'

Tom flicked his lighter on and off then laid it carefully back down on the table.

'Tom?'

'It seems that once again, Nicky set too much store by the principles of our government,' he replied grimly. 'I'm afraid the MoD intend to suppress it.'

78

She had surely not heard him correctly. The words floated up, barely audible, jumbled and rewritten by the wind. 'It's okay,' he had shouted. 'He's here now. Dada's here.'

Alba forced herself to breathe, to respond calmly. 'Jamie, listen to me. I'm going to get help. I need to find Alick and bring a rope.'

'Alba, I'm going to jump.'

'Jamie, no!' she shrieked.

'Dada will catch me.'

'Jamie, please. No!' She was sobbing now, running this way and that, trying for a better sight of him but there was only the thinnest scrap of his anorak wedged between the dark rocks. Holy God, what was he thinking? She looked down. Through the dense mist, she could just make out a near-solid brown mass at the bottom of the ravine, yes . . . moving, gently swaying on top of the water.

'Oh, Jamie,' her voice rose, then broke with understanding. 'No, it's just seaweed. It's *seaweed*.'

'It's okay, Alba. The bear will catch me. Dada will catch me.' Jamie no longer felt the rain or the cold or the ache in his knee. A delicious warmth had enveloped him. He was dimly aware of the fade of Alba's voice, pleading, yelling, but it was no longer the voice he was listening to.

Jump, his father said. *Jump and I'll catch you.*

Jamie peered down. The sides of the cliff began moving in on him.

Let go and I'll catch you. I promise.

'I'm scared, Dada.'

Don't be scared, Jamie. Trust me and let go.

Jamie hesitated, then he rolled away from the cliff wall and dropped into the emptiness. From somewhere high above him came a scream, but he felt no fear. He felt nothing in his slow, gentle spiral down, only a powerful and serene peace.

79

Letty stood silent, her forehead pressed to the glass of her bedroom window.

This island is where I belong, she'd told Nicky. *It's where I feel the possibility of hope and faith, and every morning when I look out of the window, I fall in love with it all over again.*

She remembered that day at Gebraith so well. She'd been so angry with him. Three-year-old Alba had been sticky with chocolate. 'Piggy back,' she'd demanded, and Nicky had wordlessly hoisted his daughter onto his back and started down the hill.

Had this been the moment, all those years ago, when the crank of fate began its slow turn?

'You seem to have an innate distrust of your own country,' Nicky had accused her.

'And you don't?' she'd retorted. 'With everything you know about their methods.'

'I couldn't very well do my job if I did,' he'd replied. Nicky, solid, truthful, passionate about his country's democratic values.

He had put his faith in the government and, when it

failed to live up to its promise, those first lethal curies of disillusion had been released. If the MoD had taken seriously the report on Gebraith's safety, had they taken action to put it right, Nicky would have considered that fair play and that would have been the end of it.

She knew now why Nicky hadn't told her. He would never have shattered her peace of mind without first finding a way to put things right. Finding a way out.

Tom couldn't have been more wrong. Nicky was exactly the man she thought he was.

'Mum.'

Georgie was standing in the doorway.

As mother turned to daughter, her face softened and it seemed to Georgie as though the steel pins that had shored up her spirit for so long had finally been removed. She looked tired, older perhaps, but she no longer looked broken.

Letty held out her arms and Georgie went to her. 'I've been such a fool,' Letty said.

'I'm so sorry,' Georgie mumbled into her shoulder. 'If I hadn't lied to those men. If I'd told you earlier . . .'

'No.' Letty released her. 'You did the right thing and now . . . well, it makes sense of so much. It explains so much.' After a moment's hesitation, she gave Georgie the piece of paper she was holding. 'I want you to read this.'

'What is it?' Its surface was soft and creased into a hundred tiny triangles from repeated folding.

'It's from your father.'

Georgie held herself very still. 'Dada left a letter?'

Letty didn't flinch under her daughter's hostile gaze. 'Yes.'

'When did you get this?'

'They found it just after he died.'

'And you didn't tell me?' Georgie's voice rose. 'Why didn't you tell me?'

'Georgie,' Letty said quietly. 'You know why.'

Georgie sank down on the bed. *My darling love . . .* quickly she scanned through the lines . . . *protect you and the children . . . the only way out . . .* She looked up wildly.

'So he did abandon us.' Her voice broke. 'He did jump.'

'No!' Letty took the crumpled paper from Georgie's hands.

'Then how—'

'Georgie, look at this. It's not what you think. It's not even a letter, it's a collection of thoughts. They found it on his desk. Do you know what I think this is? *All* I think this is? A practice run for a conversation he dreaded having, nothing more. Trust me, if your father wanted to leave a suicide note, he would leave one – in an envelope, and properly addressed. He would never have left us like . . . well, like this. I know Dada, he would never do that.'

'But he'd smuggle someone out of East Berlin in the boot of our car?' Georgie said cruelly. 'Did you know he could do that?'

Letty sat down beside Georgie. 'I think he felt desperately guilty about the danger he put you in, his *moment of madness*, and for whatever reason, perhaps he was besieged by so many worries, perhaps because I didn't make it easy for him, he couldn't find a way of telling me about Gebraith.'

'But then how did he—'

'Georgie, I don't know what happened on that roof. I doubt we'll ever know, but I have to believe, I *do* believe your father's death was an accident.'

Georgie sat silent for a minute. 'Do you think what he did was so very bad?'

'I think it's as he said – he was trying to protect us,' Letty said simply. 'Protect a place I love.'

She stood up and moved to the window. Outside, clouds had merged to form a solid bank of grey. The wind had dropped and an eerie stillness had descended over the island.

'You have to tell the others,' Georgie said eventually. 'Jamie will work it out eventually and Alba will work it out sooner.'

Letty nodded. She couldn't have got it more wrong, she knew that now. An imagined truth was always more frightening than the actual truth and she should have understood that long ago. She stared at the sky, her attention caught by a low humming noise. All of a sudden, an orange naval helicopter appeared from the east, flying low over the machair. She frowned. 'Where are the others, anyway?'

80

She had as good as killed him. Hunted him down and driven him off the cliff like a wild pig. She sank to her knees and rocked backwards and forwards, a low keening noise coming out of her. Hoarsely she kept calling out his name, until finally, recklessly, she grabbed at a bunch of heather growing around the top of the cliff's spine and lowered herself over the edge. She no longer cared if she lived or died but she had to get to him before the water took him. The rock was slick, the moss covering it spongy with water. She managed the first twenty feet in seconds, and when the descent steepened, spread her arms wide as Jamie had done and slid on her front, holding her face as far away from the cliff as possible. Almost immediately the corner of a ledge caught between her ribs and she had to fight for breath. As her speed increased her arms felt as if they might snap out of their sockets. Something ripped across her cheek but even had she wanted to, there was no way of stopping. It was over fast. Her legs hit the ground, jarring her spine. She stumbled and turned, only to be caught full in the face by an incoming wave.

Choking, she rubbed desperately at her eyes, then blinked in disbelief.

Jamie was not there.

She shouted. A couple of nesting fulmars ruffled their wings back at her. She yelled his name again. It was impossible. She could feel the undertow sucking at her calves, but the water was surely not deep enough to have taken him back out to sea. She tried to grasp the enormity of what had happened. He must be there, he must. Floundering in the storm, a greater black-backed gull flew drunkenly towards her, veering away at the last minute with a screech. Another wave made her legs buckle. She struggled towards the tunnel and braced herself against the arch, scanning the water repeatedly, but as her eyes slowly adjusted to the light, realization came to her that the shadows and contours of the opposite wall possessed an oddly three-dimensional quality, a gradation of black in the rock. She rubbed viciously at her stinging eyes but yes, it was still there and all of a sudden she remembered. Her father's cave. She pushed away from the wall and splashed wildly across the channel.

He was lying inside, on the floor. When she saw him she forgot she had killed him. She forgot he had dropped sixty feet. He was curled in a foetal position and the way his legs were hiked up, the way his arm was thrown over his face made the air snag in her throat. How many times in this last year had her mind veered away from this image? How many nights had her dreams transported her to the wasteland beneath the embassy? And not once had she found the courage to walk around the body of her father. To look at his face; to face his death. 'Jamie,' she whispered. She fell to her knees. What if his head was crushed? What if he was disfigured? She forced herself to touch him, to lay a hand on his arm but his eyes were closed and his skin clammy.

'Jamie,' she pleaded. 'For God's sake.'

A tremor shook him. His eyes jerked under their lids. 'Why do you hate me?' he mumbled, but his eyes remained closed.

Alba pushed back her tears. The air in the cave was arctic and he had to be badly hurt. People died of hypothermia, they died of shock or internal injuries. People died so bloody easily. 'I don't hate you.' Quickly she stripped off her anorak and spread it on top of him. She could keep him warm. He wasn't dead and she could keep him warm. At least she could do that.

'Yes, you do.'

'I hate everyone.' She said it automatically, but her mind was clicking. Behind them water was surging along the channel, but aside from the immediate entrance, the cave was dry and another good foot above sea level, though how much higher the tide would rise was anybody's guess. She had to move him.

'But you hate me the most.' Jamie blinked out into the dimness.

'Jamie, how are you even talking?' she whispered. 'How are you not dead?'

'I told you it would be okay.' He touched his chest. 'A fulmar was sick on me and then I was sick too.'

'Well, you smell like a donkey's bottom. Can you move your fingers and toes? Can you walk?'

'Will you still hate me when I'm older and not so annoying?'

Alba shook her head impatiently. 'How did you get in here if you can't walk?'

'Dada carried me.'

'Jamie,' she beseeched.

'Dada carried me in his mouth.'

'Jamie, please.' Her voice cracked. 'Stop staying that.'

'But it's true,' Jamie insisted. He had felt the jaws of the bear like a father's kiss on the back of his neck.

'I told you not to move. I told you I'd get help.' She knelt on her hands to stop her wringing them. 'Oh God, why did you have to jump?'

'Dada told me to.'

'Why, for God's sake? Why would Dada tell you to jump?'

'Because he knew he'd catch me.'

'I thought the bear caught you?'

'Yes, Alba,' Jamie said with infinite patience. 'I told you already.' He closed his eyes. He had put his arms around the bear's neck and held him close. He had felt the warmth of his father's body. He had felt the beat of his father's heart restart his own.

Alba took a deep breath. 'Jamie, there's no bear here.'

'He went back to get help. He ran away from the wrestler and now he's gone back to fetch him.'

Alba suddenly noticed a milky wash of blood seeping from under Jamie's head. 'Did you hit your head?' she asked, deliberately casual.

'A bit.'

Alba moved her fingers around the back of his skull until they connected with a pulpy area – two seams of ragged flesh. Blood was welling over her fingers in slow rhythmic pulses. She felt dizzy with fear. Was it blood or spinal fluid? Either way he needed help, he needed a doctor. She thought back to the bird skulls she'd left on the table. Her mother was used to her children's feral, subsistent lives. Why would she even notice they were missing?

'Is my brainbox leaking?' Jamie asked.

'Your what?' Alba forced herself to concentrate. What were the basic rules of first aid? *Keep them calm, keep them warm, keep them alive.*

'My brainbox. It's where I keep all my information and words and intelligence and I don't want any of them to leak out.'

'God forbid.' Alba wrenched off her boot and dragged down her damp sock.

'What are you doing?'

'Jamie, why do you think the bear is Dada?'

'He just is, Alba.'

'Keep still.'

'I know why you don't believe me.'

'Why?'

'Because you don't believe in anything. You don't believe in the bear, you don't believe in God or Father Christmas and you don't believe in Dada.'

Alba bit her lip and held the balled-up sock to the wound in his head. A spray of dirty foam blew in off the thundering channel and drifted across the threshold of the cave. The water was rising.

'Jamie, you understand that Dada is dead, don't you?'

Jamie turned his head carefully towards her. In the dark, his bright falcon's eyes gleamed. 'You worked that out too?'

'I didn't need to work it out.' She looked at him strangely. 'Jamie, Dada died. He fell off the roof of the embassy and the fall killed him.'

'No,' Jamie said.

'It was an accident. It was the day of the circus. Mum told you, don't you remember?'

'No! Mummy never said anything like that, Alba, never.'

'Well, that's what happened.'

'That's not what Mummy told me,' he said stubbornly. 'She said Dada had an accident and then after that he got lost. Everyone said he was lost. No one said he was dead. I only worked it out because he never came back.'

'Jamie, if you had jumped off that cliff and died, do you know what people would say? They'd all talk in soft voices to Mum and say, "I'm sorry you lost your son." Nobody ever says the word dead. No one ever says it because . . . because it's just too awful.'

Jamie pushed her hand away. 'How could he fall? He's a grown-up. Why does everyone lie to me? Why?'

Alba opened her mouth to reply then remembered her mother's silent weeping. She tried to imagine reading her father's suicide note out loud to Jamie like some dreadful bedtime story and she understood then she couldn't cross that line. Her father was a coward, Alba thought bitterly, to leave them like this, but especially he was a coward for leaving Jamie and she didn't know whether she could forgive him.

'He was watching the circus being built from the roof,' Jamie went on. 'Every day, he told me.'

'Jamie, he could have tripped or felt dizzy, people have stupid accidents all the time.'

'Well, it doesn't matter anyway, Alba, because he's here now. He promised to come back and he did. This is his cave. This is where he's been waiting for me. These are all his things.' There was an almost fanatical timbre to Jamie's voice, Alba thought as she looked distractedly around her. Collected against the walls of the cave were tangled lengths of seaweed and a few scattered bottles. In the corner, she could just make out the outline of an old mine, salted and pockmarked with rust.

'He's coming back for us, Alba.' Jamie's eyes were closing. 'He promised me.'

Of course I promise, the bear had said. *Don't I always come back?*

'Jamie,' she whispered. 'Don't go to sleep.' His lips were colourless. Small flecks of saliva had dried in the corners of his mouth.

'He promised, Alba. You believe me, don't you?'

She hesitated. 'Okay, yes, Jamie, I believe you.'

Jamie stretched out his arm and touched the tips of his fingers to hers.

Alba looked down at the small white hand, so close, so hopeful. After a moment she took it in her own and squeezed.

She'd been staring into the darkness a long time before

she noticed it – a pinprick of light, far back in the cave. Carefully she extricated her hand from Jamie's and felt her way along the wall. The floor was on a steep incline and as she moved deeper into the cave, the light mysteriously disappeared. The air smelt oily, earthy. The ceiling began closing in on her. She crawled on, eventually banging her head sharply as she came to a dead end. Disorientated, she tried to turn. There was the light again, now coming from a tiny hole, right above her head. She worked at enlarging it with her finger until she could get a fist through. Encouraged, she scrabbled at it with her hands, but her nails scraped against rock. She sank to her haunches, hope unspooling.

'Alba!' came the plaintive cry. 'Alba, where are you?'

'I'm here, it's okay.' In the murky light she could just make out the blue of her anorak covering Jamie and she frowned at an idea half-forming.

'Jamie, it's okay. I know what to do.' She fetched a piece of seaweed, stripping off the ribbons until she was left with a bare, three-foot-long stick. Easing her anorak off Jamie, she wrapped it tightly along the whole length, winding the hood strings diagonally back over the brightly coloured nylon until the thing resembled a makeshift umbrella. She crawled back to the end of the cave and pushed the stick through the hole. Initially it resisted, the seaweed bending wilfully, but she forced it upwards, loosening the hood strings and poking them through after it. The wind took it immediately. She hunched her knees and gripped the stick with both hands, holding it steady, keeping it upright as it jerked and quivered. After a while the ache in her arms consumed her. She squeezed her eyes shut against the pain and so she could not have known that Jamie kept forcing his eyes open, checking she was still there. Checking that she hadn't left him.

81

He ran. There was little strength in him, but he ran anyway. Behind him was a confusion of shouts, the rumble of Land Rovers and tractors, the thump and drone of a helicopter. For the second time that day he ran towards the cliffs. The first time he'd left the wrestler behind. Now he would guide him to the cave. The wind was sweeping the last of the storm away in quick, efficient gusts. A clean light washed over the sky. Beneath his feet, the ground was spongy and heavy-going. His legs were weakening but he was so nearly at the loch. It lay ahead of him, shining like a silver spill of mercury. From there it was a straight line to the sea and if the end came after that, well, no matter. Life, death – neither ever worked out the way people imagined. Who can predict how the fate of one person will interlock with the destiny of another, and as he struggled on a phrase came to him out of the blue. *Everything and every event is pervaded by the Grace of God.* Yes, he thought. Yes . . .

To have watched the boy jump; to have been able to count on that sweet trust one last time. The moment he'd felt that small heart beating against his, it had made sense to him, the hunger, the nostalgia, the unbearable yearning to be who he once was. At last the memories began to fall out of him, each more poignant than the last; the way Jamie rubbed his bare feet together for comfort; the way his eyes turned owl-round when he listened to stories; the way he gnawed the skin off an apple and let the exposed fruit turn to soft pulp in his hand. How he wished these had come to him sooner, but now he had them they would belong to him for eternity. And still he ran. He was right at the loch when it caught his eye – the bright daub of blue, fluttering in the colourless aftermath of the storm. He knew instantly what it was. Alba's anorak, bloated with wind. It was the children's signal, their SOS, and it should have been the flag of his own finishing line. In the background motors were idling. Above him the helicopter hovered like an angry wasp and to his dismay he realized that exhaustion had beaten him. His body had failed and he was no longer moving. He felt the sting of a dart and the world began to slow. 'No,' he tried to shout, 'not yet,' but the only sound to come out of his mouth was a croak, a hoarse animal growl, and he knew his time was running out. He pushed one leaden foot forwards. He had promised to return and he could not, would not rest until he did. At that moment, from somewhere in his peripheral vision, he saw a lone tractor breaking away from the mass of vehicles, veering erratically towards the flag. There was no mistaking the wiry islander at the wheel, his side-rolls of hair blowing in the wind, his upper body craning sideways to see around his broken windscreen, and he understood then that it would be all right.

When the sting of the second dart pricked the bear's

skin what took him by surprise was how very familiar it felt. His heart skipped a beat, like a stone skimming across a pond. He felt the acute burn of longing in his chest, for home, for forgiveness and peace. As the drug took hold, there was no pain, only the sound of rain in his head and an incredible and welcome sensation of falling.

'Goodbye, boy,' he whispered and he knew he would be heard.

On the floor of the cave, the boy's eyes drifted open in his heart-shaped face and his answer came back on the last thread of the wind.

'Goodbye, my Dada,' he said and smiled.

82

Stornoway, Isle of Lewis

'Your son has a fractured skull and a torn knee-cap. I've put in a dozen or so stitches but he's going to be fine. What I'm trying to understand is that your daughter claims he jumped, though I'm assuming she meant he fell – ' the doctor checked his notes – 'sixty feet?' He arched an eyebrow in expectation of being corrected. 'You must be familiar with the geography of this place, Mrs Fleming – is that even possible?'

Letty spread her hands, unable to trust herself to speak. Had Jamie landed an inch to the right, had the bottom of the Kettle not been cushioned by seaweed, had the tide been higher, the water deeper. What if Alba had not gone after him – or Alick not spotted her makeshift flag? And what if a helicopter hadn't been on hand. Right there! Less than a hundred yards away, with the unconscious bear tangled in a net suspended underneath and half the island in pursuit with shovels and sticks, ready to dig out her children from under the ground. She gripped Tom's arm.

'Of course you get these cases from time to time,' the doctor was saying. 'There was one during my first-year internship. A toddler fell from the twelfth floor of a Sydney high-rise and walked away – so to speak – without a scratch.' Letty thought of her recurring nightmare. Jamie on the stairwell, his thin arms extended to catch his father. Alba had told her as well that Jamie had jumped. Could he have thought he could join his father in some way and if so, then why hadn't she noticed, *why hadn't she been paying attention*? But what had she paid attention to these last few months other than her own pain? When, earlier, she had been taken into the curtained cubicle to see Alba, she had barely recognized the young woman lying on a narrow trolley bed. Alba looked so wan, so grown-up, her pointed little face positioned to the wall, hiding the giant wad of cotton wool taped to her cheek. Then she had turned and an expression of such child-like relief had passed across her face that Letty had sprung forward and gathered her up. 'Oh Alba.' She cradled her. 'Alba, Alba.'

For a second, Alba remained limp, then Letty felt thin arms slowly encircle her and tighten.

'I want to give you something,' Letty said when she'd settled her back against the pillow. She pressed a small square of folded paper into Alba's palm. Without looking up, Alba turned the paper over, her eyes brimming as she'd seen the letters IOU written on the other side.

'Open it,' Letty said.

Very slowly Alba peeled the note apart.

'Read it.'

Everything will be all right. Alba had read out her mother's promise in a whisper. *From now on, it will be all right.*

'How is it possible, medically, I mean?' Tom was asking quietly. 'What do you think happened?'

The doctor made a frustrated gesture with his hand.

'If the child knows no fear. If the body is completely relaxed. If someone up there is watching over him. I have no logical answer for you. The fact is, however, it happened, a miracle is a miracle and all we can be is thankful.'

'Can I see him yet?' Letty asked. Her hold on Tom's arm loosened – not that she had any intention of letting go entirely. She'd taken possession of it ever since the phone had rung and Tom had quietly assumed charge. She'd clutched it in the army plane he'd commandeered, and even tighter in the waiting room where she'd sat rigid on the edge of her seat. Opposite her were other people's family and friends, all rinsed, as she was, with a sickly tinge from the strip lighting and all struggling, as she was too, to ignore the smell of fear that no amount of disinfectant could disguise. Letty stared at these strangers, wondering who would be lucky and who not, whose lives would work out and whose would change forever, all the while trying to reassure Georgie, thank Tom – all the while sending up entreaties to God, to Nicky, to the devil himself. Those two insignificant words, 'if only', were no longer a hopeless exercise in wishful thinking. She would renounce whatever future she was entitled to, she would offer up her soul for sacrifice along with anything else of hers that might be of interest – *if only* her children could be safe – *if only* she could be given another chance.

'We're still conducting tests,' the doctor said, 'but as soon as I have those results, I'll come and find you.'

'Tests for what?'

He hesitated and Letty frowned. With his Australian accent, there was something utterly incongruous about him, incongruous yet oddly familiar.

'Mrs Fleming, your son was hypothermic when they brought him in – both children were – and initially I put it down to that. Sometimes cold can account for these things.'

'I'm sorry, account for what?' she persisted.

'When I originally assessed him, apart from quite severe concussion I noticed he had VPB, not enough to cause a—'

'VPB?' Tom interrupted.

'Yes. It stands for ventricular premature beats. When your heart skips a beat – I'm sure you've both experienced that?' He looked up for confirmation. 'Well, that would be due to VPB. Do you follow?'

Tom nodded.

'Anyway the point is that Jamie's was not enough to cause his blood pressure to drop dangerously low, but . . .' He shrugged apologetically. 'I've just completed a fellowship in cardiology at the Peninsula General, so I'm probably a little more neurotic about matters of the heart than most residents. Jamie's blood pressure was low enough to sound a few warning bells so I thought to myself – better get the boy an ECG and echo after you have had that head seen to—'

'Echo?' Letty queried faintly.

'That's an electrical and sound wave test of the heart called an echo cardiogram.' He flashed her an apologetic smile. 'It will tell us a bit about the heart structure.'

'Are you saying there's something wrong with Jamie's heart?'

'Let's hope not, Mrs Fleming, but if there is, we will deal with it. In any event, I'm going to speak to your daughter again and I'll come back to you as soon as I know what's going on.'

83

'I'm prepared to offer you a Fruit Salad.'

'Which is?' Alba inspected the doctor with narrow eyes.

'Fruit Salad is a collective phrase for a group of stroke patients, or if you like, there's Vegetable Garden which is a group of brain-damaged patients.'

'Okay,' Alba conceded. 'One stitch for each.'

'Too kind.' He tilted her chin and threaded the needle through her cheek.

'Ten Fs is a good one, but I want three stitches for it otherwise we'll be here all day.'

'Go on, then. If you must.' Alba's posturing helped cover the fear. She'd had the shakes ever since arriving in hospital and, despite the blankets and hot sugary teas, she could still feel a tremor in her hands and the weakness in her legs.

'Fat, fair, fecund, fortyish, flatulent female with foul, frothy, floating faeces.'

Alba giggled in spite of herself. 'Where did you learn these?'

'Med school, Sydney. Keep still.'

'You're from Australia?'

'The accent didn't give it away?'

'What are you doing here from Australia?'

'My great-grandparents originally came from the north of Scotland so, you know, I thought I'd check the place out.'

'Sounds tedious.'

'It's actually a pretty romantic story.'

'I'm not the slightest bit interested in romance but I'll take more medical slang.'

'Last one for four stitches and the knot then?'

Alba glanced hopefully towards the curtain but she knew that her mother had finally been taken in to see Jamie and would not be out for a while. She took a deep breath and offered her cheek. The tug of the needle through flesh made her feel sick. She felt for the note in the pocket of her hospital gown. More than anything she had wanted her mother to stay, hold her hand, but she'd forgotten how to ask.

'You're quite brave for a Sheila.' The doctor knotted and snipped the thread. 'I hope you're proud of your sister,' he said over his shoulder. 'Saving your little brother's life and everything.'

Georgie sat, legs folded, in the tiny upholstered chair in the corner of the cubicle. She looked at her sister, spindly as a lab monkey in her hospital gown, her cheek distorted by the railroad track of stitches. Alba had climbed down a cliff and saved Jamie's life. She knew she ought to feel proud, but she couldn't rid herself of the suspicion that somehow – quite how, she had no idea – Alba was responsible for at least some portion of the accident. Still, Jamie's loyalty was such that even were this true, he would never tell. She resigned herself to the inevitability that all her future life achievements, however accomplished, would forever be overshadowed by Alba's childhood heroics.

'I didn't save his life,' Alba said.

'Oh, who did, then?' The doctor fiddled with his bleeper.

Alba touched a finger to the ridge of stitches. The thing was, she couldn't erase it from her head. The ragged edge of Jamie's wound, his plunge through the mist, the sound of the helicopter – and then that animal, the beast, so small and shrunken looking, balled up in the net. *Dada will catch me*, Jamie had shouted, and every time she closed her eyes she saw the mass of seaweed, moving, floating at the bottom of the Kettle. 'I don't know,' she said quietly. 'I honestly don't know.'

After the doctor took himself off, the two sisters eyed each other like battle-weary generals. Since they'd last come together, only twenty-four hours earlier, they'd discovered between them sex and spirituality. In other words, pretty much all the complexity the world had to offer, but the accumulation of prohibited subjects that had stacked up over the last six months prevented them sharing any of these revelations. They continued to stare at each other in uncompanionable silence until Alba finally blurted it out.

'I burnt your university offer letter.'

'You did what?' Georgie said, startled.

'I burnt your university offer letter,' Alba repeated hollowly. 'And your A level results as well.'

Georgie gawped at her. 'You little bitch! Why?'

Alba pulled the thin sheet up to her chin. 'Because you're nearly grown-up.' She faltered. 'Because you get to leave home and start a new life. Because I'm stuck here for another three years, for an eternity. Because there's no way out for me.'

Georgie felt strangely disassociated from the endless drama of her sister's selfishness.

'You don't understand.' Alba's voice rose. 'You've escaped, but I'm doomed. "Oh, poor Alba,"' she mimicked, '"how could she not have turned out bad, I mean, those wretched Fleming children, they had the most awful childhood."'

'We haven't had a really awful childhood.'

'Well, losing Dada happened for me at a more damaging time than it happened for you.'

'What are you talking about?'

'I think my formative years might have been ruined.'

'Rubbish, your formative years are something like two to six. These are your teenage years.'

'I know, I know,' Alba said piteously. 'I'm in the middle of *puberty*!'

Georgie sighed and closed her eyes. She saw Aliz's arm resting against hers. She heard the papery noise of waves against the sand. What Alba said was true. Her own clock was ticking again. She was growing up, moving on. 'Do you know something, Alba? You're not nearly as interesting as you think you are.' She pushed out of her chair.

Alba's head was turned into the pillow. 'Please don't leave me, Georgie,' she whispered. 'Please.'

'You're going to be fine.' Georgie pulled aside the curtain.

'I don't want to be fine. I want to be better than fine, I want . . .' Alba's voice caught then broke. 'I want Dada back.'

The minute that Georgie allowed to pass felt like a year. Then she turned and sat back down on the edge of Alba's bed. Her sister still existed in the before, whilst she had moved into the after. And the after was okay, it was better. In the way that most mattered to her, she had got her father back. 'Do you know what I think about sometimes?' she said softly.

'What?' Alba wiped her nose on the sleeve of her gown.

'That one day I will come across a door and through that door will be a room and in that room I will find all the precious things I have ever lost; that beautiful necklace Grandpa gave me, my old teddy, the Biba cardigan with the striped sleeves, and . . . you know . . . Dada.'

A fat tear trailed down Alba's cheek.

'Look, I'll make you a deal.' Georgie reached forwards and pushed a damp length of her sister's hair away from her stitches. 'If I defer university for a little while, if I stay with you a bit longer, will you tell me what I got in my A levels?'

84

All Letty remembered afterwards was the absoluteness of her exhaustion. She and Tom had been fetched out of the children's ward by the doctor and having failed to find a quiet spot, had taken up position between the shiny cream walls of the second-floor corridor. The air had been warm and unpleasantly scented. Bad ventilation, Letty thought. No windows to open. No wind to blow through. Outside she could hear the noise of a siren then the rolling slide of doors opening and shutting; voices, shouting. Somebody else's trauma was beginning.

'And no history of heart disease in your family?' the doctor was asking her. She'd tried to restore rhythm to her thinking, to articulate her responses, but anxiety had wound her down to nothing.

'Not that I know of.' She didn't like the way he was looking at her – concern mingled with a certain ghoulish curiosity adopted by the medical profession when they were in the throes of diagnosing some halfway interesting condition.

'On either your or your husband's side?'

'No.' Letty's teeth began to work at the inside of her lip.

'And Jamie has the two sisters, correct?'

'Yes.'

'Any health issues affecting either of them?'

'None.'

'What about yourself and your husband?'

'Jamie's father was killed in an accident earlier this year,' Tom intervened quickly.

The doctor made a note. 'I'm so sorry. What about Jamie's grandparents, are they still living?'

'All died of old age – well, apart from my husband's real mother who died in childbirth.'

'From anything in particular?'

'I don't think so, I mean, she was never terribly strong. How is this relevant exactly?'

A janitor moved through them, a dungeon-sized bunch of keys dangling from his leather belt. How late was it? Letty wondered vaguely. How long had they been there? Time in hospitals was not measured in hours and minutes but in shifts and rounds, the wait between painkillers, the number of fluid ounces pumped into arms.

'As I mentioned earlier – ' the doctor knuckled at his eyes, as if the sight of the night janitor had reminded him of his own fatigue – 'I initially questioned whether Jamie's irregular heartbeat was due to the cold, or too much adrenalin, but the results of his ECG show that he does, in fact, have a slightly dilated heart.'

'What does that mean exactly?' Letty reached unconsciously for Tom's hand again.

'I believe your son is suffering from cardiomyopathy.'

Then, when this pronouncement elicited only a shocked, blank silence, he took a pen from his coat pocket and began sketching on his notes. 'Let me see if I can make this simple for you. The engine of a heart is driven by electrical waves. The sort of waves, say, a pebble would make if you dropped it into a still pond.' He squinted up at them.

'Go on,' Tom encouraged.

'Those waves send out a signal to the muscles of the heart which, in turn, pump the blood through the body. Now, if there's an interruption in those electrical waves, it causes an abnormal heartbeat – as in when your heart skips a beat.'

'And this is what Jamie has?' Tom asked. 'An abnormal heartbeat?'

'Well, yes and no. For most people, skipping the odd beat happens from time to time and normally when the electrical waves are interrupted the heart simply reboots itself – but in those suffering from cardiomyopathy, the heart lacks the capability to reboot. Instead it panics and this causes a sudden and potentially fatal drop in blood pressure.'

'Fatal?' Letty stumbled over the word. 'Wouldn't we know if Jamie had something wrong with his heart?' She tried to exorcise the shrillness from her voice. 'Wouldn't we have found out before now?'

'Well, patients are almost always asymptomatic. There are literally no clues whatsoever. Sudden Cardiac Death can happen at any time during a person's life. Too much exercise, one coffee too many, an over-strenuous walk, a shock to the system. It can happen in your sleep, or when you're quietly reading in a chair. A person might experience palpitations or feel faint but that would be all. One minute they're here, the next they're gone. And I have to say – ' he shook his head – 'given the enormous amount of physical and emotional stress your son has been subjected to, it's quite amazing that . . .'

'Yes, thank you so much, doctor.' Tom stopped him with a warning look.

The doctor took in Letty's ashen face. 'Oh no, Mrs Fleming, please don't worry. Jamie is in no immediate danger. Now we know what we're dealing with, we can treat it.' He put the pen back in his pocket, hesitated. 'Look, the miracle isn't that your son survived a sixty-foot fall. The miracle is that he fell in the first place. If he hadn't been brought to hospital, his condition might have gone undetected.'

Letty felt like a weak imprint of herself, a cardboard cut-out. She leant against the wall. 'Thank you.'

'Yes,' Tom said, 'thank you very much.'

The doctor grasped Tom's outstretched hand. 'We have a few more tests to run and then we'll have a talk about treatment.'

'Of course.' Letty stared through him unseeingly. He turned to go. The first light of dawn was seeping between the shutters on the window.

'By the way.' Tom put a hand on his arm. 'Why were you so interested in the family history? You never explained.'

'Yes, well, I'm afraid usually it's the family of the sufferer we get to treat.' The doctor crinkled his eyes at the light. 'Cardiomyopathy is very often a hereditary disease, and in those cases where it *is* hereditary – well, it's almost always passed down from father to so—' He cut himself

431

off. 'That's right. You told me earlier that Jamie's father had an accident.' He looked eagerly at Letty. 'Exactly what sort of accident was it?'

It had happened then. In the weightless gap between not knowing and understanding. Letty realized that she had stopped breathing, she realized that in truth she hadn't really been breathing for a very long time. And just like that, she'd gone down.

85

The Island, September 1979

Letty was sleeping a dreamless sleep. She slept as if sleeping was a new hobby, one that she'd lately discovered and now couldn't get enough of. She had finally understood what it meant when people said they slept like the dead.

It meant they were at peace.

When she woke, her thoughts veered off to the same place they had gone every morning since she'd returned from the hospital. To the embassy in Bonn, to Nicky's office and the desk where he'd sat writing, practising his confession, crumpling up his first draft, summoning up his courage. She imagined him stealing up to the roof, smoking a cigarette and smiling as he watched the ropes tighten on the Big Top of the circus below. Then, perhaps a frown as pain sliced across his shoulder to his chest. A moment of dizziness as his faulty heart skipped that beat, *like a stone*, the doctor had said, *skimming across a pond* or the final guttering of a candle. Either way, he'd have been dead before he hit the ground, dead before he even fell, and she could come to terms with that. It was a death she could live with.

Nicky's arrhythmic, asymptomatic heart. It would not have shown up on an autopsy. It might have looked somewhat pallid in appearance, but no suspicions would have been aroused.

'I told you,' Jamie said in the hospital. 'I told you there was something wrong with my heart.' He hadn't remembered much about what had happened on the cliff, but Alba remembered. Alba remembered everything.

If the child knows no fear, the doctor had said. *If the body is completely relaxed. If somebody up there is looking out for him.*

'He jumped,' Alba said simply. 'He just rolled away and let go.'

Jump. Letty saw Nicky under her bedroom window, his arms opened wide.

Let go and I'll catch you.

So much unfinished business.

Jamie had inherited his father's heart and his father had come back to warn him. At least that's what Jamie believed. Letty didn't know what she believed, but maybe she didn't have to. It was no longer a requirement of life that it should make good sense or even reasonable sense, only that it should make Jamie sense. And recently Letty had begun to understand that sense to Jamie was a complex and wonderful thing.

Squirrelled away in his brainbox were soaring columns of words and phrases, fragments of song and the frayed edges of poems. There were tall stories and short stories, the vibrations of truth and lies and a thrumming of tiny fibs between; there were the spores of magic, the residue of dreams, a few sharp splinters of reality and then there were the shapes and patterns of wishful thinking all merging, intersecting with overlapping dimensions of hope and optimism. These elements together had created an infinite number of dots and dashes that constantly orbited his brain, sparking, colliding and joining in an ever-changing, multifaceted kaleidoscope of possibility.

Life or death. Nobody understood the workings of either. There was only what you believed – what you managed to hold on to.

And what Letty believed was that Jamie's logic had a cohesive quality that had glued their broken family together again. It had been the unfairness of tragedy, the agonizing futility of 'if only' that had trapped her in the past, but now all the interlocking connections of fate and chance which had saved Jamie's life had rebalanced the scales of fortune and tipped her into the present.

Tom had taken the report back to London with him. It would have to be put into the right hands, he'd said. Someone outside the MoD. Someone powerful who could and would have questions asked in Parliament. A minister senior enough to oblige the MoD to commission a new report. 'This is something I can do for Nicky,' Tom said before he'd left. 'Something I can do for you.' And he'd kissed her, briefly, on the cheek.

Downstairs, she could hear Georgie moving about in the kitchen, putting on water for the porridge. In just over two hours, they would go to the church by the loch for the memorial service. She had brought Nicky home, back from Bonn, to a place where he belonged. Letty looked at

Alba and Jamie, both hot with sleep and stretched across her bed, their bare feet inadvertently touching. There was a lot of growing up left to do.

Life was unfinished business. It was time to begin living it.

Epilogue

 In the summer of 1980, an eight-foot-four-inch grizzly bear named Hercules was taken for a swim in the sea by his owner, a rambunctious Scottish wrestler called Andy Robin, whilst filming an ad for Kleenex in the Outer Hebrides. His rope snapped and he was subsequently lost on the islands for nearly four weeks. It was widely feared that the bear, in order to survive, would quickly turn wild. A high-profile search was instigated involving the army and the navy, not to mention the islanders and the bear's indefatigable and heartbroken owners, Andy and his wife, Maggie. Nevertheless, he was eventually given up for dead. When Hercy was finally sighted and netted by helicopter it was estimated that he had lost more than half his body weight during his long weeks on the island. The bear, despite being on the point of starvation, never hurt a single living creature.

In 1981, the Naval Radiation Protection Services on behalf of the MoD commissioned a safety report on the missile firing base at 'Our Lady of the Isles'.

Epilogue

It was discovered that the range head and its surrounding area of land and beach had been contaminated by high amounts of Cobalt-60 – a radioisotope used to track missiles. The report concluded that 'both the ammunition technicians at RA Range Hebrides and the general public were placed at considerable and unnecessary radiological risk'.

This report was suppressed by the Ministry of Defence.

Acknowledgements

First and foremost I'd like to thank my parents for just about everything.

My continued thanks to my friend and agent Sarah Lutyens for her support, patience and timely advice. The same in spades to my beloved editor Maria Rejt.

And all at Lutyens & Rubinstein and the stellar team at Mantle and Pan Macmillan.

Thanks, too, to both Kim Witherspoon at Inkwell and Elizabeth Schmidt at Grove Atlantic for their invaluable contribution.

Also to:

Carole van Wieck, as always, friend, reader and critic.

Marcela Bombieri for her contribution to charity on behalf of her daughter Leticia Bombieri Ganoza, after whom my lead character is named.

The wonderful Maria Fairweather, who died in March 2010.

Acknowledgements

I am more grateful than I can say to all those friends and family who have read, advised or helped me with research on *The Summer of the Bear*:

Maya Schönburg, Julia Samuel, Robert Salisbury, Katrin Henkel, James Henderson. Gina Thomas, Geli von Hase, John Alec MacLean, Angus Ferguson, Angus Macdonald, Annie Macdonald, Alisdair MacLean. Lisa Bryer, Minna Fry, Sylvie Rabineau, Susie Pollen, Hoagy Pollen, David Mac, Sarah Hodsall and her girls, Esme, Alba and Georgie. Eddie Wrey. Caspar and Madeleine Glinz. Torsten and Margaretha Mlosch. Christa D'Souza, Daisy Sworder. Dr Rodney Foale, Henry Porter, Lady Nicholas Gordon-Lennox, Dr Brian MacGreevy, Debby McGregor and Nick Haddow.

In fondest memory of:

John MacLean of Baile Raghaill

Donald Ewan Macdonald of Baile Raghaill

Mrs Macdonald of Baile Raghaill

Roddy Ferguson of Hogha Gearraidh

Hugh Matheson of Baile Sear

Donald Macdonald of Loch Eynort

Annie Macdonald of Loch Druidibeg

Doone and Jamie Granville of Grimsay

Marcia Leveson-Gore of Grimsay

Angus John Maclellan of Baile Raghaill

Katy Mary Ferguson of Baile Raghaill

Callum Macdonald of the Glebe

Donald John Macdonald of Baile Raghaill

Acknowledgements

And with great affection for all friends of the townships of Baile Raghaill, Taigh a' Gheàrraidh, Ceann a Bhaigh and Hogha Gearraidh.

Finally, a thank you to Andy and Maggie Robin for their inspirational story.

If you enjoyed The Summer of the Bear *you'll love* . . .

Midnight Cactus

by Bella Pollen

On the run from her claustrophobic marriage in London, Alice Coleman moves her two small children to the Arizona desert with the intention of renovating an abandoned mining town on the Mexican Border – and there finds an escape and solitude she hadn't thought possible.

But in the dusty, alien atmosphere, where it seems that everyone – from Benjàmin, the town's Mexican caretaker to the laconic cowboy, Duval – has something to hide, Alice is uncertain whom to trust.

As winter moves to scorching summer, what seemed idyllic turns deadly as Alice is drawn deeper into an obsessive quest for revenge, until finally she must decide how far she is willing to go to cling on to her freedom and what exactly she will have to sacrifice.

Fierce and compelling, *Midnight Cactus* explores the territory between unrealized dreams and the pull of family. In a blistering climax Alice discovers it is only by risking everything that you learn what is really worth living for . . .

Out now in Pan paperback

The first chapter follows here . . .

1

January 2002

Thousands of feet up, somewhere between space and earth, night seems to go on forever. For hours, a never-ending sunset has been doggedly following the plane, trailing its woolly strands of orange and purple like an exotic jellyfish. Only now as I press my nose against the perspex window do I see that we've finally left it behind. There is nothing out there any more – just a world so black and vast it makes me want to topple into it and disappear.

I check my watch: two a.m. English time. New Year's Eve. Looking around at my fellow travellers, slack-jawed and mute with exhaustion, I wonder what will happen to us all in this year to come. Who on this plane will die? Who will become a grandparent, embezzle funds or burst into tears at their first grey hair? And the idea makes me unaccountably sad. What is it about flying that makes people so hopelessly sentimental? Something to do with the lack of air, I suppose, too much breathing in other people's anxieties and emotions. The DNA of strangers. The man across the aisle, corpulent by even the most liberal of standards, loosens the leather belt from around his trousers, no doubt feeling the acid burn of dinner's coq au vin. The rest of the passengers shift uncomfortably under blankets or scratch drowsily at itches they can't quite locate. The atmosphere of somnolence in the cabin is so overpowering that were the pilot to streak naked through the aisles, just for a lark, I doubt very much anyone would notice – much less care. Even Jack and Emmy have passed out, mouths open, as though sprinkled mid-bicker with sleep dust by a kindly British Airways fairy.

God knows, I wish I could sleep on aeroplanes. Disconnected and temporarily excluded from life on earth below, it seems the only sensible thing to do, but as soon as the plane reaches cruising altitude, the moment the signs are switched off and the clink of the drinks trolley soothes the nerves of even the most neurotic of flyers, I fall prey to philosophical musings. While down on earth babies are being born, wars are being fought and couples argue over burnt steak dinners, I sit buckled into my seat and make endless pacts with God. I can spend long hours in this way, plotting personal revolutions, planning get-outs, but always with the safety net of knowing that as soon as the wing begins its downward tilt and the reality of hard ground rises up to meet us, this brave new me, this ghost of my future, will fade back into the ether where it belongs.

But not tonight. As the blinking lights of Phoenix airport appear below like a defiant grid of life on an inhospitable planet, I feel a surge of adrenalin. Tonight will be different. Tonight there is no turning back. In about an hour's time we will be at the head of the immigration queue. Poised for entry. The customs official will give me and the children no more than a cursory once-over before stamping our visa forms.

'What is the purpose of your visit?' he will ask.

The pickup truck has a side-swinging motion that the Mexican corrects every few seconds, bringing it back into line on the right side of the road. Every time my eyes begin to close with the rhythm, the wrench of the wheel forces them apart again. Right now I'd give anything to slip between clean sheets, sleep until it's time to let tomorrow begin, but the silence in the truck feels reproachful. No doubt the Mexican is pissed off at having to pick us up – well, too bad. Quite apart from the fact that I would have killed the three of us falling asleep at the wheel, the town is so remote I would never have found my way there in the first place.

I study his profile surreptitiously. He is more Spanish looking than I remember – though it wasn't until we cleared customs that I experienced a moment of panic: what on earth did he look like? What if I didn't recognize him? What if he didn't remember me? What if he didn't show up at all? I'd held a vague picture in my head over the last few months of a shortish middle-aged man with tightly curled hair greying at the edges and a brushstroke of a moustache, but the truth is, all I could be really sure of was that he looked, well . . . Mexican, and at Phoenix airport, as it turned out, that wouldn't exactly have made him stand out from the crowd.

It's cold in the truck: 10 degrees above zero, if the crackle on the radio is to be believed. My hands are numb. I burrow them between my legs and check the heating dial on the dashboard. The thin white line is swivelled to maximum and I can feel pockets of warmth coming from somewhere, but they're no match for the freezing air leaking through the distressed seals of the cab's windows. The cold takes me by surprise. The last time I'd driven down this road it had been over a hundred degrees, hot enough to bubble the tarmac and melt the soles of my trainers, hot enough to sting the back of my throat and lodge there like some solid mischievous thing. It had been late September then and, on both sides of the road, grassland had rolled towards the hills like a golden sheet billowing in the wind. On the other side of the windscreen now, there is nothing to be seen. The road ahead is completely deserted and whatever might lie on either side of it hidden by the density of night.

Jack sighs from the back seat and I turn round to check him. His fringed suede water bottle, bought at the airport, is slung around his neck in a potentially lethal knot. His face is filthy. A still-life of the journey's bribes and snacks. The corner of his mouth droops slackly and a trail of dribble has leaked down his chin onto his neck where it has dried into a chalky mark. He sleeps in his customary upright position, a pose I'd always assumed was the result of all those years imprisoned in unforgiving baby car seats, but recently have come to understand is simply a mark of his independence, his two fingers up to the adult world. Jack has always had a certain irritation and impatience at being small, as if his babyhood and now youth were no more than inconveniences unfairly foisted on him, and consequently he's always treated them as something of an affliction, an accident of birth that he'd have to overcome, like a club foot or a squint.

'When are we there?' Emmy slumps self-pityingly against the opposite window. 'I'm sooo tired.' Her voice cracks with exhaustion and tears. As I prop her up again, she opens a cyclopian eye in order to fix me, the mother of all her woes, with a baleful accusing scowl.

How can my children possibly understand what's going on? Why they've been dragged on this endless painful journey, away from their home, from their friends, their father – and for what? To spend a year in some jerry-built cabin in the middle of God only knows where because of a whim, some barely explicable desire for escape that I had no longer been able to ignore.

'I still don't understand why you insist on going on ahead,' Robert had said for the umpteenth time as he'd kissed the children at the departure gate. 'It could be months before I can get away.'

I hadn't answered him because what was there to say? Once you lose the power of communication with someone, nothing makes sense between you any more and months were exactly what I was counting on.

Unhappiness is a dangerous thing, like carbon monoxide. You don't smell it, you don't taste it, it's formless and colourless, but it poisons slowly. It seeps into every pore of your skin until one day your heart just stops beating. And I've been wondering. How did my mother put it? The summer she took off? A wind was rising over the Orkneys the day she upped and blew out of my world forever. But before there's any debate about repeat behavioural patterns and the hereditary nature of bolters, I have to point out one significant difference. In the summer of 1983 my mother didn't take her children with her. She didn't pack their favourite chewed teddies and leaking finger paints and Emmy's clock with the cat's eyes, whose tail wags along in time with the seconds. No. My mother left me behind, sitting on the beach, the underside of my trousers packed down with cold wet sand as I dug for lug worms, happy, oblivious, dreaming of beans on toast while my father knelt behind me and cried fat salty tears into a pile of nearby seaweed.

Sleep must have somehow come then, because when I open my eyes, the truck has stopped. I unclip the seatbelt and feel stiffly for the door handle. The Mexican is hauling suitcases out of the back and tossing them to the ground, small puffs of smoke gusting out of his mouth at the exertion. Even unconscious, Jack is not an amenable child, his limbs remaining obstinately rigormortified. I shake him awake and push him out into the cold night air, then scoop Emmy into a fireman's lift and the three of us stumble towards the cabin's deck where the Mexican stands silently, holding the fly screen open. Once we're safely inside he nods his head curtly and climbs back into the truck, leaving all the luggage in a sloppy pile outside the cabin door. I bite my lip in irritation as the ignition fires into life.

I push the children up the narrow wooden staircase, tossing Emmy onto my bed before going back to rescue Jack, who has somehow got left behind and is hunched, wide-eyed, on the top step as though shot by a sniper in the first wave of a surprise attack. At least the cabin has been made habitable. There are sheets on the bed and a shrunken striped woollen blanket on top. The sink in the corner still has rust stains down one side but hot water trickles from the taps, and the loo, whose incessant gurgling drove Robert crazy last time we were here, appears to have been fixed. Most luxurious of all, a reading light has been rigged up via the central overhead beam and connected to a yellowing switch on the wall. The children quickly lock themselves into their familiar sleep positions. Emmy, stretched out horizontally across the pillows, her long black hair splayed around her head in tangled Medusa locks, while Jack lies in repose in a T-junction with her shoulder. There is a bout of feral growling when I attempt to wash their faces and I give up. What does it matter if they spend the next year encrusted with dirt? What do I care if they run naked through the brush and their feet grow over with soft fur like baby wolverines? In this 'big adventure' of ours, there must surely be perks for them too. Jack's hair smells of cauliflower and urine. The H&M label on his T-shirt is sticking up against his neck. Height 125 cms, 7/8 years old, it reads and for a second I sit down on the bed, overcome by a wave of emotions I am simply too tired to identify.

After a few minutes of dozing upright I have the brilliant notion of peeling off my own clothes and getting into the bed, but as I move around the room I feel a nubble of something on the floor which, though solid initially, yields under the pressure of my foot. I kneel down and flip back the rug. It's a dead mouse. Or the putrid, rotting remains of one. Squashed flat, its legs and paws are spreadeagled across the floorboards like a miniature hunting trophy. For an optimistic moment I wonder whether I can get away with leaving it till morning, but the revulsion factor is too high. There's no obvious mouse-scraping utensil to hand

and a quick rummage through the overnight cases produces nothing helpful. In desperation I yank open the drawer of the bedside table and finally luck out with a box whose hinged lid lends itself nicely to the task. Balancing the corpse gingerly on the lid with one hand and fumbling with the rusted catch on the window with the other, I shake the whole disgusting mess out. Then as soon as it's safe to, I laugh, thinking of the fuss Robert would have made. 'I mean surely it's not unreasonable to be angry!' I can hear him shouting. 'Haven't we been paying him to caretake the place? I mean, haven't we, Alice?'

Up in the sky, the stars are out in force. Cold air blows around the room. It smells earthy and unfamiliar. Except for Emmy's snoring, a faint puckering of air in and out, there is absolute quiet. What a miracle this silence is. No car parking outside, no slamming of doors, no heavy tread on the staircase to the bedroom, no reek of cigars or hand laid expectantly on my shoulder. Ha! We're here, we are finally here and to hell with poor little dearly departed Mickey Mouse, to hell with Robert's bombastic rants, because this is it, we've made it, and as I climb into bed, curl around my children and wait for sleep to come, I feel as smug as a cat who has taught herself to swim.

Hunting Unicorns

by Bella Pollen

American Maggie Monroe is a journalist for New York's hard-hitting current affairs show *Newsline*. Independent and fearless, the more cutting-edge the story, the happier she is. But when her next assignment turns out to be an in-depth documentary on the decline of England's ruling classes, she's furious at being sent to cover a bloody tea party.

Meet the Earl and Countess of Bevan, eccentric, maddening and with family secrets to hide.

Meet Daniel Bevan – their eldest son. Funny, attractive and hopelessly alcoholic.

Meet Daniel's responsible brother Rory – angry, self-mocking and strictly teetotal.

When Maggie discovers Rory to be an uninvited chaperone on the first stop of her journey, the two look set to clash. Maggie finds herself torn between her journalist ideals and coming to terms with a greater understanding.

This unlikely romantic comedy paints an endearing portrait of a family, which, like so many others, holds itself together despite its evident frailties.

Hunting Unicorns was voted the favourite
Richard & Judy Summer Read

Out now in Pan paperback

extracts reading groups
competitions books new
discounts extracts extracts
reading groups
competitions extracts discounts
books new events
events books reading groups
extracts reading groups new titles
interviews events books
events extracts extracts
discounts
new books events
events new events books
discounts extracts discounts interviews new books extracts
www.panmacmillan.com
extracts events reading groups
competitions books extracts new books